Year Of The
HOOPOE

A JUSTIN AND SOPHIE MYSTERY

A NOVEL

by

JEFF SOUTHARD

Copyright © 2021 Jeff Southard
All rights reserved
First Edition

PAGE PUBLISHING, INC.
Conneaut Lake, PA

First originally published by Page Publishing 2021

ISBN 978-1-6624-4888-1 (pbk)
ISBN 978-1-6624-4890-4 (hc)
ISBN 978-1-6624-4889-8 (digital)

Printed in the United States of America

Also by Jeff Southard

Year of the Dolphin

This book is dedicated to the memory
of the nearly 500,000 Americans who died
of COVID-19, many of them needlessly, while
it was being written.

AUTHOR'S NOTE

This is a work of fiction set in the year 1016 A.D. Most of the action takes place in Constantinople (now Istanbul), in what is referred to as the Roman Empire. Readers may find this confusing, in that modern historians refer to Constantinople as the capital of the Byzantine Empire. I have used the term "Roman" throughout, in keeping with the conservative practice of the inhabitants of the empire of that time. So, even though they spoke Greek, were Christian and had not ruled over Rome for centuries, 'Roman' they were, and remain so in this book.

J.S.

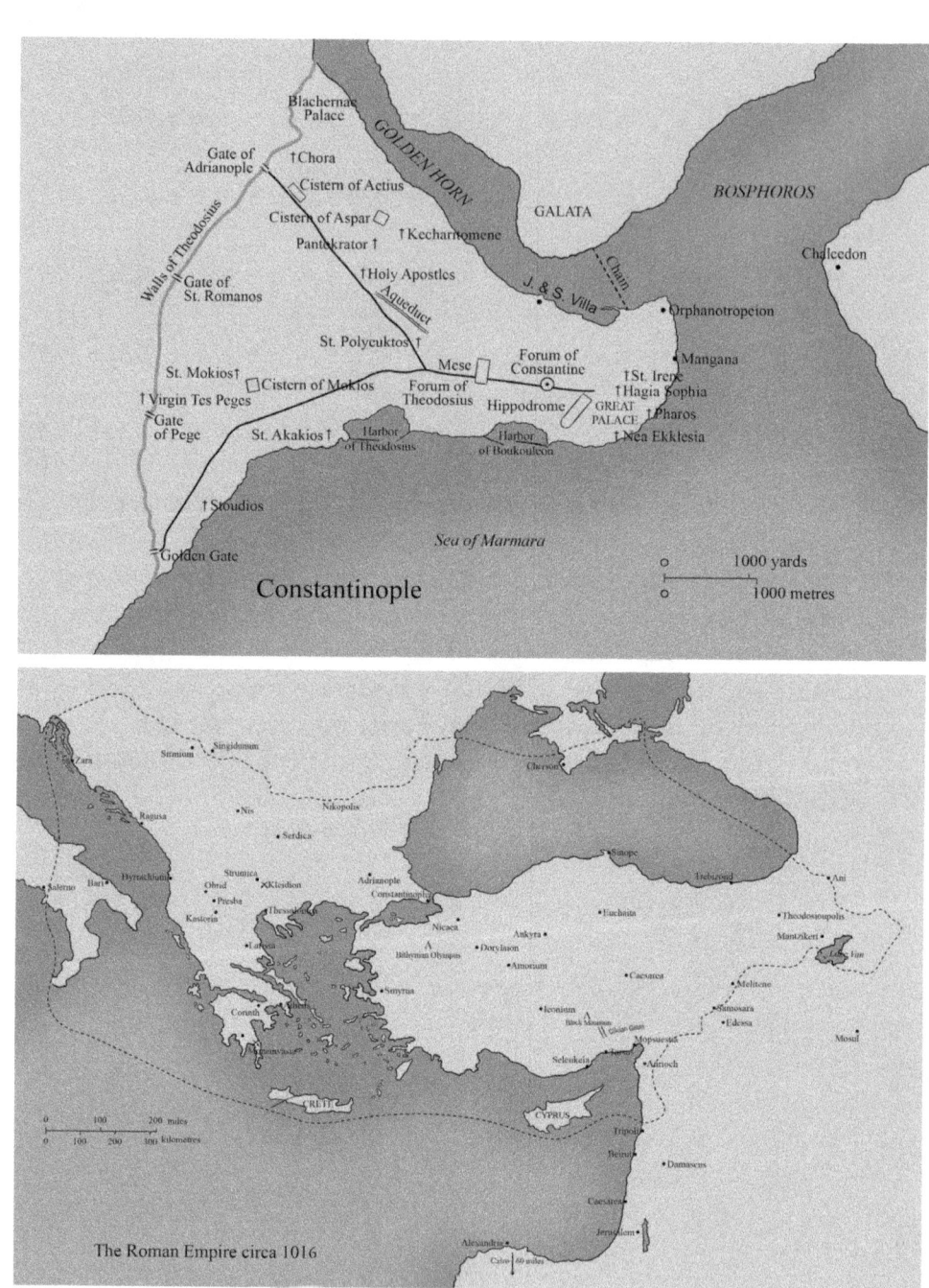

PROLOGUE

The hoopoe carried the lizard it had just caught back to its nest in a hole on the side of a building. The building stood atop a hill men called Muqattam on the east side of a river they called the Nile, overlooking a city they called Cairo. His mate was there, along with the four fledglings which they had raised since May. Now it was June, and the male was tired from doing all of the hunting it took to keep them fed. Still, prey was plentiful, and the men who were around the building sometimes left scraps out for the bird since hoopoes were specifically mentioned in the Koran and thus protected. Now as the sun was setting across the river, the hoopoe looked forward to bedding down for the night.

Below, activity continued, for it was the night before the end of Ramadan, the month sacred to Muslims as the time the Koran was revealed to the prophet Muhammed, peace be upon him. Tradition dictated that each devout Muslim should fast between sunrise and sunset, with allowances made for children, the elderly, the sick, pregnant women and travelers, especially those in lands which were still under the control of non-believers. Now, as the sun was setting, it was time to eat.

The staff of the building, which was an observatory, was to be joined in their evening meal by their benefactor and ruler, Defender of the Faithful Abu 'Ali Mansur Al-Hakim bi Amr Al-lah, the 6th Caliph of the Fatimid dynasty. Coming from northern Africa decades ago, the Fatimids had seized Egypt from the failing Abbasid Caliphate, and had gone on to control the Muslim holy cities of Mecca and Medina. Only Baghdad remained to be seized, but circumstances had conspired against them in that regard, at least for the present. Not the least of their problems was that they adhered to the party of Ali, and so were known as Shi'ites, when most of their subjects were orthodox (Sunni). The year was 396 A.H. (After the Hegira), which for Christians was 1016 A.D.

The staff, who were astronomers, astrologers and scientists from across the Muslim world, were more than a little intimidated by the presence of the Caliph. Widely known as a mercurial ruler, he changed viziers as often as he changed his robes, and while successful servants were rewarded richly, failure was not tolerated. As a result, the staff ate in silence while watching their lord with every bite. This night, as on most nights, he was in an introspective mood and ate his dinner in silence. When he was finished, everyone was on edge as he deigned to speak.

Now 31, the ruler of the Fatimid Caliphate was the absolute master of a realm that stretched across northern Africa into Syria and the Arabian Peninsula, including the holy cities of Mecca and Medina. Still slim, with eyes that were deeply sunk into his face and yet glittered with subdued passion, he rose after dinner resplendent in his white robes. "In the name of the Prophet, peace be upon him, we bid you greeting," he said in a low voice. "We are here to confirm that the end of Ramadan will occur tomorrow, when the new crescent moon will be observed. Chief Astronomer, can you swear to this upon pain of your life?"

The astronomer, an older man with a wispy-white beard, stood and said in a halting voice, "Yes, Eminence, that is what our observations tell us. The Eid-al-Fitr may proceed tomorrow evening."

"That is well, for so we will proclaim it. Now go in peace. We wish to remain and contemplate the heavens this night."

As everyone else left and returned to the city that stretched out in below, al-Hamid went out and sat on a bench which was reserved for him alone. Despite the lights of Cairo, the heavens above were quite dark, and he could clearly make out the stars. He had always been fascinated by the night sky, and remembered fondly the times he had spent with his father Caliph al-Aziz in the desert at night. While the stars were distant and unfeeling, they also posed no threat to him, and after a lifetime of fending off threats from all sides he could take comfort from their isolation.

Looking up, he could see Arcturus shining in the southwest, not far from the bright light of Zohaal, one of the wandering stars that his astronomers had identified as planets. To the north, the dipper-like shape of Dub-al-Ekber hung straight down, with the immovable light of Polaris shining in its familiar position. All was in order, all was good.

As he sat in solitude, he was aware of footsteps behind him which came to a stop. Without turning around, he said, "Good evening, sister. What brings you out on such a fine night?"

After a pause, he was joined on the bench by a hooded figure, whom he knew to be his half-sister, Sitt al-Mulk. At 46, she was still slim and very attractive, and had not married only because of the prohibition levied on her for the past 20 years by her half-brother. She made no attempt to hide her opinions that he was intolerant of many of his subjects, including Christians and Jews, while he missed no opportunity to hint that she was promiscuous, particularly among his high officials and generals. Only her position as his closest living relative (apart from his son) kept her immune from punishment. She knew this, and was not shy to exploit it.

"Greetings, brother. How did you know it was me?"

"Because you are the only person whom Kassim would permit to approach me. I trust you saw him?"

"Oh, yes, your giant Nubian eunuch. Yes, I saw him. I would say we exchanged words, but for the fact that he is also mute. As to why I am here, since you go out of your way to avoid me in the Palace, it seemed the only way we could talk."

"All right, you are here, so talk."

"Believe it or not, brother, I am concerned about you. You lock yourself up in the palace for weeks on end and interact with no one except Kassim. Even for you, this is excessive. There are matters of state to attend to. My sources tell me that the Umayyads are making trouble on the Moroccan frontier and the Yemenis are doing the same in Arabia. The harvest has been poor in Palestine and the price of bread has doubled. Finally, the demands coming from the Romans are getting more pre-emptory by the day."

The Caliph gave his sister a side-long glance which he held long enough so that she looked away in discomfort before saying, "And how, may I ask, do you know about the demands? Through your 'sources'? What else do they tell you—that I am insane, unfit to rule?"

"No, Ali, no, nothing like that. This is your sister talking to you now. I am doing so out of love, love for you and for your son. He's only 11, and he needs you. I remember you were the same age when our father died, and it was hard on you whether you admitted it or not."

"All right, sister, all right. I promise that as of tomorrow, I will resume my duties. I have been burdened by the memories of events of two years ago, but when Eid-al-Fitr is finished, I will move on. Satisfied?"

Now it was Sitt al-Mulk's turn to pause in thought before she said, "Two years? Oh, now I remember—your Roman 'guests'—too bad I didn't get to meet them in person. I saw them from across the room at the Eid-al-Fitr meal, but that was as close as I got. Are you still mourning the loss of your fleet?"

At this the Caliph gave a short, hard laugh. "Hardly, sister, hardly. Look there," he said, gesturing toward the Nile, where the sails of many ships reflected the lights of the city, "the Romans did me a favor—I now have a completely new fleet, the equal of anything they have."

"Perhaps, but for the little matter of Greek fire. What of the other problems I mentioned?"

"Troops will be dispatched next week to handle the Umayyads—they are too tied up in Andalusia to give us much trouble in Africa. I can buy the Yemenis off as usual, which will let them get back to their favorite pastime of cutting each others' throats."

"But what of the latest communication from Emperor Basil—I have seen it, and it simply says, 'Syria or Sicily—you choose.'"

"Never fear, sister. As for the Romans, I have several things in the works which they will never see coming. My network is still in place and may be carrying out my commands this very night. In any event, I may see the Romans shortly. A meeting is to be held on Crete where money for various church reconstruction projects is to be transferred, and other matters discussed. Perhaps I will attend in my persona of 'Ali', or, for a change, I may send you. The patriarch of Alexandria will be there, along with the pope of the Coptic Church. That reminds me—I need a new vizier to officially preside."

"I thought you just appointed one—what happened to him?"

"Oh, he accidentally hanged himself. It is of no importance."

The half-siblings sat in silence for a while. The Caliph contemplated the night sky, while his sister contemplated him. Finally, she broke the silence.

"You miss them, don't you? I mean the Romans who were here."

Her brother gave a snort. "Miss them? That empty-headed princess? Hardly. Besides, they are Greek."

His sister persisted. "No, not her. The deputy treasurer—what is his name?"

After a moment, the ruler of the Fatimid Caliphate replied, "Justin. His name is Justin Cataphlates, and he is the Treasurer of the Empire now. He is one of the biggest enemies we have, and yet I do miss him."

"Because he was not afraid of you?"

"No, no, he is too intelligent not to be afraid of me. Still, I felt free to talk with him. He was also honest with me, at least up to the point where he burned my entire fleet. Even then, I'm sure that was nothing personal. I look forward to following his career, even if he and I don't meet in Crete."

At this, Sitt al-Mulk thought to herself, '*I wonder if Justin feels the same?*' but elected not to offer that observation. Instead she said, "Well, brother, thank you for this time. We must do it again soon. With your leave, I will return to my carriage and leave you to your thoughts. Go with God."

"Go with God, sister." After she had left, the Caliph sat in silence for a while longer, watching the stars do their silent dance around Polaris. When he finally walked back to where his silent attendant waited, the world was left to darkness and the hoopoe, who had escaped the close confines of its nest to sit on the roof of the observatory. Even at night, the summer heat was starting to build, and the bird could feel that a change was coming.

Change did come for one man later that evening several hundred miles away in Constantinople. A member of the Varangian guard, the elite force recruited by the Roman Emperors from the forests and fjords of northern Europe, staggered out of a tavern into a dark alley. A veteran of many battles, he was no stranger to death, but he had seen something earlier that evening that caused even him to blanch, and to seek solace in many drinks. He therefore felt little pain when his head was suddenly jerked back from behind and his throat slit from ear to ear. In a reflex action, he pulled his knife and swung blindly, even as the light left his eyes. Slumping to the pavement, his last conscious thought was 'Loviatar!'

CHAPTER 1

Earlier that morning a few hundred miles away, another hoopoe had been trying to find food for his own brood. Unlike his distant cousin in Cairo, this bird had migrated south for the winter, and had come back with his mate to their summer haunts in New Rome, popularly known as Constantinople. Now the capital of the Roman Empire for almost seven hundred years, it stood on the border between Europe and Asia, with its emperors ruling over a land which was, for the most part at peace. The long war against the Bulgars was winding down, and all of its other potential foes, Russians, Pechnegs, Magyars and Fatimids, were quiet. As to all of this the hoopoe was ignorant, as all of his present attention was focused on a grasshopper. The insect was basking in the sun on a stone wall lining a veranda overlooking the Golden Horn, a deep harbor on the north side of the city. At the right moment the bird swooped, the prey was caught, and he was off to the nest where his mate waited with five hungry chicks.

On the veranda, this little drama had gone unnoticed by a woman who was playing with her child. The woman was Sophie Cataphlates, chief lady-in-waiting to one of the imperial princesses of the empire. Now 36, the still-slender brunette had the entire confidence of her mistress, the Princess Zoe, with whom she had now spent half of her life. Their friendship, always close, had been cemented forever in the pilgrimage they had made together two years before to Jerusalem, where they were kidnapped by the Caliph and taken to Cairo. Through the efforts of Sophie and her husband Justin, now Treasurer of the Roman Empire, they had escaped, although it had cost the life of Zoe's confessor, former army officer-turned monk Simon, who had given the last full measure of devotion for the sake of his friends.

In part as recompense for the long hours Sophie had spent working during Lent and Easter, Zoe had given her a few days off which were greatly appreciated. Less appreciated were the messages which Zoe sent several times a day, asking for advice/direction. While the messengers were very good about waiting for Sophie to compose responses, it made being away from the Palace less restful than it could have been. Now rest time was over, and Sophie was resigned to returning to her position tomorrow.

Simon's memory lived on in the presence of his namesake, Sophie and Justin's son. At a year-and-a-half, the younger Simon was fast becoming the terror of the household, particularly the family dogs. Shadow, the oldest of the lot, had taken to scrambling up onto the highest couch available upon hearing his coming, while the younger dogs simply made themselves scarce. At present they were safe, for Simon's attention was entirely fixed on a ball which Sophie batted in his direction. Thus engaged, Sophie did not initially hear the words of Philip, the steward of the household, when he approached from the dining area.

"Excuse me, mistress, but do you expect Master Justin back for dinner? The kitchen staff would like to know."

After first making sure that Simon was nowhere near the edge of the terrace, Sophie sighed and said, "Oh, Philip, I don't know. He's got so much going on now, what with the officials from Asia in town and all. Why don't we assume that he'll be late—just have the cook set something covered aside for him. The children and I will dine at 6. Speaking of children, have you seen Maria?"

Philip thought for a moment then said, "Yes, madam, I think she is in the study, finishing her mathematics lessons with that tutor fellow."

At that, Sophia laughed a laugh that sounded like a waterfall made of a cascade of jewels. Hearing it, Simon laughed too, and ran over to jump into her lap. Recovering her breath, she said, "Oh, Philip, he's not 'that tutor fellow'! As you well know, his name is Anwar. Just because he is an Arab is no reason to dislike him. Maria adores him, and he's teaching her that new system of numbers that works much better than Roman numerals do."

"That's right, soon all of us Romans using the old system will be out of a job!" said a male voice coming through the door. Simon gave a squeal of delight, and hopped down from his mother to run to his father, who stood there beaming. Now 36 as well, Justin Cataphlates was of medium height and build, with sandy hair that was already beginning to thin. He looked very much the part of the Imperial bureaucrat he happened to be, albeit at a rather high level in his post of Treasurer for the entire Roman Empire.

Justin had no sooner uncoiled himself from his squirming son than he was tackled from the back by 10 year-old Maria, who grabbed his legs and cried "Papa!"

Giving her a hug, Justin exclaimed, "My goodness, child, you'd think that I'd been gone for months—it was just this morning! Hello, my dear, did you enjoy your last day off? It must be nice." With that, he turned to sweep up the still-clinging Maria and deposit her next to Sophie, giving both a big hug.

Beaming, Sophie said, "Thank you, I did. Now that you've graced us with your presence, let's have dinner." Turning to Philip, who was watching a scene he'd seen played out so often before, she said, "Dinner for four, please. We'll have it here on the veranda."

And so it was that the family ate their evening meal in their home which overlooked the Golden Horn. The mansion, though well-built, was modest by the standards of even mid-level imperial officials. Now, as Treasurer, Justin could clearly have moved up in the world by taking a larger, more luxurious villa. The couple had never entertained the thought of moving, however, for they both loved the home which had served them well. Both Justin and Sophia prized the veranda and the garden that lay below it at the rear of the mansion, with their view of the harbor known as the Golden Horn and its many brightly colored ships.

While the family ate, Justin quizzed Maria on her lessons. As someone for whom numbers held no magic or fear, he was secretly thrilled that she seemed to feel the same. When he asked, "What's eight times seven", she immediately replied "56". When he upped the ante to "And what's 12 times 25," the answer, while a little more hesitant, was nonetheless a correct 300. Not bad, he thought, for 9 years.

At this, Sophie could only smile and shake her head, for while she was wise in the ways of the world and incredibly observant, numbers had no charm for her. In any case, she was occupied with Simon who, sitting in his highchair, seemed to put about as much food in his mouth as he found ways to feed the three dogs who formed a chorus around him. Shadow, the oldest and wisest of the bunch, had learned to let the younger two fight over a scrap thus giving her Simon's undivided attention. But, as all good things do dinner eventually came to an end, and it was time to sleep.

Justin carried a now-drowsy Simon up to his room, while Sophie got Maria ready for bed. As an observant mother, Sophie knew that the louder her daughter talked, the more tired she was, and so let the process play out. Eventually, after stories and songs, the younger generation were put to bed and placed under the watchful eye of the night nurse. Justin and Sophie retired back to the veranda, where they were rewarded with a magnificent sunset over the hills of Asia to the west. Far off to the south, the lone peak of the Bithynian Olympus rose, its snow-capped peak shining in the setting sun.

As he nursed a glass of a rather pedestrian Thracian white wine, Justin looked at the peak and said, "It was very nice to catch up with your father over Christmas," referring to Sophie's physician father who, after retiring from a very illustrious practice in the city, now oversaw a leprosarium near the mountain.

Sophie, after taking a sip of her own, nodded and said, "Yes, he so loved seeing his grandchildren. He would really be pleased to see how much Simon has grown since then."

"When do you think he'll come back to Constantinople?"

"I don't know. I think he feels useful where he is, but there is only so much he can do there."

After a moment of silence, Sophie continued. "So, what's the news from the outside world—good, bad, or indifferent?"

Justin sighed, for the news was mostly bad, as it is in the nature of good things to pass unnoticed and unmentioned until they either are gone or are replaced by less pleasant ones. Preparations continued for the 40th anniversary of the accession to rule of the current emperors, the brothers Basil and Constantine, and with that there was always a need for money. A delegation had just arrived in the city from the pope in Rome, although Justin was not clear what their intentions were. Due to the prefect's involvement, Justin had been tabbed to journey to Crete for a diplomatic cause involving churches and money. As for the man who was and always would be enemy number one for them and the empire, there was nothing new about the Fatimid Caliph.

Sophie digested this for a moment, and then quietly said, "And the project? It continues?"

Without answering out loud, Justin nodded.

Comfortable in each other's company, the couple watched the twilight come on and the early stars begin to appear. Sophie was about to announce that it was time for bed when Nathan, the night porter, appeared and stood by the door.

Making allowance for the fact that he was new, she said, "Yes, what is it?"

Nathan stammered and said, "I, uh, I have a message that was just delivered for the Treasurer."

Justin, who had been dozing off, came awake and said, "Well, let's have it." After looking at the note, he said, "Thank you, Nathan, that will be all," and wordlessly passed it to his wife after the porter had left them alone.

Sophie, catching the look in her husband's eye, looked at the paper and read: "The Alitheia Society cordially extends an invitation to you to attend its next meeting. Beta 6. Please bring the Scalpel."

She nodded, and immediately arose, followed by her husband up the broad staircase to the upper portion of their villa. They moved wordlessly but with purpose, and only spoke once they were securely in their bedroom.

"So, here we go," she said. "What does the grid tell us?"

These remarks got no immediate response from Justin, who was engaged in pushing a sequence of knobs on a dresser, so as to disclose a hidden drawer that contained two large parchments. One was a map of the city of Constantinople, while the other was a translucent grid with numbers across the top and letters down the side. By laying the second on top of the first, they determined that the cryptic 'Beta 6' instruction directed them to a site near the southeast waterfront between the Boukouleon Harbor and the palace of the same name. Justin showed Sophie their destination and said, "Well, 'Scalpel,' ready to go?"

She responded with a wordless smile, and immediately began to change her clothing, putting on a dark gown. After Justin had selected a black cloak, he was as concealed to the night as his wife. So attired, the couple came downstairs to get into the coach which was waiting for them at their gates. They moved as silently as possible, and slipped away into the night of the city, with Sophie carrying a bag which contained things she might find useful.

Still, their movements had not gone unobserved, and a smaller wagon started after them. The street, like most main thoroughfares in Constantinople, was lined with lamps which contained oil that was lit every evening by a small army of city employees and then extinguished in the morning. Pulling a mirror from her bag, Sophie held it up and noticed the trailing vehicle. Leaning over to Justin, she whispered, "We have company."

Nodding, Justin replied, "Then we'll make the switch," at the same time rapping three times on the roof of the coach.

They continued several blocks to the east, and then halted at the Church of St. Irene, where Justin and Sophie got out. Entering the church, they slipped through the nave and out through the garden, where another carriage picked them up on the far side of the church and continued down a side road. The couple were soon satisfied that they had beaten the tail that had been put on them.

"So, the hunt begins again in the greatest city in the world," murmured Justin to his wife, who smiled and replied, "I wonder what tonight will bring?"

CHAPTER 2

After informing the new driver of their destination, they trotted along in silence for a few minutes. Ahead, they could see the great stadium/racetrack of the Hippodrome on one side and the soaring bulk that was Hagia Sophia, the Church of Holy Wisdom, on the other. Turning left at the Hippodrome, it was a short drive past the Senate House and the law courts to the Chalke Gate on the north end of the palace complex. So-called for its bronze doors, now closed for the night, the gate was surmounted by a giant icon of Christ Pantokrator whose visage was stern even as his right hand was lifted in blessing. The buildings of the Great Palace formed an interconnected maze that was over a mile in length, and contained individual structures that dated back to the time of Constantine 700 years before.

"Are we there yet?" said Sophie mischievously.

"Have we stopped?" replied Justin. "You'll know when we get there, I promise."

In a more serious voice, Sophie said, "Given the handwriting on the note, it had to be from Alexius. Why do you think he wanted me here? After all, I'm not in the 'society' like you are."

"Oh, come on, you know that is just something Alexius made up for security purposes. We can hardly be getting notes from the Secret Empire Committee Opposing External Threats, can we? And, after all, *alitheia* means truth, so it fits."

Sophie sighed, "Whatever. It has to be a murder—that much is obvious, but where is the security issue?"

"I think we'll find out shortly. The grid reference has us going by the Boukouleon complex where your Varangian friends are quartered, but not all the way to the harbor itself."

Soon after passing the last of the ramshackle collection of buildings which housed the Varangian mercenaries, they could feel the carriage start to slow down. Justin stuck his head out the window and saw several people standing by the side of the road. Turning to Sophie, he said, "All right, dear, here we go—showtime!"

As they alit from the carriage, the first man to greet them, as they expected, was Justin's deputy treasurer, Alexius. Alexius was of an indeterminate age, due to his smooth bald head and equally hairless face. Justin had often intended to ask him how old he was, but always decided that it was none of his business, as was Alexius' life as a eunuch. Either way, Alexius was worth his weight in gold, despite a sharp tongue which he never hesitated to display. While his ability to balance budgets was matchless, he had recently also demonstrated a knack for the clandestine, with his knowledge of the seamy sides of life in the city coming as an added bonus.

"Hey, Boss, thanks for coming on such short notice!" Bowing to Sophie, he continued, "And I see you brought the Scalpel, too!"

Sophie forced a smile. "Ha-ha, Deputy! Seriously, this had better be good—we were settled down for a quiet evening."

Alexius frowned and then said, in a much quieter voice, "Serious—yes. Good—I don't think so, but then again, solving murders is what you two do best, isn't it? The body is over here." He turned and walked off the road into an alley on the west side.

As Sophie began to follow, she noticed that there were a number of men holding torches ahead in what appeared to be a circle. What caught her eye was the fact that even in the flickering light she could see that they were Varangians, the Vikings who had come to the city they called Mikkelgard in search of employment as mercenaries. Admission standards were high, and the men's loyalty was unquestioned. The fact that they stood on average about half a foot higher than the Romans added to their overall impression, as did the shoulder-length blond braids in their hair and the long, single-bladed axes they carried everywhere.

As they drew nearer, Sophie could hear a murmur of men's voices saying, "Jarnlayden koma, Jarnlayden koma!" {"The Iron Lady comes, the Iron Lady comes!"}

By now, Justin had noticed this too, and tugged on Sophie's arm. She shook him off, for now her mind was in full-perceptive mode as she took all of the scene that lay in front of her. For starters, the main attraction was the body lying in the middle of the circle. Clad in full-dress Varangian garb, the man lay on his back with his hands folded across his chest. No weapon was apparent but it was clear that the man's throat had been cut from ear to ear and that his nose had been slit. He was clearly dead, his sightless eyes facing the sky. Given the nature of the wounds, there was surprisingly little blood. He was fully clothed in the dark off-duty tunic and cloak favored by the Norsemen, with his sword and dagger still stuck in his belt. Sophie immediately noticed that the dagger appeared to be half-way out of its sheath.

As they moved forward, the men holding torches crowded in for a better view, which led Sophie to call out, "Einn armr doegr, Vikingr! Augen framen—hedhra inn nar!" {"An unfortunate day, Norsemen! Eyes front—honor the dead!"} In response, as a unit the men stepped back and came to attention.

Justin reflexively crossed himself in the approved Orthodox style using two fingers, up and down, right to left. While he and Alexis were still registering the dead body, Sophie scanned the scene taking everything in. She stepped forward, watching where she stepped, and noticed a ruby earring in the dead man's right ear. She did not touch it nor anything else on the body save the dagger at the man's belt. Pulling it out, she noted that there were traces of blood on the tip. After placing it back, she looked side to side wide-eyed, seemingly in a trance. She then began talking to herself as she examined the scene and the body.

"Victim is a male, approximately 6 feet, 2 inches tall, lying on his back. Hair on head is blond and curly, as is full beard. Appears to be in his 20's. Apparent cause of death is a stab wound from a dagger which slit his throat. From the incision, this was done from left to right, indicating that the killer is right-handed. Victim's blue eyes are open. He is fully clothed and there is little blood, too little in fact for such a wound." Peering closer, she added, "There appear to be no other cuts or marks on the body which would be the source of the blood on the knife blade, indicating that the dead man may have injured one attacker before he was overcome by a second from behind. Slitting of the nose was done post-mortem, given the minimal amount of blood on the face."

Justin was used to this and said nothing. Alexis had never seen Sophie in action and whispered. "Is this normal?"

"Oh, yes," said Justin. "Let the woman work."

The two men stood silent for several minutes while Sophie roamed about the scene, looking intensely at everything. At one point, she took a torch from one of the Norsemen, and bent low over the man's face, as if sniffing. Then standing, she turned and addressed the men around her.

"Dreifask, felangi! Sjask um til blod!" {"Spread out, friends! Look for blood!"} Sophie motioned Justin and Alexius to remain while the Varangians scattered while still holding the torch. When they were a sufficient distance away, she whispered, "All right, I want you to turn the victim on his side—I want to see what is underneath the body."

As Justin bent down to do so, he was conscious of a strong smell of wine, and even the dead man's clothes were wet with it. When he and Alexius had the body on its side (no easy task), Sophie looked underneath and said, "Ah-ha, I thought so. All right, you can put him back down now."

Seeing Justin's quizzical look, she continued, "You noticed the same smell I did—but Varangians usually don't drink wine, at least not to excess, only beer and mead. I was looking to see if there was any wine under the body—there was an entire pool."

Unable to restrain himself, Alexius burst out, "So, so?"

Sophie gave the faintest of eye-rolls and said, "The murderer or murderers wanted us to think that this poor man was falling down drunk, so he or they actually poured wine over the body after it was already placed here. The question now is, where was he actually killed?"

News on that front was quick to come, for within a few minutes there came a shout, "Hi, Snotti, Hi!" {"Here, Lady, here!"}.

They looked up and saw a Varangian waving a torch across the street in an alley directly across from theirs. With Sophie in the lead, everyone moved in the man's direction. However, before people could trample the scene Sophie turned and yelled instructions in both Greek and Norse that everyone should stay back. With Justin on her left and Alexius on her right with torches, she surveyed a sizeable patch of blood on the pavement. Of more interest to her were splatters of blood on one side of the alley wall. She stood silent for a moment in front of the blood patch, and visually measured the distance to the wall. Satisfied, she nodded to Justin and they returned to the street.

As was his wont, Alexius wanted directions. "All right, Bosses, what now?"

With a nod from Sophie, Justin replied, "Very well, here is what we want. First, have the body removed with honor—I'm sure the Varangians have already started work there. Second, we want to know who he is—he must have a name. Third, we will need to speak with any men he was with earlier tonight, as well as his commander, or supervisor, or whatever they call it. Finally, activate the Alitheia Society network—we need to have all of our informants and spies working overtime on this one. This may be nothing, but one never knows. Understand?"

"Got it. Sorry for the late call. Good night."

"Good night—I'll see you in the main office tomorrow—I have a feeling that the Prefect and others are going to be asking about this."

"'Others', Boss? Like who?"

"As I recall, the civil official who oversees the Varangians is the Akolouthos, who is currently a retired general whom Basil made a senator. Apart from that, I don't know anything about him. I suspect we'll be meeting soon, though."

As he and Sophie rode in the carriage back to their villa, making sure to take a circuitous route, Justin felt torn between feeling weary and exuberant. While some husbands would have interpreted their wives' silence and motionlessness for sleep, Justin knew better. Beside him, he knew Sophie was still going through what she had just seen, and would be analyzing it for some time. He also knew that it was his place to remain awake, so as to be fully available to her when she needed to have her conclusions validated.

By the time their carriage turned north past the Hagia Sophia, Sophie was ready to break her silence. "Your deputy, Alexius, is a good man, you know. You need to keep him."

While he wondered for a moment where this was going, Justin replied, "Oh, I know, I know. Still, why do you say that?"

"Because this is no ordinary murder. Sure, I know that the Varangians look rough—that's part of their effectiveness—and they are not above getting into the occasional brawl in a tavern which sometimes leads to a killing. However, I also know that they have an internal code of honor that they hold themselves to, and that for every man who comes to the empire there are at least three more who want to. This was not a random act, although it was staged to look like it. Dear, I think we're looking at an assassination here, although I have no idea why."

"Because of the way the body was positioned?"

"Yes, that, as well as the fact that it was moved so that it would be more easily found for maximum effect."

Sophie paused for a moment, and then sighed. "Of course, it could have been the settlement of a private grudge in which case it will go no further. Still, this seems to have been a calculated killing done without passion. Enough for tonight—we'll see what tomorrow brings. On another topic, what are you going to do about the tail we had on us tonight?"

Justin gave a low laugh. "Absolutely nothing. There is no way you could have noticed the man across the street from our villa—there are several that take shifts and wear various disguises. When we shook off our friend tonight at the church, Alexius' people put a tail on him. We'll find out tomorrow if anything comes of it."

Sophie cocked her head and gave her husband a side-long glance. "Well, played, well played. You are taking this spy thing seriously."

Frowning, Justin was quiet for a few seconds, and then said, "We have to, Sophie, we have to. The people on the other side mean business, so we have to be vigilant as well."

At this, the carriage pulled up into the circle drive in front of their house, and the couple went inside and prepared for bed. Lying together, Sophie grasped Justin's hand. "Sleep well, dear. I know I will—knowing that your people are out there, guarding the city and the empire. Good night!"

CHAPTER 3

Morning came early in Constantinople in June, and it did not help that the hoopoes were yammering outside the window of Justin and Sophie's bedroom. Justin finally gave up and rose, only to find that Sophie was well ahead of him. On what she called her "palace days", she had to be suitably attired, as befitted the chief lady-in-waiting for her Imperial Highness Princess Zoe. It was a fine line she had to walk—being well-dressed without out-shining her mistress—but years of practice served Sophie well. Only in the art of drawing her long, black hair up into braids did she need assistance, something provided by her maid Donna.

Now that she had not one but two children, Sophie had perfected the art of getting along with as little sleep as possible. Well before Justin had arisen, she had been up, seeing to Simon (who now, thank the Virgin) slept through the night, as well as hearing from Maria, who wanted to take her pony to the palace to show Aunt Theodora how big it had grown. Unfortunately, given that Poppy (the pony) had a penchant for leaving odiferous calling cards on a frequent basis, Sophie had declared it to be *equinam non gratia*, with the result that never again could it make the trip to the palace.

Maria took the news with surprising good grace, a fact which Sophie filed away as a warning of something else to come on her daughter's part. By the time Justin came down to the dining hall to join them, all three of his family were playing together with the dogs.

Although it was the same every day, he still felt gratified when both Maria and Simon rushed over to him with cries of "Papa!" and gave him hugs. He reciprocated, and then, as was another still-gratifying custom, gave Sophie a warm kiss. Breakfast was a little bread and cheese, washed down with apple juice made from the couples' own trees, which grew in the terraces below the back of the villa.

Maria had taken to quizzing both of her parents as to their daily plans, something which she continued today. Occasionally, when there were no significant activities planned, she would accompany either Justin or Sophie to "work". While today was not to be such a day, in the manner of 10 year-olds everywhere, she quickly moved on to the next challenge, which involved riding Poppy. Sophie accordingly called for Agatho the groom, and then made sure that Simon was secure and happy with his nanny. While Justin was usually far more eager than she to get to the Palace, Sophie was still feeling the exuberance of being involved in a new investigation, even though, as she had sometimes noted to Justin, this feeling came at the cost of another person's life. So, she surprised her spouse of 16 years by being in the carriage when he stepped out onto the front portico.

"Well," she said, "finally ready to go?"

Justin could only smile, and then sit down beside her. As he did and the carriage began to move away, there came a cry from inside the house, from a voice that could only be that of Philip, their steward.

"No, Miss Maria, you can't bring the pony in here, no, no, you can't!"

Justin looked to Sophie who only smiled and said, "He'll work it out—drive on!"

Soon the couple was riding in their large open carriage across the broad avenues of Constantinople. It was a sunny day, bringing everyone to the streets. Their progress was slowed by the crowds, but neither one minded.

As they passed the many venerable structures, Justin thought with a smile how his first "job" in the city had been to make an index of all the city's public buildings. Fresh from his home in Thessalonica, he had come to Constantinople at the age of 18, with nothing but high hopes and a letter of recommendation from his uncle to the man who was Prefect of the city at the time, Romanus Phocas. A poorer relation of a great noble family, Phocas had chosen public service as a career, and had been in office when Emperor Basil decreed that the large estates should be either broken up or heavily taxed. He had earned a reputation as someone who enjoyed furthering the careers of bright young men who, unlike he had done, were starting at the bottom. Only after completing the Prefect's assignment did Justin realize that it had been a test to see if he had the right make-up and background for imperial service. Though it had now been 16 years, he found he could still name off the many buildings without even really looking. Since they had just passed the Palace of Botaneiates, the Church of Urbicius had to be next, then the Forum of Constantine, then…

"Naming the buildings, dear?" Sophie whispered in his ear. "Are they all still here?"

Justin smiled and patted her hand. "Yes, they are, and we're coming to your favorite one now." As he said this, they turned onto the shopping center of the entire empire, the Mese, a broad avenue that ran from the land walls to the plaza between the Hagia Sophia and the Palace complex. "What would the merchants of the city do without you?"

"Oh you, don't exaggerate! I'm sure there are some I don't know."

Given the reception they received as they rode past the many stalls filled with merchandise, however, a neutral observer could well doubt the truth of that statement. Truly, the Mese, the Middle Street, was the world's marketplace, where the wealth of many nations was on display. Here were metal dealers—gold, silver, bronze and copper—while further on were the sellers of glass, ivory, perfumes, leather, silk and jewels. Next came the merchants of household items like lamps, vases, embroideries and rugs, while further down meats, cheeses, fruit, honey, spices and bread were available. No matter the item, though, their passing universally evoked the same response, as many voices greeted "Lady Sophia" and implored her to stop and inspect their wares. Her response to each was a smile and a wave, which continued even as Justin leaned forward and told the coachman to keep driving.

Traffic was clogged, however, and the carriage slowed to a stop to let a wagon carrying barrels of Thracian wine cross the street. While they were stopped, a scruffy beggar with a patch over one eye came up to the side of the carriage. While Sophie professed to be unconcerned, she was internally alarmed when Justin, her mild-mannered husband, began to engage the tramp in conversation.

"Good morning, my good man! How can we help you?"

"May Saint Theodore and the Virgin bless you sir!" the man croaked. "My name's Sergius, I'm a veteran of Emperor Basil's wars, I am, and have lost an eye in his service. Could you spare a follis or two for a meal? I'm powerfully hungry!"

Justin nodded, and then, to Sophie's amazement, said, "We can do better than that, friend. Why don't you get in with us and we can take to where you need to go?"

To Sophie's consternation, the beggar, showing surprising agility, hopped into the carriage beside her. Turning to her, he said, in a completely different voice, "Good morning, Lady Sophia—I trust you had a pleasant evening, apart from the dead body, of course?" Then he flipped up the eye patch over his left eye, to show a fully-functional blue eye that was twinkling along with its companion on the right.

As quick as Sophie usually was to absorb information, this revelation set her aback for a moment. Then, her mouth agape, she recognized the Deputy Treasurer of the Roman Empire, and exclaimed, "Alexius, you wretch! How dare you!" Then, pausing to smile, she continued, "but still, well done!"

"Thank you, Lady, thank you—please forgive me my little jest—I have been awake for over a day now and I'm feeling a little woozy."

Justin, who had recognized Alexius from the start, decided to draw the line. "Indeed, sir, what are you playing at? Do you think you can fulfill your responsibilities in an exhausted state? You're not a one-man department, you know!"

Alexius hung his head, but only for an instant, before he brightened up and said, "So, can I have the rest of the day off?"

"Certainly not, you don't get off that easy. What are you doing out here anyhow?"

Lowering his voice, Alexius replied, "I'm checking with my contacts to see if anyone knows more about what happened last night."

While not fully taking in the import of Alexius' words, Sophie nonetheless said to Justin, "So, it's that serious?"

"Maybe, maybe not, but that's what the network is for, to investigate matters out of the ordinary."

Sophie frowned, "So, when were you going to bring me in? Aren't we a team?"

Looking appropriately humble, Justin replied, "We haven't had a crime of this magnitude up to now—there was no reason to. Believe me, you're in now."

Before things got more heated, Alexius made a timely intervention. "Yeah, that's right! I always wondered about that—how did the two of you get into this sort of stuff anyhow?"

Justin smiled at Sophie, and then, taking her hand, said, "Well, it's a long story, and since we're getting near where you, 'Sergius', need to get out, I'll give you the condensed version. It's been 16 years since our first case—we just married, and I was a junior official in the Prefect's office—not the current one, but his predecessor. Anyhow, we showed that the manager of a troupe of players from out-of-town had not killed the Master of the Notaries, who was involved in a shake-down scheme targeting those people coming to the city for the Millennial. We caught the eye of the emperors, and I was named the new Master of the Notaries. So, from time to time, we've been brought in on other matters, and have done pretty well, haven't we, dear? How many has it been—20, I think?"

Sophie smiled. "No dear, it's 21—you always forget that one where we cleared the Master of the Fisheries."

"Aughh, that guy—the one who sent us herring every week for a year to show his thanks! I hate herring!!"

"Well, at any rate, Alexius," Sophie continued, "we haven't had one since the emerald dealer affair two years ago, which turned out to be a triple killing."

Alexius nodded. "Who can forget that one, Lady? Although as I recall, the ultimate killer is still at large."

"Very true," said Justin, "although we know where he is." Then, looking up, he noticed that the carriage was nearing the large square where the Mese ended that separated the Hagia Sophia, the Great Palace and the Hippodrome. "All right, 'Sergius', it's time you got out. I want you back in the office today by early afternoon—I have a feeling the Prefect is going to want an update on what we know—I hope you have something good to tell him."

"Right, Boss, see you then. I'll check in with the annex first."

But before Alexius could get out of the carriage, Sophie motioned to her left eye, reminding him to put the eye-patch back down. Looking sheepish, he did so, and quickly disappeared into the crowd.

"'Annex'?" said Sophie to her husband.

"Yes, it's the secret location of the Society headquarters—if I tell you, I'll have to kill you."

"I'll take my chances."

"Well, you'll recall that entire debacle which happened two years ago with the former treasurer and his nephew—you know, the one who got tossed off the sea wall?"

"Sure, he got killed by that Serbian who was found the next day on the shore across the Marmara with his throat cut, courtesy of your friend the Caliph."

"Not my friend, thank you, but yes that's the nephew I mean. Anyhow, it turns out that with his uncle's connivance he had a separate suite of offices in a different building from the rest of the Treasury. When we rolled those into the main office, we had some space open to us and that's where Alexius keeps his stable of informers, low-lives, no-goods and general miscreants. We call it the annex."

"Thank you, husband. At least I can die happy. Still, duty calls—here we are."

The carriage stopped in front of the Chalke Gate on the north end of the palace complex. Justin helped Sophie alight from the carriage, and the two strode through the entry hall, walking under mosaics of Justinian and Theodora that still gleamed five centuries after their creation. As they approached the inner door, they could see what appeared to be some kind of confrontation in process. A group of men wearing western garb were gesturing and yelling at the palace officials and churchmen standing in front of the doors.

After a nod to Sophie, Justin walked up to the Italians, as he perceived them to be, and said, "Buongiorno, Signori, posso aiutare?" {"Good morning, sirs, may I help?"}

For the next several minutes, Sophie was an amused onlooker to a scene in which her husband was the central participant, translating between the Italians on one side and the palace officials on the other. Finally, after much gesturing and hand-wringing, some resolution was arrived at, and the visitors were admitted, with profuse cries of "Grazie, Grazie!" in Justin's direction.

"Well, don't leave me hanging, what just went on?" she said when her husband came back to her.

"A simple misunderstanding, it appears. This group is a delegation from His Holiness in Rome to see Patriarch Sergius on some theological dispute. They ran into trouble when they insisted on calling themselves 'Romans'. Since only those of us under the authority of the true emperors can say that, they were denied admission."

"And you worked that out? I must say, I'm impressed. What did you say?"

"Oh, after first determining that none of the Italians really understood Greek that well, I told the palace officials and churchmen that while these men were only pretending to be Romans, it pleased his Majesties that they be allowed to continue their charade. So, they were happy, the Italians were happy, and everyone wins."

Sophie gave a rueful smile and shook her head. "Sure, until somebody finds out otherwise—of course, you'll be long gone."

Justin smiled back, "Timing, my dear, timing. Now, it's time to get to work. Expect a message from the Prefect later today—I'll meet you there. After that, we need to talk to the Varangians who knew the victim—you can sound them out."

"Way ahead of you, husband! See you soon." And with that and a kiss on his cheek, she swept off down the corridor, carving a path between courtiers, court officials and visitors who bowed as she passed.

CHAPTER 4

Sophie soon came to the portion of the palace reserved for the quarters of the royal family. Zoe, as princess imperial, had her residence in the suite called the Porphyra, so named for the abundance of purple silk hangings and even purple marble. After serving in such a place for 17 years, Sophie had developed a hearty dislike for the color, and forbade it to be displayed anywhere in her own house. Access was limited by decree, and enforced by the presence outside of the Varangians who served as members of the Emperor's own personal guard. Constant contact with them had led Sophie to listen to them talk, and when she responded, albeit haltingly, one day, she was thrilled when they spoke back. Daily practice from then on had led her to be able to converse with them freely, something which had already proved to be of an immense benefit to her and Justin, and had also given her the nickname of Iron Lady.

As always, two were on guard outside the door where Sophie would take her leave of Justin. While they always looked grim, Sophie thought that today they looked particularly so. Deciding to test them, she turned to the Varangian on the left and said, "Godr dag, Vini. Ek bida yovarr wel?" {"Good day, Leader. I hope you are well?"}

With no change of expression but with a slight bow, the blond giant responded, "Ek fagha vel, Snotte. Yovar all kyn. Beste gesornd." {"I am well, Lady. You are very kind. Be of good health."}

"Bakka mjok, Vini." {"Thank you very much, Leader."}

Then, in a lower voice, the other guard said, "Snotte, leggja fyrir Magnus." {"Lady, give Magnus justice!"}

Sophie stopped, looked at them both and gave a slight nod, then passed through into the inner chamber. The world that she entered was as different from the one outside the Palace as could possibly be imagined. All was luxury and wealth and pomp and comfort, as well as silence, or at least very little noise, for noise was held to be common and potentially disturbing. Room after room held more wealth than did many cities in the barbaric West, and the days passed without being counted. For the royal inhabitants, reality was something to be created and not endured, and the life of those outside the palace walls was, up to recently, neither imagined nor understood. Now, however, things were changing, thanks to Sophie's mistress.

The woman whom Sophie served as chief lady-in-waiting was Zoe Porphyrogenita ('born in the purple' when her father Constantine was already emperor). She was 38 years old, but did her best to look ten years younger. Her appearance was aided by having never had to work a day in her life or to ever want for anything. It was also helped by her generous use of various creams, lotions and potions designed to keep her skin smooth and white. Indeed, several rooms had been set aside for the preparation of such nostrums, and a staff of herbalists and alchemists worked ceaselessly to come up with new preparations. Sophie had found it vaguely ridiculous, but kept her opinions to herself, out of self-preservation as much as a genuine feeling of affection for her mistress. Zoe was also very pious and engaged in prayer for two hours a day. She had been engaged to marry twice, but in both cases the prospective grooms died before the weddings could be held.

For her part, Sophie had become a junior lady-in-waiting when she was 18. As a daughter of a notable family in Constantinople (her father was a well-known physician), she won the position due to her beauty, her grace and her wit. Like most young women who held such a position, it was expected that she would serve for one year, perhaps two, before becoming married and leaving the royal service. However, she and Zoe bonded in such a way that leaving was unthinkable, at least for Zoe, and that was all that mattered. Even her betrothal and marriage to an unknown young man from the provinces did not diminish her standing with the Princess.

That standing was even more enhanced by the experiences Zoe had shared with Sophie and Justin two years earlier, when a pilgrimage to Jerusalem badly misfired, first through an attack by Turks in the pass known as the Cilician Gates, and then in Jerusalem itself, when they were kidnapped by the Caliph of the Fatimids. Transported to Cairo for purposes of ransom, Zoe had been freed by the ingenuity of her friends and the self-sacrifice of her confessor Father Simon, the man Sophie and Justin had taken as the inspiration for the name of their new son.

Since their return, Zoe was in some respects a changed woman. A reconciliation with her younger sister Theodora had followed her return. This had made Sophie's life easier in at least one respect, for during the years that Zoe and her sister were estranged, great care had to be taken they were never seen in public together wearing the same or even similar outfits. Fortunately, due to cooperation with Theodora's head lady (also named Sophia), harmony was preserved. While the 'other Sophie' had retired since the reconciliation, things had gone well, at least up to now. With Zoe, Sophie knew, it was always a day-to-day matter.

More importantly, at least to Sophie, was Zoe's changed outlook on life. Up to the time of her pilgrimage to Jerusalem, her world had been very narrow, confined entirely to the city in which she was born, 'in the purple.' Travelling across the empire to cities and towns which had seldom seen a member of the royal house was an eye-opening experience, which Sophie had subtly used to remind her just how the wealth she enjoyed was generated. Even more significant was the time she spent in Jerusalem and in Cairo, where an audience produced hundreds of Christians who lived their lives as minorities subject to periodic oppression. The final impact was made by the sacrifice of Father Simon, who died in the successful attempt to permit their escape down the Nile to freedom. All of these experiences had led Zoe, with the cooperation of her, sister to sponsor a series of soup kitchens around the city, which in reality meant one more duty imposed on Sophie. Fortunately, with the Treasurer of the Roman Empire for a husband, finding money for the cause was generally not a problem.

Given this history, Sophie found it surprising that Zoe did not greet her after her absence for several days. Instead, she was greeted by Irene, age 28, who had been with Zoe for 10 years. After Sophie had broken with tradition and made the position of lady-in-waiting a potential lifetime appointment, others had followed. Some had not lasted, but Irene had. Sophie thanked God and all of the saints for Irene on a regular basis, for her presence enabled Sophie to have a life of her own. For her part, Irene did not seem to be interested in marriage, yet was perfectly willing to serve Zoe through the oversight of Sophie. As for the other ladies, the group had gradually grown older as Zoe herself aged. Very early on, Sophie had perceived that Zoe's identity was largely based on how she looked. As a result, there would inevitably be tensions if Zoe found herself surrounded by women who were increasingly younger than she was. Sophie's solution, quietly managed, was to have a decreasing number of ladies in the 20-year old range, with a greater number in their 30's, but still not older than Zoe.

"Irene, good to see you," Sophie said with a hug.

"You too, my lady. I hope you are rested and refreshed?" Irene replied with a smile.

"Well, I was, at least until last night. Justin and I have got another case. I should be working on that, but I couldn't miss lunch today, what with Princess Theodora coming."

Like most of Constantinople, Irene was familiar with the couples' reputation, and could only exclaim, "Another case—that's wonderful! What can you tell me?"

"Very little at this point, and I'm not being coy. A Varangian was murdered, but exactly why and by who we still don't know."

Irene smiled even more broadly. "But you will, Sophie, you will. Zoe will be thrilled to hear all about it!"

"Speaking of the Princess, where is she?" Sophie's question was immediately answered when two three-year old children came running out of a side room, closely pursued by Zoe herself. All three were laughing. When Zoe saw Sophie, she stopped and adjusted her blond hair, which was pulled up into a bun on her head.

In a stern voice, she said, "About time you came back!" and frowned, which was quickly replaced with a grin. "It's good to see you!"

"And you as well, Princess, although I would note I was only gone for two weeks," Sophie replied. "I see you're entertaining yourself anyhow."

Another of the ladies-in-waiting had rounded up the children, one of which was her own, and herded them back into the adjoining room which had been converted into a nursery and day-care. Sophie was responsible for this change in palace routine, for following her announcement of her pregnancy with baby Simon, Zoe was ready to do anything to avoid cutting ties with her. This change had the unexpected benefit of broadening the pool of women who were interested in becoming ladies-in-waiting, which eased the burden on Sophie, Irene and other long-timers. Zoe loved the change, and did her younger sister Theodora, who had instituted a similar practice in her own living area. If their father, Emperor Constantine, or their uncle, Emperor Basil, knew of the situation, the two men said nothing.

"Oh, we get along," replied Zoe. "But where are Maria and Simon? I haven't seen them today."

"Well, they're not here, and for a very good reason." Then, lowering her voice, Sophie added, "Justin and I have a new case, and we may be working some long hours."

The face of the princess lit up. "Oh, how wonderful! It will be like old times! How can I help?"

Knowing Zoe as she did, Sophie had anticipated a response of this sort. Not wanting to offend her boss, who also happened to be a member of the royal house, she smoothly replied, "I'll tell you all about it at lunch. I imagine your sister will want to hear about it, too. Now, let's get you ready—you need to look your best!"

Getting Zoe to look her best was not difficult, given that Sophie had virtually unlimited resources at her disposal. While every day was a formal day for the Imperial Princess when it came to her attire, some days were more so. With the luncheon planned for that day, Sophie decided to err on the side of formality. She accordingly selected a new light blue knee-length silk gown which had lower sleeves of dark green and bronze accents up and down the sides. The lower inner skirt which reached almost to the floor was also bronze, as was Zoe's tiara, which was attached to a silver headdress which reached down to the middle of her back. The finishing touch was provided by a magnificent emerald necklace which Zoe had acquired two years earlier from merchants who had come from India. Initially stolen in a theft which involved a murder, it later was recovered by Sophie and Justin. Zoe pronounced herself "thrilled" by the results, and they emerged to await their guests.

So it was that, sometime later that morning, Imperial Princess Zoe greeted her younger sister Theodora, who arrived with her entourage of six ladies-in-waiting and her own guard of Varangians. The soldiers stayed outside with their compatriots already there, while the ladies mingled with their counterparts in Zoe's household. Sophie took the opportunity to peek outside, and was careful that she not be seen by the Norsemen. She saw many of them standing in a group, and while she could not hear most what they were saying, they appeared to be nervous, even tense. Among the few words she was able to make out were "Jarnlayden"{"the Iron Lady"}, which she knew from experience was the men's nickname for her. Another was "Loviatar", which meant nothing to her.

Not wanting to be discovered, she closed the door and rejoined the group. In keeping with long-established protocol, seating for the luncheon was strictly regulated. When Zoe was dining with her ladies, she sat at the head of a triangular table, with Sophie on her right and Irene on her left. The other ladies were arranged in order of seniority, with the new women at the base of the triangle. Every meal that Zoe ate, unless she took food in her chambers, was a formal affair, and the stewards served the courses of fruit, cheese, fish and bread with wordless efficiency. Today, though, the table had been enlarged so that the two royal sisters sat side by side at the head of a long table, with each one's respective attendants sitting down each side. It was customary for the ladies-in-waiting to stand until their mistresses had taken their seats.

As Sophie stood next to Irene, she cast a practiced eye cast on Theodora's outfit, and she was impressed with what she saw. Although somewhat shorter and plainer than Zoe, Theodora nonetheless looked stunning in a gold robe which was wrapped around her, accessorized with a jeweled belt, golden bracelets and a gold tiara from which a long train flowed down her back, almost to her feet. Sophie could tell that this was not lost on Zoe either, and made a mental note to be ready to hear about it when next they were alone. She also wondered where Leonida, Theodora's new dresser, was getting such innovative ideas.

When the sisters had gotten settled the stewards began the parade of dishes. It was also a matter of custom that no one was to speak until one of the sisters had first done so, but, Zoe being Zoe, that was not long in coming. "So, Lady Sophia," she began, using the formal title that she employed for Sophie in public, "we understand that you and your husband are involved in a new investigation. I am sure we would all like to hear about it, provided of course that it is not a state secret."

Sophie knew Zoe well enough to know that the princess was not really that interested in the details of the crime, but was using her acquaintance with Sophie to show everyone, particularly her sister, how fortunate she was to have such a clever person in her household. So, she gave only a brief overview of what she had seen, although her description of the deceased as a Varangian caused raised eyebrows around the table. Theodora in particular was taken by this.

"That's very interesting, Lady Sophia," she said, "I noticed that the guards were unusually tense this morning. Perhaps this was why."

At this, Zoe gave a broad smile and broke in, "And you can be sure that Lady Sophia will find out—do you know she can speak their awful language?"

With this, Sophie decided that things had gone far enough, and so announced that while she really couldn't say anything more, she was going to be interviewing the soldiers later that afternoon. This got her knowing nods from around the table, and the luncheon conversation turned to more conventional subjects like the soup kitchens that the two sisters had started to support following Zoe's return from her Egyptian ordeal.

With lunch concluded, Theodora and her entourage departed, with mutual exchanges of "See you next week," and the like. Sophie was spared the task of having to deal with Zoe over any possible dress issue with the timely appearance of Brother James, who was the latest in a long line of monks who served as the spiritual advisor to the Princess. He had been in his position since Zoe's return, and tolerated the bustle of the palace better than most of his predecessors, who resented taking time off from the life of spiritual solitude which they had sought. He strongly supported Zoe's work among the poor, which put him at odds at times with Patriarch Sergius who looked down on such interaction between royalty and the common people. Sophie liked him, but found him to be much more withdrawn than Father Simon had been. Still, he acknowledged her presence and her importance in Zoe's life, and the two had worked out a mutually-harmonious existence. Afternoons were Zoe's prayer time, something for which Sophie had more than once herself given thanks in prayer.

Before she could head to the Prefect's office, Sophie checked with Irene that everyone knew their duties for the rest of the day and evening. When she was finished doing so, Irene asked, "So, did you see Theodora's gown today?"

Sophie groaned. "Yes, I did, and I am sure Zoe did too. Where is Leonida getting these ideas?"

Irene shook her head. "I don't know, but you had better find out, or come up with something better. The 40th anniversary banquet is coming up next week, in case you've forgotten." Then, taking Sophie's hand, she went on, "You poor dear, having to investigate murders and design gowns all at once! I don't envy you."

Sophie gave a wan smile as she headed towards the outer door, "All in a day's work, I guess. See you tomorrow."

As Sophie passed the Varangians still standing impassively at the outer doors, she made a point to say in a low voice, only for their hearing, "Magnus munu hafa jafnadr!" {"Magnus will have justice!"}

CHAPTER 5

After leaving Sophie, Justin walked past the old throne room built by Heraclius, then a newer one constructed by Basil I, who was the founder of the dynasty of which Basil and Constantine were the latest members. After passing through a majestic garden containing numerous fountains he finally came to the Treasury complex, which was made up of two adjoining buildings which had originally been the residential areas of Leo III and his descendants 300 years before. It was hard not to be aware of the history, given the number of mosaics of Leo's dynasty that were all around. Leo III had been an iconoclast, as every orthodox Roman knew, and while he was remembered for having saved the Empire from the last siege by the Arabs, he was more often reviled for having waged war against the religious pictures which the common people revered. More than once, Justin had found this ironic, given the number of times Leo, his son Constantine V and the rest of the dynasty apparently had not been troubled by having their own pictures preserved in stone.

On this day, however, all of the splendor around him was lost on Justin. He had long been conscious of the different worlds he lived in as an Imperial bureaucrat and as a husband and father, along with his occasional duties in investigating crimes. Now, he had to juggle the additional role of counter-intelligence agent, a position he had accepted following his return from Egypt at the request of Emperor Basil himself. This job consisted of overseeing Alexius and his network of agents in the city, who kept tabs on the known agents of the Caliph who were in Constantinople and attempted to identify new ones. Justin conferred with the Prefect of the Empire on a regular basis, with Emperor Basil participating behind the scenes.

As befitted an Empire that was expanding and for the most part peaceable, the Treasury department had expanded so much over the years of Basil's rule that it now required the work of over 400 people in Constantinople alone. Including the tax assessors and collectors throughout the entire realm, the number employed exceeded 2,000. While in the past most of those men never saw the capital in their lives, Justin had moved to change that once he was appointed Treasurer two years before. This had occurred after his predecessor, Michael Taronites, had been involved with wealthy landowners in a plot to frustrate Basil's taxation rules. Because of his connections, Taronites had merely suffered lifetime exile, and was currently 'serving' as governor of some third-rate island in the Aegean. Lately, there had been some days that Justin had cause to envy him.

After entering the Treasury complex, he went past the salutations of the guarding Varangians and the many workers who appreciated his diligence and honesty. Justin then went into the office he had had for several years and sat at his worktable, which was made of mahogany with a marble top. From the window, he had a fine view of the southern part of the city and could, on a clear day, even see the tops of the towers on the land walls several miles to the west. On the left was the Boukouleon Harbor, and the ever-changing assemblage of ships of all sizes and nations never lost its fascination for him. While he had been entitled to claim Taronites' old office, he valued the view that he had, and so had allocated the space otherwise.

After a few moments of reverie that were too quickly over, the first man to greet him inside, as he expected, was Alexius. In addition to his unparalleled ability to work with numbers, he seemed to be able to function with very little sleep and to transform himself from one persona to another, as there was now no trace of 'Sergius' the one-eyed beggar.

"Good to see you, Chief," Alexius drawled. "Glad that you could make it in today."

"You are insufferable, you miscreant! Still, there is work to be done. Despite what you may think, I can cover the department heads' meeting this morning and the meeting with the Prefect—I need you to line up interviews with the key Varangians for later this afternoon."

"Got it, Chief! Anything else?"

"Yes, has your network picked up anything yet?"

Alexius frowned before he responded. "Yeah, Chief, and what I'm hearing isn't good. The Varangians are troubled, really shaken up, and we can't figure out why. I mean, it's too bad about Magnus—oh, that's the name of the dead man—but he was just a junior officer. I know this wasn't a bar fight, but let's face it, these men live pretty rough—after all, that's why they're here in the first place."

"All the more reason for the interviews. Let's conduct them at the banquet hall the Varangians use, but keep the men separated before we talk to each of them individually. Sophie and I will meet you there. Oh, one more thing—how did the tail you put on our visitor go?"

Alexius shook his head. "I don't think whoever it was is on to us, but it ended like it has so often before—he disappeared into the merchants' quarters along the Mese. The alleys are like a maze along there. If we get too close, our cover will be blown. Sorry, Boss."

Justin patted his disconsolate deputy. "Well, if Rome wasn't built in a day, then we'll need to be patient. See you later! I'm off to the staff meeting."

He entered the conference room which was adorned in good iconoclastic manner with mosaics of antelopes, deer, peacocks and other more fantastic animals, along with extensive foliage. Around the table were seated his seven assistants, one for each of the principal taxation sources for the budget; land, head, hearth, commercial, guild, franchise, and the newest, gaming. Apart from one man, they were all older than he but he had, through hard work and insight, won their respect over the preceding years. The one younger man was Levi Ben-Isaacson, who headed up the gaming division, an innovation of Justin that was proving to be very profitable.

"Good morning, gentlemen," said Justin. I will not take very much of your time this morning. As you know, we have a busy week planned for next week, what with our guests from the Asian themes in town for their conference. I trust that each of you will meet with the officials in your various areas and update them on the latest changes to Imperial policy, with the exception of Levi, whose area is confined to the capital. I know that it's a lot to ask, given that there are over 20 themes represented, but I am sure you will do what needs to be done. For today, I would just like to have a brief update of where you think the midyear numbers will be. I won't hold you to them, and, as you can see, Deputy Alexius is not with us today, so you won't have to hear him throw them back at you." At this, there was a general chuckle around the table, for Alexius' amazing ability to retain and analyze numbers was legendary.

Each official then went through an update on his numbers—land tax (based on agricultural production), head (each person in the Empire paid something), hearth (chimney), 10% value added tax on all commercial sales, guild fees, franchise licenses and gaming revenues. Most were flat, although the land tax numbers were still below their five-year norms, due to the continuing re-allocation of estates seized after the landowners' conspiracy that had been part of Justin and Sophie's ordeal two years earlier.

The one shining light continued to be the gaming numbers. Upon his appointment as Treasurer, Justin had sought approval of the Prefect and, indirectly, the Emperors, for a system to license (and thereby tax) the gambling which everyone knew occurred on races in the Hippodrome. For centuries, horse and chariot races had been held there four days a week from May through October. Thousands of spectators showed up for each day of races, and gambling, though illegal, had been widespread. As Treasurer, Justin argued that it made fiscal sense to bow to reality. In part due to his success in extracting Princess Zoe from the clutches of the Caliph, he was given permission to proceed. A 5% tax on bets and a 10% tax on winnings had generated 10,000 gold solidi in the first year, with double that produced in the second. This was enough to provide an additional mounted regiment for Emperor Basil, with enough left over to help restore two crumbling churches in Constantinople and to help pay for Zoe's soup kitchens for the poor of the city.

The church aid helped to disarm the opposition of Patriarch Sergius, who had initially opposed the idea on moral grounds, namely that Christians should not associate themselves with such practices. While this position cost the patriarch what little respect Justin had for him, it also freed Justin to offer the position to a non-Christian, namely the Jew Levi Ben-Isaacson. When Levi delivered the first bag of gold to the patriarch, the holy man had a sudden conversion experience and gave thanks to the God of Abraham, Isaac and Jacob. Since then, he had voiced no opposition to Christians participating in gambling and Levi stayed in his position.

After hearing Levi's report, Justin thanked his staff, and then thought it prudent to add, "One more thing—as most of you know, from time to time my wife and I are called upon by the Emperors to investigate serious crimes. One such crime occurred last night. Although I cannot really say anything more about it at this time, I will try to be here as much as possible, but some absences undoubtedly will occur. At my request, Alexius also will be assisting with the investigation. That's it for today—keep up the good work!" With that, he set off for his meeting with the Prefect.

To get there, Justin had to walk for several minutes, for the Prefect's offices were at the north end of the Palace complex, on the opposite end of those of the Treasurer. If the latter's offices were large, the former's were vast, for the Prefect was the chief civil official of the entire empire, with thousands of employees spread from southern Italy to the Crimea, Armenia and Syria. As the overseer of all civil officials in a very centrally-organized empire, he was responsible only to the emperor, or emperors as the current situation dictated. While the final decision to appoint or remove officials lay with the emperors, the sheer volume of appointments meant that the Prefect's word was largely law, whether the emperor was a warrior who was largely absent like Basil, or a man who preferred to pursue his own pleasures like Constantine. Given the inherent power of the position, the appointment of the Prefect was one of the most important a ruler of the Empire could make.

As Deputy Treasurer, Justin had not had much interaction with the current Prefect, Leo Comnenus, prior to the events two years earlier involving Zoe's pilgrimage. Since then, they had spoken on at least a weekly basis. Leo had now been in office for several years, having replaced Justin's mentor Romanus Phocas, who had taken a much-deserved retirement with an appointment to the largely ceremonial Senate. Like many imperial officials (although not Justin), Leo came from a wealthy and landed family, but himself had no ownership in any estates in Asia Minor. As such, he was the perfect candidate to administer a bureaucracy whose impact fell largely on the landed aristocracy.

The offices were opulent, and were marked with mosaics dating back to the time of the Emperor Maurice, whose reign marked the last time that the Empire had stretched to its current extent. Justin was ushered into the Prefect's office by a staff member who was as obsequious as possible and was greeted by the Prefect himself, sitting behind a large marble table, who gestured to a cushioned chair across from him. He was a large man with a head full of white hair and a beard to match. Sitting by his right side was a middle-aged man in military regalia, who, with his stocky build and salt-and-pepper beard, looked much like Emperor Basil.

At the same time he took this in, Justin also noticed that a bust of Constantine the Great was on the left side of the prefect's desk. If it had been on the right, it would signal that Emperor Basil himself was in attendance, concealed behind a screen on the right side of the room. While Justin was not clear why the emperor liked to engage in this charade, he was willing to play along, and on occasion use it to his advantage.

"Good afternoon, Justin," the Prefect said in a deep voice. "Would you like some wine?"

Justin nodded and replied, "No, thank you, Prefect, it's a little early for me, although when Sophie arrives she'll likely have a different answer. While I'm glad we have this opportunity to talk today, we'll need more time to talk about the Crete trip—perhaps we can meet first thing on Monday morning?

"Sounds fine. Now, may I introduce you to General Nicephorus Xiphias, who is in the city for the anniversary celebrations. I have asked him to join us, in that he has knowledge of the Varangians whom he has commanded in Italy and elsewhere for many years."

Justin bowed his head in acknowledgement. "Ah, the hero of the Battle of Kleidion, I believe. It is an honor to meet you."

The general gave a slight smile. "I did my part. The plan for the battle and the danger in its execution were the responsibility of His Majesty. It is I whom am honored, for I believe you are the man who burned an entire Fatimid fleet?"

Before Justin could reply, he was interrupted by a familiar voice.

"Gentlemen, may I interrupt the mutual admiration society?" There, at the door, stood Sophie, with a smile on her face and a sparkle in her eye. "Oh, wine—thank you, I believe I will," she continued as she poured herself a glass.

Justin shook his head ruefully. "General, may I introduce my wife, Sophia Cataphlates, First Lady-in-Waiting to her Highness Princess Zoe. Feel free to say anything in her presence you would in mine. As you have already seen, she feels free to do the same."

"I have my orders, and will follow them," the general replied with a smile.

"Now to business," said the Prefect. "I understand that a member of the Varangians was killed last night. I know it's early, but have you two drawn any conclusions yet?"

"Only that the dead man held the equivalent rank of sergeant, that he was murdered, that there were at least two assailants, that his body was moved and that his death was intended to send a message," Sophie said. "We'll know more when we've interviewed some of the dead man's associates later this afternoon."

While he had seen it often before, Justin never tired of seeing the look of surprise on men's faces when they witnessed Sophie's deductive powers. General Xiphias was no different as he listened to her matter of fact recitation. Prefect Comnenus took it all in stride as he asked a follow-up question. "Any speculation as to what that message is?"

After glancing at Justin, Sophie continued, "No, I'm afraid not. While I did find it curious that the man's nose was slit after he was dead, I don't know enough about the Varangians to know if this has any significance."

"I might be able to help with that," said the general. "It's been my experience that while the Russians have adopted Christianity, many of their Varangian cousins from Scandinavia have not. It's possible that this kind of ritual mutilation would render a warrior less able to enter Valhalla, as they call the place of their afterlife. Still, it's often hard to tell what these men are thinking."

"Ah, General," said the Prefect. "That's where the gifts of these two are so valuable to the Empire. Justin here speaks Bulgarian, Russian, Italian, Armenian, Turkish and Arabic, while Sophie knows how to speak to the Varangians in their own language."

"Prefect, you are too kind," replied Sophie demurely. "I have a working knowledge only. Still, it should prove useful."

"Please proceed with your investigation, and keep me informed of all your significant findings. As you know, it was Emperor Basil who himself started the Varangian regiment. What you may not be aware of is that there are over 5,000 of these men serving across the Roman Empire. Any disruption of this would have very serious consequences—consequences which would be beneficial to a certain unnamed foreign ruler."

Justin nodded in agreement. "I understand, sir. We'll let you know. Uh, isn't there another official involved here, too? His title is Akolouthos, I believe?"

The faintest of frowns flitted across the prefect's face for a moment before he replied. "Yes, you are correct. He is the civil official overseeing the Varangians who are stationed in the city. The position is currently held by Senator Paul Kalokyros, a retired general who served with Emperor Basil and General Xiphias in the Bulgarian war. If you have any difficulty with him, please let me know."

Surprised, Sophie turned to the general. "Are you familiar with him, General?"

General Xiphias looked at Sophie, then at Justin, and finally the Prefect before responding, "Yes, I know him," without saying anything more.

On this puzzling note, Justin could not think of anything else to say but "Thank you, Prefect, we shall." With a bow, Justin turned to Xiphias and said, "General, it was good to meet you—I hope we have time to talk again while you're in the city. Shall we, dear?"

As they entered into the outer hallway, Sophie said in a low voice, "'Certain unnamed foreign ruler'? I hope not, husband, I sincerely hope not."

"Believe me, that makes two of us. Let's see what we can find out."

CHAPTER 6

It was a short carriage ride down to the warren of buildings north of the Boukouleon Harbor where the Varangians in the city were quartered. The buildings were not new, with some dating back to the time of the Empire Heraclius nearly four centuries before, who used the barracks and storehouses as a staging area for his eastern expeditions against the Persians. Nicephorus II, who ruled during the minority of Basil and Constantine, had most recently done the same for the expedition which re-took Crete from the Arab pirates who had held it for a century. The buildings stood empty for several years until Basil started the Varangian corps in 989. Although the entire Varangian contingent in the empire numbered around 5,000, only about 800 were at the city at any one time, serving as the elite guards for the emperors and other royalty and acting as palace security. The rest were on duty at the frontiers, primarily in Syria and Bulgaria, where they served as the empire's best shock troops coming into battle at the crucial moment.

Alexius was waiting to meet them outside the front entrance to the main dining hall where the Varangians held their weekly feasts on Friday night. With him was a Varangian officer who was even taller than most. He was in full-dress regalia, with a breastplate over his chain mail shirt that was decorated with what appeared to be fantastic beasts. In place of the broad-bladed ax which such soldiers usually carried, he had a long sword in his belt, contained in a jeweled scabbard. A dark red robe attached around his neck with a gold collar completed his ensemble. The two rubies in his left ear showed that he was a man of some rank. Unlike most men of his kind, he was clean-shaven, with brown hair and eyes to match.

Before Alexius could make an introduction, the man stepped forward to Justin and Sophie, bowed deeply, and said, "Welcome Treasurer! Welcome Iron Lady! I am Hetman Sweyn Siggurdsen, in command of the Varangians here in Mikklegard who serve their majesties. Thank you for your help in bringing us justice! I am here to assist you in any way I can!"

Justin returned the bow. "Thank you, Hetman. We will greatly appreciate any help you can give us—these are deep waters, and we are only starting to find our way. I trust my deputy Alexius has conveyed to you what we want to do here today?"

For an instant, Justin saw the Varangian's eyes narrow before he said, "Yes, of course—please come this way!" With that, he entered the dining hall and motioned them to follow. As Justin did, he gave a side glance to Sophie.

She had also picked up on the hetman's response and so lagged behind to whisper to Alexius, "What is going on?"

Alexius shook his head. "It's nothing. Let it go."

Sophie persisted, "Oh no, you don't! Out with it!"

Pausing a moment, Alexius responded, "The hetman doesn't care for my kind."

"He doesn't, does he? Well, we'll see about that!"

The banquet hall they were led into was extraordinary in several ways. First, it was large, and could accommodate several hundred people, although the tables which were laid out only covered about half of the available space. On the east side, which faced the very southern end of the Great Palace, the hall was lined with windows so polished that, given the right light, they could act as mirrors, albeit wavy ones. The west side had two levels. The bottom level consisted of the kitchen and various storerooms. The upper level, which looked out over the hall, was dark and appeared to be unused. The entire hall was used only on Friday nights, when the men gathered for their banquets. During the week, the men ate in their barracks or at the locations where they were on duty.

In the center of the hall, the tables had been pushed back to form an open area. It was here that the interviews were apparently set to take place. Before the hetman could take control, Sophie pre-empted him and said, "Very well, let us begin! Deputy Alexius, what have you arranged?"

In a gesture that no one but Sophie could have seen, Alexius gave a quick nod of his head, and then said, "Very well, Treasurer and Lady! We have identified five witnesses—one Greek, four Varangian—who may have information relevant to the investigation. Per your instructions, they have been kept in separate rooms before being interviewed. With your permission, I will conduct each one out here for your examination."

Justin, wanting to get into the act, responded, "Fine, Deputy. If you have any innate feeling as to the order of importance, please let that be your guide."

During this comment, Sophie kept an eye on the hetman who appeared to be unhappy with the course of events. Thinking 'good', she decided to conduct a charm offensive, and said with a smile, "With your permission, of course, Hetman."

"As you wish, Lady," came the less than enthusiastic reply.

While she knew that her next tactic would take Justin by surprise, Sophie had long ago accepted that this was sometimes necessary. Speaking to the hetman again, but this time in Norse, she continued, "As you know, Hetman, I have some knowledge of your language. Recently, though, I heard Varangians use a word I was not familiar with—'Loviatar.' Does that mean anything to you?"

If Sophie expected to get a reaction from Siggurdsen, she was disappointed, for he merely nodded and replied, "Yes, Lady, it does. 'Loviatar' is a goddess who is recognized in the eastern part of Scandinavia and is said to rule over death and chaos. Why do you ask?"

Not to be put off that easily, Sophie persisted. "You answer as a Christian. Do all of your Varangian brethren feel likewise?"

This shot hit home, for Siggurdsen shook his head before answering, "No, Lady, they do not. Some men are very affected by even the mention of her name. I pray you to be cautious in doing so."

Switching to Greek, she continued, "Thank you, Hetman, the fact you refer to Loviatar as 'her' says worlds to me." Turning to Justin, she continued, "I'm sorry, dear, I didn't mean to leave you out. How do you want to proceed?"

Feeling somewhat mollified, Justin replied, "Let's speak to the city resident first—the one who found the body. We can do that in Greek, but I'll let you take the lead as usual—men don't realize that they're being led to tell the truth by a woman until it's too late. As for the others, you'll have to speak to them in their own language—this investigation is too important to take a chance on having something lost in translation. No offense, Hetman," he concluded with a nod to Siggurdsen.

"None taken, Deputy," came the reply.

"All right," said Alexius. "Let's proceed—the first man is named Stephan—he works at a tavern down the street from where the body was found."

The afore-mentioned Stephan proved to be a disappointment, for in Greek or any other language he was monosyllabic. He confirmed that he was a bartender at an inn called the Lion, that he had seen the deceased some time before closing, and that all he observed the deceased drinking was wine. Since Varangians normally didn't consume wine, this was noteworthy. After the man left, Stephan had had to clean up, and so was not sure how long it was before he left the bar. He had not gotten very far along the street before he turned up an alley (why he did so was unclear) and found the dead man. He was simple enough that he cried out upon making this discovery, so the constables who soon arrived initially considered him a suspect. He had no knowledge of what happened after that.

As Sophie thanked the man for his testimony, Justin found himself hoping that the remaining four witnesses would have more to add. In this, he was not disappointed, although he absorbed what they said only indirectly. Without exception, they were Varangians, and their knowledge of Greek was sketchy at best. When Sophie tried to initiate conversations with each of them in Greek as they came out one by one, it was quickly apparent in every case that much would be lost if they tried to struggle through a language that was foreign to them.

Fortunately, Sophie was able to translate as they spoke in Norse, so Justin and Alexius were aware of the flow of the conversation. While it was all unintelligible to Alexius, Justin began to pick up some patterns, although he found Norse to be simple and complex at the same time. Although he was fluent in several languages, he found the language of the Varangians to have a unique tonal quality, in that every sentence ended with a downward, almost melancholy, tone. '*I wonder if that reflects the view they have of the world,*' he thought.

The first two men had come to Constantinople about the same time as had the deceased, a period of time which Sophie elicited was about five years. One, Sweyn (or was it Olaf?—Justin had trouble telling them apart), said that he and the victim had worked as guards that day outside Emperor Constantine's quarters, and that the latter had been his usual taciturn self. Sweyn had not noticed anything about Magnus that seemed odd, although he had recently been pining over his homeland, a place which Sweyn referred to as "Suomi" that was even further north than Sweyn's homeland of Gotland. Sweyn did not seen Magnus again that day, for he had passed up the banquet for a chance to earn some extra money doing additional guard duty. Sweyn explained that he hoped to return to his homeland sooner than many men did, and this was a means to an end to help him achieve an earldom when he did.

Trying to salvage something from what had otherwise been a dry and unconvincing narrative, Sophie turned the conversation to a different tactic, and asked Olaf (or was it Sweyn?) if he was familiar with a goddess called 'Loviatar'? At the mere mention of the word, the man's face turned white, and he began stammering. Having seen enough, Sophie reassured him that she must have gotten the word wrong, thanked him for his help, and directed him on his way, after he was strictly enjoined to say nothing about the interview to anyone one. From what Justin could see, this latter part was a waste of breath, for Olaf/Sweyn intended to do nothing of the kind. Still, short of having the man locked up, which they could certainly do, there was nothing to be done.

Before the next man came in (and it was in fact Olaf), Justin thought it appropriate to call for a recess to confer with the others. Sophie and Alexius, having noticed the same reaction to the mention of the word 'Loviatar', thought that it should be avoided extraneous and distracting. Justin was glad to find that Siggurdsen was on his side, and asked him to explain more fully.

The Norseman thought for a moment, and then said, directing his comments to Sophie, "Lady, I know I advised caution, but if 'Loviatar' is an object of fear, the subject must be discussed. I know that you people here in Mikkelgard regard all of us Varangians as the same, but we are not. From my tradition, 'Loviatar' means nothing, and that is not because I am a Christian. In the lands of the north, there were many gods before the Christian God was known—Odin, Thor, Frigg, and so forth, some of which are known to me, others not. If 'Loviatar' means something to these men, you need to find out and I need to know."

"Thank you, Hetman," Sophie said. "I appreciate your concerns. It is just that we are only beginning to understand what is going on, and we need to proceed carefully. Alexius, please bring Olaf in."

For his part, Olaf confirmed what Sweyn had said. He had had lunch with Magnus, but had not seen him after that. He was shocked to hear that Magnus had been killed, and adamantly refused to believe that his friend had done anything to bring his fate upon him. 'Loviatar' meant nothing to him. Given Siggurdsen's background information, this was not surprising, for Olaf was from a land even farther west, called 'Danemark.'

Following this interview, two more Varangians remained to be heard from. In talking with the first three men, Sophie had noticed while Alexius and Siggurdsen had studiously avoided eye contact, the underlying animosity between them seemed to be dying down. Giving Justin a poke in his ribs, she used one of their agreed-upon looks to show that he should notice this as well. As they were waiting for Alexius to escort the next man into the hall, he nodded his understanding, and they then waited to see what was next.

Things began to pick up immediately, for when the next Varangians came into the room, there were two rather than one. When Sophie quizzically looked at Alexius, he just shook his head and said, "These two men refused to come out unless they were together. Their Greek isn't very good, but I was able to understand that much. I think they also said that they were together when they saw Magnus at the banquet. They may know something you need to hear."

The two men, Eric and Ragnar, had known each other for many years, even before they jointly came to Constantinople. When Sophie learned that they came from the same area of Scandinavia as had the dead man, she made sure to glance at Justin as she translated. Looking back, he mouthed the words 'Say her name.' In the interests of getting home to her children as soon as possible, Sophie was happy to do so.

Once she did, asking if the two men were familiar with a goddess of that name, the effect was immediate. Both men's ruddy faces grew a shade paler. The effect was particularly marked on Eric, who was the taller and blonder of the two. Neither said anything as they looked blankly at her, then at Siggurdsen, who was equally impassive. Suppressing a momentary hesitancy to continue causing them discomfort, Sophie pressed on, with a new note of hardness in her voice.

"Jarln, kunna hrausligr! Segja nu!" {"Gentlemen, be strong! Speak now!"}

Her words had the result she desired. After looking at Eric, Ragnar began to speak, slowly at first, then more rapidly, to the point where Sophie had to tell him to slow down so that she could translate. Yes, the two men knew Magnus, and yes they had sat near him at the banquet on Friday night. No, neither they nor Magnus had not been drinking in excess, although what constituted 'in excess' to them was unclear. At some point, they had both seen Magnus, who was sitting across from them, rise half-way off of the bench on which he was sitting, with a look of terror on his face as he mouthed the word 'Loviatar!' Reflexively, they had turned to see what Magnus had seen, but they saw nothing. By the time they turned back, Magnus was heading for the door at a rapid pace. Thinking that he was going to use 'the facilities' (Sophie had some difficulty translating this), they did not follow him. When he did not return, they concluded he had drunk his fill for the night, and thought no more of it. Only the next morning did they learn the awful truth.

Sophie thanked them for their words, and then turned to Justin and Alexius. "Right, what now?"

Justin thought for a moment and said, "I'm still confused about what happened. Let's have them show us where they were sitting."

Alexius nodded in agreement, and added, "It would help to make some permanent record of the scene."

Sophie proceeded to do both, and the results were interesting. Eric and Ragnar got up and went to a spot in the middle of the banquet hall, toward the rear. During the banquet, they had been seated looking away from the glass, which meant that Magnus had been looking towards the east side, where the mirrors were. While they both qualified their comments, they did agree on the general location. Having seen Sophie work in the past, Justin was not surprised to see her use the heel of her sandal to mark the spot on the wooden floor with an 'X'. Seeing his look, she smiled and said, "Well, it works, doesn't it?"

While Sophie tried a few follow-up questions, it was clear that the two men had said enough. Siggurdsen dismissed them with strict instructions to say nothing to anyone else about what they had seen. After the Varangians had left, they sat in silence for a minute. On an inspiration, Justin asked him what funeral arrangements had been made for Magnus.

Surprised, Siggurdsen replied, "Well, the body will be cremated and the ashes scattered at sea. I would invite you to attend, but these matters are generally private, unless a man of high rank is being honored. Thank you for asking, however."

Sophie, Justin and Alexius agreed to meet the next afternoon, following Sunday morning services. It was obligatory that Sophie attend Zoe at Hagia Sophia, and Justin was expected to attend as well, as a high-ranking official. Alexius did not pretend to have any use for such things, a feeling he shared with Emperor Basil, who, Easter being over, considered his royal religious duties to be finished. His brother Constantine could be reliably counted on to carry the imperial standard at such functions, although Justin had noticed lately that even his attendance had been getting spotty.

As they rode back home, Sophie wanted to process what she had just heard. From long experience, Justin knew better than to try to make conversation during this time, so he concentrated instead on what lay ahead for him. While these murder investigations never came at a good time, now seemed particularly bad. What with his treasury officials in town for conferences about the budget, the Prefect having to deal with churchmen from the west, uncertainties about both of the emperors, and an unknown quality in Senator Kalokyros, Justin was at a loss. Still, as he watched the evening sky glint over the domes of the Church of the Apostles, he could smile in the knowledge that things would work out, as they always did in this city that was under the Virgin's protection.

CHAPTER 7

The next day found the couple attending divine worship at the Church of Holy Wisdom, the Hagia Sophia. As she had done for many years, Sophie went to the palace well before Justin, in order to prepare Zoe for the service. While the ritual of preparation was well-established and one that Sophie had practiced for many years, she found herself increasingly nervous while doing so. Every public appearance by Zoe was a statement of the majesty and wealth of the empire, and Zoe expected to look her best. Sophie always delegated junior ladies to start the process, beginning with layering the undergarments, so that she could finish off with the jewelry, hair and tiara of the princess, the latter of which was literally the crowning achievement in preparing Zoe for her public. As the princess grew older, the task became more challenging.

Justin came later, accompanied by Maria. While Simon had been christened after only a few weeks of life, he was not technically a full-fledged member of the church until the time of his baptism, which would occur only when he was old enough to appreciate the significance. In any event, it would have been out of the question for him to sit and stand through a Sunday service. They left him playing with the dogs in the garden, under the watchful eye of Anna, his nurse. When they arrived at the church, they entered on the right side and took their places in the front center section, all as prescribed by protocol. Since it was unusual for a treasurer to be as young as

Justin was, let alone to be accompanied by a young child, they were surrounded by other bureaucrats and their wives who were significantly older. All of them knew Maria, though, and she reciprocated, addressing them by their titles and, in case she did not know, by simply saying, "God's peace be with you." While he was used to seeing this every week, Justin could not help but think to himself that he was in the presence of a natural-born politician.

Justin and Maria were seated when the royal women's procession began to fill the balconies above the altar. While the royal box for the emperors was on the lower level, it was unoccupied today, save for the Prefect, who was standing in for the emperors, and a token Varangian guard. This took Justin by surprise, for while Basil was well-known to have little personal piety, his brother rarely missed an opportunity to be seen in public, even if this meant sitting through a two-hour service. *Maybe there is something to these rumors about Constantine's health,* Justin thought to himself. Looking around further, he saw Russians on the left and the western Christian delegation on the right. Their clerical members were dressed in their formal garb, and the difference between their red robes and the somber black of the local clergy was striking.

Above, the ladies had precedence, with first Zoe on the right side and then Theodora on the left being seated with their accompanying retinues. While Justin did not really know about such things, from his vantage point the gowns of both princesses looked to be about the same. When he caught Sophie's eye from where she stood behind Zoe, she acknowledged as much with an ever-so-slight nod of her head. Justin reciprocated and thought to himself that she had never looked lovelier. For her part, Sophie had satisfied herself of the couture equivalency much earlier, and had breathed a silent prayer of thanks to the Virgin. The banquet three days hence was another matter, and more prayer would be needed.

The presiding officials now made their entrance as the choir struck up a plain chant. The incense bearer was first, with the fragrance symbolic of the prayers of the saints as recounted in the book of Revelation. A column of priests and archpriests followed, with Patriarch Sergius at the end, bearing the gold chalice of consecrated red wine to be used for communion. Watching the display, Justin could not help but notice Maria's reaction, wide-eyed and attentive. *'I was like that, too,'* he thought, *'the first hundred times. Now, after over a thousand times, not so much.'*

From the opening blessing through the Divine Liturgy of St. John Chrysostom, with its familiar chorus of "O Death, where is thy sting? O, Hades, where is thy victory? Christ is risen—He is risen indeed!" Justin observed the crowd and thought about the coming week. He noticed that while some of the visiting Russians were wide-eyed with wonder, at least one bored Varangian was carving runes in a wooden railing. When the Nicene Creed was read, he made a point to see the reaction of the visitors from Rome when the words "from the Father though the Son" were read. Predictably, they were not amused. The homily on a passage from Galatians was a good time for him to examine the problem of the Varangian murder—why now, why this way and why the mention of 'Loviatar', whatever who that was? He had not reached any conclusions when he felt a poke in the ribs.

"Papa," whispered Maria, "it's time for communion!" With an emotional voice Patriarch Sergius intoned said: "Your own of Your own, we offer to You, for all and through all." All present knelt and the voice of the choir director could be heard chanting: "We sing to You, we bless You, we thank You, Lord, and we pray to You, our God." This was followed by the "Our Father," and the "With the fear of God, faith and love draw near," and all those who had been baptized approached to commune from the Immaculate Mysteries, including Maria, who had been baptized by immersion a year before. In order to facilitate the flow of the service, priests took communion to the royal princesses and their retinues, along with others who were in the balcony.

When the service ended with the final chorus and blessing, the royal party processed back to the Palace. Justin and Maria went home, to be joined soon thereafter by Sophie, who, true to form, proceeded to kiss Justin, hug Maria and Simon, and get a full glass of wine. She collapsed on a chair on the veranda, and slipped off her sandals. "Oh, why did the Lord make His Service so long!" she exclaimed. "You'd think he would have some mercy or pity on us poor ladies-in-waiting, but no, we have to stand the entire time! I'm getting too old for this!"

Sophie's mind was put considerably at ease after a change of clothes and lunch on the veranda, which consisted of a sampling of fish fillets, cheese, fruit, bread and olives. Simon was now eating solid foods of all kinds, and was not shy in taking seconds or even thirds, although more than one piece would get slipped to the ever-watchful dogs. As they finished, Justin was looking forward to a peaceful afternoon with his family when Philip approached Sophie and said, loud enough for all to hear, "Her Highness Princess Zoe is here." Seeing the look on Justin's face, Sophie could only reply, "Fine, please send her in." Then, to her loving husband, she gave a little smile, a brief chuckle, and said, "Well, you know, that's our understanding—she can come by on Sundays when she's in the mood."

This Sunday was apparently such a day for such a mood, for the Imperial Princess of the Roman Empire, Zoe Porphyrogenita, then walked into their veranda, dressed in a very ordinary day gown. This was not new to Sophie and Justin, for they had grown used to seeing her in such attire during their trip across Asia Minor two years earlier, on their way to Antioch, Jerusalem and eventually to Cairo. Now, time and miles removed from those events, she reserved such attire for times when she wished to 'connect' with the common people through her friends Sophie and Justin. The fact that they had children was even a greater plus, for while she had never been married, let alone have a child, Zoe still felt a need to know what it was like to do so, and they fulfilled the need perfectly with complete discretion.

In this way 'Aunt Zoe' came to visit the Treasurer and his wife, free of the constraining atmosphere of the palace, as she periodically had done over the past two years since their escape from the Caliph. Still, she could not entirely shake off the life she had led for so many years. For example, the idea of having a dog in the palace was entirely unthinkable. So it was that when she came to visit her friends, the sensation of having a large dog lay its head on her lap was completely unsettling. While on one level she knew that Shadow and the other hounds were completely harmless, she still found it difficult to do anything more than smile and nod in their presence. The ability to actually touch such a beast was out of her skill set. So, she smiled and nodded until Sophie, noticing her discomfort, called the hound away. Shadow was happy to give Zoe a final sniff and head off to the kitchen.

Maria was happy to see 'Aunt Zoe' and ran to give her a hug. Justin smiled at her response, and nodded to the Princess. While during their time together in the pilgrimage to Jerusalem he and Zoe had spent many weeks together, he had never gotten to really feel at peace with her. Still, he knew that Sophie needed to have a relationship with Zoe, and was ready to play along. Zoe smiled at him and nodded back, and then got engrossed by Maria. Justin felt relieved and wandered off to join Simon, who was searching the lawn below the veranda.

"So, what is that you're working on, Maria?" inquired Zoe. "Are you making squiggles on the chalkboard?"

"No, Aunt Zoe, these are numbers. Alexius, who works for my dad, showed me how to make them. They're called Arabic numerals instead of Roman numerals, but Alexius says they're really from India, so…"

Knowing what a talker Maria was, Sophie decided to intervene. "Now, Maria, I'm sure Aunt Zoe would like to hear about things besides numbers. Why don't you tell her how your pony is doing?"

"No, no," Zoe replied, "this is fascinating. Maria, please show me how it works."

Thus encouraged, Maria proceeded to demonstrate how much easier Arabic/Indian numerals were to use in adding, subtracting and multiplying. Zoe, whose education in such matters was non-existent, smiled and nodded as Maria explained. However, when the subject of zero came up, she was baffled—how could one have a number that was nothing? Sophie let the demonstration go on for as long as she thought proper, and was getting ready to intervene when Simon did it for her. Outrunning his father and grasping a dead lizard that had likely fallen out of the hoopoes' nest, he triumphantly placed it on Zoe's lap.

Summoning all of her regal aplomb, Zoe Porphyrogenita, Princess of the Roman Empire, looked at the still form lying on her robes and managed to croak, "Sophie, get it off! Get it off!"

Before Sophie could react, Justin, having first grabbed Simon, gave a slight bow to Zoe, said, "With your permission, Highness," and picked up the lizard by the tail. Unfortunately, the creature had been dead long enough that the tail was brittle and came off in his hand, depositing the rest of the carcass back on the lap of the panicked princess.

Order was eventually restored. Unlike some of her previous visits, which seemed (at least to Justin) to go on overlong, Zoe was quite ready to return to the sanctuary of the palace. On her way out, she swept by Alexius, whose best court bow earned him only a side-long glance from the princess. He watched as the imperial carriage rattled off before shaking his head and entering the front door which Philip was still holding open. As usual, he found Justin and Sophie on the veranda. What was unusual was finding them both convulsed with laughter.

"Is this a private joke, or can I get in?" he asked when the merriment died down.

"Sorry, Alexius, but I think you had to be there," Sophie replied with a final chuckle. "Let's just say that Her Highness will remember this visit for awhile."

Justin was about to make a jocular remark of his own when he sensed something in Alexius' demeanor that was unsettling. Sophie picked up on this as well, and the general mood grew serious.

"All right, Alexius, what's going on?" Justin asked.

With a sigh, Alexius began, "We lost an operative last night—his body was found in the Golden Horn around noon. He was a trusted man who had done good work for us over the past several months. We think he was killed around midnight. His throat was slit."

At this apparent intrusion into her area of expertise, Sophie interjected, "And how do you know the time of death?"

Alexius replied, "Because the tide was coming in and carried his body up the inlet. Otherwise, it would have been washed out to sea."

Looking at the downcast face of his deputy, Justin felt a wave of sadness. "His name—who was he?"

"Nazir al-Amadi. He worked in a stall on the Mese. In this position, he was able to note what was going on. Apparently, he got too close to someone or something. The service is tomorrow morning at the mosque. I thought you'd like to know."

"Thank you, Alexius, I will certainly attend the services. It will be a good time to pay my respects to Imam Ali—he has always been a friend to us, insofar as he can, given his position."

Surprised, Sophie said, "The service is tomorrow? The poor man just died!"

"That's Islamic custom, dear—burial within 24 hours if possible. Besides, it's not like he's going to have friends and family coming from Egypt."

"But do you have time to go? I thought you're meeting with the Prefect tomorrow and perhaps Basil, in addition to getting your office ready to go to Crete. Perhaps I'd better go. I'd like to examine the body to see if this poor man was killed by the same men who dispatched the Northman."

"My schedule is what it is, and I'll manage. Also, while I'm sure you'd do fine at the service, there are several problems with that. First, you don't speak Arabic. Second, autopsies are forbidden by Islam, even if you were not a woman, and Islam enforces some pretty strict divisions among the sexes. Besides, the banquet is in three days. Do you have everything ready to go for Zoe?"

"Oh, for the most part. I've done this so many times I could do it in my sleep. The hair is the most time-consuming part, and then there's…"

Alexius could take no more, and gave vent to a rare fit of anger. "Stop it, you two, just stop it! That's the problem—you always have to have everything just right, and what's worse, you honestly think you can do it, each and every time!"

Shocked, Justin said, "What on earth do you mean?"

"It's just the way you two are. You effectively run the Empire, or what's worth running, and you make it look so easy that everyone expects you to always get the answers. If Emperor Basil wants more money for his wars, no problem, Boss, you'll get it, while rooting out graft and corruption along the way. If Princess Zoe wants to outdo herself for the hundredth time, just leave it to Sophie to come through. And, along the way, you both solve every crime you're presented with, and have kids and run a household in the bargain! What happens when you can't keep it up?"

"Then we don't," Sophie said in a quiet voice. "I really am sorry about the death of your agent, Alexius, and we'll do what we can. That's all we can do."

Deflated after his outburst, Alexius put his bald head in his hands.

After a moment of silence, Justin said, "Go home, Alexius, go home. We'll deal with this tomorrow. You've done enough for now."

Later, when Justin and Sophie were lying in bed, they continued the conversation.

"Are we really like that, Justin? Really?"

"Maybe so. We've both been doing what we do for so long, it seems like second nature. Don't be mad at Alexius. He carries the same burdens we do, but he has to do it by himself."

Sophie lay in silence for a minute, and then gave Justin a kiss. "I'm glad you're there for me, dear, just as I'm there for you." Pausing a moment, she added, "Still, you have to admit, we are pretty good at what we do."

"Quiet, you. Now good night."

CHAPTER 8

On Monday both Justin and Sophie had to be at the palace early. Sophie had to review the final layout for Zoe's banquet outfit, in addition to interviewing the candidates who had made the final cut for the next lady-in-waiting opening. One was the daughter of a prominent senator while the other was the great-niece of a retired admiral. Although the senator had more political pull at court, Sophie personally liked the second young woman better. The final test would be to see how each woman reacted when delegated to work in one of the princesses' soup kitchens. While, as always, the final choice was Zoe's, she placed complete trust in Sophie's judgment leaving the burden on Sophie alone. When Irene told her that the dressmakers were running late, Sophie knew it was going to be a long day.

Fortunately for Justin, the complex of the prefect's offices was located at the north end of the extensive complex of buildings that constituted the Great Palace. After being waved through by the Varangian guards (did he imagine sidelong glances from them?), he entered the anteroom of Prefect Leo Comnenus, and was waved in again by the chief clerk. Prefect Comnenus was at his desk, where he seemingly spent every waking hour of the day, and rose to meet Justin with a smile and a nod. At the same time he took this in, Justin also noticed that the bust of Constantine I had been moved to the right side of the desk, the signal that Emperor Basil himself was in attendance, concealed behind a screen on the right side of the room.

Basil was 58 years old, and had been emperor for forty years, following the death of John I Tzimiskes, who had ruled for seven years during his minority. Basil was of average height, had a beard that was flecked with gray and piercing blue eyes. As a man who had from his youth carried himself as a soldier, he was direct in his dealings, and found the protocol of the court stifling. It much suited him to deal with his senior officials informally, although woe to the man who failed to give him direct and honest answers. Justin knew from personal observation, although thankfully not from personal experience, that "I don't know" was much preferable to a dissembling evasion.

"Good morning, Treasurer," began the prefect in his deep voice, "I trust you are well?"

"Yes, Prefect, very much so, although it often seems that there are not enough hours in the day."

"I understand perfectly. I am sorry to impose this Crete trip on you, but I simply cannot leave the city at this time, given my duties as mediator between Patriarch Sergius and the visiting churchmen from Rome. Believe me," he continued with a shake of his head, "I would gladly trade places with you."

"Sorry to hear that. Are things not going well?"

"You might say that. The legates from Pope Benedict are led by his brother, a man named Romanus, who is the chief civil official in Rome and whose theological knowledge is roughly that of my horse. His sole negotiating technique is to be outraged by everything, starting with the quarters that they were assigned to use during their stay here at the Church of Chora and the attached monastery."

Surprised, Justin replied, "I know that place—it's quite beautiful. What's the problem?"

"Only that it is about as far away from the palace and the Hagia Sophia as it is possible to be and still be within the city's walls."

"Oh, yes, it is out by the Blachernae complex, isn't it? Well, I'm sure that was not by design, or was it?" From the prefect's silence and knowing look, Justin could only say, "Ah," and leave it at that.

"Well, we all have our crosses to bear," the prefect went on briskly. "I'm afraid yours is Crete. You will take the down payment for the reconstruction of the various houses of worship, although I must tell you there were some who questioned why we included the synagogue in Jerusalem. You leave next Monday."

"Very diplomatic, sir, very diplomatic. I don't need to be told that the 'some' were the patriarch and his churchmen, and I don't really care. Emperor Basil knows what help we received from the Jewish community in Cairo, help that was vital to our return, and he's the only one that counts." For emphasis, Justin paused just long enough to glance at the screen to his right. "I will see that the transfer is completed. What other business needs to be done?"

"Oh, the usual. There is an agreement to be signed about the treatment of ship-wrecked sailors in Italy and Sicily, another one about the joint use of water wells on the Syrian border, and so forth. I expect that there will also be the usual banquets and receptions, that sort of thing. I imagine you have attended more of those than about anyone, apart from the royal family and of course your wife. Speaking of your wife, will Sophie be accompanying you?"

"Regretfully, no. She has her own duties to attend to as chief lady-in-waiting, and there is still the matter of the Varangian's murder. Of course, my deputy Alexius is on the case as well, and we hope to make progress soon. At this point, though, we have no suspects and no motive, and the Varangians are difficult to get to know."

Suddenly, the screen slid away as if on ice, folding up into the corner as it was pulled by a servant. There, seated an ordinary chair, was Basil II, Senior Emperor of the Roman Empire. Standing beside him was a gray-haired man with a weathered face and a grim expression. Bidding them to stay seated, Basil looked at Justin for a moment before speaking.

"Very true, Treasurer Cataphlates, very true. We have had them under our command for many years now, and we still do not understand them. Still, they are brave, devoted, loyal and honorable according to their own code. Spare no effort in giving them justice. Be aware, though, that they often do not reveal themselves easily to outsiders like us."

Then, as if suddenly aware of his companion, Basil went on. "May we introduce Senator Kalokyros, whom we have appointed to be our Akolouthos over the Varangians in the city. He will serve as our liaison with you in the investigation."

Justin nodded and said, "Senator, I am honored to meet you, and look forward to working with you."

In response, the older man gave the slightest of bows in return, but said nothing.

Deciding to focus on the real power in the room, Justin then addressed Basil. "Highness. I can report that our investigation is on-going. While I have my deputy working on the matter as we speak, it is too early to say if this was an isolated incident or a part of something larger, as we encountered two years ago. I fear it may only the beginning, for we lost one of our agents, a Muslim, over the week-end. The same people may be responsible for both murders."

"Um, thank you for that report, Treasurer. If we can be of any assistance, please advise. We bid you good day." With that, the emperor rose, and as Justin and the prefect bowed, started through a rear door that led to a corridor used solely by royalty. Basil paused, turned, and said, "Oh, yes, Treasurer, we will see you at the audience for your people tomorrow," before departing with the senator in tow.

When they were alone, Prefect Comnenus looked at Justin with raised eyebrows. "Do you know, that is the first time in awhile that the emperor has said anything during the meetings he has attended. I guess the Varangians mean a lot to him. While I know that Kalokyros can be difficult to deal with, I wish you, your wife and your team Godspeed in your work."

"Thank you for that, Prefect. Now, if you will excuse me, I need to attend a memorial service for our agent at the mosque. I may be able to find out something more there."

On his way out of the anteroom, Justin stopped and scribbled a note. Handing it to the chief clerk, he said, "Could you see that this is delivered to the Deputy Treasurer, please? His name is Alexius."

The chief clerk, who also appeared to be a eunuch, acknowledged the request with a bow of his head. "Of course, Treasurer, it would be my pleasure."

To reach the mosque, Justin was required to head north from the palace complex and pass through the city walls through one of the numerous gates. Though less massive than the land walls on the west side of the city, the sea walls had served their purpose well, although it had been almost three centuries since a full-scale siege had been mounted. While in many places the walls ran very close to the shore, along the tip of the peninsula which held the city there was an area of about three hundred yards between the walls and the harbor of the Golden Horn. The one mosque in the city had been located there for many decades, mainly to avoid conflict with the numerous churches found within the city proper. Here the call to prayer on Fridays could be given without causing offense. As the number of merchants from various parts of the Muslim world grew, so did use of the mosque, although relations between the Sunni and Shia factions were often tense.

Leaving his carriage and escort outside of the wall that surrounded the mosque, Justin approached the building on foot. From the number of others doing the same, he guessed that Nazir had many friends who had come to mourn his death. He had remembered that morning to wear darker robes consistent with the funeral service, and so blended in fairly well, apart from his sandy hair, lighter skin and lack of a skull cap. Unlike its larger counterparts in Cairo and Jerusalem, this mosque lacked a minaret. A beautiful garden lay in front and on the sides of the building, with a fountain in the courtyard.

The Sunni imam who presided at the mosque, Hasan ibn Ali, was well-known to Justin, and greeted him with the traditional handshake and hug as he entered. The interior of the main room of the mosque was unadorned, and was as far removed from the interior of one of the city's churches as it was possible to imagine. While Friday prayers were done with the worshippers kneeling (men segregated from women by the use of screens), for this service chairs were to be used. As he made his way to a seat on the back row, Justin was able to disarm most, but not all, of the looks he received with Arabic phrases such as "May the peace of Allah be upon you."

The service, like the mosque itself, was simple. The imam presided, and read passages from the Quran which spoke of the mercy of God and the fate of believers and non-believers after death. When he was finished, the wooden casket was borne out by four pallbearers who led the congregants to the Muslim cemetery which adjoined the mosque. No graveside service was held as the burial occurred with each person left to his/her own thoughts. Finally, Imam Ali concluded the service with the traditional blessing, "May the peace, blessings and mercy of Allah be with you." However, rather than disperse as Justin expected, most of those in attendance headed back inside the mosque, where a light lunch was provided in one of the side rooms. The conversations were convivial, and sometimes even humorous.

Seeing his reaction, the imam gently said, "Surprised, Treasurer? This is our way—we have commended Nazir to Allah, and now the life that Allah has given the rest of us goes on. We appreciate the honor you have done him by being here today. Such a thing does not often happen. I suspect that there is more to this than meets the eye."

"Yes, Imam, there is. May we talk?"

"Certainly. Come, walk with me in the garden." A few moments later, in the shade of the plane trees, the imam continued, "May I assume that Nazir was a man of importance to you?"

Justin paused for a moment. He had not thought through a response to such a question, and hesitated to give too much away. "Uh, yes, he, uh, was, uh, letting us know about people who mean ill to the empire."

"And by that do you mean Muslims?"

"Perhaps, well probably, but not necessarily," Justin replied, thinking back to the Serbian who had been involved in the jewel theft and murder two years before. Sighing, he continued, "All right, Imam, I'll be plain. Based on past events, we believe that the Fatimid Caliph seeks to subvert the Empire by various means, using agents in the city. Nazir was helping us keep an eye on such men. Now, whether that cost him his life or if it was something else, we don't know at this time."

At the mention of the Fatimid Caliph the imam nodded. "Nazir was a good man and a good Muslim. Tell me, Treasurer, what do you know of Shia Islam?"

"Not a lot, apart from it is different from the Sunni Islam that is practiced in this mosque. Oh, and that it is the faith of the Fatimids. That's about it. I guess I have thought the differences were like those between that of the patriarch here and the pope in Rome."

"I would say that the differences are more than that, but that is a good analogy. Mostly, our practices are the same. For example, there were a number of Shia believers here today, like two of the men Nizar worked with at his stall on the Mese. Still, the current Fatimid caliph tends to be rather more doctrinaire than most."

Justin shook his head. "Believe me, Imam, I know that. You mentioned a stall—do you know what Nazir and the others were selling?"

Iman Ali gave a little smile and said, "No, I'm afraid not. Now, I need to be getting back. Again, thank you for your presence here today. May Allah go with you in your search for justice for Nazir."

Now it was Justin's turn to smile. "Thank you, Imam, you're the second person today who has said something along those lines. If I may ask one thing of you—if you hear anything that might be helpful to us that you can reveal without disclosing a confidence, would you let me know?"

"I shall, Treasurer, I shall. Good day."

As he walked back to his carriage, Justin resolved to have Alexius check out the information the imam had given him, namely that Nizar had worked in a stall on the Mese. Because of the message he had left at the prefect's office, he expected to have the opportunity to do just that very soon. As he entered the carriage, he noticed that the driver appeared to be different than the one who had driven him earlier, this one being rather bulky.

"So, feeling better today?" he asked as they pulled away and headed back towards the city walls.

"Yeah, Boss, I do," said Alexius, "sorry about that little episode yesterday. Hearing about Nazir was hard to deal with—he was a really nice guy."

"Think nothing of it, we've all been there. It comes with what we do. Now, do you want to do something about it?"

"Do I? Keep talking."

"All right, but this has to come in addition to the on-going investigation about the Varangian, understand? I have this straight from Basil himself."

"Fine, fine, whatever. Start with Nazir first."

"Well, the imam confirmed that Nazir worked at a stall in the Mese. He may have seen something going on at another one which got him killed. Check that out!"

There was a pause from Alexius, and Justin, who couldn't see his face, wondered what the problem was. He got his answer when Alexius, in a disappointed voice, said, "That's it? Do you have any idea how many stalls there are in the Mese?"

"Judging from the last sales tax figures I can recall, about 1,200."

"At least. It will take a while to check each one." There was another pause, and the ersatz driver went on as they rolled through the gate in the sea walls. "Still, it's a beginning. I'll have our people start with the stalls which employ Muslims, which should speed things along some. Very well, what about the other matter?"

"Deputy, let me just say that if you didn't like the last one, you really won't like this one. Do you remember Hetman Siggurdsen from the interviews we did?"

At this point, Alexius did more than keep silent—he brought the carriage to a full stop (much to the annoyance of a wagon driver behind them carrying barrels of olive oil), and turned to glare at Justin. "How could I forget him—he made it clear what he thinks of 'my kind.'"

"I can't help that, I really can't. The fact is we need him and there is nobody else. Based on what Basil said today about the Varangians, I am sure he has not told us everything he knows. Don't you see? This can be your chance to pay him back in kind."

Eyes narrowing, Alexius said, "You have my attention—keep going."

"Lean on him. Bring the full weight of the empire down on him. Invoke Basil's name if you have to. Just get him to tell us everything. Don't ask, demand. Tell him you know he's not been forthcoming with us, and you're giving him one more chance. He either talks now or pays the penalty."

"What penalty?"

"How should I know? Just say it with feeling. I'll be amazed if you don't get results. Agree?"

A wry grin spread across Alexius' smooth face. "Sounds like it has possibilities. When do I start?"

"As soon as possible. Drop me off at the villa and then your time is your own. I just know we need to keep moving on this before the trail grows cold. Now, could you please start driving again?"

"Sure, Boss, you've got a deal. I'll try to report to you tomorrow."

"In the morning, I'll be in the office. We're still meeting with the local officials from Asia, so if you do get something important, don't hesitate to have me pulled out of whatever meeting I'm in."

As Justin finished, the carriage pulled into the circular drive in front of the villa. "All right, Boss, here you go. Have a good evening."

"You, too, Alexius. Thanks for everything."

So it was that when Sophie came home later that day, she found her husband playing with the children in the library, after they had been driven off the veranda by a sudden shower. She smiled to herself, and gave thanks to the Virgin for all of the blessings she had been given. Sometimes, especially at the palace, it was easy to forget. Her prayer finished, she stepped into the room and announced, "I'm home!"

CHAPTER 9

Tuesday morning found the couple travelling back to the palace together for a change. Both had full schedules apart from whatever they could fit in regarding the Varangian investigation, and both appreciated the brief time the carriage ride afforded them before the demands of the world closed around them.

"So, who exactly are you meeting with today, dear?" began Sophie.

"Oh, these are local treasury department officials from the various districts across Asia, about 60 men in all. As far as anyone can determine, this is the first time they all have been together. We'll do the rest from the European side in a few months."

"Did you meet these people when we travelled to Tarsus two years ago?"

"Yes, exactly, and some of them should be here today. Others have been replaced for various reasons."

"Associates of the former treasurer?"

Justin nodded with a knowing smile. "Yes, Treasurer Taronites did have a number of cronies here and there. I think by now we've got most of them weeded out."

Sophie persisted. "What's on the agenda, then?"

"The usual—a review of the tax structure, how to deal with delinquent properties, application of the new assessment rules, and, in a subject near and dear to Basil's heart, the allocation of vacant lands to veterans."

Giving an exaggerated yawn, Sophie said, "Sounds like fun."

Feigning outrage, Justin replied, "All right then, I suppose your day will be action packed?"

"In a way, I suppose. Zoe and the rest of us get to go on a field trip to one of the soup kitchens we've set up. This will take all our minds off the banquet tomorrow night, and will let Zoe get out to see 'her people' as she calls them."

"What about her outfit for tomorrow? Is it finished?"

Sophie sighed. "As finished as I can make it—the dressmakers are adding the final touches, but I can't be of any help to them now. I hope it will be enough. I really pulled out the stops on this one, but somehow Theodora's people are always one step ahead. Maybe when we get this thing with the Varangians done, you can," lowering her voice, "direct the attention of the Alitheia Society to determine how they do it."

At this, Justin laughed out loud to the point their driver turned his head to see if there was a problem. When he was able, he merely nodded to Sophie and said, "Consider it done. Well, here we are. Let the fun begin!"

The couple walked together for a little while before Sophie had to enter the quarters that were off-limits to everyone who did not directly serve the royal family. With a kiss, she headed between the Varangians who formed part of the guard that was on duty 24 hours a day. Justin walked on, greeting various other imperial officials as well as the foreign dignitaries and delegations who were in the palace for various reasons. Russians, Arabs, Italians—all were there, all wandering down the halls staring at the artwork that Justin had long since taken for granted. In response to their salutations, he greeted them as best he could, resolving to spend more time each week brushing up on his languages.

As he was drawing near the treasury offices, he saw at least part of the delegation from Rome coming toward him. As they passed, he nodded and said, "Buongiorno!" This prompted looks of recognition from several of the men, including one who seemed to be their leader. When he stopped, Justin did the same, and listened as the man spoke in passable but halting Greek.

"You're the one who speaks Italian, aren't you? Have you been there?"

"Yes, but it has been a number of years. I presume you are the delegation from Pope Benedict?"

"Yes, we are. I am Romanus, Senator of Rome, and brother to His Holiness. And you would be?"

"Justin Cataphlates, Treasurer of the Roman Empire." As he said "Roman," Justin could see the Italian's eyes narrow slightly, so he thought it best to continue. "Will you be coming to the banquet tomorrow in honor of Their Majesties?"

"Yes, we will. So far, it is about the only thing we will have accomplished here, but we appreciate the invitation. Tell me, what do you know of our mission?"

"Very little, actually. I assume there are some theological points involved which as a laymen are beyond my ken. Perhaps some political ones, too, but again I don't really know. It's been good speaking with you, but I really do need to go."

As Romanus and his entourage moved on, the Roman called over his shoulder, "Oh, Treasurer, do you speak Latin, too?"

Surprised, Justin replied, "Well, no, I don't. Does anyone speak it now? I do read it fairly well."

With a faint smile on his face, Romanus said, "Good enough, Treasurer, good enough. I bid you good day."

'One of the benefits of being the head man,' Justin thought as he entered the main hall in the treasury offices, *'is that things can't start without you.'* His presence was announced to the officials, who grew silent as he took his place at their head. Justin knew from experience the assembled men weren't there to hear him drone on about statistics and percentages, so he kept his remarks short and to the point, thanking them for coming (not that they had a choice), urging them to ask questions, and hoping that they would take what they learned back to their local offices. Finally, as he noticed the attention of many start to wander, he decided it was time to spring his surprise.

"I can't emphasize enough how important the work is that all of us in the Treasury department do, and that starts with each of you in your own provinces. Believe me when I say that the results that we either get or don't get are noticed at the highest level, and I mean highest. In fact, there are two men who would like to personally express their thanks to each one of you, namely their Imperial Highnesses."

The effect on the room was all that he had hoped for. Heads snapped around, eyes grew wide, and there was absolute silence. Then, everyone started talking at once. One wizened older man (from Ephesus, maybe?), raised his hand so insistently that Justin felt compelled to call on him.

Standing, the man said, "Excuse me, Treasurer, but I don't think I am dressed for such an occasion. May we have time to change?"

Suppressing a grin, Justin said, "No, I'm afraid not. We're going directly from here to the audience chamber. Besides," he said after a pause, "you don't want to present yourself in too fine a robe—the emperors may wonder where you got the money to purchase it." At this, there was general laughter from around the room.

Seeing the downcast look on the official's face, Justin tried to make amends. "Besides, don't worry—since you are all invited to the 40th anniversary banquet tomorrow, you can wear your finest then. I know everyone else will."

The older man nodded happily and took his seat.

From Justin's viewpoint, the audience was something of a letdown, although for most of the others it was the first, and very likely last, time they would have such an experience. For starters, only Basil was in attendance, and there was no mention of his brother's whereabouts. As the chamberlain read the name and title of each official in attendance, they would step forward and bow. Basil nodded and the process was repeated. It did not take long, however, for boredom to set in, and the imperial nods got more perfunctory. Justin was glad when the proceedings were concluded upon the emperor's departure, and let his assistants conduct the attendees back to the Treasury.

As Justin was bringing up the rear, he heard a familiar voice. "Well, you made it to Treasurer, did you? It's a long way from looking through records in Amorium!"

Turning, he saw a thin man with black hair and beard, wearing the insignia of a provincial treasurer. The man's eyes were twinkling and he had a broad smile on his face.

"George Taronites! How are you? Still hanging out in taverns?" Justin said with delight.

"Not so much anymore—the quality of wine available in Iconium leaves much to be desired. But, a man goes where the jobs are, and thanks to you, I've got my own office! Things are going well, although I have to tell you—I inherited a real mess out there."

"Oh, that's right! You've got to deal with the reallocation of all those properties seized from the large landowners. Here, walk with me. How are things going?"

"About as well as can be expected. From a revenue standpoint, of course, it's been a disaster. We may never get the revenue back we had when the properties were intact. On the other hand, it's been very satisfying. For example, the land owned by Simon Byrennius alone was split up to provide homesteads for 18 of Basil's veterans, and there have been many others. Tell me, whatever happened to him?"

"The last time I heard, he was in Cherson in the Crimea. Those who have been there describe it as having two seasons—winter and nearly winter. Still, one has to be alive to experience winter. Thirty years ago Basil would not have exiled Simon—he would have been executed on the spot."

George shook his head, "Good riddance. Anyhow, thanks for the promotion. I'll do my best for you and the emperors. Will I see you tomorrow night?"

"Of course, although I may not see you. The master of ceremonies wasn't too happy to include another 60 people. I think you'll be in the dining hall, but you may not be able to see the head table." Justin was interrupted by the blare of trumpets, which grew steadily louder.

"What in the name of St. Demetrius is that?" exclaimed George.

"A member of the royal family is passing—let's see who it is." It did not take long for them to find out, for as the trumpeters passed, they were followed by a column of Varangians, and then Zoe and her ladies. First among them was Sophie, who passed by with a stately tread, interrupted only by a wink at Justin.

George saw it too. "Did you see that, did you? That beautiful woman winked at you—you better hope your wife doesn't find out!"

"Fine, George, I won't tell if you won't. Now, please tell me more about Iconium..."

Seeing Justin was just the boost that Sophie needed as she and the other set forth on the 'field trip' to the soup kitchen. One of eight across the city, it was located in the southwest quarter near the harbor of Theodosius and St. Akakios Church. When Zoe had resolved to 'do something' for the common people following her deliverance from captivity in Egypt, she turned the whole matter over to Sophie as she always did. While Sophie had a much better feel for the city than did her royal mistress, she in turn relied on Alexius to pick out the locations. Once that was done, an infusion of money from the royal clothing and jewelry fund did the rest. To keep things fair, Theodora, along with her money, was part of the effort as well.

Today, both royal sisters would be in attendance, along with their retinues. Zoe and Theodora rode in the first carriage, which followed the trumpeters and the Varangian guards as they marched along. Sophie was in the second carriage with Leonida, who had taken over as chief lady-in-waiting for Theodora in March. Not by coincidence, at least in Sophie's mind, it was shortly afterwards that Theodora's outfits began show elegance and sophistication of a kind never seen before. While Leonida was outwardly convivial, Sophie's guard was up whenever they were together. '*Yet another mystery*,' she thought, '*that's all I need.*'

For her part, Leonida was in a talkative mood, and was apparently oblivious to Sophie's one-word responses. It was only when the subject of gowns for their mistresses came up did Sophie's attention come into focus.

"Yes, as only you would know, it is difficult to keep coming up with new designs, isn't it?" Leonida blathered on. "I must say, I don't envy you—after all, Zoe has got to be, what, at least ten years older than Theodora. Still, as they say, youth must be served."

By now thoroughly annoyed, Sophie was saved from making a snappy come-back by the trumpets announcing they had arrived at their destination. '*Still, I won't forget this*,' she vowed.

While in the beginning Zoe and Theodora actually handed out the bowls of soup, this was discontinued when it was discovered that people were taking the bowls (and spoons) home with them as the next best thing to holy relics. Sophie fondly remembered Justin's reaction when she approached him for replacements ("Five hundred bowls and spoons after one time!"). So now the royal sisters simply presided doing what they did best, namely smiling, nodding and wearing their tiaras. There was no need to advertise they would be in attendance, for the spectacle of the trumpeters and the Varangians marching ahead of the carriages drew a crowd every time. Preparation of the food was handled by parishioners from St. Akakios, with the opening blessing given by the archpriest assigned there.

In addition to Sophie and the other eight ladies-in-waiting, the two candidates for the one open position were also in attendance. Sophie made sure that each one was on a separate serving line and had positioned herself so that she could observe the young woman, Julia Kritikrites, great-niece of a retired admiral, who was her personal favorite. Meanwhile, Irene kept an eye on the other, Eudocia Menas, the daughter of an influential senator. Sophie had arranged for two actresses to play the role of older, infirm women coming through the lines. Now it was time to sit back and see what happened.

It was Julia's turn first. She had been doing a good job in keeping up the flow of people coming down the line, often greeting them as they passed by. When the first actress drew near, she stumbled after getting her soup, dropping the bowl and spilling the soup on the floor and table. Giving out a wail, she slumped to the floor. Immediately, Julia was at her side, consoling her and getting her cleaned up and back on her feet.

Wiping away her tears, the actress said, "God bless you, child, God bless you!" With more thanks, she moved on down the line. Sophie noted this with approval, and waited for act two.

It was not long in coming. In the other line, Theodora and Leonida stood at the end, with various ladies and women from St. Akakios in the line distributing the food. Sophie had arranged things so that Eudocia was there as well, standing next to Irene. As the second actress gave a repeat performance like that just concluded by the first, Eudocia stood dumb-founded and stared. When the actress decided to turn up the pressure by looking directly at Eudocia and wailing, "Help me, help me!" the latter's response was to look to the church woman standing across from her and snap, "Here, you, take care of that!" At that, Irene's eyes met Sophie's and mutual nods were exchanged.

The rest of the lunch was anti-climactic from Sophie's viewpoint, and she felt buoyant enough to bring up the subject of the banquet with Leonida as they travelled back to the palace, albeit in general terms. Leonida agreed that creating original gowns for royalty was a challenge, but would go no further. When Sophie attempted to learn where Leonida had learned to design, her counterpart was non-committal. Frustrated, Sophie let the matter drop—for now.

Later that afternoon, satisfied that she could do more that day, Sophie prepared to leave for home. Before she did she asked to see Zoe. The princess was still coming off an emotional high from 'seeing her people', something Sophie was counting on. So, when she informed Zoe that her recommendation for the new lady-in-waiting was Julia rather than Eudocia her mistress said "Sounds fine to me," and that was that.

When Sophie arrived home, Philip indicated that Maria was finishing her lessons in the library, while Simon was playing in the garden with Justin. She changed out of her court dress, got a glass of wine, and relaxed on the veranda. Far to the south, the white peak of the Bithynian Olympus glinted through the clear air in the afternoon sun.

When dinner was served, Justin appeared to be uneasy. Finally, Sophie could stand no more. "Dear, are you expecting someone?"

Justin smiled wanly. "No, darling, just feeling a little out of sorts," as he rubbed his right ear. By prior agreement, this was a signal that meant *Not now*. So, the matter was dropped and the rest of the dinner was devoted to listening to Maria recount how she had played that day with two of the maids' children who were about her same age, and encouraging Simon to eat his food rather than throw it on the floor.

Later, after the children had been put to bed, the couple were seated on the veranda.

"Yes, I'm anxious," Justin began. "Alexius was supposed to talk with that Varangian we met at the interview—Hetman Siggurdsen I think his name is—and find out what it is he's holding back, if anything. I thought I would have heard from him by now."

"Well, dear, you know how Alexius is. He probably decided to help loosen the hetman's tongue over some wine or mead or whatever, and time got away from him."

As if on cue, the night porter came to the door and announced that the deputy treasurer wished to call on them. This was actually a useless gesture, in that Alexius was right behind the man and proceeded to sit down across from the couple. From the look on his face, both Justin and Sophie could tell the news was not good. They were right.

"All right, Boss, I have to say you were right about the Varangian. He did know more, and I did just what you said to do. I threatened him with the wrath of Basil, the fires of Hell, and whatever they do in Valhalla, and it worked!" At this, he paused, and caught his breath.

"Well, come on, man, out with it," said Justin.

"Here it is—the murder of Magnus wasn't the first one of its kind—there was another one a few weeks before that! The first victim's throat was slit and was mutilated the same way Magnus was!"

"Why didn't we hear about that?" exclaimed Sophie.

"A lot of reasons, I think. According to Siggurdsen, the man who got killed was disliked by everyone. He was often drunk, was sloppy in his duties and was on the point of being sent back to the Northland when he showed up dead. Since the list of people who were happy to see him dead was fairly long, it didn't get reported. Plus, it seems that the Varangians despise the senator who oversees them, and knew that they would only get grief from him should this come out. Only now though, with the second killing, does it seem important."

"Along with impossible to cover up," said Sophie wryly.

Justin frowned, then commented, "Well, I'm glad you and the hetman got along so well. Turning to Sophie, he continued, "I see this news as both good and bad. Agree?"

"Oh, yes. Good in that Magnus was not killed randomly, which would be very difficult to solve. Bad in that we have appear to have a serial killer. The only question now—when will the next murder be?"

The three were silent for a moment before Alexius spoke. "So, Chief, what's our next move?"

"Assuming the next banquet is this Friday, I think we need to convene a meeting of the Alitheia Society there, just in case 'Loviatar' makes another appearance," Justin replied, getting a nod from Sophie as he finished.

"Sounds like a plan, Chief, sounds like a plan," Alexius responded enthusiastically. "I'll get on it."

"And I," said Sophie, "will break out my best inconspicuous outfit. It won't do to have the Iron Lady make an appearance—it might scare off 'Loviatar.'"

At this, Justin smiled. "Oh, I'm sure it would, assuming the goddess knows what's good for her!"

CHAPTER 10

The big day of the 40th anniversary banquet arrived at last. Sophie never attempted to keep track of how many such affairs she had attended since her career with Zoe started, but was well aware that each one would quickly go from being the center of her universe to a memory of no real importance. Still, she enjoyed them immensely, even more so now that, as wife of the Treasurer of the Empire, she actually got to sit down during the proceedings. Getting ready was half the fun, and with Justin having gone to his office first thing in the morning, she had time to herself, first to take a bath and then to begin the dressing process. In this, she was assisted by Maria, who, like most 10-year old girls, loved dressing up with her mother. Dressing up was merely part of the package though, for Maria was smart enough to grasp that part of Mommy's job involved clothes, and lots of them.

Sophie's position involved clothes far more than Maria grasped. For a lady-in-waiting at the highest level like herself, every day was dress-up day, and the difference was only a matter of degree. A banquet like the one that night was show time in every sense of the word, and Sophie had been preparing for weeks. Unlike jewelry, which could be selected through a simple shopping trip to the Mese, clothes had to be hand-sewn just for her, and she kept a team of dressmakers on call. As a result of their efforts, she had a variety of outfits to choose from, all of which had never been worn by her or anyone else.

All had multiple layers, but since all but the outer wrap were made of silk, wearing them was not oppressive, nor were Sophie's movements constrained. Looking at them spread out on every available flat surface in the bedroom, Sophie was pleased—they looked nice, but not too nice—rule number one was not to outshine Zoe. Still, since she would not be standing behind Zoe at the banquet, perhaps the emerald earrings would not be too much?

"Mommy, is Daddy going to the banquet tonight?" asked Maria as they surveyed the array of capes, blouses, stoles and robes.

"Yes, Maria, he is, and we get to sit together, since he's the Treasurer."

"But doesn't Aunt Zoe need you?"

"Yes. In fact, when I get dressed, I need to go to the Palace to help her get dressed."

"But can't she dress herself?"

Sophie was spared the trouble of tackling that question by a knock on the door. A familiar voice said, "Hello? Are you decent?" as Justin poked his head around the corner.

Sophie laughed and said in a low voice, "Since when do you care?" Then to Maria she said, "All right, Daddy's here to help Mommy get finished. I'll see you before I go. Why don't you go check on your pony?" And with that Maria was off, with a quick hug to Justin as she went by.

Surveying the outfits laid out in the bedroom, Justin could not help but give out a low whistle. "All of these for tonight? What are we going to, a play where you change every act?"

Smiling as only she could smile, Sophie replied, "No, silly, it's a banquet. The ones I don't wear tonight I can wear later. That's the way it works—if I was ever to wear the same outfit to two different formal affairs, my career, such as it is, would be over—people would talk."

Justin, not in a mood to give up easily, came back with a retort. "Hold on, the Empire pays Zoe's clothing allowance—don't I know it—why can't it pay yours, too?"

"Coming from the Treasurer of the Roman Empire, that's an odd statement. Why don't you just make it happen?"

"Oh, you know I can't. It would come out of Zoe's budget, and Basil watches that like a hawk already, I can tell you. Sure, it's all well and good to have Zoe be a princess for the people, but you can only stretch that so far. Still, I'm sure you'll look marvelous," he said, finishing his mini-tirade with a kiss.

"Thank you, dear. If you ever wondered why only the female relatives of rich men get to be ladies-in-waiting, well now you know."

At this, Justin objected, "But your father wasn't rich—professionally successful, yes, but not old money rich."

Giving another sweet smile, Sophie replied, "Well then, that's just another example of how truly unique I am, isn't it? Here, make yourself useful, and help with these fasteners on the back."

Justin got to work, marveling at the complexity of women's clothing, but kept his thoughts to himself. In an attempt to pass the time, he tried another tack.

"I talked with Alexius some more today about what he found out about the first murder, and he said..."

Sophie cut him off. "Please not today! I have got enough to worry about today without starting into that. After all, that just concerns the security of the empire—here we're talking about whether Zoe's ensemble is going to outshine Theodora's! What makes it worse is how long it takes to get ready. You men are so lucky—what does it take you—five minutes?"

His voice raised in feigned outrage, Justin said, "Hey, wait a minute! That's not fair... If I shave, it takes at least ten minutes!"

Ducking the pillow thrown at his head, Justin headed for the door. As he left, he heard Sophie call, but not in anger, "Please send the maid up—it's time for my hair!"

After doing as he was told, Justin retired to the library and collected his thoughts. Taking a piece of paper as was his habit, he recorded his thoughts about the Varangian murders. When finished, he read over the following: (1) Suspects—none; (2) Motive—none; (3) Method of killing—consistent in each case; (4) Target victims—Varangians in the service of the empire; (5) Consistent elements—both victims attended feasts periodically held in the Varangian quarters.

Shaking his head, he thought, '*Right now, we've got a whole bunch of nothing.*' His thoughts were interrupted by Sophie, who stuck her head in the library and announced that she was leaving to assist Zoe.

Turning to look at her, Justin could only say, "You were never lovelier," with all his heart. Deciding to heed her advice, he folded up the paper he had been writing on and went off to find his children.

Sophie took their best carriage to the north entrance to the Grand Palace, where she was met by a special escort sent courtesy of Zoe. When she arrived at Zoe's chambers, she was greeted by Irene, who had handled the initial steps of getting the princess ready. With no husband or children herself, Irene was invaluable to have in such situations where Sophie's attention was diverted. For a moment, Sophie considered repaying her trusted aid by offering to take her place behind Zoe that evening. Fortunately the moment passed, and Irene would remain where she was.

"Sophie, I have to tell you that outfit you laid out for the princess is amazing," gushed Irene. "None of the other ladies and I have ever seen anything like it! Where did you get the idea for the blue and silver robe with the jeweled rosettes that go clear to the hemline? It's a perfect match for her tiara with the sapphire pendants!"

"It took many sleepless nights, I assure you. How does she like it?" replied Sophie with more than a little relief.

"She's over the moon, I can tell you. Here, see for yourself." Irene then took Sophie back into the inner sanctum and saw Zoe, who was positively glowing as the aides worked on her hair, jewels and other accessories. While it did not take a village to get her ready for such an occasion, it was close. Upon seeing Sophie, Zoe paid the highest honor within her power—she rose, acknowledged Sophie, and gave a slight curtsey, to which Sophie replied in kind.

Sophie then went to the banquet hall to check the arrangements. Having attended Zoe through dozens of such affairs over the previous eighteen years, Sophie knew that the best way to make sure things went off without a hitch was meticulous preparation in advance. Since the attendance for this banquet was set for about 600 people, it was to be held in a refurbished hall initially constructed in the time of Justinian I, and then re-done by Basil I, the great-great-

great grandfather of the current emperors, 150 years ago. The use of this particular hall was in keeping with the theme of the banquet (celebrating 40 years of their joint reign), even though there were other halls in the palace that were larger and more opulent.

Since the entire royal family was to be in attendance, there was a raised platform at the head of the room, upon which was placed a curved table. Basil and Constantine were to be seated in the middle, with Zoe and Theodora on one side and the prefect and the patriarch on the other. Senior officials of the empire like Justin were to be seated on a table immediately below, facing them. The rest of the diners were to be at tables that held 12 people each. Because of the very real space limitations, those in the back, like Justin's visiting treasury officials, were seated close enough to make movement difficult. Still, they were in the room for what promised to be an unforgettable night of luxury.

By tradition, the diners sat on embroidered couches, although they were not expected to recline as did their distant ancestors in Rome. In his younger days, Justin had tried to get through a three-hour banquet in this fashion, and found it absolute torture to prop himself up on one arm the entire time. As for Sophie, Zoe and the rest of the ladies, the gowns they wore made reclining a physical impossibility, to say nothing of the lack of modesty. Still, while the diners would sit erect, they would dine off golden plates and drink from silver cups. As a final nod to tradition, the only utensils would be forks and knives, eliminating the possibility of having a soup course.

Finding the physical layout to be satisfactory, Sophie as an afterthought checked with the Master of Protocol and determined where she and Justin were to be seated. Their location in front of the prefect would let her keep an eye on Zoe. Although she had no doubt that Irene could handle anything that came up, she was relieved to see that they could still make eye contact on occasion. Looking up from the table, she saw Justin come in the side door, and waved him over to her side.

In a break with tradition, before the banquet began a select group of officials and dignitaries, along with their wives, were invited to what was billed as 'an informal audience' with the emperors. For his part, Justin thought a more complete oxymoron could not be invented, and so it proved. Following an announcement by the Master of Protocol, Basil and Constantine entered from a side door. Basil was in his full ceremonial military garb, while his brother, who had never seen action, wore a richly-brocaded robe of purple and scarlet. Both wore their crowns. The two men took up their seats on small thrones at one end of the room, there to await well-wishers. To keep attention focused on the royal brothers, Zoe and Theodora did not make an appearance.

One problem immediately became apparent—no one came forward to speak with them. Years of having been kept at a distance in audiences and public appearances had conditioned most people to regard the emperors as other-worldly. Fortunately, Sophie had no such feelings and, with Justin in tow, made a bee-line for them. While Basil seemed as cordial and relaxed as he ever did, which wasn't much, their attention was drawn to his brother. When they got close enough to exchange greetings with Constantine, both Sophie and Justin noticed that he appeared pale and seemed to slur his speech. They had no time to linger, though, for with the ice broken others were lining up behind them, and the chamberlain hustled them on. Among the dignitaries present were the prefect, who greeted them warmly, and Senator Kalokyros, who ignored them.

Eventually, the audience was over, and the banquet began while it was still daylight, reflecting the years Basil spent on campaign when he rose early and turned in early. Banquets held in his absence, presided over by Constantine, would go considerably longer with a correspondingly greater wine consumption. The guests filed in from four different entrances, with the Master of Protocol and his assistants directing them to their assigned seats. Nothing was left to chance, lest the imperial demeanor be ruffled.

When Sophie and Justin took their places, Sophie whispered, "Did you see Constantine? He looks terrible! What's going on?"

Before Justin could answer, the rest of the head table processed in with the emperors first. While most of the guests' eyes were fixed on them, Sophie only had eyes for Theodora, and she didn't like what she saw. Theodora's gown was truly eye-catching, covered as it was by jewels and pearls all outlined in silver. The colors were by themselves amazing, combining red, orange, yellow and pink in combinations Sophie had never conceived. Worst of all, from the look on her face, Sophie could tell that Zoe had noticed all of this too, and was not amused. *'I'll hear about this tomorrow, if not before,'* Sophie thought, for while Zoe was not particularly intelligent, the princess grasped very well the truth that such banquets were both social occasions and opportunities for the Empire to display its opulence to the assembled gathering.

The Patriarch then mumbled through what Justin assumed was be a prayer, and everyone could finally sit down. A small army of servants then started to bring out the food and wine. Of the latter, there was white wine from Crete and what Justin was told was a very good red vintage from Italy. Unlike most of his contemporaries, Justin did not consume much wine, although he did not completely abstain like Basil. Justin found it useful to let other men get into their cups, for in wine there was truth. He therefore sipped at his goblet, intending to nurse it through the evening. Sophie, with no such limits, resolved to try both at least once.

Included in the hall were separate tables for foreign guests. The Venetians were on one side, and were distinguished by the green feathers in the hats which they seemed to wear at all times. The Russians were on the other side, nearer to the couple, and were already well into their allotted amount of wine which Sophie had heard was two bottles per man. As he feared, Justin's people were in the far back, just behind the delegation from Rome, who were looking none too pleased. There was even a table for some visiting Arabs from Mosul, who were no friends of the Caliph. He didn't bother looking for Alexius—his deputy had no use for such affairs.

During the course of the meal, Justin got ceremonial cups from the Russians (vodka) and the Venetians (grappa). On receiving each, he looked toward their respective table, gave a toast which was reciprocated, and then pretended to take a sip. Sophie observed this with amusement. Based on their observations at the audience, Justin also kept an eye on Constantine. To his surprise, Constantine belied his reputation for being a heavy drinker. He drank very little and very slowly, and seemed uncomfortable. Since making small talk with Basil would have been fruitless, he did appear to exchange some words with Zoe who studiously avoided looking at Theodora.

Eventually, Justin lost count of the courses which came out. At various times, the diners were served fish, lamb, bread, olives, apples, pears, cherries, plums, nuts, honey, eggs, cheeses, carrots, squash, leeks, figs and sweet pastries. Sophie, more a veteran of such feasts, knew how to pace herself and so was not totally stuffed when the final course of pudding was brought forth. That is when things got interesting.

As had been the case for each course, the eyes of the diners were fixed on the emperors when the pudding was served, for it was considered a major breach of etiquette to begin to eat before they did. This usually was not a problem, for given the size of the room there was no way to serve everyone at once, even with a large wait staff, and the emperors were always served first. Out of habit, Basil and Constantine started together. This time though, Basil sat, fork in hand, waiting for his brother who sat staring at the dish in front of him. Then, without further warning, Constantine collapsed face first into the pudding.

After a moment of total silence, several things happened. A woman several tables back let out a scream, the Master of Protocol rushed forward with a towel, Justin and Sophie jumped to their feet, and Basil simply sat and stared at his brother. With Justin lifting from the front and the master from the back, they were able to pull Constantine, who was a large man, into an upright position. He was semi-conscious and did not respond to questions. As murmurs in the room grew louder, Basil exercised his imperial function and rose to his feet. At once, silence fell again.

In a commanding voice, he said, "Peace, good people! Our brother is merely under the weather, nothing more. The physicians will attend to him now. This banquet is concluded." As Basil turned to leave the room, both Justin and Sophie caught a glimpse of his blue eyes which were blazing with fury.

Sophie had gone to comfort Zoe, who was trying her best not to weep in public. Together with Irene, she escorted the princess out, following the aides who bundled Constantine out through the royal entrance. As she passed, she caught Justin's eye, who nodded in understanding, as if to say *"Do what you need to do, I'll be fine."* On impulse, Justin looked into the cup at Constantine's place. What he found confirmed his earlier observation—it was almost full.

Turning back to the remains of the banquet, Justin's attention was drawn to what appeared to be an altercation near one of the exits. It seemed to involve some of the Venetians and two Varangian guards. Since the guards spoke only marginal Greek and the Venetians only Italian, tempers were escalating when the Master of Protocol came to Justin in a panic asking for help. When Justin spoke to the men, it became apparent that somehow one of the guests had several silver forks and knives in his purse. Translating back and forth, Justin worked out the 'misunderstanding' and the cutlery was returned.

Knowing that Sophie would have a carriage provided whenever she wished to come home, Justin rode by himself back to their villa. While Constantine's reputation as a big drinker was well known, Justin was convinced that on this occasion at least the man was not intoxicated. *'Well, that's his physicians' problem now,'* he thought, *'I've got enough to worry about as it is.'*

Later, as he lay in bed, Justin was aware that Sophie was crawling in beside him. Only half-awake, he gave her a pat. The words she spoke caused him to come fully awake.

"Zoe is terrified that her uncle has had enough. She's afraid her father is to be exiled!"

CHAPTER 11

As she rode to the palace the next morning, Sophie could not remember when she felt more unsettled. The sight of Zoe losing her composure at the banquet was something she never thought she would witness. Even when they were under attack by the Turks or held captive in Egypt, Zoe had maintained her bearing as befitted an imperial princess. Seeing her father helpless and publically humiliated at the banquet apparently was too much even for her. Given what Sophie knew of Basil, Zoe's fears were well founded, for there were few sins more reprehensible in the eyes of the senior emperor than embarrassing the empire even if the offender was his own brother.

At her direction, the driver took her to a side door in the Great Palace, which allowed her to get to Zoe's quarters for the most part unobserved. The door was still guarded, however, as were all entrances into the areas where the royal family lived. Given her status and fame, Sophie was well-known to the Varangians on guard, who admitted her with nods. She had not planned to engage them in conversation, but found herself doing so when the commander of the group of five addressed her.

"Ver vita fyrir yor wit, Jarnlayden!" {"We know you are with us, Iron Lady!"}

As she looked up to the man, who stood almost a foot taller than her, she was at a loss for words for a moment. Then, drawing herself up to her full height, she answered, "Bakka yor, Drengr! Ed munu idja minn bezt!" {Thank you, warrior! I will do my best!"}

At that, one of the others, perhaps more pious than the rest, chimed in. "Christus aen Frigga visa yor um binn soku!" {Christ and Frigga guide you in your quest!"} With this, he and one other man made the sign of the cross as Sophie went on her way.

When she arrived at Zoe's rooms, Irene met her at once. From the look on her face, Sophie feared the worst.

"Oh, Sophie, it's been a long night. Zoe's been crying and praying and dozing and then the cycle starts over. Finally, she got the word that her father was conscious and was asking for her and Theodora. She's been in his chambers since first light and wanted you to join her as you came in. I've never seen her like this!"

"All right, Irene," Sophie said in her taking-command voice. "You're in charge of things here while I'm gone. Keep everyone calm, especially the new women. They haven't dealt with things like this before, at least not here. You know what to do."

"Very well, Sophie. May the Virgin guide you."

The distance to Constantine's quarters was not that great, but it was a path that Sophie had rarely taken before. By Zoe's own past admissions, Constantine had not been a very attentive father, and in recent years father and daughter had seen little of each other except on festive occasions. The Varangians at the door did not seem surprised to see her, something which Sophie attributed to a word passed by Zoe earlier. The same was not true when she entered the outer chamber and confronted Constantine's aide, a grim-faced young man who appeared to be from one of the eastern provinces.

"You can't come in here! How did you get in! Leave now!" he barked.

From long experience, Sophie knew how to deal with officious types like this. Looking at him for a moment without replying, she then kept on walking. Only when he made a move to grab her arm did she speak.

"I am the Lady Sophia Cataphlates, chief lady-in-waiting to her Imperial Highness Zoe Porphyrogenita! I am here at her majesty's command, and if you touch me, I will see that you live to regret it, although not for long! Now, where is the princess?"

Stunned into silence, the man could only point to a door at the far end of the room. Sophie marched on and entered. There, she found a surreal sight. At the center of everything was Constantine, who was lying in an enormous bed covered with silk sheets. He was propped up on pillows and was awake and alert, although he looked tired and drawn. On one side of the bed were Zoe and Theodora, looking very un-imperial and very much like concerned adult daughters, with Leonida standing behind Theodora. On the other side were a trio of men whom Sophie took to be the imperial doctors, who were chattering among themselves like a flock of crows. Behind them stood a number of courtiers, eunuchs and servants. As she surveyed this scene, she saw a door open in the far side of the room, through which entered the senior Augustus of the Roman Empire, Basil II. His face was impassive, but Sophie noticed that he did turn his head to her and give a slight nod. From what Sophie could tell, he had had a difficult night, too.

When the rest of the occupants of the room became aware of Basil's presence, they fell silent. Sophie saw Zoe look to her with a face filled with apprehension, which was quickly suppressed as the princess made the obligatory curtsey to her uncle. Sophie glided to Zoe's side, and could tell from her body language that she was near exhaustion. She grasped the princess' hand, and Zoe gripped hers back with determination.

Basil looked at his brother impassively for what seemed a long time. Then he quietly said, "We wish all here who are not family members to depart, now!"

Zoe looked at Sophie with alarm, something which her uncle apparently noticed. "Everyone, that is, but Lady Sophia. She may stay."

As those who had been dismissed filed out, Sophie tried hard not to look at Leonida. In this, she was unsuccessful, for as her counterpart passed her with what appeared to be a glare, Sophie could not help but give a slight shrug of her shoulders and a faint smile.

Once the room was cleared, Basil looked at Constantine and spoke, not as an emperor, but as a brother. "How did it come to this, Constantine? Have we been together so long that you must play the fool in front of hundreds? What can I do to help you? Do you have to be exiled? Please tell me, I beg you!"

The silence that followed was palpable, finally broken only by Constantine's muffled coughing, which led into prolonged sobbing. After what seemed an age, he spoke. "I am so sorry, brother, I really am! I know I drink too much, but I have been trying to cut down, I really have! I don't know what happened last night—I really didn't have that much. Give me another chance, please—this will not happen again, I swear!"

As long as Sophie lived, she would not forget the sight which followed as one of the two most powerful men in the Roman Empire hugged the other as both wept. Zoe was weeping too, and held on to Sophie's hand so tight that her fingernails turned white. At last, before all feeling was lost, Basil nodded 'yes' without saying anything, and the tension in the room was released as the two brothers looked at each other with affection. A wave of Basil's hand brought others back into the room, and Zoe gave her father a hug before leading Sophie out into the ante-chamber. As Sophie left, she noticed Basil again giving her the slightest of nods before he barked to the attending doctors that his brother should under no circumstances be bled.

When they left the chamber, they passed by the young man who had addressed Sophie so rudely when she entered. This time, he barely gave her a glance, although he was all too obsequious to Zoe, bowing low as the princess passed.

As they went on, Zoe, noticing that Sophie had stared at Constantine's aide, said, "Oh, that's Maurice, or Mauricius, or something like that. He's been serving my father for several months now. He's very clever, I think. Would you like to meet him?"

Sophie could only shake her head before replying, "No, we've met. Where is he from?"

"Syria, perhaps, or one of those eastern provinces. I never was too good at geometry."

Sophie decided to let that last comment go, for her mind was already moving ahead to the coming days, for how could Constantine really ever change behaviors years in the making? If, or rather when, he relapsed, what would that mean for the Roman Empire? As she accompanied Zoe back to her royal quarters, she could only shake her head in weariness. *'All of this on top of the murders,'* she thought, *'May the Virgin sustain us now!'*

Justin's day got off to a considerably more subdued start than Sophie's. After making sure the children were set for the day at home, he was ready to go to his office to finish preparations for the trip to Crete. To his consternation, he was unable to find a clean linen outer robe of the type that he was entitled to wear as treasurer (white, with a blue collar and blue stripes down each side and on the cuffs). While there were wool ones aplenty, the early June weather in the city was already getting warm, and he really did not want to go that route. But, in that necessity knows no law, he made the decision to wear wool, one that he was already regretting by the time he arrived at the treasury complex.

When he arrived, he found that Alexius had already been in the office for some time, but had now moved on, likely to the Alitheia Society headquarters, where Justin would meet him later. Justin had always marveled at his deputy's ability to get by with little sleep. Could the fact that he was a eunuch have anything to do with that? Justin decided that it was best not to find out, for Sophie might take such an experiment amiss.

As the two clerks who were to accompany him on the journey took turns reciting the details of the financial transfer, he found himself staring out his office window at the Boukouleon Harbor. Seeing the many ships from many lands moving in and out, he wondered, *'If I got on one of them, could I ever get far enough away from both Basil and the Caliph? But what of Sophie and the children? Perhaps I could send for them—after all, I do speak Italian. Then there is Ireland—I understand it's nice this time of year. I wonder if there are Varangians there?'*

His reveries were interrupted when the droning of Mark, the senior clerk, broke through.

"Treasurer, here is the official receipt to sign for the delivery of the funds. You need to sign here, here and here."

Recovering quickly, Justin frowned, and replied. "I am not entirely convinced that these numbers are accurate. Can you break them down again for me please?" He then sat back and waited, all the while ignoring the looks between Mark and Andrew and thinking *'It's good to be king!'*

Undaunted, Mark responded, "As you will, Treasurer. There will be a total of 20,000 in gold solidi transported on four ships. Of this amount, the Church of the Holy Sepulchre is to receive 10,000, while the Patriarch of Alexandria and the Coptic Church in Cairo each get 4,000. The remainder is to go to," and here Mark was so hesitant in his response that Andrew, the junior clerk, stepped in.

"To the synagogue in Jerusalem, sir. They will receive 2,000, which will be transmitted via the Patriarch of Jerusalem, who has agreed to serve in this function."

Now fully focused, Justin responded. "The allocation seems fine, but that seems like a lot of money for a voyage of only four ships. Are you sure about that?"

After exchanging glances with Andrew, Mark responded, "I am sorry, Treasurer, if I gave that impression. While the funds will be on four ships, there will be a total of twenty in the fleet. Will that be sufficient?"

Trying his best to keep a straight face, Justin nodded, "Twenty? I should think so—we need to leave some for the rest of the Empire. Very well, that will be all—oh, wait, what's that?" as a noise erupted in the outer room.

Justin's clerks, who were on the point of leaving, paused when an unexpected visitor came through the door. It was Senator Kalokyros, and he was not happy. The clerks gave way before him, and exited upon seeing Justin's nod that they do so.

Before Justin could even invite the elderly man to have a seat, the senator rasped, "So, Treasurer, you think to supplant me in charge of the Varangians? We will see about that!"

It was a measure of how imperial service had moderated Justin that he initially made no response, but let the tension lift, if even for a moment. Then, when he was sure that his emotions were under control, he answered in as a measured a voice as he could.

"And good day to you, too, Senator. What makes you think I wish to supplant you? It is not often that an imperial official steps down to take a lesser office, is it?"

If looks could kill, Justin would have died several times over. As it was, the senator looked at him through narrowed eyes, as if grasping that here was a man who was not to be pushed around easily. When he spoke again, it was in a calmer voice.

"Forgive my initial comments, Treasurer Cataphlates, I spoke out of zeal for the Empire. It is just that, as the official who has a direct link between their Majesties and the Varangians, I need to know what is going on here."

At that point, it dawned on Justin that the Varangians themselves had no use for this man, and so felt no need to talk with him. This further tempered his initial dislike, and led him to attempt further reconciliation.

"Of course, Senator. The fault is mine. While I have been Treasurer, my wife and I have not had to investigate the kind of matters that we did before, and certainly none involving the Varangians. As someone who is focused on financial matters, I have not been concerned about the…uh, other offices of the Empire. I offer my sincere apologies. As to the current state of affairs, here is what I know."

Justin then gave a true, but abbreviated, version of what he and Sophie had found so far, all the while watching the senator's body language. When he was satisfied that he had said enough, he concluded, "and that's where we are—not very conclusive, I'm afraid."

Senator Kalokyros nodded in affirmation, and then, to Justin's surprise, rose and offered his hand. In a voice much subdued from that which he used initially, he said, "Thank you very much, Justin, if I may call you that. I am much relieved—please keep me informed. Go with God! Oh, and one more thing—the Varangians—you may think you understand them, but, trust me, you never really will."

Justin took the older man's hand as a matter of course, and nodded in deference. At the same time, he made a mental note not to tell the senator anything of a secure nature—something about him did not ring true. He escorted the senator out of the treasury by stating that he was leaving anyway (which was true), and waited until the older man disappeared into the crowds. After waiting to make sure, he then headed for a door on the west side of the palace. A few minutes' walk brought him to a non-descript building with no exterior markings. The door was crooked and barely opened onto an anteroom that was empty and dusty, with only a solitary man at the far end. This shabbiness was by design, for the building was the headquarters of the Alitheia Society, the undercover agency which the emperors had authorized following the return of Zoe, Sophie and Justin from their captivity in Egypt. Designed to combat the subversive schemes of the Fatimid Caliph and his minions, the society was run by Alexius, under the supervision of Justin, who reported only to the emperors, via the prefect. Justin did not come by the place very often, lest his movements be observed, but today was an exception—the Friday banquet of the Varangians was approaching, and he needed to talk with Alexius.

Alas, that was not to be, for the man at the desk shook his head and said, "Apologies from Alexius, Treasurer. He was called away, but will be in contact with you tomorrow. Any messages for him for now?"

Alexius shook his head in turn and gave a slight smile. "No, Stephan, I'm sure I'll see him when I see him. How's the leg doing?"

Stephan nodded in response. "Very well, Treasurer. The exercises that your wife's father prescribed are really helping—the pain is much less and I have a lot more motion. Thanks for asking."

Justin paused, and then replied, "Thanks to you, Stephan, for being there for me and my wife and the Princess Zoe at the Cilician Gates. It's the least I can do."

As he left the building, memories came back to Justin of the desperate fight two years earlier, in which so many good men died at the whim of Caliph al-Hakim. Stephan had taken an arrow in his leg which had left him with lameness and constant pain. Still, he could still perform limited duties, as did two other men who had also survived and who were employed by the society. When the prefect expressed doubts as to the men's capacity, a note from Emperor Basil—'proceed'—settled things.

Both Justin and Sophie were ready to retire early that night. After seeing the children to bed, which involved some full-body wrestling involving all four of them plus the dogs (at least as long as the beasts would stand it), they settled down to some refreshments on the veranda. In Sophie's case, it was wine, while Justin was satisfied with pomegranate juice. As they often did, they reviewed their days.

"So how did you know that Constantine was not at death's door?" asked Justin. "It sounds like things were pretty grim."

"Oh, things were, but when I saw that Eudocia wasn't there, I knew things were not that far along."

Justin paused for a moment. "That's right, I had forgotten about her. She is, what, Zoe's older sister? She had some physical problem?"

"Yes, smallpox. That led her to adopt the monastic life. She's still in the nunnery attached to the monastery out by the Theodosian walls. Zoe and Theodora go to see her every few months. She's not a very pleasant person, although her life has not been very fortunate. Anyhow, this senator you had to deal with—he doesn't sound like a very pleasant person either. What's his excuse, and why haven't we run into him before?"

"Sophie, your guess is as good as mine on the first point. As to the second, you know as well as I do how many bureaucrats there are in the Roman Empire now—as Assistant Treasurer, what was I in the pecking order—143? Then again, we've never had to deal much with the Varangians except as soldiers on guard or in the field. Senator Kalokyros may have been there all along. We'll just have to deal with him." Slumping in his seat, Justin sighed and continued, "I have to tell you, Crete can't come soon enough—each of the past few days seem like years. Now, we have one more thing to do tomorrow night."

"Right, the Varangian banquet. Does Hetman Siggurdsen know?"

"Alexius was supposed to have cleared it with him. I haven't made contact with him today—you know how he is—always in the field, up to something. Anyhow, you and I will be there, I promise.

Then, we can have a peaceful two days together until I leave. I think we both deserve it!"

The couple sat in silence for a while, enjoying the view and the cries of the owls. Then Philip knocked and entered carrying a message. He coughed, and then said, "Excuse me, sir, a courier just came from the Prefect."

Justin sank even further into his seat as he took the paper. After reading it, he sighed. "Great! Now I have a meeting with the delegation from Rome. Another thing on my plate!"

Sophie smiled wanly and patted his arm. "Crete—here you come!"

CHAPTER 12

While Friday morning began at the regular time for Sophie, she had had a restless night, and she found herself looking forward to Saturday. Then she could (maybe) sleep in, assuming she was undisturbed by husband, children, servants, royal mistress or the problems of the Roman Empire at large. Leaving Justin still sleeping in bed, she got up and went into an adjoining room to get prepared for a trip to the Palace, assisted by a drowsy maid. On the way, while she was wrapped in her thoughts, she could still appreciate the beauty of the rays of the rising sun glinting off the dome of Hagia Sophia. '*This is a city worth fighting for*,' she thought.

She relied on this sentiment to carry her into Zoe's chambers, where she was met by a smiling Irene. There was no sign of Zoe, but Sophie was not surprised after the emotionally wrenching scene she had witnessed the previous day. Irene confirmed this by using the code word they had devised for days when Zoe just did not feel up to playing the part of imperial princess.

"Good morning, Lady Sophia! Our royal mistress is 'indisposed', but instructed me to show you in to her as soon as you arrived. I take it things were a little tense yesterday?"

Sophie could only shake her head. "You might say that. Still, maybe this time Emperor Constantine will turn things around. I wouldn't put money on it, though. See you soon." And with that she knocked on the door to Zoe's inner chambers and then entered. As she expected, Zoe was still in her dressing gown, sitting on a sofa and reading a psalter she used for her daily devotions. Now 38, she was still quite beautiful, even without her make-up, gowns and jewels. She looked up at Sophie and smiled, saying, "Good morning, friend. Please, sit here with me."

Sophie obliged, and thought that she had not seen Zoe this relaxed since they had been on pilgrimage to Jerusalem two years earlier. "Thank you, and I want you to know that you have my earnest prayers for your father's recovery."

Surprisingly, Zoe frowned at this seemingly supportive remark. "As always, your prayers are appreciated, but I fear they not may be enough. My father's spirit is willing, but his flesh is weak. I do not know how many more times he has to fail in public before my uncle will banish him and, worse yet, make me the heir to the Roman Empire. The thought of that is terrifying! Sophie, you must help me!"

Thoroughly confused, Sophie could only exclaim, "Of course, but how?"

"Your father—he's a great doctor, isn't he? Could he help my father conquer his demons?"

Sophie was taken aback but only for a moment before replying. "He is very good, but you know where he is now—we saw him when we were on pilgrimage—he's helping those people who really need to be helped in the leprosarium."

At this, the 'old' Zoe reasserted itself. "As if my father, an Emperor of the Romans, doesn't need to be helped? He's certainly more important than lepers!"

Only Sophie's many years of friendship and service let her respond as she then did. "As a daughter of God, did you hear what you just said?"

Zoe's eyes widened, and then closed. After a moment, she quietly replied, "That was uncalled for—I shall confess that to my father confessor when I see him." Pausing, she continued, "Sophie, I only said that because I am desperate—please tell me—would he come if you asked?"

Hearing the question phrased like that was enough for Sophie. She could only take Zoe's hand and nod, "Yes, of course, he would come."

The senior princess of the Roman Empire bowed her head for a moment, and then said, "Thank you, Sophie, that is all I can ask. It's times like this that put other things into perspective—like dresses, for example." Here, she stopped, and looked at Sophie with a sly smile until Sophie got the idea, and then nodded, giving a wan smile in return.

The ice broken, the two talked for a while like the old friends they were, until Zoe changed the subject. "If you can't say, I totally understand, but if you can, how is your latest investigation going? I do try to keep up on these things, you know."

Back on familiar ground, Sophie felt relieved. She explained (briefly) where matters stood, and mentioned her intent, with Justin, to attend the Varangians' banquet that night, without going into great detail. Zoe listened intently, and, when Sophie was finished, squeezed her hand, saying, "I will pray earnestly for your success in bringing justice to these poor men, who died in the service of our Empire, so far from their homes."

Since this seemed a good time to excuse herself, Sophie did so, needing to see to other matters of the princess' household before she left by late afternoon to meet Justin back home and finalize plans for the evening's expedition.

Justin's day was equally intense, but in a totally different way. After stopping by the office to see if there were any fires to attend to (there were not), he found a message from Alexius on his desk which said, "Chief—I'll be by your place later in the afternoon—big things going on tonight for the Society, right?"

While he was still smiling at the whimsy of his deputy's irreverent note, a clerk came to remind him that Prefect Comnenus was ready to begin that morning's session with the churchmen from East and West. Justin accordingly went to the old audience hall that was first built in the reign of Constantine VII, the grandfather of the current emperors. When he arrived, he found two large tables set up along both sides of the hall, with churchmen lining each, and a third table set up at the top. The prefect was already in place, and rose to meet Justin as he entered. Justin could tell the gravity of the situation by the tenor of the older man's greeting.

"Welcome, Treasurer Cataphlates. Thank you for taking time out of your busy schedule to sit in with us. Now, I think some introductions are in order. I think you know the men who are here from the Roman Empire, beginning with the Ecumenical Patriarch Sergius."

That worthy gave Justin the slightest of nods, to which Justin responded with a minimal one in kind. His nine assistants, clad in black as was the patriarch, did not even do that much. '*Wonderful,*' thought Justin, '*here's another fine mess I've gotten into!*'

The delegation from Rome were introduced next, beginning with Romanus, the senator whom Justin had met earlier. While he was dressed in the white clothing Justin recognized as the classic toga, his entourage, being churchmen, were in bright red garments which showed that they were cardinal priests from various churches in the city. While they initially looked at Justin with blank faces, when he greeted them with, "Buongiorno, Signore! Piacere di conoscerti!" {"Good morning, gentlemen! I am pleased to meet you!"}, the mood lightened considerably and he even got a nod from Romanus.

The atmosphere in the room lifted even more when the prefect informed the assembled group that Treasurer Cataphlates had an announcement to make regarding the Church of the Holy Sepulchre. When Justin looked puzzled, the prefect leaned over to him and said, "Sorry to catch you off guard like this, but the papal delegation has been insisting that Emperor Basil take action to revenge the destruction of the church by the caliph."

Justin nodded his head in understanding, although he could not help but think, '*They do know that it's been seven years, don't they?*' Putting this thought aside, he forced a smile and turned back to the assembled clergy. First in Greek and then in Italian, he explained how in just a few days he would personally deliver funds donated by the Emperors Basil and Constantine for the reconstruction of that very church, along with other holy places that had been damaged. While Justin caught a passing glare from the patriarch due to the inclusion of the synagogue in Jerusalem, the overall reaction from both sides was very positive. Fortunately for Justin, before matters turned to theological points on things like the *filioque* clause (whatever that was), he was excused and left with a sense of profound relief. '*Mediation, my foot! One might as well try to mediate between wolves!*' he thought on the way home.

This feeling of relief was still with him as he discussed the day's events with Sophie as they dressed for the evening's adventures. After talking with Hetman Siggurdsen, they had decided to go to the banquet hall incognito, reasoning that if the Iron Lady made an appearance, the normal flow of the banquet would be entirely thrown off. As a result, they donned dark cloaks over inconspicuous clothing. Alexius had decided not to meet them at their villa, but instead sent a message that he and 'some friends' would meet them at the hall.

As they drove in their carriage through a lovely June night in Constantinople, the street lighters were out igniting their lamps, one by one, down the broad avenues of the city. Thousands of people went about their lives, some coming home from the shops where they worked during the day, others going out to the restaurants and taverns that were scattered all across this part of town. Anyone looking at the carriage would have seen nothing remarkable, for they both had dressed very modestly and had taken the smallest, oldest vehicle that they owned. They drove along past the Hippodrome, where the first big series of chariot races were to be held the next day. '*Levi's people will be busy,*' thought Justin. '*I hope the crowd enjoys themselves, but not at our expense.*'

Sophie's mind was fixed on other matters. The idea that 'Loviatar' was actually real was one that she had never entertained for a moment. While it seemed odd that numerous Varangians had reported seeing something, from experience she knew that they tended to be superstitious and were largely uneducated. The link between the sighting and the murders was more troubling, but again could be simply a matter of coincidence. Whatever the explanation, she hoped that the evening's jaunt would shed some light on what was now a very murky situation.

During their first visit to the banquet site they had examined the main hall, which was large, albeit somewhat shabby. On this visit, they both felt it best to arrive early and to enter through a side door. Waiting to meet them was Hetman Siggurdsen. Behind him were the serving staff who were getting the banquet fare ready. From what Sophie could see, the Varangians ate very well, with large roasts, haunches of venison, bowls of vegetables and platters of rolls lining the counters. Beer there seemed to be in abundance, along with the peculiar liquor much beloved of the Northmen that they called mead. Made from honey, it had a unique taste that Sophie had long ago decided she did not care to acquire.

Seeing her gaze at the preparations, Siggurdsen asked, "Is this to your liking, Lady?"

Sophie blinked once, then said, "Forgive me for staring, Hetman, but am I to understand that you and your men eat like this every Friday?"

Misunderstanding her intent, Siggurdsen nodded. "Yes, Lady, I'm afraid so. Once a week is all we can afford."

Since this prompted a muffled guffaw from Justin, Sophie quickly sought to change the subject. "Your serving people—there seem to be quite a few."

Siggurdsen gave what, for a Varangian, was a huge smile. "You noticed that, did you, Lady? There's someone here who had something to do with that." Looking over across the serving room, he called, "Sergius—there are people here to see you."

Justin gave Sophie a glance which she returned. Sure enough, when 'Sergius' came over it was Alexius, complete with eyepatch, albeit on the other eye than they had seen earlier. To accompany it, he was also sporting a patently false beard.

"Good to see you, Chief, and 'Scalpel.' What do you think of my new look? I'll really blend in, don't you think?"

Justin sighed and shook his head. "Only if the circus is in town. Either lose the eyepatch or the beard—your choice."

Alexius looked stricken and made a wordless appeal to Sophie, who shook her head in the negative. Taking matters in stride, he removed the beard and threw it in the trash. "Well, it was worth a try. Anyhow, I have got ten picked agents here from the society. We'll spread out across the room and keep our eyes open as we serve the food."

Sophie frowned. "If you're serving the food, who handles the drinks?"

Alexius said nothing, but pointed to the far side of the room, where the drink servers were assembling. They were women, Russians to be precise, and from the size of most of them, they could have been Varangians themselves. Sophie nodded in approval, and made a mental note to observe whether any of them were lady-in-waiting material, or at least lady-in-waiting bodyguard material.

Hetman Siggurdsen then gave them a rough idea of how the banquet would go. Soon, members of the various Varangian units who had been on duty across the city would start to filter in, apart from those who were scheduled to man posts on either Saturday or Sunday. Given the rigors of what would transpire at the banquet, such men were proscribed from attending. This meant that only about 400 of the 800 Varangians who were in the capital could attend on any given night.

'Well, that accounts for all of the long faces I see on week-ends,' thought Sophie.

Once the banquet started, it would last for several hours, and would mirror those which the men would have known in their homelands. In addition to the food and drink, songs would be sung and stories would be told by skalds, who were a professional class of poets and storytellers who carried the oral history, literature and mythology of the Northmen in their heads. From what Justin and Sophie could determine from their previous interviews, 'Loviatar' appeared later in the evening. This fact alone predisposed Sophie to think that there might be more of mead than magic about the goddess.

Before the revelers showed up, Justin and Sophie looked out again to re-familiarize themselves with the layout of the hall. They saw that the tables that were laid out only covered about half of the available space. On the east side, the polished windows were now lit by the torches which lined the walls. On the west side, where the kitchen was located, there were also storerooms and an upper level that was unused. The rows of tables ran north-south, parallel with the east wall.

As it grew dark outside, the Varangians began to trickle into the hall in groups of five to ten at a time. With the exception of Sigurdssen, who always seemed to be in full-dress attire, it was a minor revelation to see the men out of their on-duty gear. Justin and Sophie agreed to take up separate positions on the west side of the hall, since the reported sighting of 'Loviatar' had been along the front side on the east. They also noted the men they interviewed had been rather vague about when the sighting occurred, although it undoubtedly had been well along into the evening's proceedings. So, with a kiss they parted. Justin was resigned to spending one of his last nights in Constantinople listening to men talk loudly in a language he did not understand. Further, since he did not drink much, no solace to be found there either.

For her part, Sophie was intrigued to hear prolonged conversations in Norse, for most of her conversations were brief exchanges with soldiers who were on duty. Early on she had noticed there seemed to be two main dialects spoken by the Varangians who served in the Empire. She looked forward to getting a brief immersion into the language, which she found both beautiful and melancholy at the same time. A little white wine along the way would not hurt either, and she had made it a point to acquaint herself with several of the serving wenches despite the language barrier.

The hall soon filled, and Hetman Sigurdssen made some opening remarks, which Sophie thought generally amounted to "Let's be careful out there" or words to that effect. The diners, who probably amounted to around 350, were respectful of his authority, but quickly grew more raucous as the meal began. Still, nothing that Justin or Sophie saw rose to the level of a brawl, save for one younger looking man who apparently got a little too friendly with one of the bar maids. A kick in his groin set him straight, as did the hoots and jeers of his fellows following his discomfiture. *Well played, sister,* thought Sophie, *'you'll go far.'*

Dinner settled down into a routine that, at least from Justin's perspective, went on interminably. Sophie was entertained by a series of bards who led the crowd in songs. Some were traditional ballads which extolled the valor of legendary warriors, while others evoked the beauty of the men's faraway homeland. The final bard, whom she took to be more of a joker, entertained the increasingly intoxicated crowd with a story involving an older man who had a younger wife who he could not satisfy, when they entertained a traveler who was happy to do so. Sophie was presented with some terms that she was not familiar with, but which sounded very naughty. *'Best not to ask the guards what hyrggrauf means,'* she thought, although from the context she had a fairly good idea.

Alexius and his men were still circulating around the room, but the demand for food was rapidly ending, and they were now in the business of cleaning up as some of the torches began to go out. The bar maids were still doing a good business, but some of the men were now starting to drift away from the tables and into the night, to whatever further destination they desired. As more and more left, Sophie was still scanning the room when she felt Justin come up beside her.

"Well, there was never any guarantee that 'Loviatar' was going to show up tonight, or that such a thing even exists," he said. "How long do you think we should stay?"

Sophie thought for a moment. "Let's wait a little longer—the room is still about…"

She never finished that sentence, for a shout about forty feet away from them was followed by others and the sound of overturning tables and benches. Men were pointing up at the east wall, but Sophie could see nothing. By his reaction, Justin was befuddled, too, but they both made their way as fast as they could to where a knot of men had gathered, including Alexius and some of his people. Looking up, they saw a sight that startled them, for the image of a woman was reflected on one of the upper mirror-like windows on the east wall, saying nothing, pointing out at them.

"Do you see that?" Justin hissed. "What is it?"

"Quiet! I'm working!" whispered Sophie. Turning her full attention to the apparition, she noticed its face, hair, posture and, most importantly, its attire. Its face was blurry, but the eyes were very dark and emotionless. Still, something seemed odd about that face, something that she could not identify, which made her focus all the more intently. In this, she was an island of serenity in a sea of chaos, for all around her Varangians were yelling and running out the doors, while Justin, Alexius and his men were rushing toward the silent figure. Still more odd was the fact that men around her were yelling, pointing and screaming 'Loviatar!' while at the same time those farther away were calling out "Vel hvat sja a per?" {"What do you see?"}. And then, as the torches were re-lit, the figure was gone, just gone.

When the tumult in the room showed no signs of dying down, Justin caught Sophie's eye and gestured toward the side door. She met him there after he had conferred briefly with Alexius, and they entered their carriage amidst the throngs of Varangians pouring into the street.

"All right," Sophie said, "maybe there is something to this after all!"

CHAPTER 13

Justin woke up the next morning in a very grumpy mood. As he had expected, their experience the night before in the banqueting hall had gotten Sophie's investigative nerve-endings excited, and she had spent the entire coach ride home discussing what they had seen. In contrast to Sophie, Justin had never been much of a night person, and while he followed and even contributed to her speculations on the way home, once in bed it was another matter. As soon as his head hit the pillow, he wanted nothing more than to sleep. Of necessity, though, his wife needed to process all she had seen, and process she did, going through each step of the evening, occasionally getting up to jot something down, which meant she had to keep the oil lamp burning. Justin kept murmuring sounds of assent as long as he could, but finally lost the fight to Morpheus. When Sophie finally fell asleep he had no idea.

She was still blissfully dreaming the next morning when, in no particular order, the dogs and the children decided that Momma and Papa had slept long enough. While long practice let Sophie doze through the onslaught, Justin had always been a light sleeper and he knew it was useless to resist. So, once he got hounds and kids sorted out, he ushered everyone out and got dressed. It being a Saturday, he had made arrangements for others to manage the office, which was only open until noon. Maria and Simon were glad to accompany him for breakfast, although they were disappointed that they had to stay inside. The morning showers in June generally moved through by mid-day, at least according to Philip, whose knee was said to give very accurate forecasts of the weather.

As predicted by said knee, sunshine soon appeared, and Maria and Simon went on to the veranda, where she delighted her brother by placing scraps of bacon on top of the stone half-wall that lined the outside edge. High enough to be out of the reach of the dogs (who nonetheless tried), the morsels attracted the hoopoes who plucked them off the wall while on the wing without a pause. Justin was enjoying this sight when Philip entered with something more than a weather report.

"Sir, Master Alexius is here to see you along with another man."

"Very well. Do you know who the other man is?"

Philip paused, and then said with an unspoken sniff, "Yes, sir, he's one of those Northmen one sees around the city nowadays. Shall I show him in as well?"

"Yes, yes, I'm fairly certain he's on our side."

This proved to be true, when Alexius and Hetman Siggurdsen came in. Alexius was still in his serving man garb, while Siggurdsen was, if anything, in more resplendent regalia than usual. From their looks, Justin was prepared for the worst.

"All right, let's have it," he said. "Was there another murder after the banquet last night?"

After looking briefly at the Varangian leader, Alexius cleared his throat and said, "No, Boss, but it was close." Seeing Justin's puzzled look, he continued, "As you know, things broke up in confusion after men saw, well, you-know-who, and they spilled out into the street. Most of them still had their wits about them and stayed in groups as they headed back to the barracks or to a tavern or to, well, you know…Anyhow, uh, Hetman, why don't you tell the Treasurer what happened then—you were there."

Gravely, the tall soldier nodded and said, "Certainly. I was following a group which contained several men who were known to me to be the kind who often found trouble, if they did not create it first. One of them gave a shout, and started running down an alley. Others followed, as did I. When I reached the leaders who had stopped, they were lifting up a fellow Northman from the street. Apparently some men in the group had seen two shadowy figures attempting to drag him away. At the noise, the figures ran away and the man in the street was none the worse for wear apart from being very drunk."

Justin stared at them before speaking. "That is very good news, Hetman. Tell me, how is the mood among your men? What do they think about what they saw?"

The blank look on Hetman Siggurdsen's face evoked in Justin's memory the parting words of Senator Kalokyros about really understanding the Varangians. For whatever reason, it lasted only a moment before the Hetman replied.

"Treasurer, I must say that while many of them are confused, none of them are afraid. Many of them are Christian, and for those who are not, they trust in the power of the God that rules over this city and this Empire to protect them. There are some, I confess, who murmur that the power of 'Loviatar' must be great to extend this far to cause the death of men here, but their numbers are, for now, not many."

This affirmation prompted Alexius to interject, "That's right, Boss! I've talked with them, at least those who will talk with, you know, people like me, and they all just want an explanation!"

"And that, gentlemen, is just what they will have!" announced Sophie in a dulcet voice. "I know how it was done!" With that, she swept into the room, to be mobbed by her children and the dogs. Even informally, on a Saturday, at home, she was dressed to the nines, and whatever irritation Justin felt with her evaporated like snow in the desert sun.

"Oh, no, don't get up, don't get up!" she continued, seeing Alexius and Siggurdsen start to rise. "We have work to do, and there's no time to waste!"

Justin could stand no more. "Oh, you!" he said with a smile. "What do you mean, 'I know how it was done!' Please, tell us!"

Reciprocating the smile, Sophie came over and gave Justin a kiss before sitting down beside him and saying to Alexius, "Sorry, that's all!" and to Siggurdsen "Var kunn, Hetman!" {"Pardon, Commander!"} Cradling Simon on her lap, she continued while brushing his hair.

"We all saw what we saw, correct? The ghostly vision of a woman dressed in white in the window last night, pointing out at the men in the room. The question is—who was it? Some would say it was 'Loviatar,' a pagan goddess from a distant land, come to bring death and destruction on the Varangians (but oddly enough, not on anybody else!) As a daughter of the Church, I cannot and do not believe that, so there must be another explanation. I confess that the sight last night was impressive, but that is no matter—here is how it was done, and here is how I will prove it!"

What followed was an emphatic, if somewhat breathless, description of Sophie's theory, complete with hand motions and facial expressions. When she was finished, the three men looked at her in varying degrees of disbelief, although with Siggurdsen it was always hard to tell.

Justin broke the silence first. "You have got to be kidding! That's insane! How are you going to get any woman to agree to be suspended by ropes from the roof of the Varangians' banquet hall?" Then, he paused, and an incredulous look came over his face. "Oh, Sophie! Not you? Think of the children!"

"Me? Of course not, silly! I need to make observations," Sophie said with a laugh. "No, I have a volunteer. Oh, Donna, come in, please," turning toward the door.

At that, Sophie's maid came in, bowing her head and blushing in the presence of so many notables. As if pre-arranged, she came up to Sophie and stopped, still saying nothing. The men in the room could only stare in silence.

Sophie could only shake her head. "Here, gentlemen, look—can we agree that Donna and I are about the height of an average woman? And that the apparition we saw last night appeared to be about the same height? So, once we lower Donna down, we can show how the people behind this plot have created the myth of 'Loviatar', and so dispel any impact it may have on the more credulous Northmen. Sound good so far?"

At this, Justin felt compelled to speak. "Uh, Donna? Do you know what is being talked about here? Are you comfortable with that? It is important that we know."

Donna gave a quick smile before answering. "Oh, yes, sir, my mistress has explained it all. It sounds exciting, and it will let me get married!"

Before anyone could inquire about this last statement, Sophie intervened. "That's right—Donna and I worked out an agreement. She needs a dowry to marry her beau—Justin, you probably have seen him—he's a fishmonger who comes by twice a week. Anyhow, it's all set, so gentlemen we will see you tonight at sunset. Agreed?"

After Alexius and a still non-committal Siggurdsen had left, Justin said nothing until Sophie felt compelled to ask, "So, what do you think?"

"Nothing, dear, nothing. You already know that what you've promised that credulous girl will be coming out of your household budget. Still," he paused with a smile, "I hope it doesn't mean that the children and I will be eating gruel for the next three months."

"Not to worry, husband," Sophie said with a smile as she kissed him. "It's all taken care of. Now, get cleaned up. We have a date at the Palace today—the royal family will be taking the air, and we've been invited to join them!"

So it was that by early afternoon Sophie, chief lady-in-waiting to her Imperial Highness Zoe, accompanied by her husband, Justin, Treasurer of the Roman Empire, and their two children were walking in the vast imperial gardens that stretched along the east side of the palace complex. To the east lay a magnificent view of the Sea of Marmara, dotted with the Prince Islands, with their pine-covered domes broken by church spires and cottages. Instead of hoopoes, gulls and ospreys circled above among the floating clouds in a cerulean sky. From the time of Constantine, successive rulers had added on to the gardens as their inclinations (and the fortunes of the Empire at the time) allowed. The various fountains, for example, were the gift of the Isaurian dynasty, perhaps because of their origins in the arid East. However, due to their involvement in the iconoclastic controversy, on which they ended up on the losing side historically, no mention was made of their contributions.

As the family moved through the gardens, Simon was thoroughly enjoying himself rolling in the grass while Maria was enchanted by the butterflies attracted to the flowers in an extensive bed. As a result, neither Sophie nor Justin noticed the entourage which came up behind them until a familiar voice rang out.

"Oh, Lady Sophia, it is so good to see you and your family today! Is it not a glorious one, the Virgin be praised?" said Her Imperial Princess Zoe. There, standing behind them, were Zoe and her entourage along with others who trailed behind.

As Sophie turned to give the appropriate genuflection, she briefly caught the narrowed-eyes look on Justin's face which she had long ago learned to interpret as '*get me out of here*!' Long accustomed to court protocol, for the moment she made the appropriate comments and gestures, noticing as she did that Zoe was accompanied by two of her junior ladies-in-waiting and, more importantly, by her sister Theodora and two of her own attendants. Maria noticed this as well, and showed the effects of her increased maturity by first curtseying to both princesses before running over to them and greeting "Aunts Zoe and Theodora" with hugs. Both women, childless and unmarried, beamed at the attention.

While his wife proceeded to engage in small talk with the princesses, Justin smiled and nodded, while keeping an eye on Simon, who was fascinated by the wolfhounds that trailed Theodora, minded by an albino eunuch. Off to his left, he saw a larger group walking across the grounds, headed by His Imperial Majesty Constantine. To Justin's eye, his Highness looked to be somewhat unsteady on his feet, but this was masked by the steady stream of nods he gave to the courtiers who approached him. His brother Basil, who avoided personal contact as much as possible, was nowhere to be seen. '*Probably picking out another country to invade,*' thought Justin with a sigh.

His attention suddenly turned back to Sophie, when Zoe, with her notorious naivete, casually asked, "So how is the investigation going into the murder of the Northman? Any leads? Any clues?"

After exchanging glances with Justin, Sophie launched into a noncommittal answer, but was interrupted by a most unlikely source, namely Maria.

"O, yes, Aunt Zoe, my parents have some great ideas! In fact, they are going out tonight to catch the ghost! To do it, they're going to hang one of our maids off of a building! Can you believe that?"

The silence that followed was absolute, but short-lived. Justin had been around royalty enough to avert his gaze, while Sophie tried to act as if nothing had been said. Unfortunately, Zoe was all ears, and immediately responded.

"Oh, that's marvelous! You two are so clever! I would so like to come and see—you have no idea how it is to be cooped up here in the Palace! Theodora—would you like to come, too!"

Theodora, as always taking her cue from her older sibling, was quick to comment. "Yes, oh, yes! Thank you, Lady Sophia, for asking!"

The rest, as Herodotus would say, was history. Sophie and Justin were still trying to absorb how this new development would affect the evening when Alexius met them later at the Varangians' banquet hall. While normally a man who kept his emotions to himself, Alexius laughed out loud when he learned of the royal visitors. This was enough to push Justin over the edge.

"So, Deputy, you think this is funny, do you? Well, we will see about that. As Treasurer of the Roman Empire, I hereby designate you to be in charge of the royal princesses tonight. You will strictly keep them out of our way, with the utmost courtesy of course. You will answer any questions they have, no matter how inane, again with the utmost courtesy. Do we understand each other?"

Alexius, who had not often seen Justin in such a mood, was taken aback, and could only stammer, "Yes, Boss, yes, whatever you say!"

After glancing at Sophie and getting an affirmative nod, Justin decided to make doubly sure. "Good, good. Keep this in mind if you fail in your task—do you recall where my predecessor is now?"

"Uh, some island in the Aegean—Chios or Samos or something?"

"That's right, Deputy, someplace warm. Fail, and you won't be going someplace like that, believe me. Think Cherson in the Crimea, on the north shore of the Black Sea. The winters there are about nine months long, I'm told. Got it?"

At this, Alexius could only gulp and nod in affirmation.

With this detail out of the way, arrangements proceeded for the events of the evening. Siggurdsen had seen to the construction of the rigging system to support the volunteer maid over the side of the building, so that she would be suspended in the same position as 'Loviatar' had been the night before. Donna was on the roof while this was done, and appeared to be taking it all in stride, although Sophie wondered what her reaction would be when she actually went over the side of the building and was 40 feet above the ground. While it was not possible to arrange that her attire would be exactly the same as that of the 'goddess', Sophie's wardrobe was extensive enough so that a close approximation was made.

Sophie insisted that, before beginning the test, they wait until the same time in the evening that 'Loviatar' had appeared the night before. As darkness started to fall, it was necessary to get torches installed in the same locations. This detail Justin left to Alexius, who, with his royal assistants, installed them in the proper locations. From what Justin could tell from his vantage point, Zoe and Theodora entirely enjoyed themselves in this activity, although they had to enlist the help of the taller Varangian guards to reach the top brackets. For security purposes, Sophie also had insisted that the usual complement of Northmen not be used, and while the Armenian swordsmen who took their place were battle-hardened, they were also rather short. The only Varangians present for the experiment were Siggurdsen and two of his most trusted lieutenants.

Finally, all was in readiness. Justin had given up trying to keep pace with Sophie, for he had seen her in these moods before and knew it was useless to try. For her part, she was everywhere, first on the roof checking on the rigging and encouraging Donna, then downstairs making sure that the lighting was correct (not too bright and not too dim), and then making sure the princesses were staying out of the way (they complied wonderfully, to Alexius' great relief), and then back onto the roof to make the final preparations.

Donna's anxiety level had been steadily increasing while she had had time to look around and see how high she really was off the ground, to the point where Sophie began to fear that she would back out. Sophie was greatly relieved to see a much calmer Donna on her last visit, and said as much to Siggurdsen. The placid Varangian gave a slight smile, and tapped a small flask on his belt.

"Glogg works wonders," he said. "Aldrnari vatn" {"Fire water"}.

It took a lot to surprise Sophie, and she could only reply, "Very well, let's proceed while she is still conscious." Seeing the effect, she thought to herself, *'I need to get some of that!'*

So the great experiment began. Sophie took the position she had occupied in the banquet chamber the night before, and had Justin and Alexius take theirs as well, with Zoe and Theodora huddled next to the eunuch. With a call of "Lieta til!" {"Proceed!"}, Sophie gave the signal to the Varangians and they all waited expectantly.

What they saw did not live up to expectations. The problem was not with Donna, for the 'Glogg' had done its work well, and she hung suspended from the harness without complaint. While the harness itself was clearly visible, this did not bother Sophie, given how little time they had had to put one together. Nor did it bother her that the rope was too short to lower Donna all the way down to the window pane where 'Loviatar' had appeared. No, the problem was more basic, for what they saw was clearly a young woman hanging from a rope, twisting in the wind. 'Loviatar' by contrast did not move at all from side to side and was much fuzzier to the eye. In that this much was clear to Justin, it had to be even clearer to Sophie, given her eye for detail. Only Zoe and Theodora were thrilled by the experience, and exchanged squeals of delight. This irritated Sophie considerably, and she resolved to try again.

On the second attempt, one-third of the torches illuminating the hall were extinguished. While Justin thought this made the room overly dark, he had to admit that he had not really taken an exact count of the lit torches the night before. Alas, the effect was the same, for the form of the passive maid was still lit up from behind by the street lamps which shone behind and below her.

Never one to say die, Sophie ordered a third attempt, this time with two-thirds of the torches unlit. While this did make Donna harder to see, the motion issue was not affected. If anything, it got worse, for the 'Glogg' was now starting to wear off, and the hapless maid became aware that she was hanging in the air in the dark an undetermined distance above the ground. She began to thrash about like a puppet on a string.

The room was silent for a long moment, until a sound of giggling was clearly heard. Furious, Sophie wheeled around looking for the source, only to find two imperial princesses tittering like schoolgirls. Seeing Sophie's face, they tried to stop, but couldn't. Finally, Sophie could do nothing but join in, before she gave the command to haul Donna back up. Justin merely shrugged his shoulders while Alexius had visions of Cherson flashing in his mind.

Donna and Siggurdsen soon came down from the roof, and from the maid's relaxed attitude Sophie assumed that she had drunk more of the Scandinavian wonder liquor. This almost had disastrous results, for when Zoe approached the maid to offer her congratulations for the young woman's bravery, she received an unexpected response.

Supported by the Varangian chief, Donna gave a sleepy smile and said, "Thanks, Highness! I gotta tell you, it was great!" Further embarrassment was spared everyone when Donna then collapsed into Siggurdsen's arms and was removed from the room.

This time it was Theodora who broke the silence. "Sister," she said to Zoe, "I must ask you—is it like this all the time with Lady Sophia?"

After giving Sophie a quick glance, Zoe nodded gravely and replied, "Oh yes, all the time. You should have been with us in Egypt! But, that's a story for another day, and I think we should be getting back to the palace." Turning to address Sophie and Justin, she assumed her regal bearing (or at least tried to) before saying, "Lady Sophia, Treasurer, we thank you permitting us to witness this demonstration. We feel certain that, with the investigation in your capable hands, justice is sure to be done!" With that, she swept from the room, trailed by a puzzled Theodora and their bodyguards.

Justin was initially afraid that Sophie would be in a foul mood during their ride back to the villa, but he was pleasantly surprised. Sophie was in a surprisingly good humor, perhaps helped by the snoring Donna who lay on the seat across from them.

"Well, I think we can rule my solution out, but at least we tried," she mused.

Justin was shocked. "Does this mean you're accepting the Varangians' belief as to the existence of 'Loviatar'?"

"Of course not, silly! We just haven't figured out how it's being done. And with you traipsing off to Crete, that may not change for a while. Still, you know how these things go—clues turn up when you least expect them to."

Justin smiled and gave his wife a kiss, the mood only slightly spoiled by Donna's involuntary choice of that moment to give a hearty belch.

CHAPTER 14

On Sunday morning Sophie was off to attend Zoe at services at the Hagia Sophia, and to no doubt deal with a myriad of questions about the previous evening's experiences. Justin begged off on attending, saying that he needed to check on the final preparations for sailing on Monday, as if he actually had anything to do with a fleet on which he was merely a passenger. Since Maria had seen Aunt Zoe and Aunt Theodora just the day before, she was fine with having the groom lead her on her pony around the neighborhood, while Simon trailed along with his nanny.

As he rode to the harbor where the fleet was assembling on the south side of the city, Justin reflected he had never paid much attention to naval matters. While he knew how much the navy's budget was, he didn't know much else, apart from it never seemed to be enough. His actual time spent on ships was limited, for like most Romans he had a distrust of the sea or at least being out of sight of land. Still, he was duly impressed when the carriage came to a stop and he looked out at the ships which were clogging the harbor. It almost seemed like a man could walk across the harbor by stepping from one ship to the next and never getting wet.

As he gazed out at the sight, his thoughts were interrupted by a deep voice.

"Impressive, isn't it? Twenty-eight ships, including some of our biggest and newest. I guess I should thank you for paying for it all, for you're the Treasurer, aren't you?"

Justin turned to see an older man dressed in the uniform of a Roman Admiral, with a bronze cuirass and dark blue tunic and leggings. His white beard was close cropped and his helmet was a round affair trimmed with gold. Justin took it as a good sign that the man was smiling and had an outstretched hand, so he reciprocated before saying, "Yes, I am Justin Cataphlates, Treasurer of the Empire. You have the advantage of myself, sir, for I do not know your name."

The admiral smiled, and said, "A thousand pardons, how rude of me. I am Admiral Romanus Kritikrites, of their Majesties' navy. I will be in command of the fleet which sails for Crete tomorrow. As our honored guest, I wanted to welcome you personally. On a personal note, I also want to extend my gratitude to your wife, the Lady Sophia, for her kindness to my great-niece Julia, whom she recently selected to be a lady-in-waiting for Princess Zoe. My entire family is thrilled by this great honor. Please let her know that for me."

Justin bowed. "It would be my pleasure, Admiral. I don't mean to take up your time today, for I know how busy you must be in making final preparations. I simply wanted to make sure that the funds for which I am responsible will be transferred to a secure location. The strongboxes holding the gold are to arrive from the palace later today."

"Of course, Treasurer, I quite understand. Please let me give you a tour of my flagship, the St. George, on which both you and one-quarter of the funds will be sailing. It's the first one there, at the end of the dock." The Admiral pointed to a ship with three masts and ports in the side for three decks of oars. It had been newly painted and the woodwork shone in white gold.

"It's called a dromon," the Admiral explained as they went aboard. "We will have a crew of over 200 for the trip, although I don't anticipate using the oars much, if at all. The prevailing winds are excellent this time of year for a trip to Crete, although coming back might take a little longer. Still, how are you at pulling an oar, Treasurer?" Seeing Justin's eyes widen, Kritikrites laughed, "Just kidding, just kidding. We'll use them to help get out of the harbor and when we make anchorage in Chandax, but only then. You're safe! Speaking of leaving the harbor, we need to leave with the tide just after sunup tomorrow, so don't be late!"

Justin was then shown his quarters, which were somewhat larger than a broom closet, and the hold where the church reconstruction money was to be kept. In order of avoid a complete disaster at sea, the money was to be divided among four vessels, all of which were to have the same safety precautions. Procedure dictated that Justin alone be in possession of the keys for each chest, which he was to keep in his possession at all times. The usual contingent of Varangians was to be in place on each ship, so, barring multiple shipwrecks, there should be no difficulty in making the transfer in Crete. Since what happened after that was out of Justin's control, steps had been taken to help insure the money got to its intended recipients, namely by having them there in person. If all went as planned, both the Patriarch of Jerusalem and the Patriarch of Alexandria would meet them in Crete, along with a representative of the Coptic pope in Cairo. The Jerusalem patriarch would forward the funds onto the Jewish community there for their synagogue.

After the tour, Justin felt much better about the trip. Still, the size of the fleet nagged at him, and he expressed his concerns to the admiral.

"This is all very impressive, Admiral Kritikrites, but aren't we leaving the rest of the Empire exposed by using all of these ships in one place?"

The admiral cocked his head before answering. "Actually, what you see here is about 10% of our fleet. We will still have ships all over the Mediterranean, the Black Sea, and up the Danube River. In fact, we have at least as many ships here as are stationed permanently off the mouths of the Nile, partially as a result of your little adventure of two years ago. Oh yes, I've read the reports and I know why they're there. Don't worry, we'll be fine. Is there anything else?"

Justin thought for moment and then said, "Yes, since you ask. I noticed the bronze tubes sticking out of the front of the ship—are those for Greek Fire?"

The Admiral's eyes narrowed before he answered. "Well, Treasurer, I suppose I could tell you that, but it's a state secret! They're there for a purpose, let's leave it at that."

For a moment, Justin expected the older man to say "Just a joke!" but when he did not, Justin decided to let the issue drop. Thanking him for the tour, he returned to the Treasury, where Alexius was supervising the transfer details.

Monday morning came early, but Sophie had everything under control. The children were so excited to see Daddy off on his trip that they got ready without complaint. Even though Justin had the trunks of his belongings ready by Sunday evening, the journey from their villa took on the trappings of a procession, as the family rode in one carriage, the luggage in another, and the household staff in a third. As they travelled, Justin reflected that he really did not get out much in his role as Treasurer. Looking around him at the miniature parade, he resolved to be more open to travel in the future.

When they arrived at the dock at the appointed time, Justin was looking forward to speedily boarding the ship. Alas, such was not to be, for he found a grand crowd around the dock, including Prefect Comnenus, the patriarch and his usual horde of black-clad priests sketching blessings on the fleet, and many imperial officials, some of whom Justin recognized and some he did not. They were all waiting with expectation, which gave Justin and Sophie a clue that the appearance of their Imperial Majesties was forthcoming. The two rulers duly appeared to the blare of trumpets, Basil looking less grim than usual, while his brother ventured a wave at the crowd while still looking gaunt. Of Zoe and Theodora there was no sign, something which seemed odd to Justin.

Sensing his thoughts, Sophie snuggled up to him and said, "Wondering where the imperial sisters are? It seems that someone leaked news of their wanderings the other night to higher powers, and so they are confined to the Palace."

Justin could only shake his head. "I wonder who that could have been?"

Sophie said nothing, but instead gave her husband a big kiss, as his children chimed in with an earnest hug. Justin responded in kind, and then boarded the waiting vessel, to be greeted by Admiral Kritikrites.

At the command of a trumpet, the entire fleet weighed anchor, and then followed the lead ship out of the harbor, each vessel guided by use of its oars. Justin waved good-bye to his family until his ship rounded the corner of the breakwater and they passed out of sight. Despite his dislike of the sea, Justin never tired of seeing Constantinople from the water. As the ships unfurled their sails and moved into the Sea of Marmara, the full outline of the city skyline was apparent, dominated by the immense dome of Hagia Sophia and punctuated by the smaller churches sprinkled around it. As they picked up speed, the city receded behind them as they passed the Princes Isles, where monasteries peeked out from between the pines. A pair of dolphins rode the bow wave of the ship, a sight which made Justin recall the return trip he, Sophie and Zoe had made from Cairo two years before when they escaped the clutches of Caliph al-Hakim. Justin missed Sophie already, and consoled himself that this trip would only be for a few days.

Justin spent the morning meeting with the four clerks who had come with him from the Treasury office. Each was in charge of one of the chests of gold and would attend to the distribution of funds when they reached Crete. This task completed, he went back on deck, where he gazed out over the rail at the distant shore. The admiral was busy attending to the management of the fleet, and Justin watched with interest as signal flags were periodically run up. In that he did not know the code, he inquired of a passing sailor and learned that some messages informed the other ships about a change in direction while others urged slower vessels to keep pace.

As he watched flocks of gulls follow the ships, he heard a voice behind him.

"May I join you, Treasurer?" said General Xiphias.

Turning, Justin smiled and answered, "Of course, General, of course. I didn't know you were going to Crete too. Back on duty?"

"Yes, thankfully, I was pleased to help honor their Majesties on their 40th anniversary on the throne, but the city is no place for me. After you finish your business on Crete, I will take several ships and proceed to Thessalonica, and then on to the front, such as it is now. The Bulgars have just about given up, but there are still a few holdouts."

Justin sighed. "It seems like this war has been going on forever. I can't imagine the stress it has placed on Basil."

The general nodded. "Still, I don't think he knows any other way to live. His entire life has been a fight for survival. If he didn't have this, I really think he would be lost. That's sad, I know, but I believe it to be true."

Justin agreed. "I wouldn't be in his position for the world. Still, even though he's usually thought of as a soldier, he really has been a wonderful emperor. To me, he personifies the perfect ruler to have at the head of the hexagon of government."

General Xiphias looked puzzled. "The hexagon of government? I'm afraid you have me there."

"It's simple really. The hexagon is a six-sided figure which also has six points. Imagine the emperors at the top point. Next point down and to the right represents the army and navy, which make their rule possible. This is followed by the Treasury, which administers the money to pay them. The bottom point represents the taxes which provide the money. Moving up and to the left we get the stable economy which generates the income to pay the taxes. Last but not least are the trained and professional administrators who serve with integrity. This gets you back to the emperors on top. Weaken any one point and all of the rest will suffer."

"Sounds simple."

Justin laughed. "Much simpler than actually doing it. Few emperors have."

"Well, I look forward to further discussions with you. Will you be attending dinner tonight in the Admiral's cabin?"

"Yes, of course. I will see you then." With that, Justin took a last look at the sea before going below to his cabin. He had brought some work with him to pass the time and before long the dinner bell chimed. Dinner was a relaxed affair, although Justin as usual partook of less wine than the other guests, most of whom were captains from other ships, along with General Xiphias. Afterwards, Admiral

Kritikrites was in a talkative mood. He had joined them after supervising the passage of the fleet through the Dardanelles, the strait which joined the Sea of Marmara to the Aegean. Even a landlubber like Justin could tell a difference in the rolling motion of the ship as it entered the larger body of water.

Seeing Justin, the admiral said, "Well, Treasurer, you were wondering about the size of our little fleet here. Any thoughts on why so many ships?"

"Uh, well, to ward off pirates?"

When some guests started to laugh, the admiral cut them off. "Actually, that would have been a very good answer, say, 60 years ago. These waters were very dangerous to travel then, largely because of the ships which came from where we are going. Crete had been lost to the Empire, not to the Caliphate, but to organized gangs of pirates. It was the Emperor Nicephorus, who acted as regent for Basil and Constantine when they were children, who took the island back. No, the size of the fleet is not for that enemy, who has been eliminated, but to impress on our current foe the Caliph how dangerous we are to trifle with. You have seen his fleet, Treasurer, does it compare to ours?"

Justin responded. "No, sir, it does not, although I do not think this Caliph or any of the Fatimids have ever really tried to compete. The test will come if Emperor Basil determines to recover Sicily."

At that point, a silence fell on the cabin, with many of the captains looking down. The admiral finally spoke. "Your powers of observation do you credit, sir. Since I know you understand what is said in this room stays here, you are correct. With the help of the Virgin and St. George, Sicily will be Roman again one day. But," he continued with a smile, "enough of such things! More wine!"

Justin allowed himself to have a goblet of wine, if for no other reason than to fit in. He did manage to extricate himself from the merriment after that, and went on-deck to gaze at the summer stars and the quarter moon overhead. His thoughts turned toward home, and to the mystery on which he and Sophie had yet to make any progress. '*Why were the Varangians being murdered? Was there a pat-*

tern? How did the dead Arab agent relate to any of this, if at all? Finally, what about 'Loviatar'?'

At about the same time, miles away, his beloved was entertaining similar thoughts. Given her nature, however, Sophie was intent on taking action. After getting Maria and Simon to bed, she retired to the veranda with a glass of white wine. Soon Philip came in and announced the arrival of Deputy Treasurer Alexius. When he entered, it was in a rather tentative manner very contrary to his unusual bluster.

"Good evening, Lady, or should I say 'Scalpel'? I got your message. I hope you're still not upset about the other night?"

His concerns were dispelled when Sophie gave one of her ringing laughs. "Upset, Alexius? Me, upset? Heavens no, I don't get mad, I get even! We are still very much in the game here—we just need to use the leads we still have. Putting 'Loviatar' aside for now, it occurs to me that we have not followed up on the murder of your Arab agent—was that random, or was it related? We need to find out."

"Well, we have made inquiries among the various shops that are run by Arabs. It's a considerable number."

"See, that's what I mean. We need to be more focused. The dead man was from Egypt, correct?"

"Yes, I think so."

"Then we should concentrate on shops owned or manned by Egyptians. That should help narrow it down, especially since we know that you-know-who is from there. Your task is to identify the ones in question. After that, I shall make a personal visit to each, in my role as Chief-Lady-in-Waiting, posing as an interested shopper. Believe me, they will fall over themselves once that happens!"

Alexius nodded. "Sounds reasonable. What do you want us to look for?"

Sophie furrowed her brow. "I wish I could say. There are just too many missing links here. We need a break, Alexius, we need a break! There has to be something I'm missing, but I can't sit around and do nothing. With Justin gone, the burden is on me!" she concluded with her voice rising.

Seeing the surprised look on Alexius' face, Sophie stopped before going on in a more normal voice. "Don't worry, I'm all right. We'll get this thing solved yet, you'll see. After all, tomorrow is another day!"

CHAPTER 15

The next day found the fleet moving steadily southward, with various Aegean islands appearing and then receding as the ships moved on. General Xiphias, who was familiar with the area, pointed out various ones to Justin as they stood on the highest point of the stern, behind the men steering the vessel. Although there were many small islands, the first large one on the left was Lesbos, soon to be replaced by Chios. Chios seemed rather rocky and desolate, at least from the western side that was visible, and Justin gave an involuntary shudder at the fate of his predecessor, Michael Taronites, who had been exiled there by Basil after the unsuccessful plot two years earlier. Of course, others had suffered worse, but for an urban creature like Justin, to be separated from the sights and sounds of Constantinople would be a severe punishment indeed.

One of the things Justin appreciated about the general was that the man was not uncomfortable with silence, and the two spent much of the morning simply watching the sea slip by. At one point, the general commented on how dark the sea looked, prompting Justin to reach back into his classic education and note how Homer always referred to Aegean as "wine-dark." General Xiphias looked at Justin with new admiration, and commented now he knew why Justin made the big money.

After a while, talk turned to the purpose of the trip.

"So," the general asked, "how much money is to be delivered?"

"Twenty thousand gold solidi," Justin replied. "This sum to be used to repair churches in Egypt, plus the Church of the Holy Sepulchre in Jerusalem, along with a synagogue there."

"A synagogue? That must have gone over well with Patriarch Sergius!"

Justin gave a little snort. "Very poorly, actually, until Basil told him to mind his place. This is in payment of a debt of sorts, and the emperor always pays his debts."

"You intrigue me, Treasurer. That sounds like a lot of money."

"Actually, General, it is only a down payment, but it's a start. It also shows the Christians living in the caliphate that they have not been forgotten. And, there is another reason which particularly appealed to Basil. Can you think what it was?"

General Xiphias laughed. "I know better than to match wits with an educated man like you, me being just a simple soldier! What is it?"

Justin smiled. "Do you have any money on you, specifically a solidus?"

"No, but I can get one. You there," he called to an aide, "bring me a solidus." One was speedily provided, and handed to the general. He looked at it for only a moment, and then laughed in his turn.

"I get it, Treasurer, I get it! Not only does it have our Lord on one side, it's got Basil and Constantine on the other! So, every time these are put in circulation in the caliphate to buy materials or pay for labor, the Arabs will have to handle them. I can see how Basil was amused. But tell me, with him, how could you tell?"

"A very good point, General! Truth be told, the Arabs don't make gold coins—they don't have the mines we do, and so they have to use silver instead. That's what they requested, but we said no—gold it is. Also, with silver it would have taken 20 chests instead of four."

They continued to chuckle over this through lunch. In the afternoon, Naxos went by on the right, and Justin marveled how the fleet then wound through a number of small islands. Finally, to their right appeared the fantastic island of Thera, a semi-circle of cliffs surrounding a round lagoon. Villages with brightly-colored houses were clustered around the cliffs and fishing boats bobbed in the water below. Justin thought to himself, '*I wish Sophie could see this!*'

Only blue water lay ahead as they passed from the Aegean into the Mediterranean later in the afternoon. Soon Justin could see a line of hills stretching from east to west, broken here and there by harbors lined with villages. They appeared to be heading for the largest harbor in the middle of the island, which the locals called Chandax. As they drew nearer, the outlines of the city became apparent, with the governor's palace on top of the acropolis in the middle. The city was ringed by walls, punctuated every so often by towers. Seeing it, Justin could well believe the account that General Xiphias had given him about the siege several decades ago, where Roman troops were forced to break into the city which was held by Arab corsairs. It must have been costly in lives, he thought.

Led by the Admiral's ship, the Roman fleet slipped into the harbor as the waning light of the evening touched the top of the surrounding walls. To the left, the Fatimid fleet, less than half the size of the Roman fleet, was already at anchor. Justin was gazing at the ships with their triangular sails when Admiral Kritikrites came up beside him.

"Do those look familiar, Treasurer? I assume you've seen them before?"

"Yes, Admiral, I have, although this time," Justin paused for effect, "they are not on fire."

The admiral gave a roar of laughter. "Well said, sir, well said! On fire or not, they would dare not face us at sea, you may count on that. When we are finished docking, the governor's staff will be there to meet you. It's my understanding that he wants to meet with you as soon as you land."

"Will you be coming with me?"

"Not for a while—I need to see to the disposition of the rest of the fleet. I will see you later at the governor's palace, for I understand that there is to be a short reception there for the Arab delegation and our Christian friends from the east."

True to the admiral's word, a delegation from the island's governor was awaiting Justin when he disembarked. There were both men and women present, attired in traditional Cretan dress, and Justin was initially touched. He was less impressed when all of the delegation seemed to be in awe of him, and could not or would not respond to his inquiries in a definitive way. After incurring a degree of frustration, he finally made it clear that he could not accompany them until he had met with his clerks from the other ships. Once he did, he satisfied himself with the final arrangements for the safety and transport of the funds entrusted to him.

Finally, with everything secure, he entered a carriage and rode up the road to the governor's palace. All that he knew about this particular man he had learned from the prefect, who had told him that his name was Andrew Chonas, that he had been a comrade in arms of Basil many years earlier, and that, having married a Cretan woman, he was willing to take the position of governor. The palace itself was extensive, but rather plain, and it occurred to Justin that it would not be listed in the top 100 in Constantinople. Neither, he concluded to himself soon thereafter, would Governor Chonas, who seemed to be only slightly less tongue-tied than his minions. After having resigned himself to a long evening, Justin was rescued by the sight of some old acquaintances coming towards him.

Two years earlier he had accompanied Sophie to Jerusalem, as she had attended Zoe on her pilgrimage. In the course of the trip, they had met the Patriarch of Jerusalem, Theophilus, an older man who had personally suffered at the hands of the minions of the caliph. Even more hurtful to him was having to witness the destruction of much of the Church of the Holy Sepulchre for no apparent reason. Now he looked much more relaxed as he strode up to Justin, hand outstretched, wearing his black robes and hat.

Accompanying him was another Patriarch in black and white robes, this time from Alexandria, who unfortunately also was named Theophilus. T2, as Justin thought of him, was considerably younger, and his beard was still mostly black, as opposed to that of T1, which was snow white. The last two years seemed to have taken something of a toll, however, and T2's smile seemed a little forced. Still, he greeted Justin warmly and inquired after his family.

The last member of the trio of holy men did not have the rank the other two did, and yet was impressive in his own way, wearing black and red robes with a distinctive black hat that looked remarkably like a flattened-mushroom. This was Cardinal Shenouda, who was the right-hand man of the leader of the Coptic Church in Egypt, Pope Zacharias. Justin had gotten to know the cardinal well during their enforced stay in Cairo, after he and the others in their party had been kidnapped by Caliph al-Hakim and held for ransom. It was largely due to the cardinal that Justin had made contact with the Jewish community there, who had suffered at the hands of the caliph as well. It was the Jews in turn who arranged for the fire ship that Father Simon had touched off to incinerate the Fatimid fleet, although at the cost of his life.

"So, Justin, you are now Treasurer of the Roman Empire! Congratulations! Clearly, God had plans for you, delivering you out of bondage in Egypt so that you can go on to do great things!" Shenoula said with a broad smile on his face. "I have heard of the birth of your son—Simon was a fine name to give in honor of a true martyr."

"Thank you, Cardinal, and to both of your Eminences as well. When did you arrive here in Crete?"

Patriarch T1 answered. "Earlier this morning. It took us nearly a week to get here from Alexandria, and it took me another two days to get to there from Jerusalem. Solid ground looked very welcoming, I have to say. Still, the Fatimid captain treated us with courtesy, and I had some interesting conversations with the chief imam at the mosque in Cairo which the current caliph constructed."

Justin nodded. "Yes, I've seen it. It's very impressive. By the same token, I understand that the Church of the Holy Sepulchre was impressive, too, and I'm sorry that I never saw it intact, or St. Mark's in Cairo, or St. Cyril's in Alexandria. I hope what we get started here over the next two days will lead to the restoration of these places, even if many of us do not live to see the work completed."

On hearing this, Patriarch T2's face brightened. "Truly said, Justin! We are, all of us, merely workers and not master builders. In this work, as throughout our lives, we are prophets of a future we will not see."

Seeing Governor Chonas moving toward them, Justin excused himself from his ecclesiastical friends and ducked out the door. According to General Xiphias, a reception was planned this evening for their Arab guests, with the full banquet scheduled for tomorrow evening. Justin greatly desired a little alone time, if for no other reason to clean up and change into some of the ceremonial robes that Sophie had insisted he bring, saying that he needed to look like he belonged there. One of the attendants directed him to a porter who led him to the rooms where his luggage had already been taken. It was not long before he emerged, new robes and all, and found his way to the reception hall. In deference to their guests, the Romans served only fruit juices and light foods that met Islamic requirements. While Justin did not miss the presence of wine, he thought it fortunate that Sophie was not in attendance.

Governor Chonas was standing at one end of the hall with a distinguished looking Arab who looked to be about 50 years old. His dark, piercing eyes were above a salt-and-pepper beard with a prominent nose in between. The two men looked ill at ease, and Justin assumed that neither was fluent in the other's language. In this he was correct, but his second assumption was not.

Walking up to the man, he gave a slight bow and said in Arabic, "Welcome to the Roman Empire, Vizier. I am Justin Cataphlates, Treasurer to their Majesties."

The man looked at him for a moment in confusion, and then gave a shake of his head before responding in Greek, "I am pleased to meet you sir, but I am not the vizier. Merely a scientist who serves His Eminence the Caliph. My name is Hasan Ibn al-Haytham."

"My mistake, sir. A scientist? If I may ask, what is your field of study?"

Al-Haytham looked pleased at Justin's inquiry. "In simple terms, Treasurer, light. For example, how do we see? Have you ever wondered about that?"

After giving the governor a sidelong glance, Justin responded, "Uh, no, I don't think that I have."

His eyes brightening, al-Haytham continued. "The Greek writer Euclid first pondered the issue centuries ago, and I am building on his work through my own writings. Unlike him, however, it is my contention that vision occurs when light reflects from an object and passes into one's eyes, which then pass the information on to the brain."

Just as Justin was steeling himself for a lengthy lecture, a bell was sounded and the conversations around the room ceased. Governor Chonas had planned on making some welcoming remarks, but after hearing Justin speak in Arabic with the scientist, he decided to delegate that duty. Justin was momentarily nonplussed, but agreed to speak. His remarks were generic in nature—hoped everyone had a pleasant trip, looked forward to meeting them, funds would open a new chapter in relations, etc., etc.—but he did make an impression by switching back and forth from Greek to Arabic. He momentarily thought about mentioning his stay in Cairo two years before, but decided not to, in that several Fatimid naval captains were present who doubtless needed no reminding about the destruction of their fleet.

The rest of the reception could not end quickly enough for Justin, for he had not slept well on the ship and was looking forward to getting to bed. *'Must be getting old,'* he thought as he said his goodbyes and made it back to his quarters, shutting the door as he did so. He sat down with a sigh, but had not been in the chair for more than a few minutes when a knock came on the door, followed by a piece of paper slipped underneath.

Justin stared at the paper for a moment and then picked it up. There, written in Arabic, was the message, *"If you are a friend of 'Ali' and wish to learn something which may be to your advantage, come now to the last ship anchored on the far end of the dock. Tell no one of this. Come alone."*

Justin's initial reaction was that the caliph had indeed chosen to make an appearance in Crete, but chose to remain hidden. On reflection, that seemed too dangerous, for while al-Hamid was notorious for his behavior, there was always a plan behind what he did, and this would not fit any logical plan. Still, his curiosity piqued, Justin had no choice but to comply, and soon found himself heading to the dock. '*After all,*' he thought, '*what's the worst that can happen?*' When he realized that the worst involved him being kidnapped and taken to Cairo, he almost stopped, but then continued nonetheless.

The last ship anchored on the far end of the dock was clearly a vessel in the Fatimid fleet. Even if Justin had not known anything about ships, the presence of two large men armed with scimitars at the gangway would have told him that. As he approached them, he decided that presenting a brave front was the way to go.

In his best Arabic, he said, "Greetings, men! I am a friend of Ali, and have been summoned here. In the name of Allah, the Merciful, I request to come aboard."

The men said nothing, but escorted him onto the ship, where he quickly found himself in a lower cabin where the lights were dim. He was aware of a number of people in the room when he was directed to sit on a cushion near the door. When lamps were uncovered, he found himself seated before and below a veiled woman who appeared to be still quite beautiful even if middle-aged. Justin was particularly taken by an elaborate ivory necklace she was wearing that glinted in the lamplight. It featured a stylistic elephant in the middle surrounded by what appeared to be flowers. To her right and left were Islamic clerics, while other veiled figures whom Justin took to be her attendants stood behind her. After a few moments, the veiled figure spoke in the type of lilting Arabic Justin had grown familiar with while he was in Egypt.

"I bring you greetings, Treasurer Cataphlates, from my brother, His Eminence the Caliph of the Faithful and Sword of Allah! Pressing matters of state have prevented him from attending this assembly, but in his wisdom he sent me, Sitt al-Mulk, his sister and humble servant in his stead. He wishes good health and long life to you, the Lady Sophia, and your family."

Bowing as best he could while seated, Justin replied, trying to use his most formal Arabic phrasing. "I am truly blessed, Lady al-Mulk, to hear these words, although I count myself the most unworthy of men to do so. I am a servant of their most Christian majesties Basil and Constantine, and convey their hopes that this meeting may mark a new day between our two peoples. I am sorry that my wife and I were not privileged to make your acquaintance when we were your brother's guests," pausing after the word 'guests' for a moment, "in Cairo. It was truly our loss."

Now it was Lady al-Mulk's turn to pause before replying, as Justin felt her dark eyes looking directly at him. When she did, she surprised Justin by the directness of her answer. "My brother, in his wisdom, decided that such a meeting should not occur, and I, as his servant, accepted that decision." Pausing as if to let the insincerity of that remark sink in, she continued, "You may wonder why I have asked you here. You may have noticed that the Caliphate is not represented by a vizier at these proceedings."

"Well, Lady, it is true that I did not see a vizier at the reception, but I cannot swear that I met everyone who was there. I became engrossed in a conversation with a man who described himself as a scientist."

"Ah, yes, you met al-Haytham," the lady said with the slightest of smiles. "If you have not already found out, do not get him talking about his passion unless you wish to spend some time listening to a lecture. Still, my brother in his wisdom has requested that the scientist be here. No, there is no vizier here—my brother, also in his wisdom, has decided to dispense with that position—it became difficult to find men who would capably fill it."

And live more than a month,' thought Justin.

"So, in his wisdom my brother has designated me as his representative. I will be signing all documents tomorrow, both those that deal with the transfer of the gold for the churches and those that concern other matters. However, due to the commands of Allah as conveyed to us by the Prophet, Peace be upon Him, I will be seated behind a screen. Now that you have met me and heard my voice, you may assure every other Roman that everything is in order."

Justin bowed again. "It is a very prudent thing to do. Your brother, in his wisdom," here he paused for the slightest moment and watched her eyes narrow, "has planned well. It shall be as you say."

"Very well, Treasurer, I bid you good evening. Go with God—this audience is over."

Sensing he had best leave while he still could, Justin rose, bowed once more to Sitt al-Mulk, and bid her companions good evening in the name of the Prophet, Peace be upon Him. This unexpected concession to their faith caught at least one imam by surprise, who nodded in affirmation.

Back in his room, Justin pondered the meaning of the lady's words, which, though polished, showed a profound dislike of the Caliph. Justin had lost track of how many times she had said 'my brother in his wisdom,' but it was several. He was still thinking about all of this when he fell asleep, wishing that Sophie was present to use as a sounding board. *She would have seen things that I didn't, I just know. She'll be interested to hear about this!*

That lady was still very much awake in Constantinople, as she found sleep eluding her. Sophie's thoughts kept going back to the previous Friday night, when she had seen what the Varangians, or at least some of them, called 'Loviatar.' With her initial efforts to disprove the existence of the 'goddess' having come to nothing, she remained troubled by what she saw. The spectral figure looked like a woman, and yet something was not right. Something about the face, something about the body shape, something was just wrong. While she could not put her finger on it, she knew that she had seen something that she had not yet grasped, and until she did, more sleepless nights awaited her. How she wished for Justin, for while he likely would not have had an answer, he would have made the wondering easier.

CHAPTER 16

The next morning Justin was on his own for a while, for the first stage of the proceedings did not involve the exchange of the funds he had brought for the churches and synagogue. He had a light breakfast on the balcony of his room, which had a panoramic view of the harbor with its many ships, Roman and Arabic, and then walked down to the armory building where the money was being kept under guard by the ever-present Varangians. While Justin unlike Sophie did not speak Norse, he was well-known as the husband of the Iron Lady, and the guards were very respectful to him. Satisfied that all was secure with the gold, and fairly satisfied that the head guard could understand the schedule that was to be followed, he walked back to the palace.

Going up the steps, he heard someone call his name, and looked over to see Cardinal Shenouda sitting at a table on the long front porch that ran along the front of the building. The cardinal waved him over, and he was glad to sit down.

Cardinal Shenouda nodded as he said, "Up and around early this morning, Treasurer? Everything in order?"

"No earlier than you, Cardinal. At least I don't have to don the layers of ceremonial vestments you do!"

"True, true. Still, it was worth it. I have something for you that is best shared without others around. Do you recall that I steered you to certain people in Cairo who were instrumental in assisting in the escape of you and your party?"

At this, Justin had to smile. "Yes, although I thought I was being kidnapped! Tell me, Cardinal, why don't you speak their name? It was the Jewish community of Cairo that helped us torch the Caliph's fleet—just say so!"

A shadow of pain passed over the cardinal's normally impassive face. "My apologies. Living under this caliph has caused all of us to act in ways that are not normal, simply for our own self-preservation. Being here for a few days is a reminder that life everywhere is not like that, but we cannot get used to it, for soon we are going back into the inferno. Yes, our Jewish friends have not forgotten you, especially since you have not forgotten them by your designation of money for the rebuilding of their synagogue in Jerusalem. To show their thanks, they have designated you as a 'righteous Gentile,' and asked that I give you this."

Opening the small package the cardinal handed him, Justin found an exquisite gold star of six points. Letters were carved on the back which Justin assumed were Hebrew, although he could not read the text. Whatever it said, it was clearly a very generous gift from a community which was living very much on the edge, and Justin felt his eyes tear up. When he looked up, the cardinal was gone, the old habits of evasion too hard to set aside.

After gazing at the token for several minutes and recalling the events of two years before, Justin came back to the present. He heard his name being called, and found that a servant of the governor was requesting his presence in the main audience hall. Upon arriving, he found things in a state of confusion. It appeared that Stephan, the chief clerk who was handling the Roman non-monetary side of things, was unsure what to do. All of the documents had been prepared—one set forth the navigation rules for the Strait of Messina, which divided Fatimid Sicily from Roman Italy, one delineated fishing rights for islands off of the Sicilian coast between the two regimes, while another defined the spheres of influence which the two empires had around Aleppo, which was in a neutral emirate which lay between them. The last, and most important to the patriarchs, both in Constantinople and Jerusalem, made clear the rights of Christian pilgrims to the holy places in Jerusalem and its environs. The problem came in what to do next.

At one end of the room an elaborate screen had been set up, just as Sitt al-Mulk had described the previous evening. Standing around it were a phalanx of heavily-armed men whom Justin remembered all too well—Turks. He stared at them for a few moments, oblivious to the clerk tugging on the sleeve of his robe. *'Did they remember him?'* he thought. *'Had they sworn vengeance on behalf of their comrades who Justin had drugged in the course of his escape, leading to their certain execution by the Caliph?'* In a position where he could not run or hide, he decided to ignore them, keeping one eye on the nearest exit should an alternative plan be called for.

From what the clerk was babbling, it seemed that Governor Chonas was not willing to have the documents executed by a mystery person behind the screen, and Stephan did not have enough rank to overrule him. Justin had no such problem, and, after demanding and getting the items, walked up to the screen, halting a discreet distance in front of the guards. As he did so, he was aware of the eyes of the governor, Admiral Kritikrikes, General Xiphias and many others on him.

When he advanced to the screen, he cursed himself for getting rusty with his Turkish, but decided to push ahead. Clearing his throat, he tried to recall how guttural Turkish felt to speak and phrased some simple, declarative sentences.

"Selamlar, erkekler! Leydi al-Mulk ile konusmaya geldimi. Onun icin belgelerim var. Lueften gecmeme izin ver." {"Greetings, men! I come to speak with the Lady al-Mulk. I have documents for her. Please let me pass."}

His desperate wish to avoid a conversation for which his vocabulary was inadequate was answered when a woman's voice called out in Turkish, "Let him pass, soldiers. He knows what to do."

At that, the Turks parted ways and Justin stepped up to the screen, which he found was surprisingly light. A space underneath was open a few inches, and on a hunch he placed the documents there. They promptly disappeared, only to shortly emerge with the flowing signature of Sitt al-Mulk, Plenipotentiary of the Defender of the Faithful Abu 'Ali Mansur Al-Hakim, etc., etc. As he picked up the documents, he heard the voice of the lady.

"You looked nervous there, Treasurer. Your Turkish is limited, I take it."

Justin answered before thinking. "Yes, I am a little out of practice. Yours seems to be better." Then, upon reflection, he said, "You could see me? You can see through that screen?"

Sitt al-Mulk actually laughed at that. "Why yes, Treasurer, the screen is intended to protect my modesty from the lustful glances of men."

Without thinking, Justin replied, "And what protects the men?"

Laughing again, she answered. "I'll see you at the banquet, Justin, even if you don't see me. Now I think we're done here."

The governor and Stephan were overjoyed to have their portion of the conference wrapped up. Justin acknowledged their thanks, but was more focused on al-Mulk's use of his first name. *I wonder how your brother deals with you?* he mused on the balcony.

The afternoon's events were considerably less dramatic. The eunuch representing the caliphate acknowledged delivery of the money for the various churchmen, with the understanding that the funds would be theirs upon their return to Alexandria, Cairo and Jerusalem. As the technical details were being worked out, Justin had time to talk again with the Arab scientist, al-Haytham, and asked him why it was that he had been selected for this trip. Perhaps his skill in mathematics?

The scientist gave a quick shake of his head. "No, Treasurer, I am here for my own purposes. As I explained, I am fascinated with the study of light. Today is the summer solstice, when the sun is furthest north in the sky. I have taken measurements of the angle which the sun's rays strike the earth at Cairo, and further south, at the rapids of Nile which the ancients called the Third Cataract. Now, I am further north than I ever have been, and have taken measurements here. I believe the comparison will help me calculate the diameter of the earth."

Justin was intrigued. "But isn't the earth flat?"

"Oh, no, it is round, like a ball. It is just that it is so large that men cannot perceive the curvature. Allah in his Wisdom has so decreed."

"Fascinating, sir, fascinating. I know there was a Greek writer, Euclid, who wrote about light, but you are breaking new ground. I would like to speak of this more. Will you be at the banquet tonight?"

"Yes, I shall."

"Then we can speak more then, or perhaps tomorrow."

The scientist frowned at this and shook his head. "No, tomorrow will not work. We are leaving on the first tide before daybreak. It will take us longer to return to our homes than you."

"Well, at the banquet then," Justin said with a bow and went on.

When it came the banquet was a much lower-key affair than the grand imperial events Justin was used to in the Great Palace. With no royalty present, there was no need for a head table. Someone (the governor perhaps?) had come up with the idea of using round tables at which a mixture of Romans and Arabs would be seated. Special accommodations had been made for the Lady al-Mulk and her ladies, as a large screen had been set up along one side of the room. Female servers had been retained for the occasion to look after their needs. The menu was also designed to accommodate Muslim requirements, which meant that the usual supply of alcoholic beverages was absent. While Justin did not mind this, he wondered what Admiral Kritikrikes and the Varangians thought of that.

Unfortunately, Justin and al-Haytham were seated across the room from each other. To compensate for this, he was at the same table with the two patriarchs and Cardinal Shenouda, along with the commander of the Fatimid fleet and his three subordinates. Any apprehensions Justin had about the incident in Cairo were laid to rest when the commander personally thanked him for making modernization of his fleet possible, via the destruction of so many outdated vessels. To this Justin could only reply, "Thank you, I think."

Fortunately for dinner conversation, all present at the table spoke both Arabic and Greek, although the former was soon settled upon as the language of choice. The churchmen were ebullient about the uses to which they would put the money, and Justin made a mental note to add eastern church subsidies as a new line item in the imperial budget. The sailors seemed less at ease, and Justin assumed that the success of the return voyage was weighing on their minds. Given what he knew of the mercurial nature of their royal master, he could well understand.

The food was tasty, and featured several preparations of lamb and fish. When the Arabs seemed hesitant, Justin assured them of the correctness of the various items, using several quotations from the Koran to make his point. They looked at him with appreciation, and the commander ventured to ask him if he had in fact spent time with Caliph al-Hakim himself. When Justin acknowledged that he had, the commander asked what kind of experience that was.

Justin assumed what he hoped was a thoughtful look, suddenly aware that everyone at the table was watching, before saying. "Well, commander, let me simply say this—your caliph is unlike any man I have ever met, for he never ceased to amaze me with what he might say or do. I think he is one of Allah's unique creations."

The Arabs seemed entranced by this, the Christians less so, particularly since they had all personally endured the caliph's uniqueness. Further discussion on this point was cut short by the governor, who gave a short speech of thanks to his guests in Greek, and then called on Justin to do the same in Arabic. Since he had expected this to happen, he was happy to respond, although many of the Romans were puzzled by his fixation on the screen that ran along the side of the room. When he finished, there was general applause and a waiter delivered a bottle to his table, courtesy of the 'Turkish gentlemen' in the corner. Finding it to be raki, Justin managed to give them an appreciative smile and resolved never to actually drink the stuff.

Finally, the banquet ended and Justin was able to take his leave. While he did not mind being with people, he knew that eventually he would reach a limit, unlike Sophie, who fed off human interaction. To minimize the chances for further meetings, he found a bench in a recessed alcove overlooking the harbor. There, he watched a particularly vivid sunset, and was about to return to his suite when he heard the voices of two men coming somewhere to his left. They were speaking in Arabic and Justin recognized one of the men as the Arab scientist, al-Haytham. The other voice was lower, more guttural, and had the type of lisp which Justin associated with people who came from the Arabian peninsula, rather from Egypt itself. As they spoke, Justin shrank back further into the darkness of his alcove, fascinated by the conversation he was now overhearing as the men passed by.

Al-Haytham: "Have you gotten it to work properly?"
Other man: "Yes, although it is not easy to do."
Al-Haytham: "How often do you use it?"
Other man: (with something of a sneer in his voice) "That is my concern, scientist. My concern alone."
Al-Haytham: (contrite) "I meant no disrespect. It is just important that you make it work—the concept is a difficult one."
Other man: "I could care less about the concept. It is carrying out its intended purpose, trust me."
Al-Haytham: (becoming fainter) "Also, here is the additional… requested."
Other man: "Good, we have been running low. We are close to success."
Al-Haytham: (becoming even fainter) "Fine. I will carry a good report back to Cairo."
Other man: (fading out) "Please do…not tolerate…of succcss."

Try as he might, Justin could not hear any more. His desire to do so overcame his natural caution, and he stuck his head out onto the balcony. The men were gone, however, and he was alone. Heading directly back to his room, he immediately wrote down as much as he could remember, although the subject of the conversation was a mystery. Staring at the words, he could only think, *'So, scientist, you lied to me. You were in no hurry to get back to your ship, were you?'* He then went to bed, where he slept a troubled sleep, punctuated by a dream in which he was chased by a horde of Turks who kept yelling "Onu aldin mi?" {"Did you get it?"}

In Constantinople, Sophie had spent the day with Zoe as they planned the outfits she would wear in the following week for the celebrations of the Nativity of St. John the Baptist. Following the religious ceremonies, it was customary for the emperors (and by extension the imperial princesses) to preside at outdoor events at the Hippodrome, the great race track which was directly to the west of the Great Palace. Zoe, though woefully ignorant about many subjects, was extremely attuned to the popular pulse, and intended to dress for the occasion.

Normally, this kind of thing was child's play for Sophie, but today she found herself struggling. The vision of 'Loviatar' was stuck in her mind, and she could not shake it. *'Like a woman, and yet not. How could this be?'* So, she did what she needed to do with Zoe, gave the necessary orders to the seamstresses, and went home to a villa where she knew Justin would not be.

Despite her inner conflicts, dinner with the children was enjoyable, as Simon had grown quite proficient in throwing scraps to the dogs and then laughing as they dove for them. Maria was proud to show off how she had learned to divide using the new 'Arabic' numbers and they all enjoyed a lovely evening on the veranda. The hoopoes had finished raising their young, and now all of them were free to explore the city as they would. The adults still came back to the trees above the villa every night out of habit, and perched to see if any scraps were there for the taking.

After the children were in bed, Sophie relaxed outdoors, watching the same sunset her husband was seeing many miles away. When Philip announced that the Deputy Treasurer was present, she felt a sense of relief, for her restless mind had finally fixed on the reason that the image of 'Loviatar' had bothered her so. An insight had come earlier that day during a luncheon with Zoe, Theodora and their ladies-in-waiting. Looking around the room at her fellow diners, Sophie was struck by the shapes of their faces, which were uniformly oval. By contrast, 'Loviatar', even with all of the vagueness, definitely had a more square face, particularly the jaw. How to reconcile this blend of man and woman? While one answer would have been simply to say that gods are different than humans, Sophie was never going to concede there was anything divine about the apparition she had witnessed. No, there had to be another answer!

So, when Alexius sat down across from her, Sophie's mind was more at ease, even if she was no nearer a solution than she had been. She spoke at length about her thoughts to Alexius, more to hear herself talk than to expect any response from him. She had never really been able to read the bland face of the eunuch, something she imagined was very useful for him in negotiations and interrogations.

This time, though, was different. After listening to Sophie expound on her conclusions, Alexius was silent before saying, "I may have a possible explanation for what you observed, although it may having nothing to do with 'Loviatar'. If you want to see what I mean, you must promise me to do exactly what I say, and I mean that without any exaggeration. Should I go on?"

Sophie, her instincts now fully aroused, quickly said yes.

Alexius went on. "Then, tomorrow night, about this time, I will come by and take you to a place I know here in the city where you will have a chance to test your theory. You must not tell anyone about it, either before or after, including Justin. You will be in no danger, believe me, but you must do what I say. Is that acceptable?"

Sophie was a little slower to agree this time, but eventually said that she would.

"Very well. When I come by, you must be dressed in that blue gown you wore for the dinner at the prefect's villa last month, with plenty of jewelry. Also, don't spare the make-up, eyeliner particularly. Understand?"

By now completely befuddled, Sophie could only nod in affirmation.

A smile broke Alexius' usually bland face. "Very well, Lady, tomorrow you will see something entirely different, I promise you!"

CHAPTER 17

After a troubled sleep, Justin was awakened by the porter's knock. There was no sunlight coming through the window, and the weather outside looked gray, but not stormy. His attention was not drawn to that but rather to the presence of a package in the porter's hand, who said he had found it on the threshold. Justin rose quickly and, after thanking the porter with a tip, took the package and examined it. It appeared to be parchment tied with string, and was not very heavy. Opening it, he found a manuscript and a smaller package, which in turn contained a pouch, inside of which was an ivory necklace featuring an elephant in the center. With a start, he recognized it as the one Sitt al-Mulk had been wearing during the audience two days before.

Reflexively, he went onto the balcony and looked down at the harbor where the Arab fleet had been. Now, there was only open water, and the only large ships remaining were Roman ones. While he earnestly desired to examine the manuscript written in Arabic as well as the necklace, he realized that the fleet was scheduled to leave that morning, with or without him. After dressing and shaving, he packed his things, making sure to include his two new possessions, and then went to the dining hall for breakfast.

Admiral Kritikrites and General Xiphias were seated at a table with Governor Chonas, who looked more at ease now that his official duties during the conference were over. They invited Justin to join them, and then looked at him expectantly.

After looking from face to face, Justin inquired, "All right, gentlemen, what is going on?"

As if speaking on behalf of his companions, the general gave a chuckle and replied, "Oh, nothing really, Treasurer. We were just wondering what it was like talking with the caliph's sister. Did you get a look at her?"

Quickly brushing aside the sight of the Lady Sitt's dark eyes looking out from above her veil aboard her ship, Justin shook his head. "No, the screen was quite effective, although it does seem like an odd way to conduct affairs of state."

The admiral shook his head dismissively, and said, "Oh, you know these Muslims! There's probably some directive in their Quran about this and now they all think it's Gospel!"

Deciding to let the irony of that remark pass, Justin merely shook his head in turn, saying "No, I think it's more of a cultural thing. I've seen many Muslim women in Antioch and Jerusalem who don't wear the veil like that."

Governor Chonas, even though not the most astute of men, in turn picked up on this comment. "Veil? How do you know she was veiled behind the screen?"

Luck was with Justin at this point, for a messenger came in and announced that the ships would begin to board, so as to make the favorable tide. As they all rose to leave, General Xiphias took Justin by the hand and congratulated him on a job well done.

"I really enjoyed talking with you, Treasurer. Those of us in the army have our doubts about the imperial bureaucracy, but if there are men like you in charge, I can rest easier. I know Emperor Basil thinks so too, although he'll be the last to admit it."

Justin smiled, really smiled, for the first time in days. "Thank you, General, you made what could have been a tedious trip much more pleasant. Have a safe trip back to Thessalonika, and then on to the front, wherever that is."

Bowing, the general smiled in turn. "Thank you as well. Safe journey to you, and good fortune in all of your undertakings."

Feeling fully at ease, Justin replied, "Oh, and just one more thing—speaking personally and not as the Treasurer of the Roman Empire, please end this interminable war!"

With a salute, the general said, "I'll do my best," and departed to his ship for the return trip.

After taking his leave of the governor, Justin walked down to the wharf with the admiral, who spoke as one who was eager to get back to sea after a sojourn on dry land.

"Well, Treasurer, you may not find the voyage back as much to your liking as the trip here. As you can see, the sky is overcast and the wind is out of the west, which portends a storm. This isn't necessary bad for us, for the sails can catch any wind that's blowing, and we can make good time. Still, it will likely be a bit bumpy for a landsman like you, meaning no offense!"

"None taken, sir. When do you expect us to make landfall in Constantinople?"

At this, the admiral laughed. "'Landfall'? Very good, you're picking up the lingo of the sailor. If all goes well, it will be sometime early Saturday morning, and when I say early, believe it. Still, if it is clear, the moon will be almost full, and we can dock even in the middle of night. Now, we are at our ship, and I must see to final arrangements. I trust you can find you way from here?"

"Yes, Admiral, I believe I can."

While the departure of the fleet actually took longer than Justin expected, eventually they all got underway. Immediately after leaving the harbor, several ships split off to go to the Empire's possessions in southern Italy. While at the beginning of Basil's reign the imperial presence there had been tenuous, it was now firmly established in the southern third of the peninsula, with only the continued Fatimid possession of Sicily remaining to be contested. While General Xiphias thought it more likely that Basil would turn his attention to Armenia and Syria first, he had confided to Justin that the re-conquest of Sicily would be a pleasure walk compared to the seemingly-endless slog through the wooded valleys and rugged mountains of Bulgaria.

The reduced fleet turned to the north, and made good time, although the swells were more than Justin was comfortable with. He decided that the waves would be less threatening if he could not see them, so he retired to his cabin. Pulling out the manuscript that he had found by his door earlier that morning, he laid it out on his bunk and tried to make sense of it. It was 78 pages long with diagrams seemingly of a geometric nature on almost every page. Some pages contained two or three. With a start, he saw the name of the author—Hasan Ibn al-Haytham!

While his knowledge of written Arabic had improved over time, it still lagged his ability to speak the language, and he found himself staring at words he was completely unfamiliar with. Unlike Greek, which made frequent use of suffixes and prefixes to construct more complex words, Arabic relied more on internal changes to stem words, almost all of which consisted of only 3 different consonants. But, since vowels were not written, one had to deduce from the context what a particular word was. Since Justin didn't know what was being meant in many cases, he found his frustration rising. Even the meaning of the title, "Kitab al-Manazir," was unclear—*'Book of Sight?', 'Book of Seeing?', 'Book of Vision?'*

Setting aside the manuscript for the moment, he then examined the ivory necklace. While he didn't know much about ivory, the craftsmanship of the piece was obvious, down to the individual petals of the flowers surrounding the elephant (lotus, perhaps?). There was no message, no inscription, nothing, just the necklace. *'Yet another mystery to solve,* Justin thought—*when do we see the light?'*

Before he could return to the manuscript, a porter came and announced dinner. The meal was a subdued affair, particularly since the admiral felt it necessary to stay on deck and guide their passage through the island chains of the lower Aegean that the fleet need to pass. While the clouds of the day had parted to reveal a bright moon, it still took an experienced sailor in command to lead the way, in that signal flags were useless at night. As a result, the admiral was not present to indicate to his servers that Justin, contrary to most imperial officials, did not drink to excess, and so should not be served the strong wine consumed by most everyone else.

For his part, Justin was not very good company for those who were there, as his thoughts were consumed by the events of the past several days, not the least of which was the mysterious manuscript. So, he consumed considerably more than his usual intake of wine (a flavorful vintage from Samnos) and only noticed that the ship was rolling more than usual when he rose to take his leave. He was fortunate to make it back to his cabin, after a brief visit to the water-closet, before collapsing on his bunk, where he slept a dreamless sleep on top of the very manuscript which was be-deviling him.

In Constantinople, Sophie's evening was starting out quite differently. The children were still not clear where Papa had gone to, although Maria assured her mother that he was "all right." Sophie had had a difficult day, for she missed Justin more than she realized she would, and found herself going over all of the possible bad things that could happen to him—shipwreck, a sudden storm, pirates, etc. That, combined with her anticipation of a new adventure that evening, caused her mind to wander as she performed her official duties with her royal mistress.

Zoe, showing the occasional empathy of which she was capable, gave leave for Sophie to depart early, telling her, "I know that your husband is on a mission of great importance to the Empire, and I shall pray for him this evening, as I know you will too."

In the event, prayer was about the last thing from Sophie's mind as she prepared to go to the mysterious destination promised by Alexius, although she could see no possible connection with the mystery of the true identity of 'Loviatar.' Still, she followed the eunuch's recommendation and had Donna assist her in putting on a blue silk brocaded gown she had only worn once before to a dinner hosted by Prefect Comnenus. She smiled at the memory, for while Justin thought that the outfit was too low cut in the front, she seemed to get plenty of attention by the other guests at the dinner, not the least of whom was the prefect himself. This time, she added more jewelry than before, including multiple rings, and followed Alexius' admonition to be generous with the eyeliner. While she could tell that Donna was dying to know the reason for all of this, the mistress-servant relationship was too strong for the maid to actually say anything. Sophie noticed this with amusement, and thought the breaking-point was finally reached when she applied some dark red lipstick. But, the wall of silence held, and only a raised eyebrow betrayed Donna's thoughts.

When Alexius arrived with the carriage, Sophie could not help but notice that the driver was one of the agents of the Alitheia Society and that he was armed with both a short sword and a large knife. She knew better than to bring this up, and so took her seat across from Alexius.

After seeing her outfit, over which she had thrown a light cloak, Alexius nodded with approval, saying only, "You'll fit in well, 'Scapel!'"

When they had ridden for a few minutes, heading south and west across the city, Sophie could take no more.

"All right, Alexius, I've been patient enough! While my husband and I both trust you implicitly, I have to know—what is it that I am looking for, and are we going into danger?"

Alexius said nothing for a moment, and then, in a lower voice, replied. "No, Lady, the place we are going is well known to me—please, don't ask why—and since you'll be with me, you will be in no danger. As to what you will learn, that is for you to find out. Any words I have now would be insufficient. Do you trust me on this?"

"Of course I do."

"Good, then you only need to remember three things. First, follow my lead and do not address anyone until I have done so first. Second, anything you see must not be discussed elsewhere, unless it is to Justin alone. Third, try not to stare—it's impolite. Understand?"

Sophie, even more confused than before, could only say, "No, but I hear what you are saying and will comply."

Alexius gave a slight smile before adding, "Oh, one more thing—watch your pronouns."

Before Sophie could even begin to digest this cryptic statement, the carriage came to a stop. They were in a part of the city that Sophie was unfamiliar with, although the fact they had gone through the Forum of Bovis and then the Forum of Arcadius told her they were somewhere in the southwest quarter. There were few, if any, churches in this area, and no grand imperial buildings. Here is where people like Donna her maid could afford to live, for Constantinople, like all capital cities, had a higher cost of living than other places in the Empire. They were in front of a non-descript building, with only two large men standing outside the entrance making it at all noticeable. After telling their driver to wait around the corner, Alexius took Sophie's arm and approached the door. While Sophie could not hear what he whispered into the largest man's ear, it was enough, for the man gave a small bow to Sophie and admitted them.

While it was lit with candles mounted in brackets around the walls, the room they entered was dark, so dark that Sophie could not at first tell how large it was or how many people were there. From the conversations she heard, the room was fairly full, and seemed to contain a number of small tables and chairs, with an open area in the middle. Alexius steered her towards an empty table, and after they were seated her eyes grew accustomed to the lack of light. At first glance, the room seemed to contain most women sitting and conversing, many of whom were very stylishly attired in the latest fashions. As she studied them further, what she saw surprised her greatly.

The 'women' were in fact either men or eunuchs. Given the amount of make-up some were wearing, it was difficult to tell for sure which was which. While many of the gowns were gorgeous using bold colors and designs, as well as being correctly accessorized, there was still something about the wearers that, to Sophie's trained eye, looked odd. As the sudden realization of why Alexius had brought her there struck home, her eyes must have grown wide, for when she looked over at him, he gave a shy smile and nodded.

Before she could say anything, a waitress came over to their table to take their drink orders. Alexius ordered white wines for them both. Before she left, the waitress, who did seem to in fact be a woman, smiled at Sophie and said, "Nice outfit, sister—are you new around here?"

Conscious of Alexius' admonition, Sophie merely smiled and nodded. Once she had left, Sophie leaned over to the eunuch and said, "This is amazing! I had no idea! One question for now—besides the waitress, am I the only other woman in here?"

"Probably, although there is one woman who comes here from time to time. She doesn't say much and seems engrossed in writing on a tablet, so no one gives her any trouble. She usually sits over in that corner—yes, there she is."

Sophie followed Alexius' nod, and got her second shock of the evening. There, wearing a plain cloak and hood, was Leonida, the chief lady-in-waiting for Zoe's sister Theodora! *'Aha,'* thought Sophie, *'so this is where you got your ideas! Well, we'll see about this later, 'sister'!'*

Turning back to Alexius, Sophie said, "I understand now—these women who are men who look like women, or whatever—this is who 'Loviatar' is. Do you have any idea who it could be?"

Alexis shook his head. "No, but there is someone here who might be able to help us. Ah, here she comes—now remember, his name is Isaac, but inside these walls she is Alexa. Got that?"

"Right, Alexa it is. So, who am I supposed to be?"

"Oh, I think being yourself is quite enough." Then, turning to the stylish figure walking over to their table, he rose and said, "Alexa, you look lovely tonight. Come, please join us."

Alexa did so with a nod, and sat next to Alexius, across from Sophie. In a voice that would have been high for a man but low for a woman, she smiled and said, "Welcome, Lady Sophia! Alexius has told me all about you and what you seek. Thank you for gracing us with your presence. We don't usually let outsiders in, considering that most of us are breaking any number of laws at this very moment. You won't be telling the Patriarch about this, I trust?"

Sophie returned the smile and shook her head. "My lips are sealed, Alexa. Believe me, I am not here to judge or gawk—I need your help in finding someone."

Alexa nodded. "Yes, Alexius has told me about the investigation you and your husband are working on. I must say, I've been a big fan of your work for years, and I'm sure there are lots of cases that I haven't even heard about. Now it seems you're up against a goddess. That's a big chore, even for the 'Iron Lady.' How can I help?"

Sophie then proceeded to explain the recent murders of the Varangians and the visions of what they called 'Loviatar,' the Norse goddess of death. Since Sophie had seen a vision of something that did appear to satisfy the requirements of such an entity, she needed help in coming up with a rational explanation, and, more importantly, bring the individual or individuals to justice.

After listening to Sophie's recitation, Alexa was silent, all the while peering intently at Sophie. She then commented, "I want to apologize—part of me wondered if you actually were here to look at 'the freaks', as some have called us. But this, this is something that you can't make up. Please, tell me more about what you saw."

Sophie then described the vision she and the others had seen, with her usual eye for every minute detail as to facial shape, height, body build and dress.

Alexa listened intently, taking it all in, and finally commented, "Lady, you don't miss a thing, do you?" As she said this, Sophie was aware that, while she had been talking, other patrons had drifted over to their table, including a number of Alexa's companions, so that they were now surrounded by a very attentive audience. Looking around, Alexa asked, "What do you think, girls? Sounds like Daphne to me," and received a general chorus of agreement in return.

"May I speak with him, I mean her, please?" asked Sophie.

"No, I'm afraid not," Alexa replied. "You see, no one's seen Daphne for several weeks now—just disappeared. It happens often to us—we're not exactly favored under the law, you know, so going to the authorities is out of the question."

Alexius, who had been sitting impassively through the entire conversation, spoke up. "Do you think she was involved in something criminal?"

Alexa shook her head, "No, no, that's the hard part to understand—Daphne is a very gentle person, and would never hurt a fly. We are all afraid for her—we'll do anything you ask if it helps get her back safely, assuming that's still possible."

"Agreed," said Sophie after a moment's thought. "Anything we find out about her whereabouts, we will pass on to you, through Alexius. Please do the same for us. One more thing, and I mean no disrespect, but does anyone know what Daphne was known as when she was not here?"

A voice in the back said, "You mean her 'outside' name?"

"Yes, if that what you call it," Sophie replied.

A murmur of voices ensued, at the end of which Alexa said, "No, we're afraid not, although some think they heard the name 'Matthew.' You understand how it is—some people don't want to advertise they come here."

As Sophie nodded her understanding, "What does it all mean, Lady" said a blond with a voice that was really just a little too low. "What's Daphne involved with?"

Lowering her voice so as not be overheard by any outside of the little group, Sophie responded, "I am afraid they're murders, deliberate, pre-meditated murders. If we don't put a stop to this soon, I'm afraid it will be the end for Daphne, for she will just be a loose end that needs to be tied up. Still, we'll do our best. Thank you all for your help. Oh, and one more thing—pearls go better with silver than they do with gold—just a thought."

Amid nods and thanks all around, she and Alexius then took their leave. On the way out, Sophie looked over to where Leonida had been sitting. While the table was now empty, Sophie thought '*I know what I saw! We'll deal with you in good time!*'

Riding back to the villa, Sophie, as was her custom, processed what she had seen and heard that evening. Alexius, who was accustomed to her methods, was perfectly at ease with the silence, broken only by the clip-clop of the horse's hoofs.

Finally, Sophie spoke. "You were right, Alexius. This was entirely different! While I imagine those people don't have it easy, living double lives like they do, they seemed very accepting."

Alexius gave a rueful little smile. "That's why I like being there. When I am, no one judges me for being a eunuch."

"Oh, come on, I don't judge you, and I am sure Justin doesn't either!"

"I didn't say you did. The Varangians, on the other hand, well, that's a different situation. But, I'm used to it by now, I guess. Any thoughts on where we go from here?" he asked as the carriage pulled up in the front drive.

Sophie shook her head before alighting from the carriage. "No, it's too early. I want to think things over a bit, and to discuss them with Justin when he returns."

The normally impassive visage of the eunuch showed amazement. "Are you going to tell him about tonight?"

Rolling her eyes, Sophie laughed. "That will be asking a lot. I guess I will have to come up with a suitable way to introduce the subject! Good night, Alexius."

"Good night, 'Scalpel!'"

CHAPTER 18

Friday began late for Justin, as he slept in his small cabin until mid-morning. When he did get up, he immediately noticed that the ship was rolling and pitching considerably more than the night before. Like a true Roman, he did not appreciate this effect, which was magnified by his hangover. Making his way to the mess room, he had some bread and cheese before going on deck. There he found Admiral Kritikrites, who was as home on the moving deck as he would have been walking down the dock at the harbor.

"Ah, there you are, Treasurer, you're just in time! General Xiphias and his fleet are getting ready to head for Thessalonica—you can see their signal flags now—'Safe journey home. Long live the Emperors!'"

Even on a cloudy day, Justin still found it a magnificent sight as twelve vessels, their flags flying in the stiff breeze, broke off from the main fleet and headed to the northwest. Looking around, he noticed that there still seemed to be more ships than had been with them on the outbound voyage.

As if reading his thoughts, the admiral nodded. "Ah, you've noticed our guests, have you? Yes, we had some merchant ships join us in Crete to go back to the capital. Some went down with us to Crete or to other ports, but over all we have more now than we did then. Not that there's any problem with pirates—it's just that now they can leave the navigation to us."

Trying to get his 'sea legs' under him, Justin still kept one hand on the rail while he took in the activity of the ship around him, and so avoid looking at the rolling horizon. To appear casual, he inquired, "So, do you still think we can make the city before dawn tomorrow?"

"Oh, yes. It should clear off later today, and with the nearly full moon, we can sail through the Dardanelles and into the Sea of Marmara with no trouble. I would estimate we should be landing one or two hours before dawn."

Intrigued, Justin had to ask, "Excuse this question coming from a complete landsman, Admiral, but how do you tell time at night? I understand in the day, based on where the sun is, but at night?"

"It's simple, really, and based on the same principle, except we use the moon instead of the sun. It's even easier with a full moon, which comes up when the sun goes down. So, if the full moon is overhead, it's halfway until dawn. As the moon goes further down in the west, the sooner the sun will be coming up in the east. Now, there you have it—amaze your friends at parties."

How much longer this lesson in astronomy would have gone on Justin was not destined to find out, for one of the admiral's subordinates came to him with an issue that needed his attention. Justin lingered on deck for a little while longer, trying to avoid the bobbing horizon, but eventually gave up and retired to his cabin. Putting the manuscript aside for a moment, he examined the ivory necklace.

While it did look like the one the Lady Sitt wore the first time they met, maybe he was wrong—maybe it was just similar? Wishing Sophie was with him more than ever, he looked at the carving until his eyes were blurry—perhaps the elephant meant something—strength, wisdom, memory? Or was it the lotus flowers—if so, he was completely at a loss. Clearly someone from Cairo wanted him to have the piece for a reason. The Christians and Jews who were there he could rule out, for they could simply have given it to him directly, as was done with the golden star. *'I need more facts,'* he thought with a sigh. *'I can't make bricks without straw.'*

That left the manuscript. Knowing what he did about the author's interests, Justin assumed that it concerned vision or light or sight. Still, how that was connected with anything he needed to know was a mystery. Ruefully, he reflected that his reputation for being a polyglot was overstated—it was one thing to have a working knowledge of a spoken language, but another thing entirely to grasp the nuances of that same language when it was written. Fortunately, he had additional resources at his disposal, for his groom, Agatho, and Maria's tutor, Anwar, were both native-born Arab speakers. With their help, he should be able to make more progress.

Dinner with the admiral and officers was enjoyable, although Justin avoided consuming the quantity of wine he had had the night before. The men sitting around the table had been all over the Mediterranean and Black Sea, with a few having ventured further, either down the Red Sea or into the Atlantic itself. For his part, Justin spoke almost every language of the lands they had visited, although he did admit that his Spanish sounded a lot like his Italian. After thanking them for their hospitality during the voyage, he took his leave and returned to his cabin, where the night steward had lit an oil lamp on the table.

While he tried to resist the urge to take one more look at the manuscript, after a period of sleeplessness he gave in and decided to try a different approach. Unlike works he had read in Greek, the manuscript did not seem to have discrete chapters. Yet, on almost every page there were drawings of geometric shapes with lines on one or both sides, sometimes parallel, sometimes converging or diverging. Justin assumed that the text which followed each drawing somehow referred to it. Words like 'light', 'sun', 'eye', and 'color' appeared frequently. Unfortunately, other, more complex words also appeared that were unfamiliar. Sleep eventually came to him while sitting at the table, and he awoke with a stiff neck some time later.

While the lamp had gone out, the bright light of the moon coming in through the cabin window let him make his way around the cabin. On a whim, he went on deck. There, off to the west, he saw a magnificent sight—the spires, domes and walls of Constantinople itself. '*I don't know if you are a city guarded by the Virgin,*' he thought, '*but you are a truly special place and one I am glad to call home.*' Now fully awake, he stayed on deck as the city drew closer.

Sophie's day had begun well before Justin's, for there were children to mind, instructions to give to the household staff, and plans to make for the day. These latter were solidified by a message she received from Alexius as she was ready to leave for the palace. She smiled as she read it, for the trustworthy deputy treasurer had, true to his word, investigated the vendors on the Mese who were from Egypt. Her smile faded when she read the list—27 in all! Well, she thought, Rome wasn't built in a day, and neither was Constantinople.

When she arrived at the Great Palace, she noticed the preparations that were already under way for the festivities that were to occur in a few days for the Nativity of St. John the Baptist. Sophie had been preparing for this event for some time, but the course of recent events had caused her to amend her plans. While the outfit she had laid out for Zoe was impressive, she intended to put Leonida through her paces, as a partial pay-back for what she had made Sophie go through in recent weeks.

She was still contemplating her revenge when she approached the doors to Zoe's quarters. As always, they were guarded by Varangians in full armor. For the first few years of her service with Zoe she had really not noticed these large men, considering them equivalent to the furniture. Only when she had learned to speak with them, even on a rudimentary level, did she begin to appreciate them as people.

Still, she was not prepared for what occurred when she entered the doors which the soldiers opened and the guard on the left spoke.

"Hurae longum, Jarynlayden, hurae longum?" {"How long, Iron Lady, how long?"}

Taken aback, Sophie paused for a moment before murmuring, "Fljotlign, Vikingr, fljotlign!" {"Soon, Norseman, soon!"}

Her mood was not improved by the news she got from Irene.

Glancing around to make sure no one else was in earshot, her second-in-command said in a low voice, "Good morning, Sophie! A word to the wise—Zoe is a little down today. I think she received some news about her father that is weighing on her."

Nodding in acknowledgement, Sophie prepared to see the princess, after first making sure the arrangements were in order for the group luncheon that was scheduled for that day with Theodora and her retinue. Satisfied, she asked for and was given admission to the inner sanctum as Zoe finished her daily devotions with Brother James. Sophie had been around Zoe long enough to know that the best way to address her was directly, since most people did not.

"Good morning, Highness. Is there anything I can help you with today, before your sister arrives for lunch?"

Zoe sighed and shook her head. "No, Sophie, I am afraid there are limits even to your amazing abilities. I am worried about my father—you know he is to lead the procession into the Hippodrome on Tuesday for the celebration of the Nativity of John the Baptist."

"What's the problem? He has always been an excellent horseman," Sophie said with surprise.

"I'm not sure his health is up to it. The doctors try to put the best face on things, but there's more there than they say in their reports, I just feel it!"

Also unlike most others, Sophie knew the best response at this point was silence, so she just took Zoe's hand and held it. As she expected, after a few minutes Zoe's mood brightened, and she asked how the investigation was going. Sophie gave a responsive but brief answer, knowing that Zoe's attention to detail was minimal. Further conversation was avoided by the chamberlain's announcement that Princess Theodora had arrived and was awaiting her sister. At this, Zoe's countenance changed as though a lamp had been lit and they went forth.

As dictated by protocol, Theodora and six of her ladies entered behind their guard of Varangians, who then retired to join their fellows in the hallway. Prior to the luncheon, the royal sisters and their entourages mingled, although most of the conversation, at least within Sophie's hearing, was trivial. Sophie sought to remedy that when she found Leonida, who greeted her with a broad smile, doubtless fueled by yet another stunning gown worn by her mistress.

Sophie cut to the case. "You're looking very nice today, Lady Leonida. Oh, yes, since you left early the other night, your friend Alexa says hello." She then smiled and said nothing else.

At first, Leonida's eyes went wide, then her face went white, and then her mouth opened in a soundless 'O'. Then, showing more aplomb than Sophie would have given her credit for, she whispered, "I suppose this is the end for me. Very well, I'm ready."

Leaning close, Sophie took her hand and replied, also in a low voice, "Don't be silly—I have no desire to destroy you. I was there for my reasons, and I'm sure you were there for yours. The others who were there seem to be nice people, and I don't judge."

Leonida seemed to deflate for a moment, but recovered quickly. "All right, what do I have to do to keep your silence?"

Sophie shook her head ruefully. "Oh, you young people, so cynical, thinking I want something? But, since you bring up the subject, yes, there is something you can do for me." Sophie then explained to a first-incredulous, and then accepting, Leonida that she admired the younger woman's fashion design skills and wanted to benefit from them. While she did not expect Leonida to provide her with a completely new outfit for Zoe for the upcoming event, she would appreciate some improvements, along with assistance in the future, "as requested."

Leonida managed a weak smile, and gave a wordless nod of agreement.

The rest of lunch went as planned, with Sophie having the pleasure of introducing their newest lady-in-waiting, Julia Kritikrites. Seeing the young woman look around at the others with the kind of wide-eyed amazement that she once knew brought back fond memories to Sophie, along with a realization of how many years had passed since she first came to the palace. Still, she thought, *I'm still here, and I'm not done yet!*

Afterwards, the retinues of the royal princesses spent a little more time together, as their mistresses talked between themselves. From what Sophie could overhear, the main topic was their father, and it was clear that Theodora was just as concerned about Constantine as was Zoe, if not more. Sophie left Leonida alone until just before Theodora was ready to leave, when she approached the younger woman.

"Say, Leonida, if you have some time this afternoon, you are welcome to come shopping with me. I was planning on going down to the Mese to just look around. But, if not, that's all right, too."

First surprised, then puzzled, Leonida agreed. It was not until they were riding together along the broad boulevards of the city that she warmed up.

"Thank you for inviting me, Sophie, it was really unexpected. Did you really mean what you said about keeping my secret about the other night?"

"Of course I meant it. I also meant the part about expecting some help from you on clothing design—you do have very vibrant and original ideas, wherever you get them from. I'd like to get your thoughts on Zoe's gown for Tuesday, if that's all right." Seeing Leonida look more at ease, Sophie decided to press on.

"So, since you brought up the other night, I have to ask—how did you learn about the place, and how did you fit in?"

Leonida paused, then replied. "I overheard two of the eunuchs who take care of Theodora's household accounts talking one day about the place, and thought it sounded interesting. As to how I fit in, I trying dressing modestly and talking in a low voice. It took the people there about a minute to figure out that I didn't belong, but they were very nice, and just ignored me. I learn so much every I time I go there—it's just amazing! But," and she paused again, "why were you there?"

"Fair enough," said Sophie. "There's no reason that you shouldn't know. My husband and I have, for a number of years, been involved in the investigation of crimes here in the city. Some have been murders, some other crimes like theft. We are currently looking into the death of some of the Varangian guards. While I can't say why, we came to the club to learn about one of the female impersonators named Daphne, who's gone missing. Did you ever see her there?"

Leonida frowned as she tried to remember. "I think there was someone like that, although she may have been there only once when I was there. Taller than most, with a rather square face as I recall. I do have to say—whoever he was during the day, he didn't make the best woman in the evening, although his fashion sense was impeccable."

"I've been wondering about that," Sophie mused. "How do they come up with such wonderful creations?"

"I've thought about that, too. I think it's because they weren't brought up to think inside the box like we were—'you can't do that' or 'you must do this'—for them, everything's on the table. Of course, not all of their ideas work, but when they do, they're magnificent. Not that you're any slouch yourself, of course."

Sophie smiled. "Thank you for that—just keep your eyes and ears open for any news of Daphne when you're there. Ah," she said as they pulled up to the beginning of the Mese, "here we are—the greatest shopping area in the world!"

As they dismounted from the carriage, Leonida inquired further. "Does our 'shopping trip' today have something to do with your investigation?"

Sophie gave an amused look as she laughed. "Clever girl! Yes, but the reason I can't say much is that I don't know much. Suffice it to say that I want to check out stalls here that are owned or operated by Egyptians—there are 27 in all, I am told. Don't ask me what I hope to find—I really don't know."

The Mese had grown over the centuries to take in many blocks, and was divided into separate areas based on the kind of items for sale. The metal dealers were in one area, while a block over were sellers of precious stones, glass, ivory, perfumes, leather and silk. Further down were the merchants of household items like lamps, vases, embroideries and rugs. One area that was largely unfamiliar to Sophie concerned foodstuffs like meats, cheeses, fruit, honey, spices and bread. Fortunately, given the difficulty of importing food from Egypt, none of the 27 listed vendors were in that area.

True to her word, as she had told her younger companion, Sophie had no real idea of what she was looking for. In every stall, the merchants were happy to greet a woman who clearly was a member of the upper class. In each case, Sophie would feign interest in an item or two and would ask to speak to the manager or owner. These were almost always produced, although few sales occurred as a result. In only two cases were the responsible men not available. In one, a dealer in silver, they were told that the owner's wife had just delivered a baby. In the other which sold ivory pieces, a rather surly Egyptian who identified himself only as "Ishaq" said that the owner, one Musa bin-Hadi, was "unavailable." Sophie was taken with the workmanship of many of the items, and eventually bought a necklace to avoid any suspicions on the part of Ishaq who, she noted, was left-handed.

On the way back to the Great Palace, Leonida expressed keen interest in what Sophie was doing, at one point stating, "I am sorry, Sophie, for seeing you as just 'a lady-in-waiting.' Anything I can do to help with the investigation, please let me know."

Sophie thanked her for this offer before getting back to real-world issues. "Thank you, Leonida, I will do that. Now, as to Zoe's dress for Tuesday, can you come see our dressmakers tomorrow and add some of your distinctive touches? That will work? Good, I'll tell them to expect you then."

Later that evening, Sophie realized with a start that she had been so busy during the day that she had not once thought about her absent husband. '*Well*,' she thought, '*I'm sure he's been busy, too. Anyhow, he should be back tomorrow, if the winds are favorable.*' She then started to plan how she would break the news of her discoveries to him when they spoke, particularly about the news about 'Daphne'. What it all meant she was not sure, but she was sure that there was no goddess here in the city, or that any supernatural force was responsible for the deaths of the Northmen. No, there were human actors at work, just like there always were, and she and her husband would find them.

Alas, before she could retire to her bedroom, a message came via the night porter. Seeing that it was Alexius, she felt a momentary rush of dread, knowing that it was Friday night when the Varangians assembled for their banquet. She felt better after reading it, for it said that while no one 'seemed' to have been killed afterwards, one man was missing from barrack's call. More information was promised as it became available.

With a sigh, Sophie took these thoughts with her to bed, along with some dogs who took advantage of their master's absence. She fell into a dreamless sleep that was only broken by the caress of familiar hands. Smiling, she responded to Justin's touch by murmuring, "Welcome back, sailor!" before drifting back to sleep.

CHAPTER 19

Justin was asleep the next morning well after the sun came up, and was awakened finally by the family's dogs, who decided that he had been immobile long enough. While he might have been able to ignore Shadow, her combined weight with that of Velvet was too much to ignore. He arose, noticed that Sophie was already up and gone, and prepared himself for the day. He had a strong urge to go into the office, having been gone for several days, but the urge to see his family was stronger, and he went downstairs. There, he was mobbed by his children, who had been strongly admonished by their mother to "let Papa sleep", the dogs, who had followed him downstairs, and the household staff who congratulated him on his safe return.

He relaxed for some time on the veranda, luxuriating in the feel of ground which did not move beneath him and a horizon which did not rise and fall. He felt a simple pleasure in looking at the everyday things of life he had taken for granted before, like the hoopoe birds, who were now completing the task of rearing their latest brood. With Maria, he watched as the parents dropped bits of food on the ground for the young to swoop down and pick up, often with comic results when two would go for the same piece. Simon meanwhile was playing with a rattle, at one point shaking it so hard that it broke.

Justin had also called for Agatho the groom, only to be informed by Phllip that it was the young man's day off. '*No matter,*' he thought, *'this way I can talk with Maria's tutor and Agatho about the book at the same time on Monday.'*

From the look on Maria's face, he could tell that Sophie had come back, and was sneaking up behind him. He did nothing until she put her hands over his eyes, at which time he grabbed her and pulled her onto his lap, with a long kiss to follow.

Finally, when the couple both came up for air, Sophie whispered, "Missed you, too!" She sat down, scooped up Simon, and said, "Do I have things to tell you! How long have you been gone—a month? There have been at least two really important things you have to know. Oh, and how was your trip?"

"Thank you, dear, yes, I was gone for a few days. And while I'm sure that you have news, I can't imagine it will be more important than mine. I also can't imagine what was so important that you've already been out this morning. Did you get a summons from Zoe?"

Shaking her head, Sophie replied, "No, for once. Actually, I did go to the palace—I have the services of a new assistant making Zoe's outfits—it's a long story that I'll go into later—and I wanted to see how she was coming along. I hope to see great things from her, and sooner rather than later, probably as early as this Tuesday for the celebration."

At this, Justin gave a groan. "Not another one of those things again! It wasn't so bad when I was a lowly bureaucrat, but now that I'm supposed to be somebody, my absence is noticed. A church service is one thing, but with the events in the Hippodrome and all, it will take all day, and I have so much to catch up on!"

"Now, dear, you sound like one of those elderly senators. It will be fun, with the races and all! Anyhow, while I was at the palace, I ran into our friend Prefect Comnenus. Actually, he was looking for me with news—there has been another killing of a Varangian." Sophie said this in a quieter voice, seeing that Simon was still in the room.

Justin could only shake his head and mutter, "Oh, no!"

"That's the bad news. The good news is that I'm sure it's not related to the other ones."

"But how can you be so sure?"

"I knew you'd ask," smiled Sophie. "I was escorted to the scene—I could hear the murmurs of "Jarnlayden koma, Jarnlayden koma" even before I got out of the carriage—and inspected the body. Unlike the others, this poor man did not have his throat slit, but had been killed by a sword thrust to the stomach. There was also no mutilation of the face. And, the most important thing of all, he had not even been at the banquet, having been on guard duty elsewhere! No, he was killed for some other reason, by a right-handed man of medium height who carries a short stabbing sword and who is also red-haired. Also, he probably has scratch marks on his face or arms. I passed all of that on to our friend Siggurdsen and then came back here. All in a day's work, wouldn't you say?"

Justin could only shake his head and say, "For you, darling, it certainly is. I take it you found something on the victim's body to let you draw the conclusions about the hair and scratches?"

"Right you are, dear. The prefect seemed much relieved. With Siggurdsen, well, one never knows. Now, what do you have to tell me? Wait, I need some wine first."

Once that important need was met, Justin gave an account about his trip, albeit abbreviated in parts. Sophie shook her head in sympathy when Justin mentioned his occasional discomfort with the movement of the ship, recalling his same complaints two years earlier when they returned from Egypt. The details of the various meetings bored her, and she was beginning to wonder what wonderful news Justin could possibly have. Her ears pricked up when Justin mentioned going aboard the Arab ship and meeting the Caliph's half-sister.

"Sitt al-Mulk? Why didn't we ever see her in Cairo? She lives in the palace, I assume?"

Justin shrugged his shoulders. "I brought that up, but she merely put the responsibility on her brother, getting in one of the many little verbal digs she made at him during our conversation. Anyhow, I would have put it off to mere curiosity on her part about us, except for what happened on the last day I was there. Take a look at this!"

With a flourish, he pulled the ivory necklace out of the pouch it had come in and handed it to Sophie.

Puzzled, she nonetheless admired the workmanship, after which she said, "Thank you, dear, I didn't realize you had time to shop. It certainly is an unusual piece."

"You don't know the half of it. That necklace was left anonymously at my room the morning I was to leave. That, and a manuscript that I am still trying to get my head around. The first time I saw that necklace, it was around the neck of Sitt al-Mulk!"

Sophie's eyes widened. "That's amazing! Are you sure?"

Justin frowned but nodded. "Pretty sure. I wish you had been there—you have much better powers of observation than I do. I do know this—if it wasn't this necklace, it was one exactly like it. I remember noticing the elephant design and the lotus petals when she was wearing it."

Sophie examined the necklace again, and then surprised Justin by putting it up to her nose and sniffing deeply several times. "It was worn by someone, even if not her," she said. "I can still smell the jasmine. Well, husband, I must say I'm impressed—I've heard stories about sailors with a girl in every port, but you were only there a few days. That's fast work, even for you!" she concluded with a twinkle in her eyes.

"Ha-ha, very funny! This has got to be important, for why else would she go out of her way to make sure I knew it was hers?"

"Good point. It was clearly meant for your eyes, and no one outside her entourage would have any way to associate it with her, so there was no risk. That having been said, what's the message?"

Justin thought for a moment. "It must be the ivory, for I think we can rule out elephants or lotus flowers here in the city."

Sophie's eyes widened. "Another good point! I know there are merchants here who sell ivory, for I checked out some last week. Of course, they were only the Egyptian sellers, but it seemed like a good place to start. I'll go back this week and look for pieces like this one—maybe it's a common design. Well, dear, you did good! Now, as soon as I get a refill on my wine, you tell me the rest."

The delay was longer than anticipated, for shouts from the terrace alerted them that Maria was riding Poppy the pony through the kitchen garden, much to the distress of the cook, who was harvesting greens for the evening meal. As soon as this was sorted out, Simon came toddling by with a dead lizard, saying "boken, boken," or words to that effect. He was persuaded to swap the reptile for a cookie, after first having his hands scrubbed, and then it was time to go down for a nap. Sophie was finally able to sit back down, brush her dark hair back, and say with a smile, "All right, where were we?"

Justin returned the smile and continued his narrative. "Well, in addition to the necklace, there was also a manuscript left by the anonymous person. It's in Arabic, and I'm having a difficult time reading it. It appears to have been written by an Arabian scientist who I actually met on Crete, although he said nothing to me about any manuscript."

"What does it seem to be about?"

"In a word, light. What it is, how we perceive it, and so forth. Why it has any importance to us I really have no idea. While I can get the help of our groom Agatho and Maria's tutor Anwar to help translate it, even then I can't see the point."

Sophie frowned before continuing. "All right, let's analyze this. First, it had to be left with you for a reason. Second, it has to be related somehow to the necklace, in that they both relate to the same mystery. Third, from what you say of this scientist, he doesn't sound like the kind of person who would be devious enough to leave such a clue for you to find. The Lady Sitt, on the other hand, has survived long enough in the palace of her brother to be practiced in the arts of deception. I would assume both the necklace and the manuscript came from her. Tell me, from looking at it, does it seem to have been used much—are the pages bent or worn?"

"No, it looks completely new. Why is that important?"

"Not a lot, just perhaps another indication that it did not come from your scientist. Tell me, did he seem like a forthcoming sort?"

After a moment, Justin answered, "Yes, at least on the surface he didn't seem like a schemer. Still, that's another mystery—why send a scientist on a diplomatic mission?"

"Unless he was to meet someone else there."

"Exactly! Oh, he gave me some line about observing the summer solstice, but he could do that from anywhere."

"Well," concluded Sophie, "good luck on the translation. I can't help you now. That's quite a story, husband. Is that it?"

Justin shook his head. "No, there is one more thing, which will make things even more confusing. The last night I was there, after the banquet, I was sitting outside on a balcony, enjoying the sunset, when I heard voices. One of them was the scientist, al-Haytham, and the other was a deep-voiced man who spoke with a lisp."

"Could they see you?"

"No, I am sure they could not. In fact, I wanted to hear more, but I couldn't after they moved off. The scientist asked if 'it' was working, and the other man said that 'it' was. There was also talk about a 'thing' being provided, with the other man insisting that the use of the 'thing' was his concern alone. It was all very confusing."

Sophie considered this information, and then asked, "If we assume that this was not staged for your benefit, it has to be accurate. We just don't know what they were talking about. You were right, this doesn't really help, at least not now."

Justin sighed. "All right, dear. That is all I have. Please let me know you have some light to shine on our difficulties."

"Maybe. When I checked out some of the Egyptian merchants on the Mese, I had nothing to look for. Now, with this necklace, I can focus on the ivory dealers to see if they have pieces identical to or at least similar to this one. Maybe that will give us some leads. It's worth pursuing, don't you think?"

"Of course, although the death of Alexius' agent may have nothing to do with the death of the Varangians. Still, given what we know now, a return visit may be useful. Is that it?" Justin waited, his eyes fixed on Sophie.

The silence that followed spoke volumes. Finally, Sophie decided to answer indirectly. "I did look into another aspect of this matter, concerning 'Loviatar.' I still don't understand what it is we saw, for I will admit we saw something. Since I will never concede the existence of a pagan goddess here in the Virgin-protected city of the Romans, I have looked for other explanations. There was the experiment with Donna…"

"Has she recovered yet?"

"Oh, for the most part. Anyhow, something I saw in the face of 'Loviatar' did not look right to me. We all saw a woman, but I wasn't convinced. To me, it was like a man dressed as a woman, dressed very well mind you, but still not a woman. Anyhow, I mentioned this to Alexius and…"

"Oh, no, not him! Where in the world did he suggest?"

Undeterred, Sophie plowed ahead. "Alexius said that he could take me to a place here in the city where I might find answers about how our goddess looked."

With a resigned look on his face, Justin shrugged, "And I suppose that is just what he did?"

"Yes, and please let me tell you of our trip without interruptions and without judgment. But, first, I perceive we have an eavesdropper…" Turning quickly, she reached under the adjoining couch and pulled out a squealing Maria by the ear.

"Ow, Mama, I was just listening!"

"Yes, dear, and that is not a nice thing to do. You know that Papa and I work on problems for the emperors and Aunt Zoe, don't you?"

Crestfallen, Maria nodded.

"Very well, these are grown-up problems and you should not be hearing about them. This doesn't mean we don't love you, but we want to keep you safe, and some of these things are sad or dangerous." Seeing Maria on the verge of tears, Sophie tried another tack. "Tell you what, you go get Poppy, and you can ride him all around the grounds!"

"Even the garden?"

"Well, try to stay out of there—we need to be nice to Cook. Now, off you go!"

Justin, who had witnessed this in silence, could only smile and say, "We are all but putty in your hands!"

Sophie smiled and gave a half-bow. Then, clearing her voice, she said, "All right, here is what we found." Then she gave a complete and unabridged account of her trip to the cross-dresser club with Alexius, noticing as she did that Justin's eyes growing wider and wider. When she finished, she tried wrapping things up saying,

"Now, as I see it, we need to find this 'Daphne' or whatever her/his name is. What do you think?"

Justin collected his thoughts before speaking. Whirling around in his head were admiration for his wife in pursuing this line of inquiry, amazement and shock that such things existed in Constantinople, and confusion about how to proceed from here. Finally, after rubbing his brow, he said, "How did you even know of such a place? Oh wait, I remember, Alexius—that man knows people everywhere! You were brilliant, dear, to make that connection, but how are we going to ever find 'Daphne' when her, or his, or whatever, friends can't?"

"That's a problem, dear, I know. Maybe she's in jail?"

Justin shook his head. "I'm just a simple bureaucrat. How should I know?" Then, after a pause, he continued, "Still, I know people who may know. I am scheduled to meet with the prefect on Monday to give him an update on the Crete trip. That would be an excellent opportunity to find out who's in custody—that's under his jurisdiction. After that, I can go to the lock-up and see. But, Sophie, I have to ask, who are these people? Where do they go during the day?"

"Everywhere. They are just people. Maybe some are in the palace. Maybe some are in your office. Who knows? What does it matter? They are just trying to live like the rest of us. The real mystery is—where do they get their sense of fashion?" Concluding with this last flourish, she smiled and patted Justin on his arm.

Justin felt a sense of peace after moments of disorientation. "You would focus on that, wouldn't you? Still, Sophie, let's say that you are right. Let's say that 'Daphne' is somehow masquerading as 'Loviatar'—why would he, or she, do that, and more importantly, how was it done? You already tried that experiment with Donna."

"Ah, husband, I think you have me there. We still are missing more than a few pieces to this puzzle. Maybe this is important, maybe it means nothing. Still, I felt like I had to do something! Now, let's get off this and live like normal people. These problems will still be with us on Monday!"

The rest of the day passed peacefully. Justin spent some time in his study catching up with messages from Alexius and his other senior treasury assistants. Sophie met with Irene, who came by the villa to give an update on the gown-making process.

"I don't know what you did to get Leonida's help, but she's been great!" Irene gushed.

"Oh, it was nothing, nothing at all, really," Sophie replied with a smile.

Sunday was a normal day, although to Justin it may have been the calm before the storm. Sophie was engaged in her attendant duties to Zoe, who seemed more subdued than her usual self. While Justin wasn't able to discern this from where he was seated in Hagia Sophia, he could see the unusual sight of both emperors being in attendance. Basil looked the same, while Constantine appeared to have lost weight and appeared wan, but did make an effort to smile and wave when the services were over.

Later that night, when Sophie was coming to bed, she found Justin lying there, deep in thought. She waited until he felt like talking, then gave him a kiss.

This shook him out of his reverie. "Thank you, darling. I needed that. I was just thinking that, even if you were right about how and why the latest Varangian was killed, it may not make much difference to the rank and file soldiers. I see trouble ahead unless we get this matter resolved and soon."

"We will, dear, we will. The strings are in our hands. We only have to sort them out. After all, if we can't do it, who can? Good night."

CHAPTER 20

As Justin rode to the palace on Monday, he was accompanied by both his own thoughts and by his wife. Sophie insisted that she go with him to see the prefect, saying that she was on her way to see Zoe anyhow, and that she might be able to shed some light on the latest Varangian slaying. With the assurance that she stay only briefly, Justin consented. He had already spent a good deal of the previous evening thinking about how much, and how little, he would tell the prefect about his time on Crete. Also, with the 'Daphne' issue, now they had new concerns that needed to be addressed.

The couple walked through the outer halls of the Great Palace, taking turns in acknowledging salutations from various officials and foreign dignitaries. Among these were the western churchmen, who were apparently still in town for their negotiations. Several, including their leader Romanus, went out of their way to greet Justin in Italian, to which he responded in kind. When they reached the prefect's offices, they were met by Hetman Siggurdsen. While Justin could not understand the brief conversation that his wife and the Varangian had, he thought it went well, a feeling that was reinforced by Sophie who, before they went into the prefect's office, put her left finger beside her nose with a wink.

When they were ushered into Prefect Comnenus' office, Justin was surprised to see that the older man was not alone, for Senator Kalokyros had beaten them there. While Justin had a fleeting hope that the senator was only there for a social call, such hopes were quickly extinguished. After the prefect welcomed them (saying nothing about Sophie's presence), the senator asked in a sneering voice, "Yet another Varangian is dead and you and your wife have no solution, do you?"

Justin considered letting Sophie take the lead in response, but an exchange of another look with her let him go forward. "Good morning to you too, Senator, and to you, Prefect. As it happens, we do have a suspect in the latest killing, which we believe to be unrelated to the others. In that I had no part in this, I will let my wife take things from here."

Sophie was never more in her element than in that moment, for she was fully in possession of facts that would make the senator look foolish. Given her breeding and intelligence, however, she let him down gently.

"Thank you, husband. I did look into this matter on Saturday, when we were alerted to it, and passed my findings on to Hetman Siggurdsen, namely that the murderer was right-handed, red-haired, of medium height and had scratch marks on his hands or arms. I now have been informed that an arrest has been made on these grounds. Hetman?" she concluded with a look in his direction.

The Varangian, dealing with a strange people in a strange land, nevertheless acquitted himself well. "Thank you, Lady Sophia. Yes, I am able to report that we have apprehended a Varangian who fit the description which you gave us, a man named Sweyn. He has now confessed to the crime. He is from the same village as the dead man, and tracked him here after the dead man killed his brother in a blood feud. Under our law, Sweyn was entitled to take his vengeance, assuming he could paid wergild to the dead man's relatives. He now has paid that amount, and so will be free to go."

At the end of this matter-of-fact pronouncement, the veins on Senator Kalokyros' neck bulged alarmingly. "You can't do that! This man committed murder! He must be punished!" he exclaimed.

After exchanging glances, Justin and Sophie looked together to the prefect, who sighed and addressed the enraged official. "Actually, Senator, the Varangians are subject to their own laws when it comes to their own people. If Sweyn had killed a Roman citizen, he would be subject to our laws. As it is, the hetman is correct. I think this matter is closed, thanks to the insights of Lady Sophia. Thank you, Lady," he finished with a nod to Sophie, who returned it with a slight smile.

"You'll hear about this, I promise you!" the senator muttered as his parting shot before he left. Impassive as ever, Siggurdsen took his leave as well, thanking the Iron Lady for all of her help. As he left, after making sure the senator was gone, he said, "This does not end things—the men are unsettled."

"Even Mondays are interesting with you two around," the prefect said, shaking his head after they had left his office. "What is it going to be next?"

Justin paused before speaking, "Uh, sir, I would like to talk to you about the Crete trip—everything went well, by the way—and another matter. First, though, my wife and I have some concerns about the events tomorrow. Is it still the plan to have Emperor Constantine lead the procession into the Hippodrome after the races?"

Prefect Comnenus looked surprised as he answered. "Yes, as far as I know. That is the way things have been done for many years, well before I became prefect. The emperor was quite a fine horseman in his youth, and this is one of the few chances the people of the city have to see him ride. Is there a problem?"

Now it was Sophie's turn to take up the refrain. "Prefect, it's no secret that Emperor Constantine has not been well recently. It's also no secret, at least here in the palace, that he has a drinking problem. We're simply afraid there may be another incident like the one at the recent banquet, only this time it will be witnessed by tens of thousands of people. Confidence in the royal family is a precious thing. Once lost, it is very difficult to get back."

"Lady Sophia, believe me, I do share your concerns. I am in regular contact with the royal chamberlain, who assures me that the emperor is making a conscious effort to cut back on his drinking. He is also being watched by members of his household, and so far the process is working, although the emperor is not very happy about it. Besides, the process will be in the middle of the afternoon—surely even Emperor Constantine will be sober at that point in the day?" Comnenus replied, although Justin thought that there was not much conviction in the older man's voice.

Sophie sighed and said, "Well, thank you for hearing our concerns. I only hope you are right. Now I must go and tend to Princess Zoe. She has a big day tomorrow, too. See you tonight, dear." She rose, gave Justin a kiss, and swept from the room. She found a scene of bustling activity in Zoe's quarters, for the princess loved appearing before the public, both in the Hagia Sophia and in the Hippodrome, where she and the rest of the royal family would watch the procession and the races which came before them from the royal box. Everything had to be just right, and even some of the experienced women were feeling the strain.

"Oh, good, you're here," said Irene. "For some reason, Leonida from Theodora's household has been looking for you and insists on seeing only you. She's waiting in the wardroom for you. She seems very agitated for some reason."

Sophie reassured her long-time assistant. "I'm sure it will be fine. I will see her right now."

'Agitated' did not really do Leonida justice thought Sophie. The younger woman looked extremely stressed, but composed herself when she saw Sophie. She went to one of the work tables, unwrapped a package, and wordlessly pointed to the contents.

Inside was a gown of green, blue and purple. It was trimmed with silver, as was the stole that flowed down from the tiara that Zoe would wear. It was in a word stunning, even to Sophie, who had made a career out of designing clothes for the rich and famous, albeit with a very limited clientele.

"Leonida," Sophie said, "this is wonderful. Thank you so much!"

A wave of relief washed over Leonida's face. "Oh, I'm so glad! I hope this is enough to keep my secret?"

At this, Sophie was moved to give her counterpart a big hug. "It's our secret, Leonida, our secret! I think that this will be the beginning of a beautiful friendship!"

So it was that when Irene came into the room a few minutes later, she found the two of them laughing and talking like old friends, sharing tips and stories about outfitting their royal mistresses. While she felt she was intruding, she finally spoke, "Excuse me, Sophie, but Zoe was inquiring for you."

Leonida then departed after another hug from Sophie. After Irene witnessed this without comment, Sophie shrugged her shoulders and said, "It's an old family saying—keep your friends close and your rivals closer. Let's hope it works."

When Sophie was shown into Zoe's chambers, it was obvious that the princess was under stress herself. Given what Sophie had seen of her father's condition, this was no surprise. She patted her friend's hand, listened to her worries, and said a few prayers herself for the coming day.

Meanwhile, Justin had given the prefect a (mostly) complete version of the events on Crete. He did feel it significant to include his interview with the caliph's sister, but he did not disclose the subsequent gifts he had received, presumably from her. The prefect found this information interesting, but seemed more focused on Justin's relations with the eastern churchmen, taking notes as Justin spoke.

"I'll have to make a report of this to the patriarch," he sighed. "Patriarch Sergius is always very careful to make sure that he is <u>the</u> Ecumenical Patriarch, and won't like any news that these other prelates are improving their lot. Still, thank you for this news—it was very valuable, and not something one would expect to get from the Treasurer of the Empire."

While the prefect's comments helped solidify Justin's already low opinion of Patriarch Sergius, he let the matter pass without comment. There was something else to deal with of more importance, and it was time to bring it up.

"Prefect, I don't need to tell you that, apart from the official duties that my wife and I deal with, there is another matter which we have been commissioned to investigate, namely the murder of the Varangian soldiers. While my wife, using her God-given talents, was able to resolve the most recent one, the Empire does still have a very significant problem—these soldiers that we rely on are being killed and not at random, and they are getting very nervous, as you heard today. I need you to do something unusual for me, and I need you to do it without asking why. Will there be a problem, sir?"

For a moment, Justin's heart sank. Then, against all odds, the prefect laughed. "Problem? For the man who burnt the caliph's fleet? For the man, despite his youth, has turned the treasury of the Empire into a money-making machine? For the man, who, with his incomparable wife, solves all mysteries? No, I don't think so. But, there is one problem."

Watching Justin sit frozen in suspense, the prefect laughed again. "You have to quit calling me 'sir'! You are the Treasurer of the Roman Empire—a senior official, despite your youth—you need to act like it. When we're alone here together, we are equals—I am Leo, you are Justin. I've given you two years to figure this out, so do we have an understanding?"

Hoping that he wasn't sweating on the outside, Justin could only smile and nod. "That would be find, s___, uh, Leo. I would like that."

"Good. What do you need?"

So it was that Justin soon walked out of the prefect's office with an order that let him enter any jail in the city, interrogate any prisoner, and, most importantly, have any of them released. The prefect had taken the precaution of using both his seal and that of the emperors', of which he had possession, in order to avoid any bureaucrat questioning Justin's authority. While he didn't really know what he would do with such power, he was thrilled to have it at his disposal.

When he went to his office, he found the staff very eager to hear about his trip to Crete. The clerks who had sailed with him to monitor the money chests had already come back and told their stories, but that was nothing like hearing it from the 'Boss' himself. Justin thanked everyone for their hard work, told them what a success the trip had been, and encouraged them to keep up the good work, in that such trips would be very likely to become a regular event in the future.

After entering his private office, he heard a knock on the door, followed by the entrance of Alexius. Justin said nothing, but motioned him to sit. The men said nothing for a few moments, before Alexius cleared his throat and spoke.

"Good morning, Boss. Have a good trip?" When Justin said nothing but only stared at him, Alexius tried again. "Ah, I suppose your wife told you about our little trip to the club? I hope that wasn't a problem? She had questions, and I thought I might have answers. Are we good with that?"

Keeping his recent experience with the prefect in mind, Justin did not leave his long-time assistant in suspense. With a sigh he said, "Of course, we're good, Deputy! Still, we would not be, if you had sent her in there by herself. As it is, we may be on to something. Yet, I have to ask you, how do you know of such places?"

At this, Alexius closed his eyes, and then, after opening them, composed his bland face. "Boss, you are a very smart man, and you know a lot about the things you know about. But, there are a lot of things that you don't know about, and that is where I come in. I have to ask you to trust me in this—you don't ask, and I don't tell. All right?"

"All right, provided you never, ever put my wife in danger. Now, you need to tell me about another thing I don't know about, namely the city jails. You do know about those, I assume?"

While Alexius paused only a moment before replying, for him that was like an eternity. "Sure, Boss, but is this on the level? You want to know about the jails?"

"Yes, Sophie has told me about 'Daphne' and his, I mean her, or whatever, disappearance. It may be that the law has gotten involved, for I can't think that this kind of behavior, however harmless it may be, can possibly be legal. Maybe she's being held on some morals charge. Anyhow, it's worth a try. Now, do you know where to look?"

Alexius grimaced as he replied, "I'm afraid I do, and it is a very vile place. Perhaps you had better let me make inquiries first."

"Alexius, I am touched, I really am. You think I can't handle myself? Well, with you by my side, and this authorization from the prefect himself, I will fear no evil. Now, let's go!"

So it was that the treasurer and the deputy treasurer of the Roman Empire were in a coach travelling to the very southwestern corner of the city, heading towards what was called the Golden Gate because of its elaborate ornamentation. Here, at the end of the Theodosian Walls, armies had sallied forth for centuries to fight Goths, Huns, Bulgars, Slavs, Russians and others, sometimes returning in triumph, sometimes not. For decades, now that the danger of invasion from Europe had diminished, part of the fortress had been converted into a jail that held prisoners charged with lesser offences, including crimes against public morals. Those who could pay the fine for such offenses were soon released, while others lingered for months.

Justin assumed that anyone assigned to be in charge of such a place would be less than attentive to his duties, and so it proved. Although it was still early afternoon, the warden was already drunk, and had a hard time focusing on the purpose of Justin's visit. During the ride to the prison, Alexius had urged Justin to dismiss any thought of asking for 'Daphne' when they arrived. Instead, only the name 'Matthew' should be used, as it was the one that Sophie had been able to derive from those at the club.

Glad that he was wearing his official robes, Justin confronted the bleary-eyed bureaucrat with all the majesty of Rome. The order he had from the prefect didn't hurt either, and within a few minutes he and Alexius were escorted into the prison, on the pretext of conducting an 'efficiency' investigation. Despite what Alexius had warned him about, what Justin saw (and smelled) made him want to vomit. Whatever their offenses, men should not be kept in semi-darkness, some in chains, with wretched food, non-existent sanitation and constant brutality. Justin made a vow that, whatever the outcome of this investigation, this would not continue.

Still, at the moment, he was taken aback. Seeing this, Alexius intervened.

"All right, Boss, here's how we'll do it. You make a speech, and I'll make connections."

Justin was more than ready to comply, and so he called all of the officials, guards and trustees together in order to thank them for their service. Meanwhile, Alexius went over to the various cells and talked with inmates. Thankfully for Justin, who was running out of fulsome things to say, Alexius gave him a wave, and the speech came to an abrupt close. Justin then came over to where Alexius was meeting with a nervous, pale-looking man. "Matthew?" he asked.

"No," the man whispered, "my name is Michael." After a look to Alexius, who gave him a nod, he continued, "I am also known as Michaela."

Justin replied, "I understand completely. If that is the offense that you are here about, I do not care. I am seeking information about another person, who may be called 'Matthew' or 'Daphne', in connection with multiple murders in the city. Can you help me?"

The man's pale face got even paler, if that was possible. "No, sir, she is not here—I have seen her perform at the club, and she is marvelous, but she is not here. It has been several weeks since I last saw her—she was very excited, said that a foreign gentleman had offered her an acting job, but nothing after that. Please, can you get me out of here?"

After exchanging glances with Alexius, Justin nodded. Then, inspired to do more, he said, "And if there are others here who face the same charges you do, they may go, too. Understand this—there must be no one accused of anything involving children, all right?"

In a few minutes, no less than eight men were escorted out of the jail following Justin and Alexius. Before they split up, Justin urged them to let him know, through Alexius, if they had any news about Daphne. Amid a chorus of "Thank you, sir," "God bless you, sir," and "Will do, sir," they went their separate ways.

On the way back to the palace, Alexius looked at Justin with new appreciation. "Good for you, Boss! You're not as naïve as I thought!"

"Thanks, I think!" Justin laughed.

"Oh, one more thing," Alexius continued. "Tomorrow, take Neptune in the third horse race—I don't care what the odds are, take Neptune. You can thank me later."

That night, sitting on the veranda and watching the evening lights come in the houses across the Golden Horn, Justin and Sophie talked over the events of the day.

After hearing Justin's account, Sophie could only say, "Well, tomorrow can't possibly be any more interesting than today was!"

CHAPTER 21

Tuesday dawned clear and warm, although there was a hint in the air of a change coming. That day, June 24, was the Feast Day of the Nativity of St. John the Baptist, who was also often referred to as the Forerunner. That term, for whatever reason, had given rise to the tradition that a full day of horse races would be held at the Hippodrome following the services across the street in the Hagia Sophia. While the day itself was only one of many Great Feast Days on the church calendar, it was special if for no other reason than the common people actively joined in. While Easter was solemn and Christmas was held when the weather was usually cold and rainy, St. John's Day, as it was popularly known, was held to be a day of good luck, when marriage proposals could be made, and a day when bonfires could be lit in neighborhoods without prosecution.

Smoke from some of the early fires was wafting through the air when Justin and Maria went to Hagia Sophia. As they drove, Justin was torn between joy in spending time with his daughter, and regret that he was missing time from his duties, both official and unofficial. Back in the days when he did not hold a leading position, he could often get out of attending a feast day, of which there were no less than 17 on the church calendar. As Deputy Treasurer, this was always true, for under his predecessor, Treasurer Taronites, Justin ran the department in everything but name. Now, though his burden was even greater with the Alethia Society thrown in, his presence as Treasurer was required and there was no escape.

Fortunately, at the points in the service where his mind would wander off, Maria was always at his elbow, whispering, "Stand," "Sit," "Nod," or "Recite," as was required. While few noticed, those that did uniformly applauded the child's piety, and more than one congratulated Justin after the service, to which he would smile and nod. Now that Maria was ten years old, and possessed of patience beyond her years, she was to be his companion at such services from now on, or at least as long as Sophie continued to wait on Zoe. As a reward for her good conduct, she was going to the races, something she had been talking about for days. Today, they would join Sophie in the royal box as she attended Zoe. It would be Maria's closest approach yet to Emperor Basil, and she had promised to be on her best behavior.

Maria had already given promise of her resolve in this regard, for she had always refrained from waving to her mother when she saw her attending Zoe in the princess' box in church. Although very astute for a girl of nine, she did not take notice of Zoe's gown, something which was very much on her mother's mind. For that matter, her father did not take notice either, for as a man he gave little attention to such matters.

For Sophie, things were on a slightly elevated level. While she knew from her own reaction to Leonida's creation that the ensemble would be perceived as being new, she really did not know how Zoe would react beyond that. As a royal princess, Zoe had worn thousands of different outfits over the past twenty years, and while she would be hard-pressed to name her ancestors in the Macedonian dynasty, she had no trouble in recalling a gown she had worn eleven years ago for the Feast of the Dedication of the Holy Cross. So, for Sophie the reaction of her royal mistress to this year's St. John Feast Day gown was important. Sophie was aware, as was her husband, that the governing structure of the empire was illogical, but it was what she had to deal with.

So, it was with more than a little anxiety that she encountered Zoe as the princess entered the church. Leonida's design, as tweaked by Sophie, was stunning, and Sophie immediately thought that she had set the bar too high for future events. Then, reminding herself of who she was dealing with, she smiled, curtsied, and said, "Marvelous, Highness!"

Zoe, every inch in her element, nodded in turn and said, "Ah, Lady Sophia, you have outdone yourself! Finally we are keeping up with the times!" gesturing as she spoke to have Sophie follow her into the church.

Sophie curtsied again as she fell into place and murmured, "Princess, you have no idea!"

After the service, conducted as it had been for centuries, concluded, Zoe and her entourage made their way to the connecting passageway which stretched over the road between the Great Palace and the Hippodrome. There waiting for them were Justin and Maria. Maria, after first giving a proper curtsey to Zoe, then hugged her mother, to the approval of all present. Theodora and her household were there as well, along with the prefect, the president of the senate, and several other high-ranking royal officials. In that all of them were either older, like the prefect, or eunuchs like the royal chamberlain, the presence of Maria was noteworthy. While the assembled dignitaries awaited the arrival of Emperor Basil, Justin excused himself, saying that he needed to check on how the betting operation was going downstairs.

The answer, as he soon found, was very well. Levi Ben-Isaacson was Justin's deputy in charge of the betting windows at the track, and the clerks were working as fast as they could to take peoples' bets on the days' contests, which included three chariot races and six horse races. Church officials, led by the patriarch, had initially objected to such immoral practices (despite betting having gone on for centuries) until their share of the proceeds restored several churches and monasteries in the city. Emperor Basil had been pleased too, when an additional cavalry brigade and four new warships could be added to the budget.

"Good work, Levi!" Justin said to his smiling assistant.

"Oh, you are very welcome, Treasurer. This is always one of our best days of the year!"

After looking around to check that no one was watching, Justin gave Levi a gold solidus. "Look, if it's not too much trouble, I'd like to put a bet down on a horse in the third race—Neptune, I think it is."

Surprised, Levi nonetheless took the coin and motioned Justin aside to an empty betting window. Waving to a clerk inside, he instructed that the bet be placed, and gave Justin a receipt. "10 to 1 odds—pretty impressive, Treasurer! I had no idea that you were a betting man!"

"Ha-ha," Justin tried a forced laugh. "I'm just feeling lucky today. Thanks. I'll see you at the staff meeting on Friday, all right?"

After they had left, the clerk who had taken the bet motioned to one of his fellows. "Did you see that? It was the Treasurer of the Empire putting a bet on this horse! It must be a sure thing!"

"Oh, yeah?" said his skeptical co-worker. "If it was such a sure deal, why didn't he bet more? And if you're so sure, why don't you bet your month's salary on that nag!"

Stung by the challenge, the clerk responded, "All right, I will! Here goes!"

Returning to the royal box, Justin found Sophie and Maria seated behind Zoe, whose attendants were on her right, with Theodora and her ladies seated to Zoe's left. In the center was of course Basil, who looked less grim than usual. In fact, unless it was Justin's imagination, the emperor actually acknowledged Justin's bow and Maria's curtsey with a nod and the faintest glimmer of a smile.

As Treasurer, Justin was entitled to his own box, but he had made a deal with the royal chamberlain to let his seats go to some of his assistants, so that he could sit with his family. Alexius, true to form, would rather have been caught dead than be found in such a situation. Justin's assistants, to the contrary, were thrilled, and Justin had the pleasure of seeing all of them, minus Levi, taking in the sights.

Joining his family, he watched Maria's gaze of wide-eyed wonder as she gazed at the Hippodrome. First constructed in the reign of Septimus Severus, almost a thousand years before when the city was known as Byzantium, it was enlarged by Constantine, when he declared the city to be the new capital of Rome. Directly across a broad avenue from the Great Palace, it was connected to that structure by a bridge so that the royal family could make their appearance in the imperial box without showing themselves to the populace. Once there, the emperor or emperors could appear as he or they chose, particularly at the climax of processions of saints. Before then, horse and chariot races could go forward, cheered on by the factions of the city, whether green, blue or otherwise. Capacity was 50,000, and the stands looked full today. With the emperors in attendance, there were purple hangings all around the arena.

Now, Maria's attention was focused on the scene before her. "Papa," she said, "what are those things in the middle of the track?"

Smiling as he recalled his first experience at the races, Justin replied, "Those tall pillars are called obelisks, which were brought here from Egypt. The figure in the middle is from Greece, and is a column holding a tripod supported by three snakes. It was brought here by the first Emperor Constantine from Delphi. Before our Emperor Constantine comes out today, there will be races, both by horse riders and by chariots. The statutes around the top are those of famous riders and horses from the past, with the four bronze horses over the entrance where the emperor will ride in leading the procession."

Sophie, who had witnessed this with pleasure, then added, "That's right, dear. The horses go two times around, while the chariots, which have four horses, go four laps. People will clap and applaud loudly if they have a favorite horse to win."

Maria, trying to soak the experience in, then asked, "Do you or Papa want any horse or team to win?"

"No, Maria, we're above that. Aren't we, dear?" she said to Justin with a raised eyebrow.

After a pause, Justin answered, "Of course we are, of course! Here they come!"

The races that followed were exciting even to non-bettors, as the horses and chariots thundered around the oval track in their individual races. Maria was taken in by it all, although she could not help but notice that her father seemed to be interested in a horse called 'Neptune' in one race, standing and clapping while it ran. When it won, he seemed to be very happy, although her mother said nothing and narrowed her eyes.

The roar of the crowd grew even louder when it came time for Emperor Constantine to enter, followed by monks on foot carrying icons of John the Baptist and the winning riders and chariots. While he had done this for years, it was one of the few times he could be the focus of attention, and he still prized it. An accomplished horseman in his youth, he still enjoyed riding in the country, although his hunting days were well behind him.

Many trumpets then announced their entrance. Constantine rode in first, holding up a sword which symbolized the means by which John was martyred. He entered and then rode slowly around the arena followed by the others, with the plan being to end up in front of the royal box. Given what they had seen of Constantine at the recent banquet, both Justin and Sophie had their eyes trained on the emperor as he rode.

It was not long before Sophie, leaning across Maria, whispered to Justin, "He looks pale, doesn't he? And look at him sweat!"

Justin nodded in agreement. The day, while sunny, was not a particularly hot one. Still, he thought, Constantine did not have far to go. His attempt to excuse the evidence of his eyes was shortly defeated, though, as the emperor appeared to sway in the saddle as he reached the half-way point and turn back toward them. By now, the crowd had noticed this, too, and a low murmur could clearly be heard. Casting a sidelong glance at Basil, Justin's fears were confirmed, for the senior emperor was twisting his beard furiously, a sure sign of disapproval.

Constantine continued doggedly on and finally made a full circuit of the race course. Just as it appeared that he had completed his task, he gave one final lurch and fell off his horse, as if in slow-motion, onto the ground. For one brief moment, the vast arena was silent, only to be pierced by a cry coming from Theodora of "Papa!"

Several things then happened. Zoe, against all expectations, took the mature step of putting her hand across her hysterical sister's mouth and shushing her. Attendants in the area rushed forward and gave everyone in the royal box a sign that Constantine was alive although unconscious. For an instant, Basil let his human side show as he planted his face in his hands. Control was reasserted quickly, however, as he gave orders that his brother be carried back to the palace. He also directed the royal chamberlain to have trumpets blown again and an announcement made that Emperor Constantine was weary from his many official duties and there was no cause for alarm. Finally, as he rose to leave with his nieces and everyone else rose in deference to them, he motioned for Justin and Sophie to follow them back. Sophie quickly arranged with Irene to take charge of Maria, and they hurried to catch up, being passed on the run by the Varangians guards who were likewise caught off guard.

When they arrived at the portion of the palace used by Constantine, they were ushered in without question. There, as after the banquet, Sophie found the royal family and numerous attendants present along with several palace physicians who fluttered about like large bearded bats. It was all new to Justin, whose attention was drawn to the prostrate form of the junior emperor of the Roman Empire, who was stretched out fully clothed on his bed. Zoe and Theodora clung to one another on one side of the bed, while Basil, looking every bit his 58 years stood near his brother's side across from them. Among others present was the waspish-looking younger man who had confronted Sophie when Constantine had had his first collapse. She had put him in his place then, and from the look he shot her, he had not forgotten. '*There is something about him,*' she thought, '*that I just do not like.*'

After staring down at his brother for a few moments, Basil gathered himself, looked around the room, and in a voice of command said, "We wish all to exit with the exception of our nieces, Treasurer Cataphlates, the Lady Sophia, and our royal chamberlain. You may go!" Once the room was clear, following some muffled protests from the physicians, Basil looked at Sophie and made an amazing request.

"Lady Sophia, we are aware of your powers of observation, as demonstrated many times in the past. Would you be so kind as to examine our brother?"

Thinking this was the first time she had examined someone who was still alive, Sophie nodded and began. True to form, she talked to herself loud enough for everyone to hear as she worked.

"Subject is male, early 50's, somewhat overweight and not in the best physical shape…"

At this, Justin shot a glance at Basil, and could have sworn he saw a slight smile.

"Breathing is shallow, but regular. Pulse is also regular but weak. Skin is clammy and pale. Pupils are somewhat dilated. There is no smell of alcohol on the subject's breath, but…" here Sophie paused as she held her face close to Constantine's, "but there is a smell of something that is not food."

At this point, she asked for a piece of paper. After some fumbling, the chamberlain produced one, which she used to catch some brown flecks from the unconscious man's mustache. Unlike Basil, who kept his beard close-cropped as befitting a man who served in the field, Constantine's was full, including his mustache, although beginning to be flecked with gray. Sophie looked at these closely, then carefully folded up the paper and handed it to Justin.

Turning to Basil to give her report, she first curtseyed and then did so to the royal princesses, who stood, white-faced, holding each other.

"*Nice touch*," thought Justin.

Drawing herself up to her full height, Sophie began, "Majesty, I do not find that your brother is intoxicated. However, I do not know why he is unconscious or why he collapsed, although there is an indication of some substance that I am unfamiliar with. His physical condition is not good, and he needs care. If I may be so bold, I would recommend that he be placed under the care of one single physician who has your Majesty's confidence, and that person be my father, Lukas Lascaris, who is well known to you from years of past service."

"*Well played, dear! You've outdone yourself!*" Justin marveled.

Basil looked at Sophie for what seemed to be an eternity without speaking. Zoe, finally yielding to her nerves, broke the silence.

"Please, uncle, summon Doctor Lascaris back! I know he can help Father!"

Resuming the familiar role of a man of action, Basil replied, "Yes, Zoe, we agree—chamberlain, take the following order!" He then directed that Lukas Lascaris, now in charge of an imperial leprosarium near Prusa, be recalled to the capital for an indefinite period of time, subject to their majesties' pleasure, in order to provide care to the royal family. Such order was to be delivered immediately, via the fastest messenger. Upon his arrival, he was to attend Emperor Constantine at the Blachernae Palace, where the emperor was to take a rest cure for as long as necessary.

Although Justin expected that this would end matters for the evening, Sophie was not content to let things go at that.

"Many pardons, Majesty, but if I might suggest something more?" she said.

Basil's eyes opened a bit wider for just a moment, as if it had been a long time he had been so addressed. Without speaking, he gestured her to continue.

"Well, it seems to me, Majesty, that in order for my father to have the best chance to help the emperor, my father needs to have control over who has access to him. I think your order should give him authority to do just that."

"A wise decision, Lady, consider it done." Then, after a pause, the senior emperor of the Romans asked. "Is there anything else?"

Without missing a beat, Sophie replied, "Yes, until my father arrives, someone needs to have that authority."

"And that would be, we suppose, you?"

"If it please your Majesty, I would be honored to do so."

"Then it is so ordered. Now, we suggest we let the emperor rest."

On the way home, Justin was still raving about his wife's boldness in her dealings with Basil. She was dismissive, saying that someone had to do it. After a pause, though, she did say in a lower voice, "You realize now that we are neck deep in not one but two mysteries. I hope we can handle them."

Justin laughed, "Dear, if I was neck deep in anything, I would want to be in it with you!"

Sophie shook her head. "Something's going on, I feel it. Do you still have that paper I gave you with the brown flecks? Good, let me have it, it may be important!"

CHAPTER 22

Wednesday found Sophie busy supervising the relocation of Emperor Constantine to the Blachernae Palace at the far end of the city. She had planned to spend at least part of the day back on the Mese, checking out ivory dealers, and had even arranged for Irene and the newest lady-in-waiting, Julia, to go with her. But since she had put herself in the position of temporary supervisor on Tuesday night, that trip had to be put off until tomorrow. Today's problems would be daunting enough, for she had to transport a weakened, if not actually disabled, emperor across Constantinople along a four mile route using busy city streets.

She had given considerable thought to the matter before she even entered Zoe's quarters, and had sent orders ahead to Irene. Her trusted second-in-command was waiting for her, and, much to Sophie's relief, was able to give a good status report.

"Good morning, Sophie! I did as you said and got the royal chamberlain to find the spare wagon that was built for the pilgrimage that you took with Zoe two years ago. It wasn't as nice as the finished one that you ended up using, but for a brief trip it should be fine. The craftsmen have given it a fresh coat of purple paint with red and yellow trim, and the emperor should be able to rest comfortably inside. There is one problem, however, or should I say two."

"While I bet I can guess the answer," Sophie replied with a sigh, "go ahead and tell me."

"Well, you see, it's the royal sisters. They insist on accompanying their father, although I think Theodora in particular has calmed down from where she was yesterday. I told them the final decision was up to you, given the authority you received from Emperor Basil, and they seemed to be all right with that. Still," Irene paused with a slight smile, "I would like to be in the room if you tell them no."

Sophie shuddered. "That would be called winning a battle and losing the war. No, they'll go, but on my terms. Where are they?"

"In Zoe's inner chambers. They're having their devotions with their father confessors—strength in numbers, I guess. They should be about finished."

"And Constantine? What's his status?"

"He had a restless night, I'm told, but is doing better now. Whatever hit him yesterday hit him hard."

"Well done Irene. Sorry about the shopping trip—we'll try again tomorrow. Today, you can take a ride with me to the Blachernae. Oh, here come the fathers. I guess prayer time is over."

Irene did get to be present when Sophie confronted the princesses about taking the trip. While Zoe at least appeared to be ready to argue about a negative decision, Sophie did not give her the opportunity.

"Good morning, Highness," Sophie said with a curtsey, using the more formal style of address she employed when others were present. "And you, Princess Theodora. I can only imagine your feelings during this trying time, and know you want to be with your father as much as his condition allows. So, as his temporary custodian, I have decided that you can accompany him to the Blachernae Palace today, but only under one condition."

Zoe looked at Sophie with tired eyes that not even her make-up could entirely disguise. "Thank you, Lady Sophia, I can speak for my sister when I say that we are both under your direction. What do you require?"

"Only that you two ride inside the wagon, unaccompanied by your retinues, and wearing the kind of cloaks you wore the other night to the Varangians' banquet hall. The trip today is not about you, but about your father, and the best trip for him will be one that is quick and quiet. Is that acceptable?"

"Entirely so. May the Virgin bless this day!"

So it was that sometime later the gates on one of the side doors of the Great Palace swung open and a procession emerged. Despite Sophie's hopes for a 'quick and quiet' trip, imperial protocol could not be so easily overridden. After seeing his brother loaded into the wagon, Emperor Basil, in full armor, gave the signal to depart with a gesture to Sophie, who was seated on the front of the wagon with the driver. She in turn waved a blue scarf to the doormen, who opened the gates and let the mounted troops go first, followed by the Varangians, who each carried the signature axe of such troops. Following Constantine's wagon were two more, containing his household staff and the emperor's possessions for his stay away from the great Palace, which was not shaping up to be a short one. In that more troops followed the wagons, any hope of anonymity was lost.

Prior to Basil's arrival, one incident occurred which had been engineered by Sophie. As Constantine's household staff was loading the wagons, she spotted the sharp-faced young man who had given her uneasy feelings before. Summoning the royal chamberlain, Sophie directed that the man not accompany them. Though voices were raised and arms waved, her order was followed. As the man was escorted out, he shot Sophie a glance that would have curdled milk. On impulse, she waved good-bye. The gesture she got in return was not a wave, but did allow her to notice that the man was missing the fourth finger on his right hand.

What followed after they entered the plaza between the palace and Hagia Sophia was unexpected, at least to Sophie. Rather than have to deal with crowded streets, they found the boulevards virtually empty, but lined with the people of the city who stood quietly to let the procession pass. The great forums were likewise empty, and they moved steadily along the Mese, first passing St. Polyeuktos and then coming to the great Church of the Apostles, in which many emperors had been interred. From time to time, Sophie looked back into the wagon where Zoe and Theodora were seated by their semi-conscious father, who did not seem to be in any distress. Irene was seated on the other side, and gave Sophie encouraging looks.

Eventually they approached the great land walls constructed centuries before which had saved the city from invaders on numerous occasions during the earlier, darker years. Now that the empire's foes (or at least the open ones) were all far away, the towers that lined the walls had become unused, and were now occupied with shops or used as storehouses. However, before reaching the walls, the procession turned right to pass the Chora Monastery, now a temporary home to the delegation from Rome, and then eventually reached the sprawling Blachernae Palace complex.

While less extensive than the Great Palace, it was still an extensive area of many palaces, churches, halls and other buildings, including extensive stables. Directly next to the land walls, some of the buildings looked out over the green countryside that stretched beyond, where Constantine in the past had gone riding and hunting. Once Sophie was satisfied that the emperor had been moved into his chambers and was comfortable, she was on the point of leaving when a eunuch approached her with a message of thanks from Constantine. Sophie looked at the man curiously, for he seemed familiar.

With a shy smile, the man said, "Yes, Lady, we've met, but it was at a certain club and I looked a little different. It is good to see you again. Any progress on 'Daphne'?"

Sophie suppressed her surprise, and answered, "Not much yet, but we have some leads. We will be sure to let all of you know."

"Thank you. We all appreciate what you're doing. Oh, there is one more thing before you leave. I have a bag here from the man you had removed, who, I must say, nobody liked. What should I do with it?"

Seized by a sudden inspiration, Sophie said, "I'll take it. Have it loaded into my carriage—I think it should be here now." Suppressing an urge to look through it on the way back to the villa, Sophie thought, *'Well, that's one problem solved, for whatever good it will do.'*

Justin had gone to his office earlier that morning, where he was greeted by his staff with cries of 'Who do you like in the second?' and 'What about Whirlwind in the fourth?" His heart sinking, his fears were confirmed when Levi approached him with a pouch containing ten gold solidi.

"Here you are, Treasurer!" Levi said with a bow. "Don't spend it all in one place! That horse was the long-shot of the races but you certainly picked it. Fortunately, hardly anyone else did, so we had a profitable day, apart from one of my clerks who bet a month's salary on Neptune. Suffice it to say I am now in the market for a new clerk, for the winner gave his notice that day."

To make Justin's morning complete, who joined in the merriment but Alexius, who had given Justin the tip in the first place. "Betting on horses, Treasurer? I'm shocked, shocked!"

At this, even Justin had to laugh. Recovering, he put on his official face. "All right, everyone, back to work! And you, Deputy, in my office now, or your next assignment will be escorting money to rebuild churches in Ethiopia!"

Soon, the irrepressible eunuch entered Justin's office. It was another warm, clear June day, and Justin always enjoyed watching the ships sailing in and out of the harbors to the west of his office. After his recent journey, he found that he disliked sailing less than he had before, and was already thinking of a trip to Thessalonica, the city where he had been born but not seen in many years. But, there were things to do here and now that could not be put off. So, he regretfully pulled himself away and got to work, first addressing his deputy.

"All right, Alexius, the Crete trip is over, and it's time to get focused on the Varangians. While it seems like all we have now is questions, there may be some answers on the way. Let me tell you what happened in Crete!"

Justin then went through the events involving Sitt al-Mulk and the two items that had been left for him before he left. When he finished, Alexius looked at him through narrowed eyes for several moments.

"Boss, I take back everything I ever said about you being dull—you really can get involved with some shady deals! The book—I can't do a thing for you there, so you're on your own. The ivory necklace—that is something else. So your wife really thinks it came from the Caliph's own sister?"

"Well, half-sister, but you get the idea."

"All right, no matter. You do know what this means, don't you? It means that while the old enemy is back in the game, we have more friends in Cairo than we thought—the Coptic Christians, the Jews and now someone inside his own palace!"

Justin threw up his hands. "Alexius, you don't think I haven't gone over all of this already? The problem is, we need to narrow things down, and that's where you can help. Sophie tells me you know the number of Egyptian vendors…"

"Right, 27."

"And the number of ivory dealers…"

"Twelve."

"So how many Egyptian ivory dealers are there?"

"Ha-ha, I know that one too, only three!"

"All right, that's where Sophie will start. She'll take another lady-in-waiting or two at first. If things look promising, I can then go on a repeat visit as her servant, since I speak and understand Arabic. I will also work on the book that was left at my quarters in Crete."

Assuming a downcast look, Alexius said, "And what about me, Boss, what about me?"

"Ah," replied Justin, "you will exercise the skills you have shown so well—we need to follow up on 'Daphne'. I admit that I don't really know why my wife has pursued this line of inquiry, apart from believing that 'Loviatar' didn't look like a woman. Still, we know that a cross-dresser who is named Matthew as a man and 'Daphne' as a woman is missing. You have the connections we need to find out where he or she is. For all we know, 'Daphne' may be the key to the whole case—find her and we solve it all."

"But, Boss," Alexius followed up, "you were there just like I was, seeing whatever it was in the windows. How could that be 'Daphne'? We tried hanging someone upside down—it didn't work!"

Justin sighed, "I don't know, Alexius, I don't know. We have to work with what we have. Please get on that for a start. Tomorrow, there may be something else, who knows?"

"Will do, Boss. Say, not that it's any of my business, but what are you going to do with your winnings? You're not going to quit your job, by chance? Just asking."

"You wish, Alexius. Actually, since you are the one who got me into this situation, I'm going to put the burden back on you. You said that I am not naïve, but I really am. Until our trip to the jail the other day, I had no idea that men were being locked up for what seems to be a harmless diversion. I want you to take this money and use it to pay the fines of men like Michael, or Michaela if you will. Understand? Get them out of jail, now!"

For the first time since they had known each other, Justin saw tears come to Alexius' eyes as he rose to leave. "Whatever you say, Boss, whatever you say! God bless you—you are a great man!"

The high that Justin experienced from this encounter lasted about fifteen minutes. After leaving the office, he decided to treat himself to a walk through parts of the palace which he did not often get to see. As things turned out, this was a mistake, for as he was walking by one of the older audience halls (Michael II, perhaps?), he heard his name called. Turning, he saw Prefect Comnenus approaching him with a look that could only be described as distraught.

"Ah, Justin! Thank the Virgin you are here! Please come inside—I am desperate!"

It did not take Justin very long to appreciate the truth of the prefect's words. One on side of the room were Patriarch Sergius and his black-robed minions, and on the other were the western Christians, led by Romanus the brother of the current pope. Their disputes seemed to involve what bread to use in communion (leavened vs. unleavened), whether the pope had primacy or supremacy, and something about the origin of the Holy Spirit—what on earth did 'filioque' mean? While the documents that were being argued about were written in Latin and Greek, Romanus and his delegation, who apart from him were dressed in red, spoke Italian. Their understanding of Greek was limited and they seemed to rely on a monk from southern Italy who professed to be proficient. After a few minutes of hearing this man's translations, Justin could stand it no longer.

With a nod from the prefect, he stood up and said, first in Greek and then in Italian, "Gentlemen, I would beg your indulgence for a few moments. Signor Romanus, may I see you and your translator, please?"

The alacrity with which Romanus complied was a good sign, and soon he, his translator and Justin were in a side room.

Justin began with an apology in Italian. "Signor Romanus, I do not profess to be proficient in all languages, and so I may have misunderstood what your translator was saying." Turning to the monk, who seemed terrified, he said in Greek, "I trust that your lodgings in the Chora monastery have been sufficient for your needs?"

Without blinking, the black-clad man responded, "Chora market full for me and all horses."

Nodding, Justin turned to Romanus and replied in Italian. "It is as I thought—this man is incompetent as a translator. While I don't know what your disputes are about, if any of them hinge on the meaning of any particular word, I suggest you take a recess and reconsider where matters stand."

Taking his hand, Romanus looked into Justin's eyes and said in passable Greek, "Thank you, Treasurer, thank you very much. I had thought we were talking in circles recently, and now you have confirmed it! What do you suggest we do now?"

Trying to fend off a rising wave of weariness, Justin kept his voice level. "Each side should write out statements in the language they feel best represents their position. We will use Greek, while you should use Latin. Then, competent people can examine them and come up with translations for the other side to read. How does that sound?"

"Grazie, amico, grazie!" {"Thanks, friend, thanks!"}

When Romanus and Justin came back out, they conferred with their respective sides. While the patriarch looked irritated that matters were to be prolonged, Prefect Comnenus breathed a sigh of relief.

"You are a marvel, Justin, a marvel! I'll let you know when we need you again!"

Justin smiled wanly and went on his way, conscious of a dull headache he had suddenly developed. It lingered through the rest of the day, although being with his children did take the edge off. Sophie arrived home shortly after he did, and while she wanted to tell her husband about her day, she could tell that now was not the time.

Later, when they had been treated to a beautiful sunset and the children were in bed, Sophie remembered the bag she had brought home that had belonged to the rude servant. Since Justin had gone to bed early, she opened the bag in the dining room and placed the items on the table. Most were ordinary—sandals, clothing, toiletries, and so forth. One item was not, and it caught her attention—a leather pouch containing a brownish powder. Sniffing it, she tried to place where she had seen it before. Then it came to her—it was like the substance she had found on Constantine's beard when she examined him while he was unconscious. Giving a silent prayer of thanks to the Virgin that her father was on his way, she set the bag aside in a secure place and resolved to show it to him when he arrived.

"*If you'd been less rude to me when we first met,*" she thought about the nine-fingered man, "*you would still have your belongings, and we wouldn't have this clue, if that's what it is. Funny how things work sometimes.*"

CHAPTER 23

Justin felt renewed and refreshed the next morning, a feeling which lasted as long as he did not think about unleavened bread or the 'filioque' clause. Sophie brought him up to speed on Constantine's situation, remarking that seeing Zoe in the back of the wagon had brought back memories, some good, others not so good.

"So do you need to go back to the Blachernae today?" he asked.

"Thankfully, no. I am getting messages sent to me regularly both here and at the palace. In fact, I already received two before you got up. The emperor slept better last night, but isn't eating very much at all and seems depressed. He is looking forward to my father's arrival tonight, so perhaps that will help. I did come away with a little souvenir from yesterday that you might like to see. It's this!"

Sophie then showed Justin the bag of brown powder, and explained her theory of where she had seen the substance before. It meant nothing to Justin, but did prompt a memory of something that he had heard which seemed unimportant at the time. He excused himself for a moment and then came back with a paper in his hand.

"You remember that conversation I overheard in Crete between the scientist who wrote the manuscript I later got and some other man? Well, not having your memory for sights and sounds, I wrote down some notes as soon as I could. Most of what I heard concerned some kind of device, but there was something else at the end. Ah, here it is—something about getting something which had been running low, and something about being close to success. That's all I heard—by then they were walking away. Maybe this is what they were talking about?"

Sophie sighed. "Who knows? I'm just glad my father will be here tonight. He's done a lot of work with plants and herbs in his career—maybe he's seen this before. Still, much to do before then! Two of my ladies and I are going back to the Mese to look at ivory vendors. What's on your agenda today?"

Justin shrugged. "Nothing so adventuresome, I can assure you. I need to take another crack at the manuscript, only this time I won't be alone in the task. Agatho and Maria's tutor Anwar are native Arab speakers, and should give me some help. The Arabic language is very simple and very complex at the same time, so I will take all I can get. I have to think that it has as much to tell us as the ivory necklace does, if we can only understand what it is saying!"

Philip then entered and informed Sophie two ladies were calling on her.

"Well, dear, here they are. I'm off to solve the case—it is all right if I have to spend some money to do so, isn't it?" she said as she gave Justin a kiss.

Justin laughed, "Since you'd do it even if I said no, sure, go ahead—we can always make more!"

As she rode along the busy streets of Constantinople that June morning, Sophie felt very much in her element. The only thing which spoiled the moment was her inability to fully explain her purposes to her companions. Irene, though she had been with Sophie for many years, was still not privy to all that Sophie did with the Alitheia Society. Julia was still very new to the entire world of being a lady-in-waiting, and was thrilled by the very experience of going shopping with someone whom she looked to as a mentor. Looking at the wide-eyed novice, Sophie sighed and thought to herself, '*Was I ever that young?*'

Accordingly, Sophie couched the trip as a girls' day out, saying that Zoe was very appreciative of the long hours that everyone had put in and wanted them to have a day off. While Irene did her best not to roll her eyes at this transparent lie, she need not have worried, for Julia absorbed it all as the absolute truth. Sophie said as she had a weakness for jewelry and it was boring to shop alone, she hoped they could help her spend her husband's money! This brought the expected titters from Julia and eyes that did roll from Irene.

Encouraged, Sophie continued. "Today, ladies, I have a yen for ivory, that exotic stuff from darkest Africa! I have had my scouts search out the most likely vendors and we shall explore them. Are you with me?"

The first two vendors, while meeting Sophie's criteria of being Egyptian-owned and dealing in ivory, were disappointing, although their owners were appreciative of the Roman gold Sophie offered. The first was owned by Coptic Christians who had heard of Sophie from their kin at home, and were fawning in their obeisance. The second operator was Jewish, and while he was more circumspect, he was none the less effusive in his praise of Sophie, going so far as to insist she buy an ivory necklace "just to let your husband see how its beauty compares with yours." To cut off the tittering behind her, Sophie agreed, all the while thinking how she really needed to have a talk with Alexius. Clearly, all Egyptians were not Arabs, any more than all Arabs were Egyptians.

Although there was only one stall left to visit, Sophie had hopes, for it was the one that she and Leonida had been to several days before. As before, they were greeted by an Egyptian Arab who has previously identified himself as Ishaq. Today, however, he had an associate who appeared to be every bit as surly named Abdor who, unlike his counterpart, was right-handed. Both of the men spoke Greek in only a rudimentary fashion. While Sophie wished she spoke Arabic, everyone has their limits.

With no less than three women of means throwing questions at them about various items, the two clerks were soon forced to call upon reinforcements, and the owner of the business came forward from the back. 'Ah-ha,' thought Sophie, '*I bet you are the owner who was previously unavailable.*' Tall, light-skinned and wearing a goatee, he bowed and gave the Muslim gesture of touching his forehead, mouth and chest.

"Greetings, ladies! I am your humble servant, Musa al-Hadi. Please feast your eyes on all of our offerings—we are here to serve you!" he exclaimed in fluent Greek.

Sophie looked at him with wide eyes and said, "Oh, thank you, sir! Ivory is so hard to assess! I'm looking for something exotic, maybe with a fantastic animal like a dragon or a chimera or, or, what is that one with the two big horns?"

If it was possible to signal 'big sale' any plainer to a man like al-Hadi, Sophie didn't know how to do it. The bait was accordingly taken, and a variety of items were quickly laid out for the inspection of Sophie and her friends. While shopping without regard to the price tag was customary for Sophie, it was a new and exhilarating experience for Irene and Julia, and they embraced it with gusto. Numerous pieces were brought out for their inspection, including some, Sophie was thrilled to see, with elephants similar to the one that had been left with Justin.

Sophie's next task was to get al-Hadi to speak Arabic, in order to see if he in fact had a lisp like that Justin described. Since his Greek was good, and did not have such a feature, this was going to take some doing. Thinking quickly, she hit upon a plan that relied on the assumption that the master did not know his wares as well as did his employees.

Picking up one necklace with an elephant design, albeit less elegantly done than the one Justin had been given, Sophie said, "Are you sure this is an elephant? I only see two horns—I thought they have four. Is that right?"

Al-Hadi suppressed a moment of irritation over such a question, and turned to Ishaq with what sounded like a question himself in Arabic. Ishaq frowned and shook his head, but al-Hadi kept querying him until the assistant threw up his hands in frustration. With a well-practiced smile, the proprietor turned back to Sophie and smoothly said, "You have a good eye, Lady. While male elephants do have four horns, or as they are also called, tusks, females have only two. This locket shows a female elephant. It is quite beautiful, no?"

"Oh, it certainly is," Sophie crooned. But, needing more, she pressed on. "So, how much is it? I hope it's not too much—my husband would be furious."

Having clearly done this sort of thing many times before, al-Hadi smiled and said, "Dear lady, do not concern yourself with such matters. I am sure that your husband and I can come to a number agreeable to us both. Just bring him by and you will leave with this beautiful locket, as if your beauty needs any improvement!"

Returning the smile, Sophie thought, *You have a lisp, you arrogant pig! I hope you are involved in this somehow—I have some Varangian friends who would like to spend some quality time with you!*, before she said, "That sounds very nice. I will speak with him today. In the meantime, my friends and I will take three of these bracelets—no need to wrap them—we'll wear them from here!"

On the ride back to the palace, Julia was giddy about her new acquisition, while Irene was more circumspect. At one point, as the younger woman's attention was diverted, she leaned over to Sophie and whispered, "I hope you found what you were looking for."

Sophie said nothing, but only smiled and nodded. Her reverie was soon interrupted by men's voices calling her name. Calling upon the driver to stop, she recognized several Russians who were in a stall where vodka and other strong spirits were being sold. Although she did not recognize them, they claimed to have seen her in Cairo when they were trading there two years before. One, whose Greek was better than the others, asked what she was doing in the Mese. Struck by an inspiration, she asked about Musa al-Hadi the ivory dealer.

The very mention of his name brought frowns and murmurs. The Greek-speaker shook his head. "You watch out from him—he no good—he cause big trouble in Egypt—much danger!" Sophie, torn between wanting to hear more and the need to move along with her comrades, thanked the man for his information and gave Justin's greetings. This cheered up the entire group, with one man even offering to give Sophie a bottle of vodka for free. Laughing, she declined and they moved on.

Meanwhile, Justin had spread out his materials in the formal dining room of their villa, in order to better analyze the mysterious manuscript. With him, hopefully to provide some much needed insights, were Agatho and Anwar. Both had come to the city from the area around Antioch, a Christian city which had been liberated under the reign of Basil from centuries of Arab occupation. Agatho had assisted Justin in the past when a reading knowledge of Arabic was needed, while Anwar's education in classical Arabic texts would be an asset. First, however, he needed to lay out some ground rules to the young men who sat attentively in front of him.

"Good morning, gentlemen, I think you will find this interesting. What we have before us today is a manuscript, written in Arabic by one of their scientists. It seems to deal with matters of light and vision and images. I cannot tell you how it came to be in my possession. I can tell you that its translation is a matter of state security. I have only one copy, and I cannot make any more. It cannot leave this house, so we will have to examine it here. I need your help to translate it, for you both grew up reading Arabic and I did not. So, while I can to all outward appearances speak the language, to read it I need help. Do we have an agreement?"

At this, the two younger men exchanged glances, and remained silent. Finally, Anwar spoke.

"Sir, I for one am ready to help you in any way I can. I do not need to know the reason for this request—although I am a Syrian and a Muslim, I can separate that from the enemies of my country, which is Rome. In your silence, you have said volumes."

Agatho, who lacked the cultural background of Anwar but had the street savvy to interpret colloquial Arab phrases, nodded and only said, "Right, what he said."

Satisfied, Justin said, "In order to make the most of our time, I would like each of you to look through different sections and write down what you believe it says. When you are done, you can switch sections and see what the other has done, adding comments of your own. I have done all I can, and you can see my notes, such as they are. I will tell you that I am particularly interested in any part of the manuscript which describes the making of a device. What that would look like or be for, I have no idea. I'll let you alone now and attend to some other work."

From time to time, Justin would look in on his interpreters, who seemed engrossed in their task. Periodically, they would switch sections, with Justin looking at their notes. Progress was being made, but things were still very piece-meal. *'What's the big picture,'* he thought, *'we're missing the big picture!'* Eventually, when fatigue set in, he thanked the men for their work that day and paid them in cash as an incentive to come back for more.

When Sophie came home, she could see that her husband was in no mood for levity. Dinner was a chance for the entire family to be together, and things were still at the dessert stage when the porter announced the arrival of a visitor.

With a mischievous look at the children and a wink at Justin, Sophie said, "Goodness, I wonder who that can be?"

They all had the answer in a few seconds, as a tall, clean-shaven older man with white hair and dark eyebrows came through the door. To the city he was Doctor Lukas Lascaris, considered one of the most gifted physicians in the empire, to Sophie he was 'Father', to Justin he was 'Doctor Lascaris,' and to the children he was simply 'Grandpa.' For the past four years, he had been in charge of a leprosarium near the town of Prusa in Bithynia, among the foothills of the solitary peak known as the Bithynian Olympus. He had been sent there at his own request, in order to get a new start and have a new purpose after the death of his wife of 40 years from a cancer he could not stop. Now he had been recalled to help treat Emperor Constantine, and would be stationed near his patient at the Blachernae Palace on the outskirts of the city. On his way, though, he had stopped to see his family.

"Grandpa," Maria yelled, and gave him a massive hug. Simon was close behind, and was scooped up by his adoring grandfather. Sophie had to wait her turn for a hug, which was not long in coming, while Justin exchanged handshakes as the family adjourned to the veranda. While the couple knew that Doctor Lascaris needed to get brought up to speed on Constantine, for a while such business was put aside as the older man marveled at how much the children had changed in the six months since he had seen them at Christmas. Maria showed how much more she had learned about arithmetic, especially using the 'new numbers', to which the doctor could only smile and shake his head. Simon was much more mobile than he had been, and while his grandfather could not really figure out what he was saying, in the tradition of grandfathers everywhere he simply smiled and nodded.

Eventually, the children were put to bed, after getting a promise from Grandpa that he would be by to see them often in the coming days. Lamps were lit to let the adults continue to sit on the veranda, and Doctor Lascaris gave an account of his last two days.

"It was at first light yesterday, Wednesday," the doctor explained, "when I was awoken with news that there were men to see me. 'Men' was an understatement, for when I went to the front gate of the compound, there were no less than 20 fully armed imperial cavalrymen waiting for me. Their commander apologized for the sudden notice, and then conveyed to me the imperial order, red seals and all. They gave me an hour to get things in order and pack my belongings, although it really was more like two, so that they could rest their horses and themselves. They did so outside the walls of the compound, though, since none of them wanted anything to do with my patients the lepers."

Doctor Lascaris paused, and then continued with a sigh. "Those poor people were devastated to lose me. I wanted to tell them I'd be back, but I couldn't—I don't know if I will be going back there or not. I hope so in a way, but it is very good to be here now with all of you. Now, before I go out to the Blachernae, what can you tell me about Emperor Constantine?"

Sophie then recounted the events of the past few weeks as they related to the younger ruling emperor, with Justin occasionally adding comments. Her father listened intently, asking no questions, until she finished with an account of Constantine being transported to his current lodgings.

After staring intently at them for several moments, Doctor Lascaris spoke slowly, almost as if he was talking to himself. Justin, who had seen Sophie do the same thing many times, was struck by the similarity.

"Constantine has been known for many years as a man who loves his wine, especially compared to his brother, who doesn't drink alcohol at all. I would be inclined to say that his drinking has gotten out of control, but for your observations that on the two times he collapsed in public, he seemed to be sober. Clearly he has gone downhill since the last time I saw him, albeit from a distance, last Christmas. He may have a heart condition, or perhaps a tumor. I'll have to wait until I can examine him. I am glad to hear that he was not bled. At least one person—Basil—listened to me when I inveighed against that barbarous practice. Does that sound about right?"

Sophie nodded, then reached into a chest and took out the pouch she had found in the belongings of Constantine's servant, along with the folded paper containing the flecks she had taken from the emperor's beard when he was unconscious after collapsing at the Hippodrome. Placing them on the table in front of her father, she said, "Here is something else for you to look at, Father. It probably means nothing, but Constantine seems to have ingested this powder before the Hippodrome incident. I have no idea what it is or what it is for, but thought you might find it of interest."

Her father took a pinch of the brown powder, sniffed it, rolled it between his fingers, and then ever so lightly touched it with the tip of his tongue. "Hm, rather bitter, but clearly not toxic in small doses, if Constantine was taking it. I can't say I recognize it, either, but I will see what I can do. May I take these with me?" he said as he stood to go.

"Of course, Father. Do you need us to drive you to the palace?"

With a laugh, Doctor Lascaris said, "Oh, Sophie, I scarcely think so. Here, take a look at my escort," gesturing as he stepped through the front doors of the villa.

There, sitting quietly on their mounts, were a dozen imperial cavalrymen in full armor, on either side of a carriage bearing the royal coat of arms.

"I think I'll be all right. Let me get settled in and we can talk again in two or three days. Giving Sophie a kiss and Justin a wave, he entered the carriage and soon was lost to sight.

As they lay in bed, Sophie and Justin discussed the events of the day.

Justin shook his head. "Manuscripts and jewelry, a sick emperor and dead Varangians, a goddess of death and a pouch of brown powder—we have too many pieces and not enough answers. At least nothing bad happened lately—I wonder how long our luck will last?"

Blowing out the light, Sophie gave Justin a kiss. "Oh, husband, I'm too tired to talk any more today. Tomorrow will take care of itself."

CHAPTER 24

As Sophie rode to the palace on Friday, she was looking forward to what would pass for a 'normal' day. There were no banquets or saint's days on the calendar in the near future, and now that her father was back in town the welfare of Emperor Constantine was no longer her problem. While there remained the little problem of the Varangian murders, they did at least have some leads—the missing cross-dresser, the mysterious ivory amulet and the scientific manuscript. Putting them together would be a challenge, but, Sophie thought, '*that's what we do, don't we?*'

Riding with her in the carriage was Maria, for Fridays were sometimes informally designated as Bring Your Child to the Palace Day. Now that the prohibition against ladies-in-waiting being married had been lifted, there were several women who had childen. Since Zoe and Theodora were not married, and had no real prospects of ever being so, they enjoyed having the children of others around, at least up to a point. As it was, once or twice a month seemed to satisfy whatever maternal instincts they possessed.

As they walked into the princess' chambers, Maria bowed to the tall Varangians on guard. Keeping with established practice, they nodded in turn, something which never ceased to delight the child. Before she ran off to be with the other children, of which she was the oldest, Sophie had cautionary words.

"Now remember, Maria, Aunts Zoe and Theodora don't have children of their own, and it's not polite to ask them why. It's all right to talk with them, but let them talk first. We won't be here all day—your father and I have some business in the city we need to do this afternoon. All right?"

With a wave and smile Maria was gone. Sophie soon got immersed in details of everyday life in the palace, first talking with Irene and then with the other ladies, including Julia. It was not until sometime later that she looked up and saw Maria in one of the side rooms with several other children. Maria was apparently holding class, as a rotund eunuch held a blackboard on which Maria was showing how to use the new numbering system she had learned to add and subtract. The children were in rapt attention, as was Zoe, who was quietly seated in the back. Sophie was unable to catch more than a quick glimpse, but it appeared that the senior princess of the Roman Empire was taking notes! *And a little child shall lead them* reflected Sophie, *'true enough!'*

Knowing Zoe as she did, Sophie was not surprised that the attention span of the princess soon waned and she came out of the room, although not without glancing around to see if anyone had noticed. Seeing Sophie, she made a beeline for her chief lady-in-waiting. *'Here we go, it's about her father.'*

In that there were others around, Zoe slipped into her formal mode of address.

"Lady Sophia, I wish to visit my father as soon as possible, as does my sister." Though Zoe tried to sound commanding, even peremptory, Sophie could detect a note of pleading. She accordingly answered in kind.

"Of course, Highness, I completely understand. You will be gratified to know that my father is now attending the emperor, and has assured me that you will be able to visit him soon, perhaps as early as Sunday. For now, your prayers will avail him much."

Zoe deflated like a balloon, and took Sophie's hand to whisper, "Thank you!"

Back in the villa, Justin was steeling himself for another assault on the manuscript. First though, there were some preliminary matters to address. Agatho had worked for several years as the chief groom, with a young man named Mark as his assistant. Now with the translation issue taking many hours a day, Mark needed help. With a sigh, Justin sighed off on hiring an assistant for the assistant. '*The things I do for the Empire!*' he thought.

Anwar's situation posed a different issue. In addition to being a tutor for Maria, the young Arab served in three other households, where his knowledge of mathematics and/or Arabic was worth paying for. Given the seriousness of the situation, Justin had no choice but to monopolize Anwar's talents, and so had to work out something with the others. Fortunately, the presence of the royal treasurer seal on his letters carried a lot of weight, along with a goodwill payment to each household.

So, feeling a little beat down before the fight even started, Justin nonetheless greeted his translators warmly and guided them to their work. Although it had not been his intention to take over the family's dining room, in effect that had happened, as Sophie had reminded him with a series of arched-eyebrow glances.

"Gentlemen, what have we learned so far?" he asked when they had gotten settled.

With a nod to Agatho, Anwar began, "Well, sir, we agree that many words in the text are unique, almost as if the writer was coining new words to describe new observations. From what we can tell, all of them seem to be about how light works and how men perceive it, something which the text calls optics."

Encouraged, Justin asked, "That sounds promising. How far have you gotten?"

Looking down, Agatho said, "Six pages, sir."

In that he knew the manuscript contained 78 pages, Justin refrained from embarrassing his groom. Instead, he said, with hopefully a cheery note in his voice, "That's very good!" At the sametime, he fumed, '*at this rate it will be until fall!*' Deciding to take a different tack, he looked at several pages which had drawings on them. On one, lines from what appeared to be the sun passed through a triangle, coming out the other side at different angles, with different degrees of shading in each section. The triangle was described as a 'prism', whatever that meant. A fine theory, no doubt, but where was the practical value?

Justin stared at the drawing for some time, the words of al-Haytham ringing in his ears—"Have you gotten it to work properly?" 'It' would seem to be some kind of device, although a device to do what? Looking up, he saw his assistants looking at him, as if seeking direction.

"Keep at it, men, however long it takes. There has to be an answer in here somewhere!"

"Yes, Treasurer, although it would help if we knew what the question was," answered Agatho wryly.

Justin's time of frustration was ended, at least temporarily, by the arrival of Sophie and Maria. Sophie gave one look at her dining room, now completely covered in manuscript pages and parchments full of scribbled notes, and merely shrugged. After a quick hug, Maria was off, as her parents prepared to go to the ivory dealer on the Mese who had aroused Sophie's suspicions. As they rode along under a cloudy sky that held the promise of a rare summer rain in the city, they made their plans.

"All right," began Sophie, "I think we need to get the owner involved from the beginning. You can pose as my servant, and don't need to say anything. I'll ask some more silly questions to provoke the owner to speak with his assistants in Arabic, maybe haggle about the price."

"It's imperative that you do haggle," said Justin. "Don't be afraid to walk away if you reach an impasse, maybe by questioning the authenticity of the piece. It's like fishing—you need to dangle the bait without pulling it away entirely. I just need to hear the man speak. Trust me, this will work."

Sophie smiled sweetly. "Oh, I'm very good at bargaining, especially when I can use someone else's money."

But the best laid plans sometimes come to nothing. On arriving at the stall, they found it closed, with a note pinned to the outside which contained writing in both Greek and Arabic. Justin confirmed that the Arabic writing mirrored that of the Greek, which said, "Closed to allow attendance at Friday prayers."

"Prayers on Friday?" wondered Sophie. "Is that normal?"

"Yes, dear, Friday is the holy day of the week for Muslims, like Sunday is for us. I will have to check with the imam at the local mosque—if these men really do attend, he will know. Looks like a dead end for today."

Their inquiry at the stall would have ended then and there, but for something which Sophie caught out of the corner of her eye. It was a man at the stall across the street which sold silver items, who was waving his arms in a rather subdued fashion, as if he did not wish to be seen by others. Sophie caught Justin's arm, and they wandered over to the stall.

"You wonder about them?" the man said in a low voice, gesturing to the ivory dealer's business. "They not really that devout—only start closing on Fridays in past few weeks. Thought you like to know."

Justin and Sophie exchanged glances, and then Justin announced in a rather too-loud voice, "That looks fine, my man, we'll take it!" while handing the man some money with a wink and a nod. This new revelation gave them something more to ponder on the way home, arriving just in time to escape what promised to be an extended downpour.

The showers continued through dinner, and intensified as the evening went on. The rain itself was welcome, in that it would help recharge the cistern system which provided Constantinople with much of its water. The thunder and lightning were another story, for while Simon would sleep through about anything, Maria was old enough to pepper her parents with questions. "Would the thunder hurt them?" "Was the lightning caused by giants who were fighting?" "What would happen if their house was hit by lightning?" This last question did prompt some thought by Justin, who then explained to Maria that since their roof was made of tile, there was nothing to catch fire.

After hearing this last explanation, Sophie took Justin aside and said, "Really?"

"Yes, probably, I mean, sure. Now don't you start, too!"

After several bedtime stories (during which it occurred to Justin that Maria was milking the situation), she drifted off to sleep. Justin was about to do the same, assuming he could deal with the dogs on their bed, when Sophie came into the room, holding an envelope that Justin knew all too well.

"Society business?" he asked.

She nodded without a word, and then got out her rain cloak. After he did the same, they were soon travelling to yet another seamy corner of the city, which though Virgin-protected, still had its share of violent crimes.

"I assume the message was from Alexius?" he asked as they rattled along through a rain that had now been reduced to a drizzle.

"Who else? Really, that man needs to get some other hobbies to occupy him in his time off, assuming he has any time off. He does get time off, doesn't he?"

Justin, who was feeling very tired at the end of a long day, was not in a mood for banter. "Of course he does, he goes to clubs where men dress as women—does that count?"

Feeling the steely stare of his spouse, he relented. "All right, that was uncalled for. But why does everybody have to get murdered at night? Why can't they get killed at noon?"

Sophie sighed. "I don't know. But I do know this—the Varangians aren't going to take much more of this. They came thousands of miles to fight for an empire that is not theirs, and are well paid to do so. Having their throats slit by some kind of goddess—not so much. Husband, I am telling you, we need to resolve this matter in a hurry!"

As Sophie finished, Justin noted they were passing the banquet hall, where all of their problems seemed to originate. They went several blocks further south so that the outline of the Church of Saints Sergius and Bacchus became clearer. That they would not get there was evidenced by the knot of men holding torches just ahead. When they drew near, Alexius approached the carriage and they could tell from his visage what the situation was. They got out, and Sophie approached the scene where the body undoubtedly lay.

Alexius remained in the rear with Hetman Siggurdsen, who looked less impassive and more concerned than usual.

Justin, lagging behind, leaned over to Alexius and said, "If anything comes up about cross-dressing clubs, don't worry about it."

Alexius, looking thoroughly puzzled, could only stammer, "Whatever, Boss!"

Having nipped this in the bud, Justin went forward to where the all too familiar assembly of Varangians was clustered around the body of one of their fallen members. Sophie was already checking out the scene and was frustrated, but not surprised, by the lack of physical evidence due to the rain that was still falling lightly. Justin could hear her litany, which again had gotten all-too-familiar. What was not familiar was a low undertone of grumbling and murmuring from the gathered soldiers.

"Subject is a male, northern European, approximately 30 years old, about 6 feet tall. His throat has been slit by a non-serrated blade, moving right to left, indicating killer is left-handed. Decedent's nose has been slit and his ears have been cut off, apparently by the same blade. Ears are not present. Due to the rain, it cannot be determined if the body has been moved here from another location. Body has been laid out in a formal presentation, with hands crossed across breast."

Sophie stepped back from the body and wiped her hands on the towel that she carried with her in such situations. Seeing Siggurdsen, she approached him amid the undertone of dissatisfied Varangians.

"Another dismal evening, Hetman. What can you tell me about the victim?"

The hetman looked at Sophie, then at the body, and then back to Sophie before speaking. "His name was Tomas Bengstsen. He was from my village and held the rank of thegn. He had been in the city for ten years. He had no enemies. I cannot make sense of this."

While Sophie's natural impulse was to let the man have his time of grief, duty called. So, she pressed forward.

"I am sorry for your loss, Hetman, as are we all. I need to ask you some questions, and I hope you can help me. Was Tomas at the banquet tonight? What time did he leave? Did he leave with anyone? Did anyone see what happened? Please, we need your help."

Siggurdsen gathered himself together, and answered. "Yes, Lady, I understand. Tomas was present at the banquet tonight, and 'Loviatar' was sighted, although most did not see her. Around midnight, he left with several other officers that he lived with, and they were walking back through the rain to their lodgings that were near here. Because of an old injury, Tomas walked slower than most men and he fell behind. There was a sudden cloudburst, and the other men lost sight of him. When they reached their lodgings, they realized he was not there, and went back at once to look for him. They found him here."

While listening to the hetman, Sophie was also hearing the comments of the men around him, many on the general theme of how useless it was to fight against a goddess, and why they needed to leave this unlucky place. With a glance to Justin, who nodded 'no' vigorously, she decided to take a bold step. While she knew that she spoke a passable version of Norse, she doubted her grasp of the many declinations and tenses and the subtle inflections of many words. So, she decided to use Hetman Siggurdsen as her translator, a task which he agreed to undertake. He called the men to attention and they looked at Sophie with expectation.

"Soldiers of the North," she began, "I am known to you as the Iron Lady! I speak to you now through the hetman because what I have to say is very important, and I do not want to be misunderstood. I am greatly grieved for the death of your comrade, and will bring his killer to justice, I swear. Some of you may think that a goddess named 'Loviatar' is responsible. I tell you she is not. Ask yourselves, men, what kind of goddess appears only in a certain building on a certain night? Not much of one, that is for sure. No, there are men behind this, and I will find them!"

From the rear of the crowd there came a loud voice. "Thaer ir lygi!" {"That is a lie!"}

Moved to speak Norse, Sophie answered, "Thaer segya?" {"Who said that?"}

A very burly Varangian stepped out of the group of men, and stared down at Sophie. (*'Oh, that's a mistake,'* thought Justin).

"Ek, Harald Torkelsson!" {"I, Harald Torkelsson!"} he growled.

"Vel, Harald Torkelsson, bessu naest luka aptr, yor aen ek maela vid!" {Well, Harald Torkelsson, when this is finished, you and I will speak again!"} Sophie replied in her sweetest voice. "Now, husband, I think it's time to go home—I've seen all I can here."

The ride back was a subdued one, as they each wrestled with their own thoughts. Sophie was weary of dealing with murders to men she really cared for, even though they were very different from her and were very far from their homes. Justin was troubled by the bigger picture, always carrying the image of the caliph in the back of his mind.

When they finally got into bed (free of any dogs), Sophie could only look at Justin and say, "I love you, dear! You are the still point in a turning world!"

Justin would have come up with a romantic response, but he was already asleep.

CHAPTER 25

Saturday dawned fair, with a north wind coming down from the Balkans to clear off the remaining clouds. Sophie was looking forward to having some time with the children, as well as directing the household staff in cleaning and maintaining the house and the grounds. Justin was still determined to get to the bottom of the manuscript, but had already decided to only work with Agatho and Anwar in the morning before taking the afternoon off, and letting them do the same. *'It's a marathon, not a sprint,'* he kept telling himself.

The day, however, did not go as planned. Breakfast had been cleared away and the day's activities begun when Philip came from the front door with a message that the presence of the Treasurer and the Senior Lady-in-Waiting was needed, at once, in the office of the Prefect of the Empire. To emphasize this, he was accompanied by a senior officer of the palace guard. Both Sophie and Justin knew that this was an offer that could not be refused, and so they soon found themselves riding in the carriage that had been specially sent for them back to the palace. Before leaving, Justin had manage to slip a message to Philip for Alexius, requesting that he wait for them outside the prefect's offices. He also informed his duo of translators that they had the day off, an announcement which they accepted with alacrity.

"This has to be about last night," sighed Sophie as they rode. "The Varangians are brave men, but they will not be slaughtered like sheep, at least not forever."

Justin nodded. "All right, let's anticipate this. The prefect will be there—he's always been on our side. Hetman Siggurdsen—he is in a difficult spot, but he's seen what we've seen, and has to have some empathy. Then there is the Akolouthos, Senator Kalokyros—I really don't know about him. He doesn't really seem to interact with the hetman and he doesn't speak Norse—I don't know what he brings to the table apart from having some connection with Emperor Basil. He's been difficult in the past, so today probably won't be any different."

"All we can do is tell them what we've done—we are making progress, if the manuscript and the locket mean anything," Sophie said in her helpful voice.

"And yet the bodies continue to pile up. Well, here we are. Chin up!"

The outlook was indeed not good when they went into the prefect's office. Prefect Comnenus looked tired, Hetman Siggurdsen impassive, and Senator Kalokyros impatient. Notable however was the lack of any signal that Emperor Basil was present behind his screen. Seeing Justin's look, the prefect confirmed this.

"Welcome, Treasurer and Lady Cataphlates! You know the senator and the hetman. Emperor Basil will not be with us today. I am informed that he has gone to the Blachernae Palace to visit his brother, who is under the watchful care of your father, Lady Sophia. In his absence, we need to deal with a matter that has come up which may approach crisis proportions. Senator, can you fill us in?"

Giving Justin and Sophie a steely glance, the senator replied, "Of course, Prefect. Because of the continued string of murders in this city, the Varangians are threatening to go on strike, if not leave entirely! That would be disastrous for the empire!"

Trying hard to suppress his shock, Justin looked to Siggurdsen for confirmation. "Is this so, Hetman?"

"Yes and no, Treasurer," the Varangian replied. "Some men are talking about taking some action, but nothing has been decided. It is my feeling that most men still place their trust in the Iron Lady," he said, giving a small bow to Sophie.

"'Iron Lady'!" the senator scoffed. "We need more than pretty words!"

At this, something in Justin snapped. Being the man who he was, he did not stride across the room and slap the older man in the face, nor did he break out in curses. Rather, he responded as a Roman bureaucrat would. "Oh, really, Senator? Let me see—in your position as the Akolouthos you hold the seventeenth ranking in the hierarchy of the empire, correct?"

In a low voice, the senator responded, "No, eighteenth."

"Oh, my mistake. Well, I am fourth, and of that there is no mistake. Now that we have established that, let me assure you that progress is being made, leads are being followed, and justice will be done. Now, Hetman, when is the next banquet?"

The Varangian frowned for a moment, and then said, "Not for another two weeks, Treasurer. This Friday is a new moon, and we do not have assemblies on such days—it is bad luck."

Hoping that a sudden feeling of relief did not appear on his face, Justin went on. "Good, then I can assure you, Prefect Comnenus, we will have a resolution of this matter before the next Varangian is murdered. Hetman, please spread the word to your men. That is all I have to say today. Sophie, do you have anything to add?"

If Sophie had not been married to Justin for so many years, she would have run screaming out of the room after seeing such a performance. As it was, she trusted he had a plan, and so decided to add some fuel to the fire.

"No, husband, apart from saying to our comrade, Hetman Siggurdsen, Aradei, Hetman! Sigr ir orr! {"Courage, Hetman. Victory is ours!"} Now, are we excused?"

Sophie waited until they were out of the door before she gripped Justin's arm like a vise and said in a low voice, "Have you thought about what you'll do after leaving government service?"

Before Justin could reply, Alexius stood up from the side bench where he had been perched. "Hey Boss, I got here as soon as I could. I've got news—you go first!"

"Alexius, Sophie and I just got blindsided about some kind of mutiny among the Varangians—what's going on?"

"Oh, it's not that bad—yet. There is some clown named Harald Torkelsson who is trying to get things riled up. So far, he's not having much luck."

Sophie frowned. "Harald! Oh, I am so going to see him again when this is over! What's your news?"

"I'm afraid we've found another body." Seeing the horrified looks on their faces, Alexius hastened to add, "No, no, it's not a Varangian—that much is pretty clear. It was found nowhere near the banquet hall, but was clear on the other side of town, in the Cistern of Aspar. Some passerby saw it this morning, and employees of the water department fished it out."

Justin shook his head. "So, why the big news? In a city of half a million people, Constantinople has murders every week. We can't investigate them all."

"No, of course you can't, Boss. It's just that, once I got a description of the body, I thought 'Scapel' might want to take a look."

"All right, Alexius, you've piqued my curiosity—this had better be good," Sophie said impatiently. "What about this one?"

"The body is of a young man, probably in his twenties, who appears to be Armenian or Arab. He has a pointy-chin and a hawk-like nose. Sound like anybody you know?"

Before Alexius had even finished speaking, Sophie was heading for the door, leaving Justin to protest, "Hey, where are we going?"

"To the Cistern of Aspar, wherever that it. Come on, time's wasting!"

While Constantinople was superbly situated for defense and trade, it did have one serious defect—a reliable water supply. Over the centuries, many emperors had constructed an elaborate system of aqueducts to bring water into the city, and a corresponding system of cisterns to hold it until needed. Some were entirely underground, like the Basilica Cistern built by Justinian I which furnished water to the Great Palace complex. Others, farther removed from the city center, were open-air. The largest of these was the Cistern of Aspar, which, at 500 feet square, could hold over 50,000,000 gallons at full capacity. It was located in the northwest quarter of the city near the Church of the Apostles, although it was not visible from there, lying as it did on the other side of a modest hill.

"So how do you know where this place is, apart from having an encyclopedic memory," Sophie playfully asked as they rode along.

"Well, number one—I'm the Treasurer and I approve the budgets for everyone, including the water department, and number two—the current head of the department is a man named Anthony Bardanes. Anthony and I have risen through the ranks of the imperial officialdom together. Back when I was Register of the Notaries, he was Keeper of the Royal Inkstand—I'm not making that up—and we have kept in touch. He's a good man, and I'll have to kid him about what is turning up in his cisterns the next time I see him."

As things turned out, that did not take very long. As they turned into the lane which led to the cistern they could see a crowd of people standing near a gate on the fence which surrounded the entire facility. In the center was a short, red-haired man who was trying unsuccessfully to disperse the onlookers. When they dismounted, he saw them and exclaimed, "Justin! I should have known it was you—you and your wife! Going about putting bodies in my cisterns! How are people going to want to drink from them now?"

Sophie was initially alarmed by the man's tone of voice, until Justin rushed over and said, "Well, if it isn't Bardanes the red-haired barbarian! Leave it to the Treasury Department to clean up your messes! How have you been, you old rascal!"

Bardanes returned Justin's hug, and then turned to Sophie, "Excuse me, Lady, I've known your husband for a long time. I assume you're here about our unwanted guest?"

"Yes, I guess you could say that," replied Sophie with a smile. "I assume that is the body under the tarp there? I need to see it for just a moment—I promise I will be fast."

The sight of the body confirmed Sophie's fears and hopes at the same time. It was in fact the surly servant of Emperor Constantine, conclusively confirmed by the missing finger that Sophie had seen that day in the palace. While the face was puffy from being in the water for several hours, the deal was closed by the absent digit. She also noted that the man's throat was slit from right to left, indicative of a left-handed assailant.

"All right, that's enough," Sophie sighed. Then, her mind going to another level, she said, "Now we need to examine the scene."

"Dear," exclaimed Justin. "He was fished out of a cistern that is 500 feet square. What is there to search?"

"He didn't get there on his own. We need to examine the fence, starting with the gate." Bending down, she looked closely and said, "Ah, look here," pointing to bright scratch marks on the lock, "someone has recently tried and failed to open it. Now we need to look at the fence."

Justin knew better than to protest about the task of searching 2,000 feet of fence, so he enlisted help. So it was that presently the Treasurer of the Roman Empire, the Senior Lady-in-Waiting to the eldest imperial princess, their carriage driver and the Head of the Imperial Water Department were wandering around a ten-foot high wrought-iron fence.

Before they had gone very far, Justin called over to Bardanes, "Did you have to put this fence up?"

"No question about it, Treasurer. We needed to keep people from throwing trash and dead animals and, well, dead bodies into the cistern. By and large, it works."

"Until it doesn't!" Sophie muttered.

The searchers went on for a few minutes in silence, until the carriage driver called out. When the rest converged on his position, they saw something worth noting—a piece of torn, blood-soaked cloth hanging on one of the points around the top of the fence. When John their driver climbed up and brought it down, Sophie was pleased.

"Well, his killer made a mistake. He has got a good-sized cut on his hand or forearm for his trouble."

Bardanes shook his head. "Couldn't that be from the dead man?"

"No," Sophie patiently explained, "dead bodies don't bleed."

At this, Bardanes clapped Justin on the shoulder. "Friend, this one is definitely a keeper!"

As they rode home, Sophie took Justin's hand. "Well, husband, this one was in the day time—better?"

Justin could do nothing but smile and say, "Quiet, you!" followed by a kiss.

Alexius was waiting for them when they arrived home. Seeing him, Justin exclaimed, "No rest for the weary, I guess!"

Looking sheepish, Alexius said, "Actually, Boss, I'm here to see Lady Sophia. She needs to take another visit to a certain club tonight. There are people there who need to talk with her."

It was now Sophie's turn to take her husband's hand. "Justin, this is the place I told you about. You are welcome to come, if it will not make you too uncomfortable."

Later, Justin would reflect on how far he had come as a person during this time of turmoil. While he initially would have recoiled from such an invitation, seeing Michael/Michaela and the others in the jail had changed his outlook. So, he held his wife's hand for a long moment and then said, "Count me in. How should I dress for the occasion?"

So it was that the three of them arrived later that night at a location which was kept out of the eyes of the authorities. Alexius had received a message from Isaac/Alexa and thought it was worth following up. Sophie was decked out in all of her finery, while Justin was cloaked in a drab outfit that would not draw attention from anyone. Alexius got them situated at a corner table, where they could see the fashion show that was already underway. It was not long before their presence (or rather, Sophie's presence) was known, and other patrons drifted by with hellos.

Justin got comfortable in his surroundings and surveyed the room around them. After a while, he thought it was obvious when a man was dressed as a woman. Then, looking at a table near them, he saw two people sitting and looking at them. One was a man (he thought) while the other really looked like a woman. He said as much to Sophie, only to hear her hiss, "That's because she really is a woman! Now behave or I'll be sorry I brought you!"

Eventually the two people in question came over and sat down with them. One was 'Alexa' while the other was Dolores, the sister of Matthew/'Daphne'. Sophie thanked them for coming, and introduced Justin.

Justin then had the singular sensation of having a man dressed as a woman take his hand when 'Alexa' said, "Thank you for coming, Treasurer! Your actions at the Golden Gate jail have become well known among us. They speak louder than any words!"

"Uh, well, you are certainly welcome," Justin stammered. "Now, Dolores, how can you help us help your brother?"

In a very soft voice, Dolores replied. "Treasurer, Lady, my brother and I have always been very close. He has always been able to be himself to me, whatever others think. Until a few weeks ago, we spoke every week. Then, I did not hear from him. I asked around, but no one seemed to know anything, apart from some rumor that he had taken an acting job. Then, a few days ago, I got a message from him. Here it is." She handed Sophie a piece of parchment bearing scraggly writing which read 'Dear Sister, I hope you are well. I am also well and will see you soon. Please tell Mother I think of her often and miss her. Love, Matthew.'

Dolores continued, "Our mother has been dead for over ten years. I fear something is very wrong with my brother, for he clearly can't speak honestly to me. What can I do?"

With a glance to Justin, Sophie spoke. "Dolores, we think that your brother has been caught up in a very complicated web of events. I would like to tell you we have the answers, but I cannot in truth do so. What I can tell you is we are doing everything we can and the solution will soon come. May the Virgin give you strength in the days ahead!"

Tears came to Dolores' eyes as she reached over to hug Sophie. Justin was touched by the woman's heartfelt gratitude. Seeing that his wife was equally moved, he took her hand as they left the club.

Later that night as they lay in bed, for a change Justin found himself able to keep up with Sophie as she processed the events of the day. She noticed this too.

"Why are you still awake? Normally I would be talking to myself—not that that's a problem. What's on your mind?"

Justin sighed. "It's that infernal manuscript. It can't be a coincidence—we see an image of a supposed goddess that we can't duplicate, and at the same time the papers of an Arabic scientist who investigates light and vision get dropped into our lap. Yet, if we can't show what the connection is, we can't do anything about it. And then I go and make that insane claim that we'll solve the whole thing within two weeks! Maybe I better start looking for another line of work. How does that line from the Gospels go—'I'm not strong enough to dig and I'm ashamed to beg?'"

"Oh, dear, we'll figure it out. We still have to check out that ivory dealer."

"Yes, so what? Even if the other voice I heard is his, what does that get us?"

"More than we have now. Time to rest—problems always look worse at night."

Soon Justin's regular breathing showed that he had taken his wife's sound counsel. Sophie, however, found sleep elusive.

'*Great*,' she thought. '*Now he's asleep and I'm stuck! So much for my own advice!*'

CHAPTER 26

Sunday was one of those days when Justin wished he held some other position, one that did not require him to publically attend the morning services at Hagia Sophia. However, as the Treasurer of the Roman Empire, that was not possible. Being emperor was one thing—after all, who was going to tell Basil that he had to attend church, or do anything else for that matter? Today was the Feast of Saints Peter and Paul, and the liturgical color was red. Patriarch Sergius gave the same homily he gave every year on this Sunday, the choir sang the same songs, and communion was the same. Yet, Maria was still thrilled to be there, and that helped Justin sit through yet another service. Sophie, as she had done for years, attended Princess Zoe, and gave Justin and Maria nods from time to time as she was able.

After the service was over, Justin and Maria went to meet Sophie outside of the royal quarters in the Great Palace. Maria took the time to study the Varangians standing outside the outer doors. While she was usually able to get them to acknowledge her presence, when Sophie appeared, none of the guards gave any notice. While Maria moved past this immediately, Justin was more concerned, as this total lack of response had not occurred for some time.

When Sophie came out, Maria flew to her and embraced her. In this, she didn't notice the concerned look on her mother's face as Sophie looked at Justin.

"I've got a message from my father," she said. "He wants to talk to us, but can't leave his royal patient, especially with the princesses visiting him today. I don't think he really believes Constantine is ready yet for such a visit, but you can't stall Zoe forever."

As they walked back to their carriage, Maria skipping ahead across floors that had seen centuries of glory, defeat and intrigue, Justin asked, "What's the problem?"

"It's that brown powder. If I had to guess, it's driving my father to distraction, just like it did me—what is it, where did it come from, what it effect did have on Constantine? We'll have to help him—he has to attend to the emperor, and yet this may be something he needs to know to provide treatment that is really effective."

From the look on Justin's face, Sophie intuited that her offer of help did not go over well. Justin did not say anything at the time, and indeed remained quiet until after they had dropped Maria off at the villa. While she was disappointed about not getting to see Grandpa, Sophie assured her that he would come to see them soon. Since Maria was also ready to get out of her formal gown into her play clothes, her protests were half-hearted. As they left, Philip gave them a message which had been sent by Alexius earlier that morning.

Once they were on the road to the Blachernae, Justin felt free to express himself.

"Really? Really? Take on another problem when we have dead bodies piling up? Sophie, we are in a serious situation, the most serious we've ever been in! Don't you appreciate that?"

Sophie, who had not spent 16 years of her life with this man for nothing, knew what say. "Most serious? More serious than being held captive by a sociopath a thousand miles from home? More serious than coming very close to being killed by Turks on the road to Tarsus? Really?"

To his credit, Justin exhaled and nodded. "All right, I overstated the case. But still, dear, we can only do so much!"

It was there, riding in their carriage along the Mese, passing St. Polyeuktos, that Sophie had the brainstorm of her life. "What if," she began slowly, "what if all of these situations are connected? What if the caliph is behind them all? Think about it," her voice rising as she started to make more connections, "Constantine's problems begin about the same time as the first Varangian gets killed, right?"

"Could be coincidence—it's a big world out there."

Sophie shook her head. "No, listen, seriously! There's more. What if the Arab scientist was there in Crete to meet someone, someone here from the city, to check on how the operative was doing. It fits—asking him if 'it' was working, and giving him something else he needed. Then there's the manuscript and the necklace, both courtesy of the caliph's sister, who apparently doesn't bear him any good will."

Now it was Justin's turn to shake his head, but he did so now with less conviction. "If there had been someone else on the ship, I would have seen him, especially if he was Arab or Egyptian."

"What if the person wasn't on your particular ship? You said that a number of ships went out and back. It would have been easy to be on one of those."

Justin sighed and took Sophie's hand. "Dear, I love you forever, but there is one problem with all of this. Fine, let's say that 'Daphne' somehow becomes 'Loviatar' for a few minutes on certain Friday evenings. While it is true that you and I have enough credibility with Emperor Basil that if we went to him and said he should expel all Egyptians from the city, he'd do it. If we did, though, that would be a temporary fix, just like banning the Varangian banquets from now on. Still, thanks for the pep talk—nobody can do it like you do."

This was followed by a kiss long enough that their driver was led to turn his head. Sophie, who kept one eye open, said, "Look to the road!"

Presently, Sophie recovered herself to ask, "What was in that message from Alexius?"

Justin opened the envelope, read it, and passed it to Sophie.

"Hmm," she read, "the man who was fished out of the cistern yesterday was named Mezezius. He was Armenian, and had last been employed in the household staff of Emperor Constantine—huh, tell me something I don't know! Well, if there was any link between this man and those behind 'Loviatar,' we're not going to find it now. His death ties up a loose end."

"Yes," nodded Justin, "like Treasurer Taronites' poor nephew two years ago. Say, driver, why are you stopping?"

"Sorry, sir, there's an imperial procession ahead of us. I have no choice."

"Oh, no!" exclaimed Sophie. "It's Zoe and Theodora! Quick, driver, turn off!"

But, it was too late. They both heard a cheery 'Yoo-hoo!' come from the first carriage following the Varangians, and knew they had been spotted. Zoe had pegged them, and so they found themselves in line directly behind her and Theodora, as they wended their way to the Blachernae. On the way, they passed the Chora Monastery complex and saw the western Christians outside enjoying the sun. Justin's wave to them was reciprocated by Romanus and his colleagues, prompting Sophie to ask, "More friends, dear? Shall we invite them to dinner?"

When they reached the Blachernae, Justin was reminded about the unique nature of the palace and its grounds. Even its name spoke its antiquity, for it stemmed from the Latin language spoken when the city was founded centuries ago. So special was it that a bulge was created in the massive land walls to accommodate the churches, palaces and halls at the very end where the walls met the bay called the Golden Horn. That no breach had ever been made in the city's walls was ascribed to the presence in the Blachernae church of the holy icon Hodegetria, which literally meant 'She Who Shows the Way.' Attributed to St. Luke, it showed the Virgin Mother holding the Christ Child, and pointing to Him as the way of salvation. Basil did not use the grounds much, preferring to stay near the scene of the action in the Great Palace. In contrast, Constantine enjoyed the riding and, in earlier days, the hunting that was available just outside of the walls, something which may have led his brother to send him there for his recovery.

The regal party entered through the opening to the Hall of Anastasius, which was the oldest part of the complex, built 600 years before. Other halls opened off on each side, including the Hall of the Danube, the Hall of the Ocean and the Portico of Joseph. Constantine was in this last one, lying half-supported by silk pillows on a bed. As his daughters ran to him, he tried to raise himself up, only to fall back with a groan. Dr. Lascaris was by his side, and helped him get repositioned again. Once that was done, the doctor came over to see Sophie and Justin, who stayed outside in the main hall.

Looking pleased but tired, the doctor said, "Sophie, Justin! It's good to see you. I would have been by the villa earlier, but things have been very demanding here. I can report that my patient is doing better, but he has a ways to go."

Giving her father a hug, Sophie answered, "We understand, Father. Medicine comes first. How is Constantine feeling?"

Looking around to see if anyone was near, Dr. Lascaris said, "He's depressed and tired and, if I may hazard a guess, embarrassed that things have come to this. He's also more than a little disoriented by these strange surroundings and having different people around him. He seems to miss one aide in particular."

"Let me guess, sir," volunteered Justin. "A man by the name of Mezezius, perhaps?"

The doctor's eyes opened wider as he replied, "Yes, how did you know? Do you know where this man is?"

"At this point, probably in an unmarked grave in the potter's field in the far west of the city. His body was pulled from the Cistern of Aspar on Saturday."

"Did he drown?"

"No," said Sophie. "He'd had his throat cut. Someone wanted to make sure he didn't tell what he knew."

"That's terrible," her father said. "Please don't tell Constantine—I'll wait until he's better to tell him that news."

"Father, what has the emperor said? What did Mezezius do for him? Did it have any connection to the brown powder I showed you?"

"Yes, yes it did. Thank you for reminding me. I asked Constantine about it, and he said that Mezezius claimed it was an herbal supplement that would give a person greater energy and concentration. I took him off it entirely, along with wine, and you can imagine how he feels. Still, he understands it is for the best. I still have no idea what this powder is, or where it came from. Given that you say this man was Armenian, it may be from Asia. There's no chance I'll let the emperor have any more, but I would like to know. From what people say, it seems the combination of the powder and alcohol had a powerful sedative effect."

"Doctor, when did Mezezius come on to Constantine's household?" asked Justin.

"About three, maybe four months ago, at least that's what I've heard."

Justin and Sophie exchanged glances, and then Sophie said, "Tell you what, Father, we'll make you a deal. We'll try to pin down what this stuff is. In return, you need to get by and see your grandkids at least once a week while you are in town. Deal?"

"Deal," her father replied with a smile, giving Sophie a hug. "I should get back to Constantine now—he probably would like being rescued from the attention he's getting!" True enough, as they re-entered the portico, they beheld the sight of the royal princesses fussing over their father, who looked appreciative but tired.

"Lucky man!" Sophie remarked as they left.

"Who, Constantine or your father?" kidded Justin.

"Either, or both," Sophie said as she took his arm on the way to their carriage.

Once they got home, they found it a beehive of activity. Simon was playing with the dogs, Maria was grooming her pony in the stables, Agatho and Anwar were arguing over what a recurring symbol meant in the manuscript, and the kitchen maid was chasing a chicken who did not care to be that evening's dinner. Only Alexius sat as an island of calm on the veranda, awaiting their return and drinking some wine.

"Afternoon, Boss! I thought I'd drop by and make sure we're coordinated on this week's activities. Based on what I've heard you said, it looks like time is running out!"

Grimacing, Justin ruefully said, "Oh, no! Who else knows about that?"

"Well, I only know of the Varangian Guard, the entire imperial civil service and everyone in the Great Palace, so you're probably all right. I'm sure there are some hermits in Cappadocia who are still in the dark."

"All right, all right. Help yourself to the wine—oh, I see you already have. Sophie's gone upstairs to change out of her formal court wear, and I need to talk to the two gentlemen in the dining room before they kill each other. We'll be with you shortly. In the meantime, think about what you can tell us about an Egyptian named Musa bin-Hadi."

Going into the dining room, he found that things had calmed down a little. With frequent interjections from Anwar, Agatho brought him up to speed on where matters stood. Recalling Justin's earlier comment to look for material that might describe a device of some kind, they had decided to focus on the various diagrams in the text. After determining that there were no less than 114 of these, Anwar wanted to reconsider. Agatho wanted to push ahead, which is where they were when Justin came home.

Although Justin was certainly a believer, he knew his faith was not of the same magnitude as Sophie's. Still, he was moved to give a silent prayer of thanks for the help of such devoted men, wrestling with utterly esoteric questions in a language that was not really designed for such issues, as was, for example, Greek. They had done enough for one day, and if he, Sophie and Alexius were to talk freely, he needed to get them on their way. So with many thanks he told them he would think about it and would let them know tomorrow.

As the young men were leaving, Sophie was making herself comfortable on one of the new couches that had somehow appeared on the veranda. Justin knew better than to ask how much they cost, for all he would get was the rejoinder "We can afford it!"

"All right," Sophie began, "we have a deadline to meet. The way I look at it, this will help us focus our minds wonderfully, rather like the man who is going to be executed the next day." Seeing Justin's eyes narrow, she pushed on. "It's a figure of speech! Anyhow, Justin and I will try again at the ivory dealer's shop tomorrow, perhaps this time we will find him open for business. With my usual aplomb I will haggle with him in such a way that he will be driven to speak in Arabic with his minions, at which time you, dear, will consult your vast memory for languages and see if he is the other man you overheard in Crete. How that links him to a Norse goddess of death who appears every Friday evening in a particular building, well, who knows?"

Alexius, whose mood had gotten darker after Justin had mentioned the name of the ivory dealer, took all of this in without comment. Seeing this, Justin had to comment, "Ivory elephant got your tongue?"

"No, Boss and Scalpel," he said. "This man you're looking at, Musa bin-Hadi, is known to the Alitheia Society as a truly bad man. He is feared among the Egyptian community here in Constantinople, and may be tied to one or more serious crimes amongst them."

"So," Sophie inquired, "he probably doesn't go to prayers at the mosque on Friday?" inadvertently timing this as Alexius was taking a drink of wine.

After they finished cleaning up what the eunuch had spit out upon hearing this, Sophie smiled and said, "I'll take that as a 'no'."

"Folks," Alexius went on, "this is serious. Bin-Hadi does not fool around, and if he is involved in this somehow, you need to take precautions. For example, Boss, whether you think so or not, you are fairly well known in this city. You can't just wander up to this man's store—trust me, someone there is sure to recognize you."

"But it has to be me," protested Justin. "Even if you or Sophie spoke Arabic, which you don't, you didn't hear the voice in Crete. I did. What do you suggest?"

"A disguise, silly," replied Sophie. "A fake beard, some make-up, a skull-cap—well, even Maria wouldn't recognize you, I guarantee it."

Justin frowned. "I'd really rather not."

"I insist," replied Sophie. "Haven't you been listening to Alexius?"

"All right, all right, if you both say so. Now, Alexius, I have something for you to do in turn. We have a parallel mystery going on involving some brown powder. It's possible someone has been giving it to Emperor Constantine and so caused him to have his recent health problems. We need to find out what it is and where it came from."

"Why not just ask the 'someone'?"

"He's beyond answering questions, since he's Mezezius. Remember him?"

"Anyhow," continued Sophie, "here is a sample of the powder—careful, we don't have much—I gave most of it to my father. See what you find from the apothecaries around the city—we are just too busy to handle this too."

Alexius stood and saluted. "Will do! I'll let you know what I can find out."

Later that evening, as they lay in bed, Sophie patted Justin's arm. "Feeling better than you did this afternoon?"

"Yes, thank you. It helps me to remember that we have a lot of good people working with us, and that we're not in this alone. I don't know how it's going to turn out, but having them with you and me is enough."

"Well," said Sophie in a drowsy voice, "if you want all of them here now, we're going to need a bigger bed!"

CHAPTER 27

Monday dawned clear and promised to be hot, which was typical for the city in late June. The cooling breezes from the sea only penetrated so far, and the crowded boulevards were already warming up by the time Sophie and Justin made their way to the palace. By agreement, their shopping trip would take place in the early afternoon.

"Muslims don't pray on Mondays, do they?" asked Sophie as they walked through the Chalke Gate's great bronze doors into the outer vestibule of the palace.

"No more than Christians do," replied Justin with only a minimal eye-roll. "Meet you and the carriage outside my office at noon—don't be late!"

"See you then, dear," Sophie said with a kiss. "Say hello to your fellow bean-counters!"

The mood of the Varangians, though difficult as always to read for Sophie, seemed to be better when she reached Zoe's quarters. Inside, Irene brought her up to speed on Zoe's mood. It had been improved by the chance to see her father on the previous day, and even more today, as she had been engaged in two hours of prayer with Patriarch Sergius. Prayer time was evidently over, as the Princess thanked the black-robed churchman, who then made his way to the door. In so doing, he passed Sophie. Stopping, he stared at her through narrow eyes and thanked her for suggesting to the princess that she pray more with him in person. The tone of voice he used was not consistent with someone saying thank you.

Giving a deep curtsey, Sophie merely replied, "Oh, Eminence, it is the least I could do. May the Lord bless you and keep you."

Still not convinced, Sergius sketched the sign of the cross and departed, ignorant of the stifled grins Sophie exchanged with Irene behind his back before joining Zoe in her inner chamber.

The chance to visit with her father, and to witness an evident improvement in his condition, had greatly improved Zoe's mood. Sophie sat quietly and listened to what passed for a verbatim recitation of Zoe's entire conversation with Constantine, with just enough Theodora thrown in to show that she was really there, too. Sophie knew from extensive experience that Zoe would eventually run out of things to say, and that eventually happened albeit on a somewhat surprising note.

"Oh, yes, Sophie, there was one more thing. I know that you and Justin are good at finding things out, and my father needs your help. For some time, he's had the services of a very loyal and helpful servant who seems to have disappeared. My father misses him, and is afraid something has happened to him. Could you help?"

Doing her best to project a blank stare, Sophie replied, "Certainly. What is the man's name?"

"Oh, I knew you were going to ask me that. It's one of those foreign-sounding names, Mazentius or Musselaous, or something like that."

Rising to take her leave, Sophie said, "Rest assured we will do the best we can. I'll be getting back to you on that."

In the Treasury Department, Justin made his usual low-key entrance, going from section to section to chat with anyone ranging from department heads to clerks. More than once, he found himself apologizing for how much time he spent away from the office, and promising that soon things would be better. Word of this apparently got around, for when he arrived at his office, he found several of the senior assistants waiting for him along with Alexius. Fearing the worst, he looked from face to face.

Alexius started. "All right, here it is, Boss. You have no business, absolutely no business, apologizing for anything you do in managing the Treasury. Isn't that right, men?"

All of the assistants chimed in with agreement. The most senior man, Timothy, was about the same age as Emperor Basil, and had been with the department about as long as the senior emperor had ruled.

"That's right, Treasurer," he volunteered. "I've served under several men who have held your position, and I honestly can say that you have been more involved than any of them. One man, who was before Taronites, your predecessor, was hardly ever here."

"That's right," added another senior assistant named John. "What was his name? Simon?"

"No," said a third man, "Simon was before him. I think it was Andronicus."

"Anyhow, Boss," Alexius concluded, "we all know how busy you are and we are totally behind you in anything you need to do. You've got good people here and you let them do their jobs. That's all we can ask. Right, everyone?"

The scattered cheers that followed were enough to bring a tear to Justin's eye, so he stammered his thanks and ducked into his office. While his feeling of euphoria was momentarily punctured by the sight of a confidential message from the prefect, the news it carried was good. The Varangians had settled down for the moment, but as long as the underlying problem remained there could be no lasting peace.

After wading through only a portion of the paperwork piled high on his desk, Justin heard a knock. "Come in!" he said with a note of resignation in his voice.

Surprisingly, it was Alexius, who actually remembered to knock for once. "Hey, Boss, it's time to get ready for the big shopping trip. Ready for the disguise?"

"If you say so. Tell me more about this Musa bin-Hadi character. Do you know any more about him that might help me today?"

"Well, he lives in Egypt, but he's not a native—comes from somewhere on the Arabian Peninsula. He makes a lot of trips back to

Cairo. We aren't sure what he does or who he sees—we have trouble keeping agents alive there. He does seem to be a legitimate ivory dealer, but is known to have a volatile temper."

"Temper, eh? That could be useful. Go on."

Alexius chuckled. "I can tell when I'm being stalled. I'll talk while I work. First, the beard."

Justin was at the point of asking his deputy where he had learned to apply disguises so well, but decided that it was probably a matter of don't ask, don't tell. The beard was not very long, but long enough that Justin wondered what other men saw in the concept. It was accompanied by a mustache, which tickled more than Justin liked. Standing back to survey his handiwork, Alexius nodded to himself.

"Good, good. Now for the crowning touch." So saying, he produced an eye-patch which went over Justin's left eye, and a skull-cap which fit snugly on his round head. Last was a change of robe, for Justin's treasury attire was much too formal for a servant. Producing a mirror, Alexius let Justin see the results.

Justin found himself looking at a scruffy, somewhat disreputable man with one brown eye staring back. At first glance, he seemed to be a combination of a hermit, a pirate and a bum.

"No, no, this isn't right!" he protested. "What well-born lady would have someone who looked like that as a servant?"

Alexius shook his head from side to side. "See, Boss, that's the difference between you as real you and you as servant you. Believe me, nobody is going to be looking at servant you, for sure if you're standing next to Sophie. It will work, and I'll prove it. Come on, out the back door!"

After going down a winding flight of stairs, they entered on the street that ran below the windows in Justin's office. Traffic was brisk, and, true to Alexius' prediction, no one paid any attention to Justin, save one woman who came up and slapped him on the back.

"Hey, Good Looking, what's up?" Sophie purred. "Ready to go?"

"Good luck you two!" said Alexius, as Justin helped Sophie up into the carriage. To preserve the illusion, Justin was to drive the carriage and then wait on Sophie as she shopped. Sophie gave Alexius a wave as they drove off, and the hunt began.

As they drove, Sophie sat with her back to Justin, the easier to communicate. "I've been thinking," Justin said after a while. "Why don't I pretend to be a deaf mute. It might make the bad guys more relaxed around me, if they think I can't hear what they're saying."

"All right, dear, then how do you and I communicate? Did you think about that?"

"Well, I could gesture to you with signs," Justin replied, although he sounded less adamant than before.

"Again, a good idea, if we had agreed on the signs before now. In that we're coming up to the beginning of the Mese, it's a little late. Now let's get this done!"

After Justin parked the carriage several stalls away from that of the ivory dealer's, Sophie walked along slowly, looking at various items from the various merchants. At one point, she had to whisper to Justin to get behind, where a proper servant would be, rather than walking beside her. Eventually they reached their destination, and Sophie recognized one of the assistants from her earlier visit with the other ladies-in-waiting. Was it Ishaq or was it Abdor? Watching him take a piece of merchandise and hand it to a customer with his left hand, which bore a prominent and recent-looking cut, she remembered—Ishaq it was. There was no sign of either Abdor or, more importantly, Musa bin-Hadi. Still, the stall was a fairly large one, with an area of unknown size behind the curtains in the back. At least a third assistant was located back there, bringing out more pieces upon command from Ishaq. As they spoke in Arabic, Sophie could feel Justin tensing as he focused on what the men said.

Sophie started the process of browsing slowly, looking first at one piece and then another, occasionally holding one up against her in front of one of the many strategically-placed mirrors. Now it was her turn to catch herself from treating Justin as anything other than a servant, as she realized she could hardly turn and ask his opinion on a particular necklace. She could feel Ishaq's eyes following her every move but he did nothing to intervene. *'So you think you know how the game is played?'* she thought, *'Well, time for Act 2.'*

After looking at virtually every significant piece of ivory jewelry on display, she went back to one of the first ones she examined and began the grilling process.

"Excuse me, yes, you there," she said to Ishaq. "I do not think that this is the piece that I examined when I was here the other day. Was it sold?" So saying, she held up an elaborate necklace she was certain had been present.

As the clerk fumbled to check, Sophie plowed ahead. "Well, never mind, I can see you don't know. Is there someone here who knows a little more about the merchandise than you do? How about him?" she said, pointing to the unnamed man who was peering out at her from between the curtains. "You there, come here!"

It soon developed that the unnamed man did not speak Greek, or least did not act like he did. Ishaq was clearly not used to being spoken to in this way, particularly by a woman, and was growing visibly upset. The hopes of Sophie and Justin both rose when the curtains parted and another man came out. Unfortunately, the new addition proved to be Abdor, who demanded (in Arabic) that Ishaq tell him what was going on. There followed an exchange in which Ishaq used some words in referring to Sophie that Justin was thankful he did not need to translate, to which Abdor replied that he was an idiot to risk losing such a well-heeled customer.

Quickly changing his countenance, Abdor turned his attention to Sophie, smiling and using good Greek to inquire if he might be of assistance. If he hoped to receive any better reception than his co-worker had, he was disappointed.

"You know," Sophie began, "I've heard that some ivory comes from other animals beside elephants. How do I know that this is really elephant ivory?" she concluded with a quizzical look on her face.

If looks could kill, she would have died on the spot, but Abdor kept his composure and assured her that Musa bin-Hadi would sell only the finest elephant ivory in his shop. This gave Sophie the opening she needed.

In an imperious voice she said, "Ah, yes, Mr. bin-Hagi or Hami or whatever, where is he? I demand to speak with the master rather than his minions!"

Abdor and Ishaq exchanged glances, as if doing a visual coin flip to see who had to break the news. Ishaq won (or lost, depending on one's point of view), and stammered, "Our master is away today, gracious lady, but he would tell you the same things we have. I swear it!"

"No, no, that will not do! Come, Balthasar, let us go. I shall return when I can deal in confidence with someone in a position of authority!" And with that she swept away, with Justin trying to keep up with her in her wake.

It was not until they were safely in their carriage and well away from the Mese that Justin was able to exclaim, "'Balthasar'? Where in the world did that come from? Apart from that, weren't you a little hard on those poor men? We'll never be able to go back!"

Although he could not see her, sitting as he was in the driver's seat ahead of her, Justin could hear Sophie's clear, pure laughter in reaction to his concern.

"Dear, you may be the Treasurer of the Roman Empire, but there is a lot you do not know about how to shop. Believe me, when those minions give their accounts of what just happened to Musa bin-Hadi, he will count the hours until I reappear at his stall. I am every merchants' dream—an empty headed-woman with a purse full of gold who can't wait to buy his ivory. Be patient and we'll get him, assuming he's the one you want to get. If not, I'll get a very nice ivory necklace out of the deal."

Back home, Justin wasted no time in getting out of his disguise, taking off the beard and eye-patch before he even went inside. If the household staff wondered about the moustache, which he forgot to remove, they didn't say anything. It was not until Shadow, the largest and oldest of their dogs, thought he was a stranger and starting barking that he realized his omission. He did keep the robe on, finding it rather comfortable.

His translators were hard at work in the dining room but had little progress to report. Fighting a growing feeling of despair, he sat down on the veranda and stared across the Golden Horn, to Galata and then across the Bosphorus to Chalcedon. Maria was playing with what seemed to be a pebble but with unusual properties. She would hold it up to the sunlight, which then split into a number of different colored rays as it came out the other side. Experimenting, she moved it farther and then closer to the white pavement, which made the rays get farther apart and then closer together in turn.

Intrigued, Justin asked her, "Maria, where did you get that?"

"The bird dropped it, Father. It was sitting on the roof and dropped it."

Justin examined the pebble and found it to be a piece of almost clear quartz. The 'bird' in question was certainly one of the hoopoes, who often found shiny objects to bring back to their nest. The effect on light passing through it reminded him of one of the diagrams in the manuscript. Giving it back to Maria, he gave her an unexpected but not unwanted hug and sought out Agatho and Anwar who he then showed the effect of the pebble. After he finished, he addressed them.

"All right, men, I have an idea. Let's look at some of the simpler diagrams and find the symbols that are alike. I think we'll find we can match them to things like distance, size of aperture, color of rays and how transparent the substance is. Then, we can start filling in the blanks for the terms we don't know."

"Sounds promising," said Anwar. "I'll take the first five, while Agatho can the next five, and then we'll go through the rest. It will still take some time but it's better than what we've been doing. Good thinking, sir!"

Justin let them get to it while he wrote a message to Alexius letting him know that the ivory dealer had still not been identified as the person he heard talking on Crete. He then joined Sophie on the veranda and surprised her by having a glass of wine with her.

Sophie smiled in sympathy. "Don't worry, husband, we'll be back at that stall soon. Even so, are you sure you will be able to recognize his voice? It's been a while now, and you've heard a lot of people speak Arabic since then."

"I can't be sure, Sophie, I can't be sure. I do recall that the man I heard speaking with al-Haytham had the kind of accent you hear in Arabia and not in Egypt. It's hard to explain, but I will know it when I hear it. That's the best I can do."

"Then that will be enough. Come, we've had intrigue enough for one day. Let's find the children and play some tag. You're it!"

CHAPTER 28

When Tuesday came, Justin was ready and willing to try their luck with the ivory dealer again. Sophie, being the seasoned shopper, advised that they wait a day or two in order to let, as she termed it, "the pot come to a boil."

"Besides," she said, "there is no Varangian banquet this week. One or two days isn't going to make a difference. Either he is our man or he isn't."

Justin could not argue with the wisdom of this, but still resolved to direct Alexius to place tails on the shop owner and his assistants. '*Note to self,*' he thought, '*must tell him to have men who are <u>very</u> discrete. We can't afford to tip any one off.*'

Since today was the day for Zoe to go with Theodora to one of their soup-kitchens in the city, Sophie went to the palace later than she usually did. As a result, Justin rode alone to the palace. Before he had gotten there, however, an imperial courtier came up to his carriage and handed him an envelope with the red seal of the prefect. The message inside requested him to attend a meeting of the highest importance in the prefect's office. Since Justin knew from experience that this was more of an order than a request, especially when the time frame was simply listed as 'at once,' he went straight there.

Entering the outer office, he saw the prefect's secretary, a eunuch who was acquainted with Alexius. While on most occasions they merely exchanged head nods, today was different.

"Good morning, Treasurer Cataphlates. The prefect is waiting you, as is Emperor Basil."

Surprised that this information was so widely available, Justin was momentarily at a loss for words. Recovering, he said, "Good morning to you, too. Thank you for that information. Please, if you know, are Senator Kalokyros or Hetman Siggurdsen also present?"

With a bland expression, the secretary shook his head. "No, Treasurer, they are not. Now, I believe they are expecting you."

When Justin entered the prefect's inner office, he was surprised to see that the room had been re-arranged. The large desk that Prefect Comnenus usually sat behind had been pushed to one side, so that two large chairs now faced a raised dias where a simple throne had been installed. Basil II, Senior Emperor of the Roman Empire, was already seated while the prefect stood to one side. Justin nodded to the prefect and then bowed to the emperor, who bade both of them sit. Basil was in his preferred garb of a purple tunic, trimmed with gold, with a sky-blue cloak. While he looked less worn than the last time Justin had seen him, his blue eyes were still somewhat sunken in his face. More significantly, he had a determined look on his face which immediately put Justin on alert. Clearly, this was not going to be one of those meetings where the emperor just listened—today was his show.

"Treasurer," Basil began in the even voice that was one of his hallmarks. "We have received reports of disquiet among our Varangian soldiers. Since each of them has sworn an oath of loyalty to us, we find this very disturbing. We understand that you and Lady Sophia have been looking into matters with your usual skill. Please tell us that you have things under control."

Swallowing once, Justin made a conscious effort to keep his voice from wavering as he answered. "Certainly, Majesty. What I am about to tell you represents the most current understanding that my wife and I have of the situation, which is undoubtedly the most complex of all the investigations we have ever conducted while in your service."

He then launched into a detailed, but not entirely complete, accounting of what he and Sophie had seen, done and concluded over the last several weeks. Notably, Sophie's trip to the cross-dresser club was omitted, as well as any mention of their search for 'Daphne.' Justin emphasized that they believed that the murders of the Varangians were part of a criminal scheme, and had nothing to do with any supernatural force, which had been used simply to prey on the fears of the more credulous soldiers. He also left out his conversations with the caliph's sister in Crete, saying only that he had "come into possession" of items which pointed to the Egyptian ivory-dealer.

Conscious that the account he was giving was a trifle on the thin side, he suddenly recalled Sophie's reflections that the brown powder incidents could also be a part of the overall scheme. So, to the surprise of the prefect, who was hearing this for the first time, he then detailed for Basil what Sophie and her father had learned about the substance that had very possibly laid Constantine low.

While Basil had been listening to his account thus far with interest, at the mention of his brother his eyes narrowed. "This substance, where does it come from?"

"Well, we are still working on that, but we do know it's not something that even a renowned doctor like Dr. Lascaris is familiar with."

"And this man who was found in the cistern with his throat cut, he was actually in my brother's household as a servant?" Basil asked incredulously.

"Yes, that seems to be the case. However, Majesty, Emperor Constantine does not know of the man's fate yet—Dr. Lascaris felt he needed to recover further before receiving such a shock. The doctor does feel that, with the removal of the powder, your brother can make a full recovery, also assuming abstinence from alcohol." Seeing a hint of a raised eyebrow from the senior emperor, Justin hastened to amend this last statement, "or, at least a reduction in consumption."

Basil paused for a few moments and then asked, "Very well, when will you confirm that this Egyptian is the man you overheard in Crete?"

"Tomorrow, assuming he is at his place of business," answered Justin.

"Given how your wife has whetted the expectations of his servants, he should be more than eager to meet her," observed the prefect wryly.

"All right, Treasurer," said the emperor in a tone of command, "if he is the man, we will have him and his men arrested immediately. Then, if necessary, we will order all Egyptians expelled from the city, in order to show our Varangians that we mean business. Do you concur?"

While most men would have immediately agreed with the most powerful man in Europe, Justin had been around Basil enough to know that he treasured men who spoke truth to power, having so few around him who actually did.

With a glance to the prefect, who nodded in support, he said, "No, Majesty, I do not, and here is why. First, not all Egyptians are Muslims, any more than all Muslims are Egyptians. A blanket expulsion would be unfair. Second, there may be others involved in this conspiracy who are not Muslims or Egyptians—witness your brother's dead servant, who was Armenian. Finally, while we do not know yet how the Varangians are being tricked into thinking they see a Norse goddess of death, we need to be able to show them how the trick works, so that their minds will be at rest. We need to catch whoever is doing this in the act, and," pausing before committing himself irrevocably, "one way or another, we will do so a week from Friday."

Basil looked at Justin even longer this time, to the point where Justin was regretting his candor. Then, his voice softening, the senior emperor of the Roman Empire said, "I want to thank you, Justin, along with your priceless wife, for all you have done for the empire. When others see events, you two see patterns. My brother and I are fortunate to have your help." Then, shifting back into imperial mode, he went on, "We note that all of your work points to Egypt. If you bring us proof that the Fatimid Caliph is truly behind this, blood will flow in Syria or Sicily. Please keep us informed of your progress. You may go!"

While Justin had one or two other matters to discuss with the prefect, it did not seem like a good time to overstay his welcome. With a bow, he took his leave. *'How are you going to explain this to*

Sophie!' he thought as he wandered down the busy hallways of the Great Palace. '*I wonder how the weather is in Trebizond, or wherever we end up if this goes south?*'

Trebizond was hardly in the mind of his better half, as she sat in one of the inner chambers of Zoe's quarters. It was time to go over the accounts for the month, and while Zoe had accountants to do the day-by-day entries, it was up to Sophie, as the chief lady-in-waiting, to check their work. While she was often sorely tempted to take the work home for Justin to look at, there were strict rules forbidding the documents from leaving the palace, and so she was stuck.

It was therefore a welcome interruption when a knock came on the door and Leonida stuck her head in. With her was a man who was obviously a eunuch, wearing the livery of Theodora's household.

"Are we interrupting anything, Lady Sophia?" asked Leonida.

"Totally, but please come in. Who is this with you?" Sophie asked of her companion.

In a very quiet voice, the man said, "I am Andrew, Lady. We have information which may be of interest to you. May I close the door?"

This last sentence was sufficient to raise Sophie's interest, so of course she said yes. After Leonida and Andrew were seated, Sophie looked at them expectantly.

Leonida began, "Lady,..."

"Oh, please," Sophia said, "We're friends—it's just Sophie."

"All right, Sophie, Andrew here is in Princess Theodora's household. You may recall that when we first spoke about a certain club, I told you I heard about it from two eunuchs in the household—well, Andrew is one of them. He knows about 'Daphne' and appreciates what you are doing to find her. He has something that may help. Andrew? Andrew?"

Andrew stayed silent for a moment and then placed a ring on the table in front of him. It was bronze, with a rather garish reddish-brown stone set in the middle. Sophie, whose knowledge of jewels was second to none, took one look and said, "Tourmaline. Rather cheap, too. What's the significance?" Then, realizing she had intimidated Andrew, she nodded for him to continue.

"Well, Lady, I was walking today in the city when I heard something hit the pavement behind me. It sounded like a rock, but when I turned around I found this. There was no one around when I picked it up so I went on. Only later did I realize that it looked like a ring that 'Daphne' used to wear—she loved rings—had one on each finger."

Intrigued, Sophie inquired, "Where were you when this happened, Andrew?"

"I had gone out of the Mese and was heading towards the seawall. I think it was near a church because I heard bells, but I'm not sure which one. There are so many churches in that part of the city."

Repressing a wave of frustration over the eunuch's lack of specificity, Sophie thanked him and asked if she could keep the ring for now while also thanking Leonida for her continuing help. After they left, she found herself pondering what this could mean. Of course, the ring may not have been 'Daphne's' at all, in which case it was no clue of anything. On the other hand, if it was hers, the fact that it was dropped just as the eunuch was passing was very significant. Perhaps 'Daphne' was being held prisoner and tried to send a message for help via the ring? Sophie made a note to pass this information on to Alexius, so that he could in turn alert his network of informants in the city. Sighing, she went back to her columns of figures. Maybe Maria could teach her that new system of numbers—anything had to be better than Roman numerals!

Justin's head had cleared by the time he got back to the Treasury complex and entered his office. He had been there only a few minutes when a knock, followed by two others in quick succession, came on the door which led to the private staircase which exited onto the street below. Recognizing the code for the Alitheia Society, he opened it and found Alexius with the imam of the mosque in Constantinople, Hasan ibn Ali. As usual, the imam was dressed in flowing white robes and wore a black skull cap over his white hair.

Justin welcomed them into his office, at which point the imam bowed, touching his forehead, mouth and heart in the traditional Muslim greeting, and said, "In the name of Allah the Merciful, greetings, Treasurer Cataphlates!"

Justin bowed in turn and bade them sit. Knowing that the imam as a Muslim did not drink wine, he offered him apple juice which was gratefully accepted. While Alexius cast a longing eye at the wine carafe, he too joined in the apple juice in a spirit of solidarity. When they were settled, Justin asked, "To what do I own the honor of this visit?"

After a look to Alexius, the imam began, "Treasurer, your deputy had contacted me about some men in this city who are from Egypt, and who on the surface appear to be Muslims. I thought it my duty to come and speak to you about them."

If the imam's visit alone had not caught Justin's attention, his use of the word 'appear' certainly would have. "Pray, sir, continue," he said.

"It is my understanding that Musa bin-Hadi is the owner of a stall which sells ivory, and that he employs others, among whom are men named Ishaq, Abdor and Ferhat. It is also my understanding that they may be involved in one or more murders here in Constantinople. Is this correct?"

"Yes, Imam," said Justin, "although I do not think we knew the name of the third man you just mentioned. We do think they may be involved, although we may know much more in one or two days. We have tried to locate this bin-Hadi, but found him to be absent both yesterday and last Friday, when his entire business was closed under the pretext of the men being at weekly prayers."

At this, the imam gave what could only be described as a snort. "Last week? At prayers? Nothing could be further from the truth! As the imam of the only mosque in this city, I know who attends and who does not. Like you Christians, we are told not to swear by the name of Allah. Still, know this, Treasurer, if I were to do so, I would swear that I have never, never seen any of these men at prayers at our mosque, either last Friday or any Friday or any day. Further, I will tell you that they have reputations as being those who do not fear man or Allah. You would do a great service to your emperors, your city and our community if you got rid of them!"

After this outburst, the imam grew quiet, as if surprised by his own vehemence. Alexius looked at Justin as if to say, 'do something!'

In response, Justin said, "Imam, I cannot thank you enough for your words. Very shortly we will know if these men are the ones we seek for these murders. Even if they are not, know this—we shall keep an eye on them and they will not be permitted to commit further crimes. You have my word on that!"

With a nod of gratitude, the imam rose. "You have been a friend of our community here in Constantinople, Treasurer. Please know this—if you ever need our help, you may count on us as friends in return. Go with Allah!"

"And you, sir, as well," Justin said. "Alexius, please escort the imam back to his mosque."

"Sure thing, Boss! Let me know what to do next!"

Later that night, Justin and Sophie reflected on the events of the day. For a change, they took in the evening on the balcony off their bedroom. On a different side of the house than the veranda, from there they could have a view of the Princes' Islands, dotted with sparkling lights, with the great vastness of Asia off to the left, centered on the Bithynian Olympus. Now, close to the beginning of July, its snow cover was diminishing, but still shone bright in the rays of the setting sun.

After hearing Sophie's account of the finding of 'Daphne's' ring, Justin concurred. "That eunuch, Alex or Andreus or whatever his name is, did us no favors. We don't know where he was!"

While Sophie had felt the same initially, she was now in a more forgiving mood. "Still, it could be something. I've sent a note to Alexius, so he can let his people know. We'll see. While it was good of the imam to come see you, he really didn't help us either. Tomorrow will tell the tale, assuming that the ivory dealer decides to show up."

Frowning, Justin said, "I thought you told me he would be wild to be there?"

"Oh, he will, dear, he will. At least I think so," Sophie said with a wink.

Justin sighed. "Even if he does and is our man, we still need to crack the code in the manuscript. Without that, we have got nothing!"

"Haven't your men made great strides?" Sophie asked quietly.

"Oh, yes. Tonight they said they are about halfway through al-Haytham's treatise, and that they have a much greater knowledge of, and appreciation for, how the eye works! Not much help!"

"So, what are you going to do?"

"Starting tomorrow, I'm going to start looking at it myself again. If necessary, I'll start from the back and work forward. There has to be an answer there—we know that there is no 'goddess' in the banquet hall, and we've tried to physically recreate how the illusion was produced without success. So, we need to see what the scientist can tell us, just like he told the other man in Crete."

Sophie sat in silence for a while before saying, "The other man you think, and hope, is Musa bin-Hadi?"

"Yes, with all my heart, yes. Are you ready for tomorrow?" Justin said as he took his wife's hand.

"Ready and willing! They will be sorry that we got involved before this is over, I promise!"

CHAPTER 29

As they had done two days before, on Wednesday Justin and Sophie planned to visit the ivory dealer in the early afternoon, which left them time to attend to other matters in the morning. Sophie had no shortage of things to do on behalf of Zoe, among which were planning for the next soup kitchen visit by the royal sisters. Sophie tried to move these around the city for maximum visibility, and was now focused on the northern side, near the Golden Horn. Settling on a church, she prepared a message to the patriarch's office to advise them of the event, given that Patriarch Sergius frequently made an appearance at such affairs.

After completing it, Sophie reflected that she could simply give it to the patriarch directly, since he was now meeting with Zoe for another prayer session. Given his reaction when he encountered her after the last session, however, she thought better of the idea and dispatched it by messenger to his office in the Hagia Sophia. She managed to avoid him when he swept by her office with his retinue, which was her cue to see the princess. Sophie could think of no good way to let Zoe know about the fate of her father's servant, and decided not to wait any longer. She approached the inner chamber in time to see Zoe close her prayer book and dismiss James, her father confessor, who looked more forlorn than usual.

Seeing Sophie brought a smile to Zoe's face, and she gestured for her to sit.

"Good morning! What is on your mind today?"

"Princess, I have done as you requested and have looked into the whereabouts of the servant you mentioned the other day. His name was Mezezius and he was from Armenia."

While no one would ever accuse Zoe of being overly bright, years of being a member of the royal household had trained her to be perceptive around people. Hearing Sophie's statement, she frowned. "I notice that you used the past tense—'was'—is he dead?"

"Yes, I am afraid so. He was a victim of foul play over the weekend—stabbed by person or persons unknown. I have told my father, and he will let Emperor Constantine know when the time is right. So, I must ask you not to say anything to him about this before then."

Zoe sighed. "Oh, what a wicked world we live in! Do you think that you and Justin could do anything to bring the criminals to justice?"

The pleading look in the princess' eyes was impossible for Sophie to ignore. "Yes, we may have a lead or two. In fact, we are going to check out one this afternoon. I will let you know what we find."

Zoe's countenance brightened at once. "That's marvelous—if anyone can do it, you two can!" Pausing, she went on, "You're not going to dangle your poor maid from the roof again, I hope?"

"No, Highness, no more roofs, not this time at least," Sophie answered in all seriousness, before she saw the twinkle in her mistress' eye. Laughing, she took her leave and went back to assembling the duty schedule for July.

While Justin was feeling more comfortable with going about in disguise, he had decided to put on his garb at their house and not at the palace. Even so, he still had some time to kill before heading back to the villa. As he walked along in his official robes, he acknowledged the greetings of many other palace officials, all of whom ranked below him in the imperial hierarchy. *'Isn't it odd,'* he thought, *'how the robe makes the man? No, not really I guess, that's the way of the world.'*

As he passed the offices of the municipal authorities, he heard a voice call his name. Turning, he was greeted by Romanus and some of the red-clad western churchmen. "Buongiorno, Signor, come stai?" {"Good morning, sir, how are you?"} Romanus said.

"Very well, thank you, sir," Justin answered in Greek. "How are negotiations going?"

Romanus gave a quiet laugh and looked around him to see if anyone was listening. Then, gesturing to Justin to follow him, he moved over to the side of the corridor. "Very well, thanks to you, or should I say, your wife! It seems that, thanks to her intercession, Patriarch Sergius is now pre-occupied with lengthy prayer sessions with Princess Zoe. In his absence, we are making real progress. We may need your help on some finer points of translation, but on other matters we have basically agreed to disagree."

"Will that be acceptable to His Holiness Pope Benedict, your brother?"

At this, Romanus gave what could only be described as a snort. "'His Holiness'? My brother is no more a churchman than I am. Our father was the de facto ruler of Rome, and Benedict got the position of pope to keep things in the family. Once our father died—it was me—I may be the next pope after him!"

"In that case, I look forward to working with you. Perhaps I will pay you a visit in Rome! Arrivederci!" {"Good-bye!"}

When he finally arrived at the treasurer's complex at the far south end of the palace, the chief clerk came to him and announced that he had visitors who were awaiting him in his office. As he went there, he thought *'Who is it now? My office is as busy as the Forum on market day!'*

To his surprise, he found the prefect and Hetman Siggurdsen waiting for him.

"Good morning, Justin," Prefect Comnenus intoned in his deep voice. "Please forgive the intrusion. Hetman Siggurdsen came to see me and I thought what he had to say was important enough that you should hear it too."

"And Senator Kalokyros?"

"Is occupied elsewhere," the prefect smoothly replied. "Now, Hetman, please tell the treasurer what you told me."

As the Varangian prepared to speak, Justin could not help but reflect that here was a man who was speaking in a strange language, in a land thousands of miles from his home, to men who were nothing like him. His size, full beard and long hair further set him apart. Yet, he acted with grace and was completely loyal to the man he had sworn an oath to, Basil II, Emperor of the Romans. He was worth listening to.

"Treasurer, Prefect, I am speaking now on my own, and not on behalf of my fellow countrymen. Still, I believe that what I say reflects what they feel, too. First, I want to say that I know how much your wife has worked to help us. It is not for nothing that we call her the Iron Lady." Then, almost as an afterthought, he added, "and I am sure you are helping too."

Justin forced himself to smile and nod before saying, "Thank you, you are too kind. Pray continue."

"Second, I have been told you understand who is behind these killings of Varangians. As I have told you, I do not believe they are the work of any goddess. Many of my men do not think that either. But many others do, and are very afraid. I believe that one more killing will be enough to cause them to leave, even if it means they break their oaths. They are that afraid of 'Loviatar.'"

Justin thought for a moment, realizing he needed to choose what he said next carefully. "Thank you, Hetman Siggurdsen, for your words. Tell me, please, what these men would do if the killers of their comrades are caught, and the goddess does not appear again? Would that be enough?"

From the look on Siggurdsen's face, it was clear that he had not contemplated such a response. After a pause that bordered on being uncomfortable, he said, "For some, perhaps. For others, no." Seeing the look of incredulity on the faces of Justin and the prefect, Siggurdsen went on. "Treasurer, you think as a Roman does, with logic and reason. You have one God, and so dismiss any concept of other gods. These men have been raised since their childhoods to believe differently. A goddess, like a god, can go anywhere and anytime as she pleases. Just because she is gone for now does not mean she will not return. There will still be a lingering doubt in their minds. As soon as a Varangian is killed for any reason in this city, the rumors of 'Loviatar' will resume. I am sorry, I wish it was otherwise, but it is not."

Justin, who thought he had felt as low as possible earlier in the week, suddenly felt lower. He then did what he did best—improvise—and replied. "All right, Hetman, now we know what we are up against. There is no banquet this week, correct?"

"Yes, it is the new moon and it is considered bad luck to feast on such a day. While those of us who are Christians do not believe this, it is a small thing to defer to our countrymen who think otherwise. The next one will be on the following Friday."

While the logical, reasonable part of Justin's mind begged him to ask why the banquets had to be held on Friday, or held at all, considering that was the only time 'Loviatar' seemed to have any power, he held his tongue. Instead, he said, "Thank you, Hetman, for coming forward like this. My wife and I are still working on several things before next Friday. When that day comes, can we count on your help to put this matter to rest once and for all?"

Siggurdsen nodded impassively. "Of course, Treasurer. Whatever you ask."

Justin arrived home before Sophie, which gave him a chance to put on his beard and eye-patch. While he had initially been hesitant to do so at the villa, lest he frighten his children, to his surprise they saw right through the disguise. When Sophie arrived home, Simon was laughing and trying to pull it off.

"I hope this works better on adults," Justin said ruefully.

"Oh, it does dear, it does. Adults see what they expect to see—children see the world as it is. You'll be fine, just like the other day. Ready to try again? Oh, and you might want to put the eye-patch on your left eye. Adults might notice if you switched sides."

As they rode to the Mese, Justin explained what he needed to have happen.

"When I overheard al-Haytham talking with the other man on Crete, I noticed that the other man spoke with the kind of lilting tone to his voice that is characteristic of Arabic speakers from the Arabian peninsula, almost like a lisp. One word he said more than once was 'shan' which translated into Greek would be 'concern', as in "that is no concern of yours." If I heard him say that, I am almost sure I would recognize it."

Sophie nodded, then said, "So, I'll just ask him what the Arabic word for 'concern' is—problem solved!"

"Oh, you, always with the jokes. No, this is serious. We can't just keep showing up at this man's stall—he's going to get suspicious, if he hasn't already."

"True, true, but I think we have one more chance at this. Remember what I said about adults seeing what they want to see—unless I miss my guess, Mr. Musa al-Hadi is going to see nothing but a fat payday when we walk up. He may be a master spy, a murderer and who knows what else, but the language of gold is universal, and everyone speaks it. All right, we're getting close—we'll walk the rest of the way. Remember, while I'm browsing, try to look bored and disinterested."

"No problem there, dear, I've had lots of practice!"

As they worked their way along the street, first passing dealers in bronze wares, and then silver and gold, they eventually came to the area where dealers in African items were located. After checking out some truly beautiful brooches made of lapis lazuli, they finally came to the ivory dealers. Sophie saw their quarry first, and she gave Justin a discreet poke in the ribs, as if to say '*keep calm!*' Ishaq was also there with al-Hadi, and it was plain that he remembered Sophie from the quick glare that he shot her. Justin, as Sophie had predicted before their first visit, was totally ignored.

It was clear from the start that Musa al-Hadi's minions must have filled his ears with complaints about this certain rich woman who came by the stall and caused nothing but trouble. Today, he was nothing but smiles as they came up to the counter.

"Ah, beautiful lady, my poor shop is honored by your presence again. I am truly sorry that I was not present to attend you the other day, but I was helping a sick relative. Now, I believe you were looking at this necklace?" he said as he removed a lovely (and expensive) piece from a drawer.

Sophie took the piece, held it up to the light, rubbed between her fingers, placed it around her neck, looked carefully in one of the counter mirrors, and then studied it again. Placing it back on the counter, she looked at al-Hadi and said sweetly, "No, I don't think it was this one."

Al-Hadi turned to Ishaq with a questioning look. While Justin had some difficulty in catching everything that was said between them, it sounded something like this:

Al-Hadi: "I thought you said this is the woman!"

Ishaq: "I know it is—she asked many stupid questions and even had the same scruffy-looking servant with her!"

Al-Hadi: "If this sale falls through, I am taking it out of your pay!"

Ishaq: "Ha, what pay? I haven't been paid since Egypt!"

While Justin hoped that the conversation would continue longer, al-Hadi turned back to Sophie and tried again.

"My shop is at your command, beautiful lady. Please take all the time you need."

Although Sophie could not tell what was said during the exchange between the two Egyptians, she knew it was time to start drawing things to a close. Smiling again, she replied, "Thank you sir, you are very patient with me. They all look so lovely, I'm just having a hard time choosing. I have to tell you, though, that this man here (points to Ishaq) was very rude to me the other day, and I almost did not come back because of him. I would like you to order him to leave. I would feel much more comfortable if you did."

When she finished, Justin thought, '*Here we go—this had better work!*'

At this point, al-Hadi apparently made up his mind. Turning to Ishaq, in Arabic he ordered him to leave. What followed was worth all the wait to Justin.

Al-Hadi: "You will leave, now, no arguments!"

Ishaq: "I am not your slave! Besides, I do not trust these people!"

Al-Hadi: "That is not your concern! Now go!"

'*That's the magic word!*' Justin thought. '*Now to get out of here before anyone gets hurt!*'

In the end, the only things which got hurt were Ishaq's pride and Justin's purse, for Sophie walked out of the stall as the owner of a gorgeous ivory necklace. All Justin could do on the way home was moan, "Ten solidi! Ten solidi!"

"Oh, quiet!" chided Sophie. "You got what you wanted—he's our man all right! So now what?"

"I'll immediately order Alexius to have al-Hadi and all of his men followed throughout the city. It may tell us if they have another location where they meet—they'll be too smart to keep everything in the stall. Besides, it's too small. Perhaps we can find 'Daphne' as well, although why they would want her is beyond me. Al-Hadi doesn't seem like the kind of man who would get his hands dirty with murder, but that Ishaq is something else, along with the others that you described. We've got our first big break, now let's see where it leads."

When they got home, there was other news of importance. There was a message from Alexius about his men's search of the apothecaries in the city—it was slow going, for there were over 150. Athago and Anwar presented Justin with a glossary of terms they had put together from the manuscript. With it, they were able to read most of what was written there.

"As it turns out," said Anwar, "we made it harder than it needed to be. Your Arab scientist friend really is a genius, but he was working with a language that didn't have the words he needed to describe what he wanted. So, he took Greek terms and used their Arab equivalents, as best as he could. The two languages are so different it wasn't obvious on the surface. Once we figured that out, it went very quickly. Agatho was the one who made the break-through."

Agatho took a small bow and replied, "You are too kind, sir. It was totally a joint effort. Anyhow, now I can get back to being a humble groom."

"And I a tutor," added Anwar.

Justin shook their hands and said, "Gentlemen, I thank you, but your work is not done yet. We still need to figure out how any of this relates to what has been going on here in Constantinople. I'll see you tomorrow and we will keep going."

Later that night, Justin sat on the balcony to their bedroom and looked at the very last section of the manuscript, using the glossary. He was amazed how much easier it was to grasp the concepts al-Haytham was describing. The last diagram seemed to be a progression from a light source to an object to what appeared to be a hole in a wall to another object. He tried to make sense of it, but was too tired. He was about to call it a day when he felt Sophie's arms around his neck.

"Hey, sailor," she whispered, "I've got my new ivory necklace on, and not much else. Care to take a look?"

CHAPTER 30

Thursday started off as a quiet day at the Cataphlates household. Justin vowed to keep working on the diagram he had found in the back of the manuscript, while Sophie was in her design room, coming up with new and different looks for Zoe. It was now July, an empty month on the church and civic calendars, with the next feast days still a few weeks off. Maria was working with Anwar, while Simon was playing with two of the children of the household staff. Sophie encouraged the maids and cooks to bring their children with them when they came to work, so that Simon would not be isolated as he grew older. It also helped to have one or more extra pairs of eyes on him, for he was now at the age where he was in constant motion.

After an hour or so, Sophie had decided to take a break when Philip brought her a message. While it had been delivered by an imperial courier, it had not come from the Great Palace but the Blachernae Palace instead, and was from her father. After reading it, she decided to share it with Justin. She found him in the dining room attempting to hang a sheet over the west wall.

Shrugging this off as a normal day in their lives, she called to him, "Dear, whatever it is you're doing, please take a break. I've got a message from my father. He would like to see us tomorrow for dinner. He has says that Constantine has agreed to let him have the evening off."

"Good, I could really use a break. I thought I figured out how to read this diagram but I end up having the image produced be upside down! It doesn't make any sense! So, what does your father have to say?"

"He'll be here before sundown. Apparently Constantine is getting well enough that he can do without his doctor for at least a few hours. My father told him about Mezezius, although he left out the part where the man was trying to poison him and had his throat slit. The emperor is getting stronger every day, but he still feels useless. I think my father is looking for help from us, since we have influence with his daughters who mean the world to him."

"It will be great to see him again. The children will go wild when Grandpa walks in. Long term, do you think there's a chance he'll stay here in Constantinople?"

Sophie thought for a moment. "Maybe. Going to the leper colony was good for him after my mother died—it gave him a new sense of purpose. Now, with the grandchildren here, he may feel differently. I know he could get his practice going again, and I'm sure he would be welcome at the city clinic. I know I'd love to have him back!"

"So would I dear, so would I. Now, back to work."

Justin decided that the only way he could really understand the device was to build one of his own. So, he set about turning his study into a replica of what was shown on the pages. Summoning Philip, he instructed the steward to get several white sheets and several lanterns. Once these items were assembled, he intended to get Agatho and Anwar to assist him.

As it turned out, this last step was going to have to wait for another day. Another messenger came to the villa, although this one was not dressed in imperial livery. By the looks of him, he was a beggar or street person. When he insisted on being escorted to Justin, Justin recognized him as one of Alexius' top agents. Justin thanked him for delivering his message, and then realized that the message he carried was oral, in keeping with Alitheia Society practice to minimize writings that could be intercepted. If writing was needed, the message would be sent in code.

With the look of someone who was not at ease in addressing his 'betters', the man mumbled, "Express orders from Alexius, sir. He also wants 'Scalpel' to be involved."

When Sophie arrived, the messenger looked up at a corner of the ceiling, as if that helped him concentrate, and recited: "To Boss and Scalpel from Alexius: Another one of our operatives was stabbed today. They think he will recover—is at Hospital of Samson—need you to come there now—much to tell you of interest. Please let messenger know you will come."

While Justin looked at Sophie and shook his head, she acted with decision. "Yes, please tell Alexius we are on our way." Then, after a moment, she added, "Thank you."

When they were on their way to the hospital, Justin asked, "Isn't this where your father sometimes worked when he was in town?"

"Oh, yes," Sophie answered. "I have many fond memories of this place."

"Dare I ask?"

"Of course, silly! How do you think I learned anatomy? I got it from following my father around as he treated patients in the clinic. He saved a lot, but there were some even he could not prevent from dying. So, even though the church frowns on autopsies, in the evening he would perform them, and I could watch."

Justin looked at her in amazement, after looking to see that the driver was not listening. "You watched as dead bodies were cut open? How old were you? Ten?"

"No, no, I was at least twelve. I remember that we got to do a full thoracic excision on my birthday!"

"And where was your mother when this went on?" Justin faintly asked.

"Oh, waiting for us at home. We had cake when we came back."

Justin could only shake his head. "Theodora was a remarkable woman. She dealt with your father and you at the same time. That must have been a challenge!"

Sophie was silent for a while before she replied. "Yes, yes, it was. I still miss her, and I'm sure my father does too. Still, it's good to have him here!"

At this point, their driver arrived at the hospital identified in the message. First constructed in the reign of Justinian I, the Hospital of Saint Samson the Hospitable stood between the churches of Hagia Sophia and St. Irene to the north of the Great Palace. The largest hospital in the city, it provided free care to everyone in Constantinople. Over the last five hundred years, the tradition had continued of physicians in the city working there several months of the year (with pay). The complex had now grown to include a number of buildings separated by gardens and parks, and had a capacity of over 1,000 patients. Alexius' wounded operative was assured of getting the best care possible at St. Samson's.

After checking in at the front desk, Sophie and Justin were directed to Ward Seven, where they found Alexius sitting in the hall. From the look on his face, they initially assumed the worst.

Seeing the look on theirs, Alexius hastened to say, "Don't worry, Theodore is going to be fine. He took one stab wound in his shoulder and the physicians have stitched him up after cleaning out the incision."

After exchanging glances with Justin, Sophie asked, "So, why were we summoned? Your message made it sound urgent."

"Well, I'll let you judge for yourself." Then, seeing a doctor emerge from the room, Alexius said, "Can Theodore talk to us now? It's very important that we do so."

The doctor shook his head. "No, that would not be wise. He's lost a considerable amount of blood and needs to rest. You'll have to come back tomorrow." As he turned to walk away, Sophie called after him.

"Doctor Stylites? Do you remember me?"

The doctor stopped and stared at her quizzically, before the light of recognition came to his eyes and he took her hands in his.

"Sophia Lascaris? Is that you? How many years has it been? You're all grown up! How is your father? Still at the leper colony?"

"Yes, doctor, it's been a while. My father is well. In fact, he's now back in the city. He's been tied up attending a patient, but I'm sure he will be around to visit when he has a chance. Oh, this is my husband,

Justin Cataphlates. Justin, this is Doctor Demetrius Stylites, one of my father's long-time colleagues."

"It is so good to see you again. But, what brings you here? Are you ill?"

"No, no, I'm fine. Doctor, I don't have time to explain, but we really need to talk to the stabbing victim you've just treated. I promise it won't take very long."

Doctor Stylites frowned, but then shrugged. "Well, I guess it will be all right, as long as you're brief! This man needs time to recover."

With this hurdle overcome, they entered the room and found Theodore propped up in the bed. His arm was in a sling and he had a bandage around his head. His face was pale, but he seemed alert as he listened to Alexius.

"All right, Theodore. This is Justin and Sophie—they are some very important people, and they need to hear your story. Tell them what you told me about what happened today. Don't be scared—they're on our side."

"Sure, if I can have a drink of water first." This need being met, he started speaking, using a dialect that Justin recognized as being from southern Italy.

"My assignment today was to keep tabs on an Egyptian who works at an ivory seller's in the Mese. I got his description from my supervisor, and took up position. Above all, I was told to avoid being discovered." At this, he gave a wry grin as he added, "I wish I would have been told to avoid getting stabbed. Anyhow, I followed the man down to near the waterfront. After he went down an alley and into a seedy tenement house, I waited in the shadows across the street for just over an hour."

"How do you know it was just over an hour?" asked Sophie.

"St. Laurentius Church is a block up the street, and I could hear the bells ring the hours. It rang ten o'clock when I got there, and had just rung eleven when someone came running up the alley I was watching, being chased by the man I had been tailing. It looked like the first man was trying to get away, and when he starting yelling for help I went to assist."

"What did the first man look like?" queried Justin.

Theodore cocked his head and pursed his lips. "Well, to tell to the truth, I can't tell you much—slight build, rather shaggy hair, not much facial hair—he looked like a man but ran like a woman, if that makes any sense."

"More than you know," said Sophie with a glance to Alexius. "Did you help him?"

"I tried, Lady, I tried. By the time I got there, the Egyptian had the other man on the ground and was throwing punches. I pulled him off, and that's when he pulled a knife. So, I pulled mine and we squared off. It was close, but when he lunged for a kill and missed, I put my blade between his ribs. He went down like a rock. I was about to check on the first man when I got jumped from behind. I saw a knife flash in front of my face and was able to parry the blow, which glanced off into my shoulder. Then it was my turn to go down. I must have hit my head on the cobblestones. By the time I collected myself, I was alone in the alley with the guy I'd stabbed, who was dead."

After a moment of silence, Sophie, doing her best to keep her voice even, said, "Thank you, Theodore. It sounds like you did your best and that you've had a lucky escape. We hope you get better soon."

As soon as they got into the garden outside, though, Sophie gave vent to the excitement she had felt growing as she listened to the agent's account.

"It was 'Daphne'—it had to be! She's been held captive and tried to get away. Remember that ring I told you about—someone found it on the street near a church! 'Daphne' must have dropped it out the window as a call for help. Now we know which church. Alexius, you need to search those buildings!"

"Already on it, 'Scalpel', but it looks like our birds have flown. We found some rooms that had been occupied, including one overlooking the street where 'Daphne' or someone else may have been held prisoner."

"What about the dead man? Was it Ishaq or Abdor?" asked Justin.

Alexius shook his head. "Neither one, I'm afraid. His name was Ferhat—had not been in the city very long, didn't speak Greek very well if at all. Sounds like the expendable kind of man to me."

"I remember there was a third man in the stall who didn't say anything—that may have been him," recalled Sophie. "So one of the other two stabbed Theodore?"

"Probably, since al-Hadi isn't the kind of man to get his hands dirty like that," observed Alexius. "Or, he may have other men we haven't identified yet."

"Do you think this will tip al-Hadi off that we're on to him?" said Justin.

"I don't think so, since it happened in the street and Theodore could have been anyone who was passing by. I think the fact that he's still alive is a good clue that Ishaq or Abdor or whoever didn't know who he was and what he was doing there. If they had, they would have finished the job."

"All right, then. Thanks for letting Sophie and me hear this from Theodore's own lips—it is another break in the case. We're so lucky he didn't add to the body count."

"I just hope 'Daphne' doesn't either," mused Sophie. "While al-Hadi needs to have her around now for some reason, when she stops being useful to him, it's over."

Alexius gave them a quick salute. "I'll keep you two posted on anything else that develops. Meanwhile, we'll keep checking on that brown powder. I haven't forgotten that!"

As they rode back to the villa, Sophie felt herself getting more agitated over 'Daphne's' situation. "She has to be somewhere! Why not just search all of the houses and buildings where she could be held!"

Now it was Justin's turn to comfort his wife. "Now, you know that's not practicable—there are thousands of buildings in the city where people live, and that doesn't count warehouses and other structures where they usually don't. Besides, once they know we're on to them, 'Daphne' is as good as dead. No, we've got to be patient and continue to weave our web. You've made your contribution in tying the ivory necklace with the ivory dealer, so now it's my turn to figure out how the manuscript is supposed to help. It will work out, you'll see!"

"Thank you, dear. I needed that. Just promise me one thing—don't tear up the house too badly before my father comes tomorrow. Promise?"

"Promise."

"Good. Now, I'll have the driver drop you off—I need to run by the palace to make sure things are running well. See you later!"

As the carriage was rolling off, Sophie could hear Justin calling, "Just how bad is 'too badly?'"

CHAPTER 31

Friday began as a day of frustration for Justin. With the identification of Musa al-Hadi as the mystery voice from Crete, the search for the source of the brown powder underway and the discovery that 'Daphne' was (perhaps) still alive, the only remaining loose end was the manuscript. Although he would never to his dying day admit it, he was proud of his proficiency with languages, and was maddened by the intricacies of Arabic, even though another Roman who spoke it well had told him early on that the first ten years learning it were the hardest.

Given all of this, why couldn't he make sense of the final pages of the manuscript? Anwar and Agatho had done their part in deciphering most of the symbols that al-Haytham was fond of using as a means of shorthand. The 'most' was important, for there was one remaining symbol on the last diagram that remained unknown. Justin's knowledge of Arabic and the way its words were formed led to him to think 'glowing', 'bright' or 'shiny', none of which seemed to work.

After racking his brains for several hours, he made a conscious decision to explain his dilemma to someone whose mind was not clouded by pre-existing knowledge. This ruled out his assistants, who were in the other room trying to out-do each other in translating the remaining pages. Sophie would be sympathetic, but a little judgmental. Besides, she had left for the palace earlier. This left Maria, who was riding Poppy on the grounds below the garden, next to the seawall, under the watchful eye of the assistant groom.

While Justin could have Philip send out a call to bring Maria up, he went himself and watched her ride about for several minutes. *'She is really growing up,'* he thought, *'and she's so like Sophie!'* Eventually, he called over to her and she joined him in the dining room, with eyes wide with wonder about what he was doing. In the meantime, one of the maids had brought several large white sheets and placed them on the table.

With the directness of a child, she immediately asked, "Does Mama know about her sheets being in here?"

"Not exactly, but after all they are my sheets, too, and yours. We all live here, don't we?" Justin tried to rationalize.

Undeterred, Maria responded, "I don't think she'd like it, do you?"

"Well, then we won't hurt them," Justin replied, then lowered his voice as he finished, "much. Let me tell you what I am trying to do here. I think it will be fun!"

Justin then attempted to explain what he had learned from the diagram and the text, going on the belief that one could not really understand something unless he could also explain it. He decided to start simple.

"All right, Maria, do you remember when you were playing with that piece of rock the other day?"

"Yes, Father, do you mean the quartz?"

"Uh, yes, that was the one. Do you remember how it made the light split into different colors?"

"Yes, it was pretty. Are we doing that with Mama's sheets?"

Thinking *'enough with the sheets already!'* Justin smiled and said, "No, that was just an example. Uh, Maria, I know you don't play with dolls anymore, but could you find that big one that Grandpa gave you two or three years ago? I think her name is Andromeda?"

With an eye-roll that belied her years, Maria shook her head. "No, Papa, she's Alexandra! What do you want with her?"

"We're going to do a little experiment. Don't worry, she won't be hurt."

"She can't be hurt, Papa. She's not alive!" Maria noted as she left to find the figurine in question.

'*Logical, just like her mother!*' he thought as Agatho and Anwar poked their heads into the room.

"What's going on, sir?" Anwar asked.

"Oh, good, you're here," replied Justin. "I've decided, more out of desperation than anything else, to try and replicate the last diagram in the manuscript. I think I have most of it figured out, but I can certainly use your help."

At that point, Maria reappeared with Alexandra and asked where the doll should go. Seeing the looks on his assistants' faces, Justin was compelled to explain.

"Ah, yes, thank you, Maria. Alexandra will be part of the experiment that I was explaining to Agatho and Anwar here. Please put her here on the table. Anwar, please go and find Philip—tell him I need three or four oil lamps here in the dining room."

With Maria watching attentively, Justin had Anwar and Agatho hang one sheet at the end of the dining room with a second sheet hung in the middle. The doll was placed several feet in front of the second sheet, with the lamps arranged yet in front of it.

Thinking it was time for truth, Justin said to Maria, "All right, we need to cut a little hole, a very little hole, here in this sheet. I'll tell your mother, so don't worry. It's all part of the experiment." So saying, he cut a round hole approximately one inch in diameter in the middle of the sheet about five feet above the floor.

The results were less than impressive. While there was an image projected on the second sheet hung against the wall, it was just a shadow that didn't look like anything.

Justin looked to his assistants. "Suggestions, gentlemen?"

Agatho looked at Anwar, and then said, "Maybe the hole should be larger?"

This was accordingly done, and produced a slightly larger shadow.

Agatho tried again. "What if we change the distances—move the sheet in the middle back or move the doll forward?" Neither made any real difference.

After studying the manuscript, Anwar took his shot at the problem and said, "Perhaps we should switch the positions of the doll and the lights—have the doll against the near wall and lit up by lamps between it and the sheet?"

At this point, Justin was game for anything, and the rearrangement was made. To the surprise of all, an image, albeit fuzzy, of the doll appeared on the sheet on the far wall, via the light that had made its way through the hole in the first sheet. Enthusiasm was short-lived, however. Thinking that if a hole that size would produce a certain size image, a larger hole would make an improved one, the hole was enlarged again. Alas, fuzziness still prevailed. "Too big a hole," Justin announced. "Get another sheet and make the hole a little smaller."

Seeking to redeem himself from his earlier errant suggestions, Agatho said, "Sir, have you figured out what the wording in the diagram means for this far surface?"

Justin had to confess. "No, I really have not—all I could come up with are 'bright' or 'shiny' or things like that. Do you have an idea?"

"Just a thought, sir, assuming the author was trying to use Arab words for Greek concepts, how about 'reflective'"?

Justin thought for a moment, and then said, "That is worth trying. Agatho, you and Anwar go up to our bedroom—the maid will show you the way—and bring down the mirror in the frame that sits on the floor. Be careful—if anything happens to it, you will both be fired and I will be sleeping in the stables! We'll try it in front of the sheet by the wall."

No one would ever know how much longer things would have gone on like this, for Sophie now deigned to make her appearance. Putting the mutilation of her sheets aside, she took in the situation at once, even though she knew nothing of the physical principles involved. After hugging Maria and shushing any comments about the sheets, she was confronted with the two assistants lugging the mirror down the stairs. With a mild protest of "that was my mother's," she directed them where to put it down.

The results were dramatic. Those assembled now could see a fairly clear image of the doll, projected through the hole in the sheet, against the mirror. While it wasn't very big, some further experimentation with the distance separating the sheets showed that this could be manipulated. There was only one major problem—the image was upside-down! It was also reversed—the right side of the doll was shown in the mirror on the left side.

This result caused consternation among the men in the room, who huddled to examine the manuscript again and determine their error. With a shake of her head to Maria, who was still watching entranced, Sophie proceeded to turn the doll upside down and then announce, "Better, gentlemen?"

There on the far wall in full color was a recognizable image of the doll.

The cheers that went up were cut short by Sophie. "This is fine, but what we saw in the banquet room was not a doll. That figure moved and was clearly a person. Can you recreate that?"

"Well," Justin offered in jest, "you could always ask Donna to come in here and let us hang her upside down by her ankles. Would she agree to that?"

"Doubtful," replied Sophie. "She is just now getting over her first experience, and that was after she was drunk. No, I can't ask anyone to do something that I wouldn't, so use me. Let's go!"

"Are you serious? I was joking!"

"I'm not! Now, send for Philip—I will need a shorter length of rope to wrap around my legs and hold my gown up, modesty you know, and we can hang a longer piece over that beam there. Tie it around my ankles and then Agatho and Anwar can pull me up—very easy. You keep my head from hitting anything. Got it?"

So it was that when Doctor Lukas Lascaris, renowned physician and caregiver to Emperor Constantine VIII, appeared at his daughter's house for dinner, he found her hanging upside down by the ankles in the dining room of the villa she and her family shared. Knowing full well that he had raised an unconventional daughter, he took it in stride, after first being mobbed by his grandchildren.

"Oh, hello, Father," said Sophie, her face beginning to glow a little red. "We're working on a case. Look in the mirror over there. What do you think?"

Walking around the sheet hanging down in the middle of the room, the doctor was astounded to see a miniature version of his daughter in the mirror against the wall. Even more amazing, the miniature was <u>right-side</u> up! As Sophie waved her arm in greeting, the miniature Sophie did so to, although on the opposite side of her body. Justin was by the mirror, attempting to move it forward.

"Here, Justin, let me help," said Lascaris. Together, they moved the mirror toward the sheet several feet. The result was that the image was both sharper, but smaller.

"Thanks, Doctor. I estimate that to get a full-size image, I'd need to have the mirror about thirty feet farther back, which is impossible given the size of the room."

"But wouldn't it be fuzzier?" asked the doctor.

Justin mused for a moment, then said, "Yes, but it still would be discernable as a woman."

"Yes, a woman who is about to pass out! Get me down from here!" called Sophie.

With the help of the staff, order was soon restored to the dining room and the table set for dinner. Agatho and Anwar were thanked for all of their hard work, with a more tangible expression of Justin's thanks in the form of three gold solidi apiece. Lascaris had a pleasant meal, at least as pleasant as one could have with one or sometimes two grandchildren in his lap. Eventually, as dinner was concluded and Maria and Simon were sent off to bed, they were able to retire to the veranda.

Justin and Lascaris were enjoying the night air and the ever-changing spectacle of the lights of the city and the ships in the Golden Horn when Sophie joined them. She had recovered from her ordeal and was talkative again.

"Ah, that's better! A little wine and I'll feel like a new woman!"

Justin was puzzled. "Why wouldn't you even ask Donna? She's your maid."

"Exactly, dear. A good maid is hard to find—I spent months training Donna. I don't want to go through that again. Besides, what's the problem? I survived, and you made the biggest break in the case yet. We know now how 'Loviatar' was created!" Sophie triumphantly said while at the same time seeing a confused look on her father's face.

"Oh, sorry, Father! Justin and I have lived with this for so long we forget that everyone else doesn't know. Here's what we've been working on." She then gave an abbreviated account of the past several weeks, with supporting details from Justin. When she was done, she said, "So, that's why today's experiment was so important!"

Her father sat silently for several moments, first looking at her and then at Justin and then back at her. Finally, he said, "Unbelievable. I knew you two were involved with some investigations, but this is beyond anything I could imagine. The emperors are so lucky to have you! So now what do you do?"

"That's to be determined, sir," replied Justin. "As Sophie has laid out, Friday nights at the Varangians' banquet are the crucial time. We have the next one coming up a week from today, and we need to conclude things there. Catching the criminals isn't enough—we need to dispel any notion of this goddess. We are still working on that."

Lascaris shook his head. "And to think that I am here in Constantinople because of this entire web of events. This brown powder—have you figured that part out yet?"

"No, Father," said Sophie. "We still are working on that part too. It was mostly an accident that we were able to help Constantine at the beginning, and to get you here to heal him after that. Speaking of the emperor, how is he doing?"

"Much better, I'm happy to say. He's gotten over the after effects of the powder, whatever it was, and is feeling better about not drinking, although that will take some time, and I don't think he'll ever be totally free of it. He's still depressed, but physical activity helps—did you know he's quite a rider? The Blachernae Palace has marvelous stables, and he goes riding outside the walls almost every day. I try to keep up with him, and he lets me until the end, when he always has to win. Part of being an emperor, I guess. He's also an archer—I don't even try to compete with him in that."

"Have you told him about Mezezius, and when I say that, I mean both about his actions and his fate?" asked Sophie.

"Yes, and he took it as well as could be expected, although he was disappointed. It did make him feel more useless, and by that I mean he feels he was taken advantage of by a servant, which royalty never likes to admit. I have to say that this brown powder, whatever it was, hit him hard. He's been drinking heavily for years, and took the powder for only a few weeks, yet it really laid him low."

"Why did he take it? What did Mezezius tell him it was for?" Justin asked.

"An energy supplement, I believe. Constantine isn't getting any younger, and he was quick to seize on something that would make him feel younger without him actually having to do anything, like cut down on his wine. I'd really be interested in finding out what it is, if for nothing else than a professional interest."

"Well, thanks, sir, it's always good to have your thoughts on these matters. Now, let me tell you what Maria and Simon have been doing..." Justin said. Business aside, they enjoyed their remaining time together as a family until it was time for Lascaris to travel back to the Blachernae.

After he had left, Sophie and Justin were left to digest what had happened that evening. By mutual agreement, they put off any further decisions until the next day.

"Things always look better in the morning," Sophie noted.

Later that night, as they were lying in bed, Sophie was decompressing from the day's events and had to make one final comment.

"I am so proud of you, dear!" Sophie gushed. "You treated that manuscript like it was a puzzle and figured it out! That was ingenious: I wish I could have seen what you saw tonight in the mirror. Did I really look myself?"

"Almost as good as you do in person, albeit smaller and fuzzier. Am I forgiven for the sheets?"

Sophie was silent long enough that Justin began to think that he was in trouble. Then he felt her hand in his and knew it was all right.

"Of course, dear!" she purred. "Given what you paid for that necklace, you can cut up a hundred sheets and I'll still be ahead! Good night!"

CHAPTER 32

Saturday started out warm and sultry, and only got hotter as the day went on. While the temperature rarely got oppressive due to the moderating effect of the breezes off the Sea of Marmara, there was so much concrete, marble and brick in Constantinople that over the summer it did not cool off much even at night. Justin and Sophie had the advantage of having a villa on the side of a hill overlooking the Golden Horn, and so did not usually feel the true effects of a summer heat wave. Still, it was hot enough. Sophie wondered how it was for 'Daphne', assuming she was still alive, as she was likely confined in a closed space somewhere well away from the sea.

Based on what had been discovered the previous evening, Sophie and Justin were eager to test out their theory where it really mattered—the Varangian dining hall. Making a shape on sheets in their dining room was one thing, while figuring out how it had been done repeatedly in the larger space was something else. Using the information from the night before, Justin, Agatho and Anwar had spent the morning working out the dimensions to create a life-sized image in the larger room. It all depended on the distance between the object and the hole through which the light passed, the size of the hole, and the distance between the hole and the surface on which the image was displayed. As Justin explained to Sophie on the ride to the hall, the ratio between the hole and the distance to the image was about 1 to 100.

Sophie smiled and shook her head, "Thank you dear, can you try that again in language that someone who is not a genius can understand?"

"Sure, you see—wait a minute—you understood that perfectly well!" Justin protested. "But, to please you, to get a life-sized image of 'Loviatar', the reflection of 'Daphne' would have to go through a five-inch hole to reach a reflective surface 40 feet away."

"Ah," recalled Sophie, "the far side of the banquet hall is nothing but glass that could act as a mirror. The question is—how wide is the hall?"

"That, my dear, is what we are about to find out. I've sent a message to ask Hetman Siggurdsen to meet us at the banquet hall, which is coming up on our right as I speak," said Justin.

"No Alexius?"

"No, I don't think he cares much for our hetman, whatever Siggurdsen says."

When they arrived, they found the banquet hall to be a very quiet place. Since no Varangians had been present the previous Friday night, no clean-up had been necessary, and they did not have to worry about being seen by maids and janitors. The only person there was Hetman Siggurdsen, who was waiting for them on the steps. At least to Sophie, he seemed more care-worn than usual, which led her to speak to him in his native tongue.

"Heill doegr, Hetman! Eru yor erfidr?" {Good day, Hetman! Are you troubled?} she said.

"Ja, Jarnlayden, minn gotar hraeddr. Iak hugsjukr," {"Yes, Iron Lady, my men are frightened. I am worried."} he answered with a response that sounded more fatalistic than even a Varangian would usually be.

At this point, Justin nudged Sophie hard enough that she switched to Greek. "Well, Hetman, we are here to clear this matter up once and for all. If we are right, there will be no more ritual killings of Varangians and no more appearances of 'Loviatar.' Will you help us?"

The face of the Northman, normally impassive, showed unexpected fire as he replied, "With all my heart, Iron Lady, with all my heart!"

"Good," interjected Justin, "now here is what we need to do." Producing a tape measure, he held the end against the interior wall and had Siggurdsen take the other end and walk out to the far wall lined with mirrors. Once the line was taut, Justin called out, "Now, Hetman, does it say 40 feet?"

"No, sir, it does not," came the reply. Fortunately, only Sophie could see the crestfallen look on Justin's face before the follow-up comment came from the Hetman. "It's 39 and ½ feet."

"Well, you asked," said Sophie with a wink to Justin. She then called to Siggurdsen, "Thank you, Hetman, now we need to go upstairs."

As they were walking up the stairs, Sophie continued to engage the Varangian in conversation.

"So, for your banquets, who prepares the food? The last time we were here, I remember seeing it served, but I didn't go back into the kitchens. Do Varangians fix it?"

Siggurdsen gave a snort. "Lady, we are warriors, not scullery maids! No, we have local people act as our caterers. They are instructed to prepare the kinds of food we like, and then they take it from there. If they provide food in sufficient quantities and of sufficient quality, we keep them. If not, we find others."

"And who has the hiring authority?" she continued.

"I do, although the Akolouthos has the final say over our expenditures." Here the Hetman paused as they reached the second floor before saying, "He does not examine them overmuch."

Sophie persisted. "Forgive me, Hetman, for seeming to belabor this point, but it is important. My husband and I have reason to think that the person or persons who are responsible for the 'Loviatar' illusion get into the building on Fridays without being seen or at least noticed. How many people would you say are involved in food preparation and serving for your banquets?"

Siggurdsen frowned for a moment, then said "I would say several dozen—50 to 60. Who knows?"

"Thank you. That tells us what we need to know. Now, let's examine these rooms!"

Justin took over. "Given that light travels in a straight line according to the manuscript, we need to find a place that looks out directly across from the window where we saw the illusion." So saying, he opened a door and confronted a small, narrow storage room that did not look out over the room below. "Hmm, this could be a problem."

"Not really," said Sophie. "'Loviatar' appears in the sixth window from the end. Allowing for the width of the doors on the end and each window, this would come to about 80 feet from the north end of the banquet hall. This should reduce the number of rooms we have to check a little."

As it turned out, "a little" was a lot. Measuring from the north end of the hall down, it only took them three rooms to find the likely suspect. Like the others, it was narrow but long. *'Perfect,'* thought Justin, *'just the kind of room I would have chosen.'*

Since it was very dark, they needed to get some kind of light to continue. There was accordingly a slight delay while a lamp was obtained by the hetman. Once illuminated, the room was found to be empty, with cupboards on either side. Justin was more interested on the far wall, and was examining it carefully. Although it took several minutes, he eventually found a weak spot in the wall, and gave a cry of triumph.

"Ha, here, you see! Look!" So saying, he pulled back a loose panel from the wall and uncovered an opening about 5 inches in diameter.

"That's the opening. Look through it to the wall!" Sure enough, the glass panel where 'Loviatar' appeared each time was directly across from them.

"But where was 'Daphne' when this was being done?" asked Sophie. "Based on your demonstration last night, she has to be upside down for it to work."

While Hetman Siggurdsen had witnessed many strange things in his years in Mikkelgard serving Emperor Basil, this was beyond anything that had come before. However, having seen a little of how these two unusual Romans worked, he kept silent and awaited what came next. He was not disappointed.

Standing at the wall with the hole, Justin walked back in a measured fashion toward the inner wall where the entrance door was located. After he paced off the desired distance, he held up the lamp to the ceiling. Once again, he was rewarded with the desired result.

"Look, right here!" Holding the lamp up above his head, he illuminated two black straps hanging down from the cross-beam."

"Give me that, please!" demanded Sophie. Taking the lamp, she walked up the drawers of a cabinet as if they were stairs. Holding it up, she examined the straps closely before coming back down.

When she did not speak, Justin asked, "What is it? What did you see?"

"Dried blood, dear, dried blood. 'Daphne' has been here, hung upside down. From the looks of it, she has bled more than once." Sophie was silent for a long time before doing something very uncharacteristic by muttering a number of Norse words and phrases with great feeling. Then she stalked off down the hall, repeating them even more loudly.

While Justin suspected that the words were not exactly uplifting, he nonetheless asked Siggurdsen what she had said.

"Nothing you want to know, Treasurer, although you likely have a good idea," the Norseman replied. Then, with a touch of awe in his voice, he said, "The Iron Lady is well named! She swears like a Valkyrie!"

Having seen all there was to see at the banquet hall, they parted company with the hetman and returned to the Palace. Sophie was still quiet, and Justin knew enough to let her process what she had seen without interruption.

As their carriage rolled up to the Chalke Gate, Sophie finally spoke in a low voice. "This is now officially no longer about justice alone—I want vengeance on the people who did this! Kidnapping, assault, torture, murder—we have never had people like this to deal with. Musa al-Hadi and his men must be stopped! Poor 'Daphne'!"

As Justin looked at his wife, he initially was surprised to see tears running down her cheeks. If not actually witness to much violent death, she had seen the aftermath of many violent acts, and for one to affect her like this was unexpected. *'But then again,'* thought Justin, *'perhaps not. She formed a bond with those people at the club, just as I did with those men at the jail.'* He took her in his arms, and told the driver to take another lap around the Hagia Sophia.

By the time they came back, Sophie was better. "Thank you, Justin. I needed that. Now, on to face the world, at least for a little while! Will you come back to Zoe's from the Treasurer's office…

"You mean, 'my office'?" said Justin with a grin.

"Yes, that one, too, you rascal! Will you come back or should I arrange a ride home for myself?"

"No, dear, I'll be by," Justin said as they walked across the great Forum of Constantine to the Chalke Gate. With a kiss, he left her after they had gone through to make his way to 'his' offices.

Sophie had considerably less distance to walk, and so arrived at Zoe's quarters first. While she normally exchanged greetings with the Varangians on guard, today the men on guard stared straight ahead and did not acknowledge her presence. Knowing that engaging in small talk would be futile, she simply nodded in their direction and entered. *'I hope that's not a sign of things to come,'* she sighed.

Inside, she found a bustle of activity. Since Irene was enjoying a day off, she found Helena who brought her up to speed. Zoe was excited about going to see her father after church tomorrow. It was to be a complete family affair, for Basil was going with her and Theodora. *'Note to self,'* Sophie thought, *'be busy with something else tomorrow!'*

Retiring to her office, she looked over the duty roster for the next week, and made a point to put Julia, the 'new girl', in positions where she would have a chance to interact one-on-one with Zoe. Before the year was out, she anticipated that one and maybe two of the other younger ladies would leave the service to get married, so it was important that women like Julia be worked into the routines now. Still, there was never a shortage of other young women who were eager to serve as ladies-in-waiting. *'The soup test was a good one, but I'll need to come up with something else next time—maybe hanging upside down?'*

When she did see Zoe a little later, she made it a point to share her father's report on Constantine's progress. The princess was predictably thrilled, and was particularly pleased when she heard about how Constantine had taken up the bow again.

"Oh, I have to tell you, Sophie!" she gushed. "One of my earliest memories was watching him shoot arrows at a target. He would always win in any contest, and it wasn't just people deferring to him because he was the emperor. No, he really was that good! How clever of your father to get him involved in that again—it will help his cure immensely."

Smiling, Sophie patted Zoe's hand. "I'm sure all of you will have a good time tomorrow. I'm sorry I can't be with you, but Justin and I are getting close to solving our big case, and we really need to work on it."

"That's exciting—you must tell me all about it—oh, wait, I realize you can't, hush-hush and all that! Well, we'll all look forward to hearing about it once it's over, I'm sure!"

Justin's office was considerably quieter. One of the innovations he had instituted when he became treasurer was to let most of the staff have Saturdays off, along with the already standard day off on Sunday. A few people were there on a rotating basis, but no one had to work more than one Saturday every six weeks.

When he arrived, he checked with Paul, the assistant on duty that day. Paul was working on the next gathering of treasurers from the themes, or provinces, which was set for August. This time officials from the western half of the empire would attend. The challenges facing them were different from their eastern counterparts, in that they did not have to worry as much about providing land for veterans. However, thanks to the wars of Basil, in places like the Balkans they had to deal with taxing land that had not been within the empire's boundaries for centuries.

Justin looked over the materials, encouraged Paul to keep up the good work, and satisfied himself that there no problems that would not keep until Monday. He decided to take a different route back to find Sophie, and walked along some of the porticos and verandas that had been built over the years to showcase the gardens and the views of the sea beyond the walls. He was enjoying a perfect summer day when he passed a hall and caught a glimpse of several men wearing red. Realizing who they were, he tried to duck down a side passageway. Too slow!

"Oh, Justin, it's good to see you!" called Prefect Comnenus. "We were just talking about you. If you have a moment, please come join us!"

With a sinking heart, Justin followed the prefect back into the hall where the red-clad western Christians, with Romanus at their head, were seated on one side and Patriarch Sergius and his people, garbed in black, were on the other. Romanus greeted him with an approving nod, while he got a look best classified as a semi-glare from the patriarch.

Taking him aside for a moment, the prefect grabbed his sleeve and whispered, "For the love of God, Justin, I need your help again! These people are at loggerheads! I am afraid we are looking at a major schism if we can't come to some agreement!"

Justin looked and saw real fear in the older man's eyes before answering, "All right, I'll do what I can."

Then, turning to the assembled group, he tried to use his best bureaucratic voice. "Gentlemen, how may I help you?"

The cacophony of voices that followed was to be expected, before Romanus rose and said in an easy voice that showed that he was also a player of the game, "Ah, Treasurer, thank you for coming. Yes, we have made great progress here, great progress! We do have one problem left, over just a word. Perhaps you can help us?"

This was enough to set Patriarch Sergius off, as he rose complaining that a layman such as Justin had no business in these serious ecclesiastical matters. His bishops and priests rose with him, to be met by the Italians on the other side.

Thinking *'this had better be good!'*, Justin raised his voice and said, "Gentlemen, gentlemen! His Eminence is entirely right," this with a bow to the patriarch, who looked confused and pleased at the same time, "I am just a layman. However, I am also recognized by their Majesties as an expert in languages." Thinking *'it's now time to lay it on thick!'*, he went on, "In fact I have assembled a team of translators that just now has solved a very difficult problem in Arabic! Compared to what they have done, Latin and Greek should be no problem. I would be happy to look at whatever issue you have and then report back to you, via the Prefect." He then bowed deeply to both sides, and headed out the door as fast he could, keeping decorum in mind.

When Sophie saw him a few minutes later outside Zoe's quarters, he was still a little out of breath.

"Is counting money that stressful?" she asked with a smile. Then, seeing he was not smiling back, she said, "Emperor troubles?"

"Worse," he replied. "On top of everything else, I am now caught up in a fight between churches. I'll give you the details later."

Sophie patted him on the arm as they headed to their carriage, "Whenever you're ready, or, if not, then fine. My faith does not depend on the quarrels of old men over obscure points of doctrine. If you can do something for them, it's more than they deserve."

Justin thought about his wife's comment on the drive back to their villa. When they were walking up to their front door, he took her hand and saying nothing, merely kissed it. She smiled in turn, and kissed him back.

Their moment of tranquility lasted that evening and well into Sunday. When Justin, Sophie and Maria came home from church, they were greeted by Simon, the dogs and a message from Alexius. The first two were more than welcome, while the third was not. Sophie saw Justin's face fall when he read the note, which he then passed wordlessly to her.

She closed her eyes, hard, and then read, "Sorry to tell you this, Boss—ivory stall is closed and there's no one there. Looks like the birds have flown. Tell you more tomorrow."

CHAPTER 33

When Alexius came to the villa on Monday morning, he did so with a heavy heart. While he knew Justin well enough to know (hope?) he would not be fired for losing track of Musa al-Hadi and his men, it was still a stain on his professional reputation. Even though it had been his men who had let the Egyptians slip through their fingers, he had selected and trained almost all of them and their failure was his.

As it turned out, his fears were misplaced, as least as to Justin. Sophie was another story.

"How could this happen, Alexius? How? Do you know what may happen to 'Daphne' because of this? She could die! She could already be dead!!" In order to avoid upsetting the children, they were having this discussion, if it could be called that, on the front walk.

"You're right, 'Scalpel', you're right. There's no excuse. We're looking everywhere we can now, believe me. If they are in the city, we will know it—eventually," Alexius offered to the still glaring senior lady-in-waiting.

"Alexius," Justin began in a measured voice that alarmed the eunuch even more, "we spent a lot of time and effort to identify these men. Please just tell us what happened."

Alexius gave a sigh and began, "Well, after the incident with Theodore, we only knew of the shop in the Mese as a location where they could be found. Starting Friday, we watched it around the clock, and saw nothing. It was closed on Friday for Muslim prayers, and should have opened again on Saturday. When it didn't, we doubled the watch. On Sunday, when there was still no sign of life, we went in, and found no one. There were living areas you couldn't see from the street that would have accommodated several people, but they were empty. There was also a passage to an adjoining building they apparently used to give us the slip."

Sophie looked at Justin with alarm. "Do you think they know we have identified them?"

Justin shook his head. "No, I think it's more a matter of al-Hadi being careful. He lost a man last week and there were bound to be questions about Ferhat. I think he is lying low for now. Still, it's clear he is feeling some pressure—a little more might be enough for him to flee the city. If that happens, 'Daphne' will end up like Mezezius. Still, we may be able to use this to our advantage—let's talk about it later. For now, what's done is done."

Seeking to redeem himself, Alexius said, "I do have some good news—we found out where the brown powder came from, or at least found someone who may know! That's worth something, isn't it?"

"Nice try, Alexius, nice try," responded Sophie. "So you finally found the right apothecary? Where is it?"

"It's run by a Jew who has a shop in one of the towers in the land walls, out by the Adrianople Gate. He was surprised to see us, but was very cooperative."

"So," continued Sophie trying to keep a straight face, "why didn't you go to him first?"

"Well, you see, we started…oh, you're kidding, aren't you?" Alexius said with relief.

Sophie sealed the deal by giving her characteristic laugh. "Yes, and good job, by the way. We'll go and see this man right now—what's his name?"

"Jacob ben-Isaacson, and he's in Tower 77."

So it was that about one hour later, Justin and Sophie found themselves heading toward the land walls that girded Constantinople on its western side. While Septimus Severus and Constantine the Great had built earlier walls, the final ring of fortifications along the land side was credited to Emperor Theodosius II in the fifth century.

Over 90 towers, each 50 feet tall, lined the wall, which consisted of an inner ring linking the towers, a middle lower ring and an outer, even lower ring which bordered on a wide moat. A number of gates punctuated the wall at intervals, of which the Golden Gate was only one. Since the empire had had no external threat from the north for many decades, many of the towers were unmanned and had been occupied by opportunistic people in the city, of whom Jacob was apparently one.

As they rode, they discussed their strategy in approaching the apothecary.

"How could a Jew be involved with al-Hadi?" Justin wondered out loud.

Sophie shook her head. "I can't see that al-Hadi would be involved with a Jew. You would think that if this man was a loose end, he would have been disposed of already like Mezezius. Maybe he was involved, but doesn't really know anything. Anyhow, we'll soon find out. Here we are, Tower 77. Dear, don't you think the cavalry escort was a little much?" So saying, she looked back at the 20 cataphracts who were following them, heavily-armored men on armored horses.

Justin was dismissive. "Not my idea, dear. Alexius is scared to death that Jacob will disappear on us like the Egyptians did—he called the prefect, and the prefect—well, here we go. Act natural!"

They both approached the tower with roughly the same image of the man they were about to meet—a wizened, all-knowing sage with a wispy beard. When a young, clean-shaven man who looked to be in his 20's came out, Justin naturally assumed that this was Jacob's assistant.

"Good day, sir, we are here to see your master, Jacob ben-Isaacson," he said with an air of authority.

"Then you are here," the young man said, "for I am he."

Undeterred, Justin went on, "Yes, well, fine, but we need to speak to the Jacob who is your father or grandfather. We are here on imperial business!"

YEAR OF THE HOOPOE

Sophie perceived what was going on better than her husband, who for whatever reason had decided to act the part of the important man, something he fortunately rarely did. She decided to intervene.

"Actually, Jacob, we are here to talk with you. My name is Sophia, and this is Justin, my husband, who really is a good man when you get to know him." Ignoring the glare that this produced from her spouse, she went on. "We are looking into a matter on behalf of their majesties involving a particular kind of drug. Do you have a moment to talk with us?"

"Do I have a choice?" answered the young man, looking at the cavalrymen who had dismounted and were standing by their horses. "Am I to be arrested?"

"No, no, nothing like that. We just want to talk, and I am sorry if I came across a little strong to start with," said Justin. "May we go inside your store?"

"Certainly, although I apologize in advance for the conditions—I don't get many visitors in person. Most of my business is with other apothecaries—I'm sort of a wholesaler, you might say."

Once their eyes adjusted to the darkness, Justin and Sophie could see the truth in Jacob's words. The room they entered was round, since it was the bottom of the tower. It was piled high with boxes, cartons and containers from many countries. While Justin could recognize the Arabic, Armenian, Syriac and Hebrew scripts, others baffled him.

Seeing his puzzlement, Jacob laughed. "Yes, I do an international business here in Constantinople, the marketplace of the world. That script there is Hindi, from India, while that one over there is Chinese—since I have no idea what it says, I have to rely on what the dealers tell me."

And the smells! Sophie was sniffing around the room, seeing how many odors she could identify. Some were familiar to her, others were totally foreign. With an effort, she brought her mind back to the problem at hand and produced the bag containing the mysterious brown powder.

Seeing it, Jacob gave a knowing smile. After opening the bag, he took a pinch of the powder and sniffed it, then touched it to his tongue. Nodding, he said, "Yes, I am familiar with this substance. What would you like to know about it?"

Justin and Sophie exchanged glances, with Sophie then taking the lead. "To start with, who have you sold this powder to?"

To their mutual consternation, Jacob shook his head in the negative and gave a curt laugh. "Sell? Would that I could, Lady, but I have no supply of it. I would say that this powder is worth its weight in gold, but that would be misleading—one can get gold, while this powder is virtually unobtainable. You probably have all there is in the city right in this pouch."

"So how do you know about it?" Sophie persisted.

"I know about hundreds of drugs from many lands—my father and grandfather before me were apothecaries, and passed on to me the collective knowledge of my people, which goes back many centuries, even before this city existed. The brown powder you have is called silphium. It is a dried essence of the giant fennel plant which is found in a very few places in northern Africa. The Greeks in the time of Herodotus called the area Cyrene. The Romans called it Libya. I don't know what its current occupants call it."

"With the current occupants being the Fatimids, correct?" Justin said.

"Correct. Anyhow, the Romans overharvested it and it is now very rare. The climate has also gotten hotter and drier in the area where it grows. How did you come by so much?"

Sophie shrugged. "It's a long story. Please, Jacob, tell us, why did the ancients prize it so much?"

"Well, according to the herb lore experts, it was an unparalleled stimulant, giving energy, sharpening the wits, focusing the mind. It was also said to be an excellent aphrodisiac, although one never knows about the truth of such claims."

In full medical mode, Sophie pressed on. "Any side effects? Any drugs it interacts with?"

Jacob paused for a moment, as though he was searching his memory. Then, he responded as if reciting a lesson learned long ago, "No real side effects, although like most stimulants its effects lessen with repeated, heavy use, so that it takes more and more to achieve the same result. Addiction is possible, but it would take a fairly large amount of the powder, which would be beyond the financial means of almost anyone. As for interactions, yes, there is one very important one—it must not be taken with alcohol. If it is, the stimulant effects are reversed, and it becomes an even more powerful depressant. Motor control is affected, breathing is disrupted and in extreme cases death can ensue."

"Could someone mix the two by accident?" Sophie asked.

Jacob shook his head, "Surely not more than once. Believe me, this stuff is too expensive to waste like that. Why are you asking so much about silphium—has someone had a bad experience with it here?"

"You might say that," said Justin wryly.

"Just one more question, Jacob," said Sophie, "and then we'll get our horses off your lawn. If someone takes silphium to excess, are there any lasting effects?"

The young apothecary's brow furrowed before he answered. "Hmm, that's an interesting question. Given how it works on the body, I would say that there shouldn't be. Coming off it would be unpleasant, just like any other addictive drug, but it doesn't seem to have the hold on the body that say, alcohol, has. Does that help?"

"Unfortunately yes," replied Sophie, "but that's a story that does not involve you. Thank you for your help. If we can ever help you, please let us know."

"You are most welcome, but just who are you?"

Sophie laughed her melodious laugh as they went out the door. "Well, I am the senior lady-in-waiting for her Imperial Highness Princess Zoe, while my husband here is the Treasurer of the Roman Empire. Satisfied?"

"Well, I am pleased to meet you, Lady! Treasurer, please say hello to my cousin Levi—I believe he works for you," Jacob called in response as they rode off, cavalry and all, heading back to the city.

"How on earth are we going to explain this to Constantine and Zoe and Theodora and anybody except your father?" remarked Justin as they rode along.

Sophie replied, "We don't, dear. Now that we know the answer and the likely outcome, we leave it alone and let my father take the credit. That's fair, isn't it? Now, we need to talk about how we proceed with 'Loviatar'—Friday is coming soon!"

That talk was put off for at least a little while when the procession rolled past the Chora Monastery complex on their way back to the Great Palace. Both Justin and Sophie saw a number of men outside the monastery enjoying some exercise. The difference? Justin was not put off by the fact that many were wearing all red. For Sophie, this was something new.

Seeing the men, Sophie poked Justin in the ribs and hissed, "Justin! Do you see that! Men in red!"

Privately gratified that here was something he knew about that his wife didn't, Justin said, "Oh, that's the delegation from the pope in Rome—they tend to wear red there, just our clerics wear black here. I've talked with them—they mean well. They have some doctrinal disputes with the patriarch."

The mention of the patriarch was enough to dispel any interest Sophie had in the situation. They would have doubtless driven on but for a tall, bearded man who saw them and called out Justin's name. Justin acknowledged his hail, seeing that it was Romanus.

"Good day, Romanus! Taking a day off from doctrinal disputes?" Justin asked in a friendly voice.

"Every day is a day off for me, Treasurer!" the Italian answered in accented but acceptable Greek. "And who would this lovely woman be? Does your wife know?"

Beaming, Sophie hugged Justin and said, "Don't tell her, I beg you!"

"Ah, I thought so," replied Romanus. "Only a loving wife would respond like that. Treasurer, do you have a moment, or maybe two?"

Sighing, Justin turned to Sophie and said, "I've heard this before from Italians—what he really means is 'an hour or two.' Why don't you take the carriage home and I can walk back after I talk with Senator Romanus. I know it's about three miles, but I need time to think about our plans for this week."

Sophie nodded. "As do I, dear, as do I. Then, tonight," she said with a look toward Romanus, "we can do our best planning in bed!"

After Sophie had ridden off, Romanus and Justin walked around the grounds of the monastery, with Justin wondering what new issue had come up now.

"Aren't these gardens lovely?" remarked Romanus. "Even the best we have in Rome do not come close to these. But then again, we live in a city of ruins whose best days were centuries ago. Everyone knows it, but we pretend we don't see what is there. Here in Constantinople the comparisons can't be ignored. I will be sorry to leave."

While somewhat shocked to hear such a frank admission from one who had been at odds with the representatives from the empire he served, Justin wanted to hear more. "And the issues that brought you here? Can they be resolved?"

Romanus laughed. "How should I know? I'm not a churchman, nor was my brother before he became pope. As I've told you, he's pope only because our father was in a position to dictate who the next pope would be, after disposing of the previous strongman in Rome, along with his designated pope. We're here because the German emperor wants to have harmony in the church, even though he's the one who caused the disharmony with his stupid 'filoque' clause. I tell you, Treasurer, if you can come up with a plausible statement that reconciles the two sides' positions, say as a matter of language differences, no one in Rome is going to say no. Who knows? You could be the next pope!"

Justin shook his head in wonderment. "You are very frank, Senator, far more than we are used to here in Constantinople. In return, let me say that I will do what I can to keep our churches together—I won't lie, but when it comes to translation, one can always be creative. That leaves the bread issue and the papal supremacy issue—I'm sorry I can't help you there."

"Don't worry about those matters, Treasurer, believe me! When we have five or six popes in ten years, we have bigger issues. It's been a pleasure dealing with you, sir, a pleasure, and if I can ever be of assistance to you, don't hesitate to ask."

During the walk home, Justin's mind ran through the various threads of their investigation, as his body walked by the Cistern of Aspar, the great church of Christ Pantokrator, and the Mese (including the shuttered stall of the ivory dealer). Eventually he came to the hill that Constantine the Great, in conscious imitation of the seven hills of the original Rome, had named the First Hill. While it wasn't much of a hill, it was the doorway to home, and soon he was there.

Later in bed, Justin talked about the coming days with Sophie. After laying out a plausible way forward in theory, they turned to discuss practical problems in bringing the plan to fruition. By mutual agreement, they agreed to leave out any mention of the brown powder, its origin, or its use on Constantine.

"We'll need to go to Prefect Comnenus tomorrow," Justin said. "I'll suggest that Basil is there too—we'll need his full support if Senator Kalokyros is his usual less-than-charming self."

Sophie frowned as she took Justin's hand, "I'm worried, Justin. This is a high-risk plan we've put together—a lot could go wrong. We both may be looking for employment if things fall apart!"

Justin smiled as he embraced his wife. "Well, if we get sent to Cherson, at least we can keep each other warm!"

CHAPTER 34

When Sophie came downstairs the next morning, she found Justin already sitting at his desk in the study. The children were getting their breakfast, and the household staff was busy preparing for another day.

"Will it be a big day today?" she asked as she put her hands on his shoulders.

"I certainly hope so," Justin said after giving her a kiss. "I've sent messages to Prefect Comnenus and Hetman Siggurdsen requesting a meeting today sometime after noon. I've also suggested that, rather than use his office, we meet in one of the smaller audience rooms at that end of the Palace."

"Ah, in hopes that Basil will also be there? Not very subtle, are you?"

Justin sighed. "One can be too subtle, that's for sure. Whatever gets the job done, I guess."

The first step of the plan was achieved when they arrived at the prefect's office, only to be informed that the prefect would be meeting them in the Marble audience hall. This small receiving area was one of the jewels of the Great Palace, and had been built by Emperor Theophilus nearly two centuries earlier. Its walls and columns were built of pink marble from Chaldia in the far northeastern part of the empire.

When Justin and Sophie arrived, they found Prefect Comnenus already present, along with Senator Kalokyros and Hetman Siggurdsen. The former was cordial in his greeting while the senator merely scowled. Siggurdsen and Sophie exchanged greetings in Norse, and they were seated to await the arrival of Emperor Basil, whom the prefect confirmed was attending. That dignitary was not long in arriving, and when they had all made their bows (in Sophie's case, a curtsey), he bade them sit and the meeting began.

"Highness, thank you for accommodating us in your busy schedule," Justin began, facing Basil. Normally, Basil would have waived off such small talk, as he made little to no use of it himself. Today however was different.

"You are entirely welcome, Treasurer Cataphlates. We know that you and the Lady Sophia have been involved in the investigation of the murders of some of our Varangians. We trust you have made progress?"

"Yes, Highness, we have. In fact, I do not think it too much to say that we are on the verge of solving the case and apprehending those responsible. We will do so on Friday!"

This speech had its intended effect, as Justin and Sophie had planned the night before. The four men in the room stared at them in silence, and even the normally sour-faced senator gave them his rapt attention. Also as planned, Sophie took the baton and proceeded.

"Yes, Highness and assembled gentlemen, the end is in sight." She then went through each of the killings they had investigated, highlighting the similarities. As she did, she noticed that Basil in particular was entranced by the details, however gory. *'There is a man who is not unacquainted with killing,'* she thought.

Before Senator Kalokyros or anyone else could point out that these facts, while worthwhile to know, did not place them any closer to catching the killers, Justin took the baton back.

"I know that some of you have heard some of what we are about to say, and I would beg your indulgence. Still, I am fairly sure that none of you have heard all of what we have to say. Now, the puzzling aspect of this case was the appearance of an image in the Varangians' dining hall on their Friday night banquets. Though fuzzy, it was discernable, and was seen by many, including myself and my wife. The more superstitious of the Varangians believe it to be 'Loviatar'. Hetman Siggurdsen has informed us that this name is used for a goddess of pain and death in Scandinavia."

At this, Senator Kalokyros half-rose out of his chair. "This is outrageous! We are a Christian realm, and have no use for pagan theories! How dare you!"

Both Justin and Sophie were gratified to see the reaction that this produced from their other listeners. Basil said nothing, but stared hard at the senator. The prefect put his arm on the senator, as if to calm him down. Siggurdsen, by contrast, stood fully erect and said, "Senator, you speak of things you do not understand. Yes, the myth of 'Loviatar' is just that—a myth—but it carries power. If we are truly to get past this, this myth must be destroyed, and destroyed fully!"

Justin nodded to the Varangian as he retook his seat, and continued. "Through means that I will not bother you with, we were alerted to the existence of an Arabic document that detailed how such an image could be produced by purely natural, non-mythical means. We have managed to duplicate such an image at our home, and understand how it was done at the banquet hall. We plan to catch the criminals in the act on Friday, and disprove 'Loviatar' once and for all."

Apart from the senator, all of their listeners nodded approvingly, with Prefect Comnenus saying, "Wonderful! Uh, and just how are you going to do this?"

Sophie took up the narrative at this point and said, "On Friday night, we are going to lay a trap for the men involved. We think there are three in all, led by one Musa al-Hadi. We are going to need the help of the Varangians and Hetman Siggurdsen in particular."

"What do you wish me to do, Jarnlayden?" the Norse giant asked.

"Nothing much, really. You just need to die," Sophie replied sweetly.

The silence that followed was tangible, as her listeners exchanged bewildered glances. After a few seconds, Sophie decided that things had gone on long enough and decided to explain.

"No, not really die, just appear to. We think that two of the men involved in the plot will be outside, looking to murder another Varangian after the third man inside provokes things by showing the image again. In order to catch all of them at the same time, we need to make them think their plan is working, the Varangians really are going on strike, and a high-ranking Varangian officer is theirs for the taking."

"A ruse and an ambush—good, good. You would have made a good commander, Lady Sophia," mused Basil. But, you still have not told us how this image is produced."

Justin intervened at this point. "While the details are technical, suffice it to say, Highness, that a real person is involved. We believe that a Roman citizen has been kidnapped and forced into this role. His life is very much at stake unless we coordinate matters properly."

"A marvelous plan," enthused the prefect. Hetman Siggurdsen looked a little more dubious, but nodded his approval. Only Senator Kalokyros was as usual negative, directing his comments to Basil.

"This is madness, Highness. Why risk any more lives? These men should be arrested now, and, if guilty, executed. Why such an elaborate scheme? Besides, it's really asking too much of the Varangians. Yes, they are brave fighters, but do they have the discipline to carry off something like this?"

From long habit, Justin was not looking at the red-faced senator during his diatribe, but at Basil. Basil's face was impassive during the first few sentences, but when Kalokyros impugned the character of his favorite warriors, Justin could see his eyes tighten and the tell-tale twirling of the beard begin. *'Uh-oh, Senator, you should have known when to stop talking! Prepare to be rebuked!'*

When the rebuke came, however, it was from an unexpected quarter. Hetman Siggurdsen stood again, laid his sword on the table in front of him, and declared, "That is a lie, sir, a lie! My men and I will do whatever the emperor and the Iron Lady ask of us. Two years ago, she saved the lives of many Varangians in Palestine. We would not be men if we did not do the same for her now!" After staring a little longer at the shocked senator, he sat down.

Before the silence that followed grew unbearable, Sophie decided to wrap things up, announcing, "So, Highness and gentlemen, that is the plan. Clearly, there are details to work out, but if we succeed, the murders will stop, the criminals will be apprehended and the Varangians' minds will be freed from the on-going threat of 'Loviatar.' With another curtsey to Basil, she resumed her seat.

As he had countless times in countless meetings in the past, Basil knew when to take charge. "Treasurer and Lady, we wish you good hunting! Prefect, you will render them any assistance they ask for. Hetman, you and your men will regard any requests from them as orders coming from us. Is everyone clear on these points? Good, you are dismissed. Senator Kalokyros, please stay with us a little longer."

When they had all gotten safely out of the audience chamber and the ever-present Varangians had closed the doors behind them, Sophie and Justin let out a collective sigh of relief. Then, it was time to get back to business.

"For now, let's do this," said Justin. "Sophie, get together with Hetman Siggurdsen and fill him on what we need him and his men to do. We'll go over things in more detail later, but this will do for starters. Prefect, I need a few more minutes of your time to address one more detail that was not brought up just now."

"Sounds like a plan to me," said Sophie. "Come, Hetman, let's take a walk in the gardens—I hear the rhododendrons are particularly lovely right now."

Justin and the prefect walked in the other direction, acknowledging the greetings of those impressed by seeing two of the most powerful men in the empire together. They eventually sat down by a fountain that had been constructed by Basil's grandfather, Constantine VII, nearly 100 years before. While the weather was growing hot, they were in the shade with a nice breeze off the ocean.

"All right, Justin, what can I do for you? While the emperor made things pretty clear, I've always found that supporting you is in everyone's best interest, whether I've been told to or not."

"Well, Leo, you remember that time recently I came to you and asked for an order releasing imprisoned persons here in the city, as part of our investigation?"

"Yes, although I don't think I ever heard what came of that, if anything."

"We did get some valuable information, thank you. As an extension of that, the person we think is being held prisoner by al-Hadi will likely need medical attention after she, I mean he, is rescued. We'd like to have him receive treatment somewhere other than a public hospital."

"Where, then?" said the prefect, his curiosity roused.

"Our villa," Justin explained. We will have a room prepared and can have Sophie's father, Dr. Lascaris, attend. From what I understand, Constantine is making a good recovery and the doctor's presence isn't needed all the time as it was in the beginning. I just wanted to let you know before we remove a participant from the scene on Friday."

"No problem, no problem at all. I trust you'll let me know what else you need. Will the Varangians be enough, or do you need the city militia called out as well?"

Justin thought for a moment before replying. "Hmm, we haven't really discussed that. I think that the Varangians alone will be enough, but if one or more of the suspects gets away, we may have to initiate Plan Omega."

Now it was the prefect's turn to pause before speaking. "Plan Omega, eh? That's serious stuff. Thanks for the advance warning. I'll have to dust off the plans for that—I think I still have them in my office somewhere."

As Justin was taking his leave, he turned and said, "Senator Kalokyros—what's going to happen to him?"

The prefect looked at him with arched eyebrows. "Haven't you heard? He needs to take some time away from his pressing duties for health reasons. Believe me, I've seen it before." Then, with a wink, he headed off to his office.

Justin then did the same, and attempted to tackle the endless piles of paper on his desk. He was grateful for a stopping point when

Alexius stuck his head in through the door with the usual "Hi, Boss!" His levity grew less when Justin welcomed him in but told him to shut the door.

Justin took the next hour or so explaining what he and Sophie had in mind for Friday. While Alexius appreciated the details of the plan to catch Ishaq and Abdor in the street, Justin could see his deputy's eyes glaze over as he explained how the image of 'Loviatar' was to be created inside the banquet hall.

Finally, Alexius said, "Whatever you say, Boss, whatever you say. I don't see for a minute how it works, but if you've done it at home, then it must work. Still, I would have liked to have seen 'Scapel' hanging upside down—don't tell her I said so! What can I do to help?"

"We have to assume that al-Hadi and his men have 'Daphne' confined somewhere here in the city, we just don't know where. We need them to think that their plan is succeeding, that the Varangians are getting disgruntled, perhaps even on the verge of revolt."

"Are they, Boss? I didn't think things were that bad!"

"No, they're not, at least not yet. Still, we have to make al-Hadi think they are. So, you need to have your agents out on the street spread rumors—the more outlandish the better—about how the Varangians have killed one of their officers, how some have been arrested, others confined to barracks, etc. Anything we can to do to instill over-confidence is needed. Understand?"

"Got it, Boss. Keep going—this is getting interesting!"

"Also, reach out to Imam Ali through the usual back channels. Let him know that something big may be going down on Friday evening and that we may need the help of his community to find any of the fish that get through the net. Finally, do the same for the patrons of Daphne's club—no specifics, mind you, just that we may need their help to rescue 'Daphne' in the very near future. That's it—so get going!"

"On my way. I sure hope this pays off—you and your wife have put a lot of work into this!"

"We all have, Alexius, including you. Keep in touch!"

That evening, Sophie and Justin compared notes of their respective days.

Sophie reported, "Hetman Siggurdsen approves of our plan and is going to add one or two touches that he wouldn't tell me about yet. He also is going to recruit about a dozen other trustworthy Varangians to help Friday night's sequence of events unfold properly. Now it's a waiting game."

"Agreed; this may be the hardest part of the entire investigation. Think positive!"

Wednesday passed without incident. Justin knew that work was proceeding, based on two events he witnessed. First, when he came downstairs to get a quick breakfast, he was treated to overhearing the cook and the scullery maid arguing about whether the Varangians were heroes or traitors, to be rewarded or executed at their Majesties' pleasure. Second, while on the way to his office, he directed his driver to take the long way around the Hippodrome to go by the Varangians' banquet hall. As he went by, he saw Hetman Siggurdsen and some of his men conducting a search of buildings across the street, as if to discover the best places to hide for purposes of an ambush. In order to maintain the façade of imperial disregard for these troops, Justin did not acknowledge the hetman as he passed,

Sophie did have at least one thing on Thursday to occupy her, for she was to accompany Zoe and Theodora on one of their periodic visits to the Blachernae Palace to visit Constantine. As they travelled, the mood of the royal sisters was much better than it had been when she first went with them and their father in the ceremonial wagon two weeks earlier. Never one to pass up a chance to be seen by "her people", Zoe smiled and waved at the throngs that gathered to see them pass after hearing the trumpets that led the procession. Theodora was less naturally ebullient, but still managed to make a good impression. Gradually the crowds thinned as they grew closer to the palace, although there were still waves and cheers from the rural workers in the orchards and vineyards lining the road.

Dr. Lascaris was waiting to meet them on the front steps of the Hall of the Danube, one of several audience halls which radiated off a common courtyard. Zoe and Theodora naturally wanted to see their father immediately, and were accordingly escorted behind the palace to the athletic fields, where the archery targets were set up. Sophie and the doctor followed behind.

"How are things going, Father? It sounds like your patient has improved a lot," Sophie asked.

"Oh, without a doubt, dear. Getting him off of that brown powder made all the difference, and eliminating alcohol didn't do him any harm either. Still, he needs a few more weeks to really get back to a stable level."

Gladdened to hear that, Sophie then explained to her father that his presence might be needed on Friday evening and Saturday to help a special patient who would be treated at their villa. Dr. Lascaris was intrigued, but understood that Sophie could say no more at present. By then, they had come to the archery range where Sophie was treated to the sight of two Roman emperors shooting arrows at targets.

"Basil is good, isn't he?" said Lascaris. "Now, watch this!"

After besting his brother in several matches, Constantine ordered the targets to be moved further and further away. At each distance, he still hit the interior part of the target until the target was 200 feet away. By now, quite a crowd had gathered to watch the exhibition. Looking around with what Sophie perceived to be great satisfaction, Constantine took an arrow, placed it in his bow, and proceeded to not only hit the target, but come within inches of the center. A cheer went up that brought a wide smile to his face, which was only made broader by the embrace he received from his older brother.

"Father, I think your work here is done," Sophie said. "We'll see you on Friday."

"I look forward to it, Sophie, and to whatever new challenge lies ahead."

Justin enjoyed hearing the story of Constantine's exploits that night as he and Sophie lay in bed.

"Sounds like he's not finished yet, doesn't it?" he marveled.

"No, dear, he's not," said Sophie with a kiss. "Now, it's up to us to make sure that other people aren't finished either, starting with 'Daphne' tomorrow. Ready?"

"Ready when you are!"

CHAPTER 35

The Varangians' banquet on Friday evening promised to be a subdued affair. In talking with Hetman Siggurdsen earlier in the day, Justin and Sophie had learned that while rumors of a 'strike' by the men had died down, there was still much unease under the surface. On a more ominous note, the hetman also told them that at least 20 men whose initial service time was up had given notice that they intended to return to their homes as soon as possible. While only a fraction of the men had this option, the loss of experienced veterans could not help but weaken the overall effectiveness of the force. Worse yet, word of the goddess had spread to Varangians stationed in other parts of the Empire, so that service opportunities in Constantinople, once seen as a plum posting, were going unfilled.

By mid-afternoon, the usual throng of food preparers and suppliers had appeared at the banquet hall, entering from the many rear entrances. When Alexius suggested placing men there to survey those going in, Justin, with Sophie's strong support, vetoed such an idea as they were making final plans at the villa.

"The one thing that we don't want to do is scare al-Hadi and his men away," Justin explained. "No, the trap is baited and we want to catch all of the rats here, tonight."

"All right, Boss, whatever you say. Where are you two going to be for the festivities tonight?"

"I think we'll stay out of sight in the back," said Sophie. "We'll have Prefect Comnenus with us—it was his request to get out and see some real work in the field, as he put it."

Alexius groaned. "'Real work in the field'? He's welcome to it, as long as he doesn't mind running the risk of getting a real knife in his ribs."

Justin shook his head. "You just have your men ready to go when we need them. Remember, when the hetman has things in hand outside, he'll sound a horn—that's your cue to storm the room."

"Why wait that long?" Alexius queried. "Aren't you afraid that al-Hadi will leave before then?"

"No," explained Sophie, "because it won't be just him. He'll have to get 'Daphne' out, too, and if she's been drugged, as is certainly possible, he can't move fast. It's our bet he will wait for the hall to clear out before making his move. If that means he has to wait for an hour or two, so be it. Trust me, he'll be in there. Your job is to capture him and get 'Daphne' out in one piece. We know she's been abused, poor thing."

"All right, let's go. Alexius, we'll see you there," said Justin.

"Right, Boss. Good luck!" Alexius called over his shoulder as he left.

"Good luck to us all. Ready, dear?"

"Just a moment, I want to get my special gown—you know, the one I told you about," Sophie smiled.

Justin shook his head. "Are you seriously going through with that? Why?"

"Because it's the only way to lay 'Loviatar' to rest once and for all. A goddess who performs tricks on command isn't something to be afraid of, and that's what we'll show the Varangians. At least, I hope we will," Sophie concluded a little dubiously.

"All right, it's your neck!"

Upon arriving at the banquet hall, they found a secluded spot in the back of the banquet hall where they would wait. Before the staff started to arrive, Sophie wanted to check one more thing. She went upstairs to the room where the image of 'Loviatar' originated and opened the flap which covered the hole. She then called out to Justin, who called back. Satisfied that she could hear voices from the floor, she replaced the flap and came back down. Soon they were joined by Prefect Comnenus, who was obviously enthused about the evening. He grew even more so when things got underway. Having never seen a Varangian banquet in person, he was impressed.

"I thought I've seen mass quantities of food and drink consumed at one of the palace banquets, but they don't hold a candle to this! How will these men function tomorrow?"

Justin smiled. "With sore heads, I imagine, although they've had a lot of practice in doing what they're doing."

As the evening wore on and the men consumed ever increasing amounts of mead, it seemed time for 'Loviatar' to make her appearance. While Justin and Sophie both dreaded the prospect that the goddess might want to take the night off, their fears were alleviated when the familiar murmur went up in the hall—"Koma a hom, koma a hom!" {"She comes, she comes!"}

Hearing that, Sophie and Justin peeked out through the door and saw the familiar ghostly shape in the mirrored glass on the far side of the hall, while the prefect looked out through the window. Sophie was shocked by what she saw—the figure was even thinner and paler than she had remembered and barely moved, only occasionally turning its head from side to side. While many of the Varangians were terrified, judging from their reaction, Sophie saw only an indescribably sad and lonely figure. Knowing that she was looking at someone she knew to be 'Daphne' for the first time only made it worse.

For his part, Justin was concerned that the men in the banquet hall were getting too unruly for the next part of the plan to succeed. *'Come on, Hetman, come on—now's the time!'* he thought. Then, as if reading his thoughts, Hetman Siggurdsen made a break for the door, followed by about 10 men. No one else got through, though, for even more Varangians jumped up and barred the doors, weapons drawn. The uproar that followed could easily have spiraled into violence, but for the appearance of the Iron Lady, as Sophie walked quickly to the front of hall and calmed the crowd.

"Logn, felangi, logn! Allr munu vel" {"Patience, friends, patience! All will be well!"}

The unexpected sight of Sophie in their home-away-from-home led most, but not all, of the Varangians to stop and see what was to happen next. The few that did not were shushed by their comrades, with one or two being shushed by means of a fist to the face. They stood uncertainly for a few minutes, until the sound of a Scandinavian hunting horn rang out from somewhere in the street outside, blowing three distinct blasts.

That horn sound marked the end of the outside part of Justin and Sophie's plan. When Siggurdsen ran out into the street, he was alone by design. The other men who came out with him all ran the other way, a fact noticed by Ishaq and Abdor, who were watching out of the shadows across the street. They accordingly went after Siggurdsen, who for some reason had slowed down to a walk. Wordlessly, they moved in for the attack, with Abdor taking the lead.

Siggurdsen, who was expecting this, measured the footfalls behind him and suddenly turned when he felt them draw near, a knife in his hand. He was not quick enough to avoid the first strike, which went across his throat and would have been serious, if not fatal, but for the metal collar he had placed under his tunic. Abdor's eyes grew wide at this, but were quickly closed when Siggurdsen struck him on the temple with the butt of his own knife. He collapsed in a heap on the pavement.

Thus forewarned, Ishaq was not to be taken so easily. He and Siggurdsen squared off and circled around each other, even as the other Varangians who had come out doubled back and came at a run. According to their tradition, the hetman was left alone to fight his own fight, and they did not intervene when they arrived.

It was over fairly quickly, for Siggurdsen had been trained to fight his entire life. While Ishaq was a killer, he was a killer of unarmed men who died in ambush. He was facing something far more formidable in the hetman, who took advantage of every mistake he made. First Siggurdsen inflicted a slash on his adversary's left arm, and then on his right cheek. Finally, bleeding and in desperation, Ishaq lunged with a killing move. Siggurdsen stepped nimbly aside and plunged his blade into the Egyptian's back up to the hilt. Then, taking the horn that was strapped to his chest, he let out three long, piercing blasts. Ordering the body removed and Abdor's still unconscious form taken to prison, he headed back to the banquet hall at a trot, entering to the cheers of those present who recognized the horn of their leader.

While Justin and Sophie did not cheer, they certainly felt like it. Leaving Siggurdsen to tell of his feats to the attentive crowd, they hurried back upstairs to find the prefect already with Alexius and eight of his top men at the end of the hall. Once Justin gave the sign to go, they heard Alexius address his men.

"All right, it's the third door from this end—everybody ready? There will be two people—one is expected to resist, one is not. Go, go, go!!"

The men ran down the hall, with the two in front carrying a ram to use on the door. While Justin longed to go with them, Sophie's hand on his arm calmed him down as she whispered, "Careful dear, you're the brains, they're the brawn—leave this to the professionals!"

The door gave way after two blows and they poured inside. There were shouts and screams, and the room went dark. Prefect Comnenus had the presence of mind to grab a torch from the wall mount and go with Justin and Sophie to see what the situation was. Before they got there, Alexius came out, followed by two of his men supporting a third figure who Sophie recognized as 'Daphne', also known as 'Loviatar.' She looked semi-consciousness and could not stand. Per their plan, Sophie took charge and directed the men to carry their patient downstairs to where Philip, waiting in a carriage, would take her back to the villa where she could be cared for by Dr. Lascaris out of the public eye.

Meanwhile, Justin went into the little room and found two more of Alexius' men attending a third, who had suffered a knife wound. The other men were searching the rest of the room for al-Hadi, of whom there was no sign. One of them pressed on a panel, which opened into a narrow stairwell. It was pitch dark, but clearly led down to the first floor.

Justin was still looking at the secret passage when Sophie came in. Taking in the situation at once, she barked at Alexius' men.

"What are you waiting for? He's not here! Go downstairs and find him!" Although this remark was not directed to Alexius and the prefect, who had followed her in, they turned with alacrity and followed the others.

When they all left on the run, she told Justin, "Good—now for the next part of the plan—make sure the room is set up to project my image when we're ready. Here's the ladder they used to get 'Daphne' up there. I'll change into my outfit while you get the lights set up. What's going on downstairs now?"

Justin peeked through the flap. "Siggurdsen is retelling the tale of his exploits for probably the third time. By now, he's fought off a horde of blood-thirsty killers single-handedly. Soon he'll have conquered Egypt."

"All right, let's get started. Don't forget to come back and undo me—our children need a mother!"

So intent were the Varangians on hearing Siggurdsen's tale that it took a few moments for them to notice 'Loviatar' had returned, or what seemed to be a much better looking 'Loviatar'. While one or two wondered where the Iron Lady had gone, soon all their attention was focused on the goddess, who for some reason was making a return appearance. Perhaps she was angry because her victim had escaped?

Justin joined Siggurdsen up at the front, who got the men's attention by another blast on his horn. Justin then addressed them with the hetman translating.

"Gentlemen, for those of you who do not know me, I am Justin Cataphlates, the Treasurer of the Roman Empire. I also have certain talents which most people do not know about. For example, when I give commands, even goddesses obey!"

This remark produced the expected hoots, cat-calls and boos, so Justin continued.

"I see there are those who doubt. To prove it, I command 'Loviatar' to wave to you." Then, to the amazement of most, the spectral figure of the goddess did just that. This caused a great deal of murmuring, which grew even louder when, in response to Justin's 'commands', the goddess blew kisses, waved both arms in the air and even appeared to sway back and forth in time to music only she could hear. The piece de resistance was delivered when Justin, acting on directions from Sophie, turned to Harald Torkelsson, who was sitting on one of the front benches, and said, "Harald Torkelsson, she has a special message for you!"

All eyes then turned to the figure of 'Loviatar' who frowned, shook her head sideways and waggled her finger vigorously directly at him, or at least so it seemed. For a moment, the hall was totally silent, and then was filled with peals of laughter. For a stoic people, Varangians knew how to laugh, and Justin was surprised to see grown men laughing so hard tears came to their eyes. The victim of this prank glowered in his seat for a moment, but then he too joined in. Amid the merriment, no one noticed that Justin had slipped away. He soon reappeared with Sophie, who was wearing a black cloak.

The appearance of the Iron Lady caused the hall to fall silent again. A collective gasp went up when she took off the cloak, and revealed the dress just worn by 'Loviatar.' She then launched into a prepared speech of how they had been deceived by evil men who wished them and their liege lord Basil harm. While Justin wished he could stay around to hear it, the fact that it was in Norse detracted a little from its appeal. Instead, he went to the back, where the prefect was still taking everything in.

"Marvelous, Justin, marvelous! It worked just as you planned, congratulations!" Comnenus enthused, a feeling which ended very quickly with the arrival of Alexius.

"Bad news, Boss—the head bad guy got away. He came down the back, knifed a man in a wagon and drove off. What do you want to do now?"

Having anticipated such an outcome, Justin immediately turned to the prefect and said, "Leo, I think it's time to invoke the Omega order."

The prefect nodded and replied, "I quite agree. And, to show you once again that you have our full support, I have with me orders already signed by Basil and counter-signed by me ordering Omega to be put into effect. As soon as I leave here, they will be delivered to the city militia, the commanders at all of the gates on the city walls and the heads of all of the guilds, calling up their members for duty. Since it is late enough in the evening that the gates are already closed until dawn, we have until then to complete the rest of the lock down. No one will get out!"

Justin turned to Alexius and said, "You know what to do—get all of your people out on the streets—if anything is going on, they will hear it."

"Say no more, Boss, on it now!" replied Alexius, who then called for his men and headed out the back doors.

When Justin and the prefect came back out, Sophie was wrapping up her oration. When she finished, a chant went up across the room of "Jarnlayden, Asynja banamadra! Jarnlayden, Asynja banamadra!" {"Iron Lady, Goddess-slayer, Iron Lady, Goddess-slayer!"} While it briefly occurred to her to curtsey in responses to these accolades, she quickly decided this would be out of character, and instead raised both arms with clenched fists. In response, the crowd went wild.

Meanwhile Justin had let the hetman know about the Omega order. He in turn addressed his men and ordered them back to barracks, to rest and prepare for long duty the next day. They rose as one man, gave one more cheer for the Iron Lady, and went forth into the night.

Justin and Sophie made record time back to their villa, with Sophie urging the driver to go faster all the way. When they arrived, they found Philip waiting for them. He told them that Dr. Lascaris was there, and was attending the person that had just been brought from the banquet hall. Sophie did not even wait until he finished before racing up the stairs to the guest room. There she found her father attending an alert but weak patient. His hands were wrapped and he had a bandage around his head.

"Hello, 'Daphne', I'm Sophie. You're safe now and in our house. How do you feel?"

The wan figure managed a smile. "Thank you but you can call me Matthew, that's my name. 'Daphne' is as dead as the goddess. In killing her, you saved me!"

CHAPTER 36

While Sophie managed to get some sleep, Saturday morning still came too early. She wanted to keep Matthew under close observation all night, despite her father's diagnosis that he was in no immediate danger and simply needed to get some rest. When she did not come to bed, Justin came in and half-walked, half-carried her out of a chair in the room where Matthew was sleeping soundly. Finding herself in her own bed come morning, she protested, but not very long.

"Thank you, dear, now back to sleep!" she murmured.

"No, no rest for you, time to get up! We can't stop now—a dangerous man is still out there and must be found! We need to get to the Palace right away!" Justin replied.

"Fine, let me know when you do. Besides, what are we supposed to do—go knock on everyone's door and ask 'Hello, do you have a trained Egyptian assassin hiding in your house? No? Just checking!'"

Changing tactics, Justin then said, "Suit yourself. Oh, by the way, there's another doctor here to see Matthew. Thought you'd like to know."

Before the words had finished leaving his lips, Sophie was out of bed throwing on a robe, exclaiming, "Well, why didn't you say so!"

Going to the guest room, they found Sophie's father conferring with his old colleague from St. Samson Hospital, Dr. Stylites. Dr. Lascaris explained that he had brought his friend in "for a consult" since Dr. Stylites was an expert in extremity wounds. Given that

Matthew's hands and wrists had been injured, it seemed prudent to seek extra help. Fortunately, in Dr. Stylites' opinion no permanent damage seemed to have been done.

Sophie then went over and sat down next to Matthew, who was awake and much more focused than he had been the night before. He smiled when he saw Sophie.

"I remember you from last night. I don't remember what I said, if anything, but I do remember your face. Are you one of my rescuers?"

"Yes, I am. I'm Sophie and this is my husband, Justin. You're here at our house and you are safe. We've been trying to get you back for some time now after talking to your friends at the club and your sister. They will all be very relieved to know that you're all right. Is it permissible to let them know you are here?"

"Sure, that would be great. I suppose you want to know how I got myself in that situation?"

Ignoring Justin, who was nodding his head up and down vigorously, Sophie said, "Whenever you feel ready. It's up to you."

"No, that's all right. Since you know my friends at the club, I assume you've been there and know what it's about. Well, I really enjoyed that and thought I was pretty good at what I did. One night a man came up to me after the show and had only good things to say about my presentation. He said he directed a group of actors and thought I could fit in well. Acting has always been a fantasy of mine, along with others obviously, and I said yes. I was given an audition time for the next day and I went. I suppose I should have suspected something when the address was by the waterfront north of St. Laurentius but I went anyhow. I wanted to surprise my sister and my friends so I didn't tell them I was going—big mistake! Anyhow, before I knew what was going on I had a sack shoved over my head and got tied up. When I asked why, the men—there were several of them, although one never spoke—just laughed and said I was going to get an acting job after all. So, I became 'Loviatar'."

Sophie laid her arm on Matthew's shoulder and said, "That's probably enough for now. You should get some rest."

Matthew shook his head. "No, talking about it makes it seem better, more real, less fantastic. They held me in an upstairs room somewhere near the waterfront and the church, for I could hear both the sound of gulls and the church bells ringing. I was gagged and tied up most of the time, except on certain days when we went out. I could tell what was coming because they would force me to eat this nasty brown powder on my food, and then drink wine. Soon after doing that I wouldn't know what was going on. I would wake up the next day with bruises on my wrists. After a few days, the same thing would happen. It went on and on—I thought about trying to kill myself."

Justin, now listening intently to Matthew's account, asked, "Did you drop a ring out of the window? It was found and brought to us—here it is." He then produced the bronze ring with the reddish-brown tourmaline setting that had been found on the street. Matthew's face lit up upon seeing it.

"Oh, so they found it after all! I was able to move close to the window one day when the men got careless in tying me up and managed to drop this out. I hope it helped you find me!"

"More than you know, Matthew," said Sophie in a soothing voice. "At one point did you try to escape?"

"Yes, I got loose one day and made it out the door. A man on the street came to help me and stabbed one of my guards. He got stabbed, too—I hope he's all right."

"He's going to be fine, thank you for asking. Listen, Matthew, Justin and I need to work on some other things right now, so we'll let you sleep. You can stay here as long as it takes to get well, all right?" said Sophie.

"That's fine. Thank you again so much, from both Matthew and Daphne!" their guest replied in a weary but steady voice.

As they prepared to leave the villa, Philip ushered in a woman who looked familiar. It was Dolores, Matthew's sister. She wept tears of joy upon learning that he had been rescued, and Sophie gave Justin a big hug as she watched the rejoicing woman run up the stairs.

"All right, 'Boss', what's the plan now?" asked Sophie as they rode along through streets that seemed strangely empty. "And what's this 'Omega' thing anyhow?"

Justin rolled his eyes and laughed. "First of all, I'm not your Boss—Alexius yes, you never. Second, the Omega plan is something the prefect and I came up with some months ago. It's designed to go into effect if we need to lock the city down to prevent people from getting in, or, in our case, getting out. It seeks to maximize the people we have to man the walls and guard the sea around the city."

"So, how many is that?" Sophie persisted.

"Well, it includes all of the Varangians in the city, which is about 800. I think it's safe to say they will be motivated to act. Then, there are about 300 city police and 5,000 militia and city guild members, plus whatever regular army troops happen to be in the city. All gates will be shut, all walls on both the sea and land sides will be manned—that's about 14 miles worth—and the navy will patrol offshore. By night, the walls will be lit by torches, so that the city will appear to be ringed by fire. Also, there will be a general curfew in the city and the streets will be patrolled. As you can see, the curfew is already in effect."

"Amazing! That explains why no one else is on the streets. Still, what if al-Hadi is just hiding in the city and doesn't try to leave?"

"Then he will be sorry," Justin concluded, "for another order is bringing troops from the nearby themes into the city, so that by Monday we can search every house, business, church and public space."

"I see—he can hide, but he can't run!"

Sophie knew better than to ask what would happen to Musa al-Hadi when he was caught, so she let that question go unasked. Instead she changed the subject.

"So, where exactly are we going now?"

"To a place where I have never been, and have never wanted to go—the prison under the Great Palace. It's not someplace that holds people for very long. Generally, someone who is to be executed the next day is held there—traitors, spies, participants in failed coups—

that sort of thing. If you are admitted, I think it is fair to say that you will be the first woman ever to set foot there."

"Sorry I asked. Does this mean Abdor and Ishaq are there?"

Justin gave a dry laugh. "In a sense. Abdor is there all right, in a cell. Ishaq is in the prison morgue—didn't you listen to Siggurdsen's boasts last night?"

"Oh, you know how they are—always exaggerating. So he did kill Ishaq?"

"As dead as can be. All right, here we are. Just act like you have every right to be here and hope for the best."

As it turned out, they were both admitted without issue. Alexius was there, along with Prefect Comnenus. Both looked haggard, and Justin and Sophie could tell they had had a long night.

"Let me guess," said Justin. "Abdor hasn't said anything about where al-Hadi is?"

"No, nothing," sighed Alexius. "Nothing we could threaten him with worked, and some of the Varangians are itching to get at him. At this rate, Emperor Basil will let them have him soon."

Sophie thought for a moment, and then said, "Let me have a moment with my husband, please." When the others had left the room, she said, "I'm thinking it's time we tried a Trebizond. What do you think?"

Justin furrowed his brow. "Ah, a Trebizond? We haven't done that for a while. Still, it's worth a try. Let's do it!"

When they came back to the others, Sophie said, "Very well, gentlemen, it's time for the experts to take over. Is Abdor being held in a room with a window or two-way mirror?"

Now it was the turn of the prefect to frown. "Yes, I think so, but there hasn't been anything to show him. Why do you ask?"

"Never mind, All right, I'm going to talk with the prisoner now. While I'm in there, Justin will tell you what you need to do. Don't question him, just do it!"

Drawing herself up to her full height, Sophie entered the room where Abdor was held, shackled to an immobile chair in the middle of the room. He looked a little worse for the wear, likely due to the less than gentle ministrations of the Varangian guards. He looked at her briefly before looking away, and then looked back, his eyes growing wider with recognition.

Sophie smiled and said, "Yes, hello, remember me? I'm that annoying woman who couldn't make up her mind about the ivory."

Abdor's eyes now blazed with fury and he let loose with a string of what Sophie assumed were Arabic profanities. This went on for a while until he had to stop and catch his breath.

Sophie took the opportunity to seize the initiative. "That didn't sound very nice, but since I don't understand Arabic, it was wasted on me. No, I just wanted to see you one more time and ask if you have any next-of-kin we can notify after the Varangians get through with you. Still, what they do will be better than what Caliph al-Hakim would devise—we all know how he hates people who fail him, don't we?"

Sophie could tell the mention of the caliph's name hit a nerve, and decided to raise the stakes. Stepping over to the wall, she opened the curtain and revealed the adjoining room. There, also strapped to a chair, was Ishaq, with his back to them. He was alone, until Hetman Siggurdsen entered the room with fury on his face and a long sword in his hand. They could hear his words clearly.

"Very well, dog! Since you won't talk, let's see if we can loosen your tongue. How does this feel!" So saying, he slashed down and cut off Ishaq's left ear.

"What, no answer? Then how about this?" Ishaq's right ear followed his left.

"Still nothing? All right, I'm through with you—take this!" Siggurdsen yelled as he thrust his sword through Ishaq's mouth so hard that it came out of the back of his head.

Sophie had been watching Abdor's reaction through this little play, and noticed that he was growing paler as things went along, and was sweating profusely. With the final denouement, he looked ready to vomit. *'Time to act'*, she thought.

"Abdor, yes, I know that is your name, I can't stop that monster from coming in here next. Your time is very short—just tell me where we can find Musa al-Hadi and you can go free, as far away from Egypt as you want. What do you owe him? After all, he abandoned you!"

Gagging, Abdor finally spoke. "I don't know, I don't know where he is, you've got to believe me, I don't know!"

Shifting subjects easily, Sophie then asked, "Very well, after the street fight when you had to move your hide-out, where did you go? Tell me the new location and you can still go free! Hurry, I hear him coming!"

"All right, all right! It's close to the docks, down the hill from St. Laurentius Church. I can show you on a map, I swear, just keep that thing out of here!"

"Thank you, that will be all. Let me call for a map. Oh," she said after a pregnant pause, "if what you're telling us isn't true, that Varangian will be back for you, and I won't be able to do a thing, nor will I want to."

A few minutes later, Sophie walked out of the interrogation room with a map in her hand after calling out "Have a nice day" to Abdor over her shoulder. There Justin, Alexius, Prefect Comnenus and numerous others waited in the shadows.

"So, did you see all that?" Sophie smiled.

"Yes, dear, no problem," replied Justin, "Trebizond worked!" Let's get going—even if al-Hadi isn't there, there may be clues!"

As they got back into their carriage, Alexius came running out. "Wait, Boss, wait! I've got to know—what's Trebizond"?

"Oh, that!" Sophie laughed. "Since we tried that tactic the first time in Trebizond, we always call it that now."

"So it worked like today, right? Come on, I've got to know," pleaded the deputy.

Sophie and Justin exchanged glances before Justin answered, "Come to think of it, no, it didn't work that time—funny we thought of it now, isn't it?"

The ride to the location identified by Abdor went quickly, aided by both the empty streets and the guard of imperial cavalry. It was not far from the site of the killing of Fermat, but would have been impossible to find except with a truly intensive search, as it was deep within a twisted maze of streets. Every so often, they could see curious residents of the city peek through shuttered windows and around closed doors as they went by.

Sophie and Justin waited until the soldiers searched the place and found it unoccupied before entering themselves. In a windowless side room, they found evidence to show Matthew had been held there, including shackles and a good quantity of the notorious brown power.

"Wouldn't Jacob like to get his hands on this?" wondered Sophie. "I'll just confiscate this, evidence you know. Oh, what do we have here—ah, coin of the realm!" she said as she found a bag full of gold solidi. "This day is getting better and better!"

Having secured the 'evidence', Sophie found Justin in another room. "What have you got there?" she said as Justin pulled some parchment sheets out of a drawer.

"It's a partial map of the city, showing the south side from the Great Palace all the way out to the Golden Gate on the land wall. It's got streets, forums and churches—really quite detailed."

Looking over Justin's shoulder, Sophie pointed to a network of other gray lines, many of which seemed to run parallel to the streets. "So, what are these?"

Justin frowned. "I don't know. There are a lot in the areas of the city that are built up and less out near the walls. But, some of the gray lines seem to go right up to the walls. Very curious. I'll take these with me."

"But why just half the city? What about the part that we're in now?"

"Again, I don't know. Well, I think we've seen enough here. Wait, hold on—what's this?" Justin took a paper containing two columns written in Arabic. After scanning it for a moment, he let out a low whistle. "St. George preserve us! It's a list of al-Hadi's operatives in the city—looks like Mezezius wasn't alone!"

"Before we leave, could we at least free these poor birds?" asked Sophie, pointing to several pigeons who sat quietly in a cage in the corner.

Justin's eyes widened as he noticed the birds. "Sophie, do you know what these are for? They're homing pigeons—you attach a message to their leg and they fly back to where their home was."

"But what would al-Hadi be doing with these?"

"Oh, I don't know—perhaps sending messages to someone outside the walls! Pigeons could care less about the Omega plan."

Sophie gasped. "Oh no, that means we've got to find al-Hadi while he's still inside the city—he may have made arrangements to get away once he gets past the walls!"

Justin thought for a moment. "Let's do a little test. We'll take the birds back to the Mese, where there aren't so many buildings around and then let them go. Maybe we can see where they fly."

The idea was a good one, but they did not reckon on how fast the pigeons flew. Apart from seeing the birds circle several times and head west toward the land walls, they learned nothing else.

"Well, at least he's not leaving by ship," Sophie offered hopefully. "Now, let's get back home and see if there is any news. I really want to see how Matthew is doing!"

News there was indeed, but it was all negative, according to a note from the prefect and Alexius in person. The prefect stated that Omega had been fully implemented and was working well. So far, eight petty criminals had been apprehended trying to leave the city, but none turned out to be Musa al-Hadi. By Monday, 5,000 more troops would enter the city. This would free up others to conduct building by building searches. Already the word was being put out that residents could avoid a search by Varangians by allowing block wardens to conduct one instead. Not surprisingly, support for this option seemed to be widespread. The prefect finished his note by asking Justin and Sophie to be at the palace at daybreak to go over plans for the day with all top civilian and military officials. '*Sophie won't care for that!*' thought Justin. The only positive note concerned Matthew, who was out of danger according to the learned physicians who were caring for him.

Having finished the note, Justin gave it to Sophie while Alexius vented.

"We know this man is clever, but he seems to have vanished off the face of the earth! The wagon that he stole was found in the north-central part of the city, near the Church of St. Laurentius. I've had dozens of militia scouring the area, but so far nothing. You'd think somebody would have seen him!"

"Hm, St. Laurentius?" mused Sophie. "Near where we were today. I wonder if he had time to go by the hide-out before he moved on? That might explain the missing map!"

"Great, now if we can figure out how to read it!" replied Justin. "Only thing is, we don't have weeks like we did with the manuscript—tomorrow is crucial! Al-Hadi has got to know that the search will take some time to get underway, but when it does, he's finished. Tomorrow is the day, I tell you!"

"All right, all right, dear," Sophie said, patting Justin on the arm, "calm down! For me, I think a little celebration is in order. We've saved Matthew, we've laid 'Loviatar' to rest, and there won't be another murder of a Varangian. Not a bad result, when you think of it. As far as al-Hadi goes, he hasn't gotten away yet. It's time for some wine. Alexius, care to join us?"

The eunuch's weary eyes brightened, "You had me at 'celebration,' 'Scalpel'! Lead on!"

CHAPTER 37

Justin was pleasantly surprised the next morning when he awoke to find Sophie already up and getting dressed, for, based on past performance, he had expected to drag her out of bed. When he stated as much, he was met with an irritated sniff.

"Huh! I can get up just as well as you can. It's just that it takes me five times longer to get ready—we're going to the palace, not for a stroll in the country. I want to feel confident in the midst of powerful men—I'll likely be the only woman there!"

Sophie's mood did not improve much as they rode through the empty streets. The sun was just coming up over the Sea of Marmara, and Justin found it a beautiful sight, as the first rays of dawn glinted off the tops of Saint Irene and the Hagia Sophia. If Sophie saw this, she was not impressed, and Justin knew better than to point it out. However, as they were walking across the courtyard into the palace, she took his hand and smiled. "All right," she said, "let's get this thing wrapped up today—I'm ready for a break!"

At that point, Justin gave his wife a generous kiss.

"Ooo, what was that for?" Sophie beamed.

"It just occurred to me—today we get excused from church!" he said, already moving ahead to avoid the punch that was sure to follow.

Per the prefect's instructions, they headed toward another of the many audience halls located in this part of the palace. Today they were meeting in the Onyxtriklinos, or Onyx Hall, so-called for the floor-to-ceiling onyx panels which lined the room. It had been constructed by the Emperor Maurice over four centuries earlier when the empire was flush with gold. Looking around at the opulence, Justin wondered if, toward the end of his reign when rebellious soldiers were marching on Constantinople to get their unpaid wages, Maurice ever wished he had used marble instead.

Today no eyes were on the onyx, as they found the room full of tables on which maps of the city had been spread. Around the tables there stood a who's who of the men in positions of power that Sophie had forecast, two dozen or so. Among others, Hetman Siggurdsen was there, along with municipal officials like Justin's friend Bardanes. While there was no sign of Senator Kalokyros, Justin was gratified to see that Imam ibn-Ali was conversing with one of the patriarch's bishops.

Prefect Comnenus came over to them immediately, and said, in a low voice, "The Lion is present." Sophie and Justin both knew this meant Emperor Basil was present and yet not present, and refrained from looking around the room for the curtain that he was behind. While the emperor was keenly interested in the outcome of the search, he also realized that his presence would have a destabilizing effect. *Being emperor isn't all it's built up to be,* thought Justin. "We understand," Sophie said, answering for them both.

"Good," said the prefect. "Now we can get down to work. But first, I will need you both to come over here and stand on the second step of the dais. That's right, here, yes that will do."

Before the couple could inquire why or even protest, the prefect asked for the attention of all present and said in a loud voice, "Gentlemen, I present to you Treasurer Justin Cataphlates and Chief Lady-in-Waiting Sophia Cataphlates, seekers of the truth and defenders of Rome! All hail!"

The applause that followed was loud and long, and grew even greater when those present realized that they had been joined by Emperor Basil himself, who had stepped out from behind the curtain. It went on until Basil stopped. All others did as well, awaiting any royal comments.

After collecting his thoughts for a moment, the senior emperor of the Roman Empire then said, "Treasurer, Lady, once again we find ourselves thanking you on behalf of our realm. We thank you also on behalf of our family, for our brother is going to recover because of you. We go now to visit him, and wish you Godspeed on your continuing quest for justice!" and with that he was gone. The prefect then asked if the honored couple had any remarks.

Justin went first. "You all know your business, so I won't tell you that. I will only say that the man we are seeking is very dangerous and will stop at nothing."

Sophie was more blunt, saying, "We need to talk to this man to find out who sent him and why. If we don't get him before the Varangians do, there won't be enough left to put in a basket. Em iak rettr, Hetman?" {"Am I right, Hetman?"}

"Yes," was Siggurdsen's stoic reply.

The assembled group then got to work, with each group looking over maps of a particular section of the city, attempting to determine where Musa al-Hadi could have gone to ground. Justin and Sophie wandered around from table to table, until Justin remembered the map that he had found at al-Hadi's hideout. When he came to a table which showed maps like the one he found in the hideout, he got it out and compared them. While he was trying to determine what the many gray lines meant, Bardanes wandered by and commented, "Oh, those, they're water, sewer and storm drainage lines. That's a nice map—where did you get it?"

Sophie's eyes grew wide with amazement, and Justin replied. "It's from what we think was the last hideout of the man we are all seeking. The one we found was only for the southern half of the city. Do you have one from the north half?"

"Of course, and between you and me, that's the interesting part!" Bardanes said as he pulled out one showing the missing half. "My predecessors have had drainage problems for centuries with that part of the city. For example, you see a ridge here. The Lycus River flows on the south side, and the Chora Monastery and the Blachernae are on the north. There are a lot of lines running on both sides but none go across. Most are old and probably blocked up by now. Every now and then a farmer will lose a goat when one of the shafts collapses."

By now Sophie could speak again, and asked, "Why do you say 'probably' blocked? Don't you know?"

Bardanes laughed. "No, we don't! We've been trying to get money for a complete survey for years, but the treasurer's office always says no! How's that for irony?"

Annoyed, Justin said, "All right, we can come back to that later. Do some of these lines actually lead under the walls?"

"Sure, don't you remember your history? Justinian II it was, I think, not the great one but a guy who came later, snuck back into the city after he had been overthrown and had his nose cut off, and actually got the throne back. Then of course he had to kill everybody he thought had opposed him."

"Charming, I'm sure," said Sophie. "So if I understand you, our fugitive could have thought to get out of the city through one of these?"

"Maybe, but it's impossible to say which one. There are dozens along the four mile stretch of land walls. Sorry I can't be of more help."

Meanwhile Justin's eye had caught a pile of messages on another table and he called a clerk to inquire what those were.

"Those, sir? We're getting reports from people all over the city saying they've seen this man. We try to check them out as best we can, but so far they've all led nowhere. My favorite was the one from a woman who reported she was being held hostage by the Egyptian. When the Varangians got there, it turns out it was her husband instead. She was tired of his constant drinking and thought this would get his attention. Fortunately the Varangians could tell the difference between an old man with one leg and the fellow we're seeking before they cut off his head."

Sophie, her interest now piqued, took another one and said, "What's this one—I can't read it," as she handed it to Justin.

"No wonder, it's in Italian," he replied. "Why, it's from my new best friends from Rome out at the Chora Monastery. They say they've seen a man matching Musa al-Hadi's description hanging around some of the abandoned buildings out near the olive grove. He appeared to be looking for something, but there was nothing there."

After Bardanes overheard this, he started to scrabble among the maps laid out on the table. Seizing one, he flattened it out with a satisfied, "Aha! I thought so!"

Justin and Sophie were immediately at his side. "What have you got?" Sophie asked.

"I think I know what this fellow was looking for. You see here? These are the buildings they were talking about. The olive grove is here—it's centuries old. You see this round circle here with an 'X' in the middle? Well, it's a storm water drain—the water was collected there and then conveyed under the wall to come out in a ravine over here that goes down to where the Golden Horn starts. The line is diagonal and is about a quarter of a mile long. You can see here where it ends, across from where the Blachernae is now."

"So is it still there?" said Sophie loudly enough to draw a crowd of listeners around them.

"How should I know?" said Bardanes impatiently. "But, since it looks like your man may think so, it could be worth checking out."

Justin then took charge. "All right, Prefect—Sophie and I and Anthony Bardanes will go and look into this. I would like Hetman Siggurdsen to come with us, along with some of his men. How many can you get for us right now, Hetman?"

"I can have 50 ready to ride in five minutes!" came the response, which for once was not stoic.

"Good, they can catch up to us on the way. We'll rendezvous at the main monastery building and then fan out from there. Prefect, let them know what's going on at the Blachernae since both emperors are there. Let's go!"

Sophie, Justin and Bardanes then ran across the courtyard through the Chalke Gate to where their carriage waited, with Bardanes trying his best to keep up. The trip to the land walls never seemed to take longer, although with the streets empty they made record time. They pulled up in front of the main building, and found that their coming must have been observed, for Romanus and several of his lieutenants were in the courtyard. Romanus seemed surprised but pleased. In deference to Sophie and Bardanes, he addressed them in his heavily-accented Greek.

"Welcome, Treasurer and others! I am pleased and surprised that our note got this response. I would have thought, however, that you would have brought more people."

"Oh that, Romanus," answered Justin, "Well, I think the cavalry will be here in a moment." With that, he turned to look behind him and confirmed that the Varangian horsemen he had seen coming down the road were turning into the courtyard with Hetman Siggurdsen at their head. "Now I think we're all here. What's the situation?"

Romanus gave a sincere bow. "I am impressed, Treasurer. The man we saw is, or at least was, in the olive grove. I have had two men watching him from a distance, with strict orders not to let him know he is being observed. However, they say they have not seen him recently. What is your plan?"

Having conferred with Bardanes on the trip out, Justin instructed Siggurdsen to deploy his men in a line, each one five paces apart from the next. They were to sweep through the grove, looking for any sign of a storm drain, water line or other opening, and then give the alarm if one was found. The man they were seeking was to be taken alive if possible, but no one was to put his own life in danger.

To make sure these orders were understood, Sophie then repeated them in Norse. Justin noted that many men nodded in response to her comments that had been impassive for his. When he commented on this, she replied, "Some people have the touch, some don't."

The sweep then began, after the observers reported no new sightings. Justin, Sophie and Bardanes hung behind and let the professionals do their work. The men worked slowly and methodically, and Sophie was beginning to think they had come up empty when a cry went up near the middle of the line. The three of them converged on that point, along with the hetman, and found an open grate which led into blackness. Bardanes then consulted his map, and confirmed that this was the entrance to the line that led under the land wall into the ravine across from the Blachernae. Turning to Justin and Sophie, he said, "So, what now?"

With a nod from Justin, Sophie said, "It's up to Hetman Siggurdsen and his men from this point. "Hetman, leitask fyrir!" {"Hetman, make a search!"}

Asking no questions, Siggurdsen sent three of his more slender men into the tunnel, equipped with swords and torches. Before they left, he gave them a blue cloth and a yellow cloth to wave when and if they emerged on the other side—blue meaning they had made the capture, yellow if they had not.

After seeing them disappear into the tunnel (and thanking God, Jesus, the Holy Spirit and any saint he could think of that he wasn't with them), Justin planned ahead and said, "Good, good! Now, Hetman, you should station some men on this end of the tunnel in case anyone comes out, while the rest should go to the other end. Meanwhile, Sophie and I will go to the Blachernae and alert their Majesties."

"So, what about me?" protested Bardanes.

"Of course, Anthony, you come too—after all, their Majesties may want to know whose line al-Hadi is escaping through! How's that?" Justin replied.

It took several minutes to get back to the carriage and even longer to get to the Blachernae complex. When they arrived, they found that Prefect Comnenus had come himself to tell their Majesties the news. Everyone was standing at the base of the tallest tower on the walls and it appeared they were about to go up to survey the scene. Constantine had apparently been interrupted in his archery practice, for he still had his bow slung across his back along with a quiver of arrows.

As the climbed, Justin and Sophie filled in everyone about the situation. When they reached the top, they had wide view of the countryside, stretching from the very upper reaches of the Golden Horn to well beyond the walls on their left. Bardanes as usual brought up the rear, and after taking a moment to catch his breath, asked a very sensible question.

"Majesties, why don't you just send troops through the gate to catch al-Hadi as he comes out?"

"Because," Basil explained, "all of the gates near here have been barricaded up from the inside under the Omega order so that no one could escape. The Blachernae sticks out from the wall like a bubble—once you get through here, you are well on your way to escaping by either water or land. It would take more time than we have to unblock them. Also, all of the troops are manning the walls—once again, there simply isn't enough time to assemble them."

Constantine, whose eyesight had not been affected by his dissipated living, either historical or recent, raised a cry and pointed off to the left. About three hundred yards away, they could see a yellow flag being waved by the Varangians who had just emerged from the tunnel. But where was their quarry?

This time it was Sophie whose eyes caught movement. "There," she said, "there in the trees by the road. Look! I think it's him!"

There were actually two men on horses, one of whom was indeed Musa al-Hadi. They were moving cautiously and trying to keep out of sight, making their way toward the Golden Horn. There appeared to be no way to stop them, at least as far as Justin and Sophie could see.

"Oh, so close," moaned the prefect, "so close! Now he's getting away."

"Not yet," said Constantine in an oddly quiet, detached voice. "Do you see that bridge? They will have to cross it or otherwise risk their horses in the rocky ravine that it crosses. They'll be in the open then for a few seconds."

His brother, a veteran of many wars and many battles, immediately grasped Constantine's intent, but scoffed. "That has got to be a good 300 feet away! No one can make that shot!"

"We'll see, brother, we'll see," replied Constantine as he fitted a bow. "Now, which one am I shooting at?" Having determined that al-Hadi was on the lead horse, he tested the wind, fitted an arrow and waited for the perfect shot. When the moment came, he let fly. Due to the distance, they all lost sight of the arrow, but could see that al-Hadi kept riding his mount across the bridge.

In a voice tinged with disappointment, Basil said, "Constantine, you missed."

"Did I? Look again!"

As they did, al-Hadi slowly rocked back and forth in his saddle, and then fell motionless to the ground, the arrow protruding through his neck. The second man looked around in panic, and then spurred his horse on down the road, riding past his companion where he lay.

Constantine turned to Basil. "Should I try for him, too?"

"No, no, let him go, we need him to carry this news back to whoever sent al-Hadi. One miraculous shot a day is enough! Congratulations!"

News of Emperor Constantine's feat travelled quickly through the city. As Justin and Sophie prepared to head back to the palace, they could hear the sound of church bells coming from all directions. Hastily issued orders by the prefect arranged an informal triumph for the hero of the moment, who rode back in a chariot at the side of Basil, who periodically would raise his brother's hand aloft in tribute, with Justin and Sophie following behind, along with dozens of axe-carrying Varangians. To his delight, Bardanes got to ride in a chariot of his own, although almost no one in the crowd had any idea who he was.

The crowds that lined the road grew ever larger as they drew closer to the senate building. There, Zoe and Theodora waited on the steps, along with their ladies-in-waiting and as many of the palace officials and senators who could be gathered on short notice. Never one to pass up a crowd, Patriarch Sergius was there as well, surrounded by a crowd of bishops and priests that looked from a distance like a flock of crows. When Basil and Constantine arrived, they mounted the stairs where a touching scene occurred when Constantine was embraced by his daughters. Basil then motioned for silence and the crowd grew still, with Justin and Sophie in the front row looking up.

Basil then called for three cheers for his brother, the champion archer of the empire! Then, in deference to protocol, he stepped aside and let Prefect Comnenus summon Justin and Sophie up to receive their plaudits in turn. Justin received a hearty handshake from the Prefect, Sophie got hugs from Zoe and Theodora, and the crowd went wild. To top it off, the several hundred Varangians present started chanting "Jarnlayden, Asynja banamadra! Jarnlayden, Asynja banamadra!" {"Iron Lady, Goddess-slayer, Iron Lady, Goddess-slayer!"} in their deep voices.

Justin and Sophie stood together off to the side of the royal family, waving and nodding to the crowd. Knowing that Justin had a limited capacity for such things, after a few minutes Sophie leaned over and said, "What are you thinking, dear?"

Justin gave her a weary smile and replied, "I don't care if the entire Senate turns up dead tomorrow, I'm sleeping in!"

With a kiss, Sophie said, "Amen to that!"

CHAPTER 38

Several weeks later on a Saturday in August, the weather was typical for summer in Constantinople—warm, dry and clear. Having raised their chicks, the hoopoes had left the nest. While they would come by the villa occasionally out of habit, it would not be long before they made their annual trip to Africa, not to return until the spring.

Sophie and Justin were relaxing on the veranda after another busy week. For Sophie, it was due to the Orthodox religious calendar getting active again. The church had just completed the Feast of the Transfiguration and there were more to come in September. Unlike in the past, however, Sophie had faced the challenge of dressing Zoe appropriately with aplomb. This was in part due to her new partnership with Leonida, and even more to her new friends at the club. After a recovery period under the watchful care of Dr. Lascaris and his colleagues, 'Daphne' was back on the runway, looking better than ever. With tips from her and her friends, Sophie had produced truly stunning outfits for Zoe that were the talk of the fashionable set in the city. In order to avoid setting the bar too high, she found herself deliberately holding back some ideas, something that would never have happened before.

The prospects of the cross-dresser community had improved too, for Sophie had directed the proceeds from the sale of the seized brown powder to their benefit, with Jacob reaping a handsome profit as the middle man. While the laws against them remained technically on the books, a word from Justin to Prefect Comnenus had led to their informal suspension. Sophie was unimpressed when she heard this, saying, "You should have had them repealed! At this point, they would give you whatever you asked! If you wanted everyone in the city to wear orange on the first of the month, they would do it!"

Justin was decompressing after the kind of week he lived for as Treasurer. He had just spent three days going over procedures and outlining regulations for the local treasurers at the theme (province) level in Greece, Thrace, Macedonia, Bulgaria and Italy. Many of them were in Constantinople for the first time, and some had enjoyed themselves a little too much, keeping Alexius busy in bailing them out of local lock-ups. During the day, though, to a man they had been focused on the task at hand, and Justin was pleased with the outcome, albeit exhausted now to the point of nodding off.

Seeing this, Sophie said, "Some more wine, dear?"

"Uh, no, thanks, I'm good. Would your father like some more?"

"I'll ask." Walking over the edge of the balcony, she looked down to the garden below where Dr. Lascaris was rolling around in the grass with Simon, who was babbling and running around more every day.

"Some wine, Father?" she called.

"In a minute, Sophie, we're finishing some game. I'm not sure what it is, but it seems to be important!"

Justin joined her in looking down. "I tell you, that boy is going to be great with languages, just like we are. I should start working on teaching him Russian!"

"Russian?" she said, shaking her head. "If you want to pick a language that sounds truly guttural, why not Turkish? Say, where's Maria?"

"The last time I saw her, she was in the study with Anwar and Agatho. They were trying to re-create another one of the experiments in al-Haytham's manuscript. I'll go see."

And in fact that is what he found. Maria was working with the two men as if they were equals, albeit adults who could understand Arabic. Justin was pleased to hear her ask what various words meant and how they were spelled. *'Forget the Russian and Turkish! Arabic's the language for her!'* he thought.

When he got back to the veranda, Dr. Lascaris had joined Sophie, as it was time for Simon's nap. He was looking more relaxed every day, for while he loved the patients at the leprosarium and they returned the feeling, he was born for the city and was out of his element anywhere else. The doctors at St. Sampson's were thrilled to have him on staff, with the understanding he could visit his former patients every few months.

"So, Sophie, this new position of yours, is it going to interfere with your duties to Zoe?" Dr. Lascaris was asking.

"No, Father, it shouldn't. I mean, being the Akolouthos for the Varangians has been mostly an honorary position in the past. My predecessor didn't do much apart from aggravate them, that's for sure. I talk to them several times a week, so we should be able to keep the lines of communication open. I was also able to get our friend Siggurdsen a promotion—he went from Hetman to Foringi, which means commander."

At this, Justin laughed. "'Lines of communication?' Dear, they would crawl over broken glass for the Iron Lady who is now also the Goddess-Slayer. As long as Siggurdsen is in charge, you won't have to worry about them. According to the numbers that have come across my desk, re-enlistments are running at almost 100% and there's a long waiting list to come here. You are set, believe me!"

"And your predecessor—what happened to him?" her father said.

"Oh, Senator Kalokyros? He was honorably retired, I think. Haven't seen much of him lately."

Having gotten answers to his questions, the doctor rose and said, "Well, dear, I need to be going. I am letting one of the younger doctors have some time off with his family this weekend, so I'm taking his shift. Dinner on Thursday?" With that, the doctor gave his daughter a kiss, gave a wave to Justin and was gone.

"I like having your father around, but sometimes I like it better when he leaves," said Justin. "Does that make me a bad person?"

Sophie smiled. "No, dear, and that's why I love you. Here's the truth—sometimes I feel the same way. Still, it's good to have him here, at least now and then. Of course, considering what he did for Constantine, he could get about anything he asked for. Speaking of our junior emperor, how is he doing? I haven't seen him around lately."

Justin laughed again. "No and you probably won't. For the first time in his life, that man is actually having to work, and he seems to have some aptitude for it. Basil got the idea to keep him occupied and out of trouble, so Constantine now gets to oversee some municipal and administrative functions. It's driving Prefect Comnenus crazy, but so far it's working out."

"And Basil—any new wars we should look forward to?"

Justin suddenly looked serious. "Actually, that's not funny—it nearly happened, and still may. When the prefect and I told him about that list of al-Hadi's that showed he had operatives in several departments and that Mezezius was not alone, Basil grew very quiet, which, if you know Basil, is when he's most dangerous. His first reaction was to expel all Muslims from the city."

Sophie was shocked. "What did you do? What could you say?"

"I just pointed out the facts. First, not all Muslims are aligned with the caliph. Some, like the imam here in town, helped us. Second, not all of our enemies are Muslim. Mezezius for example was Armenian. Finally, I made an appeal to Basil's sense of duty by pointing out that Nazir al-Amadi, the shop clerk who was killed while working for us, was Muslim. I think this calmed him down for now, but I still think his mind is set on going after Syria and Sicily, possibly in that order."

Sophie nodded approvingly. "That was smart—if there is one thing Basil understands, it is duty."

"That's for certain. Upon hearing about Nazir, he even let the prefect sign off on letting the imam have a minaret for his mosque. That will get Basil a mention in the Friday prayers, but don't tell him that!" Justin replied with a grin.

"I had forgotten about Nazir—poor man—there were so many bodies piling up there for a while. Did you ever figure out why he was killed?"

"Alexius did—he took Nazir's death very personally, as he was the one who had recruited the man to work for us. Before we let Abdor go, Alexius extracted all the information he could from him—no, no, he wasn't tortured, I made sure of that!" Justin said with emphasis. "Then, Siggurdsen suggested that we might show al-Hadi's body to him before we turned it over to the imam for Muslim burial. That's all we did, just to show him for certain he was now completely and totally alone in the city. After that, he told us fairly quickly that Nazir had somehow learned where 'Daphne' was being held, and was killed before he could report that. Of course, he denied doing it."

Sophie shook her head. "How meaningless! Did he say anything else of interest?"

"He didn't know much—al-Hadi kept most things to himself. Abdor knew about the pigeons—it was his job to feed them and clean out their cage, something which apparently is very degrading for a Muslim to do. Al-Hadi had someone outside the walls he could send the birds to in the event he needed to make a quick escape, leaving men like Abdor behind to face the consequences. He also said that Mezezius had been killed when he came to al-Hadi in a panic and reported he'd been sacked and his supply of the brown powder had been seized. At that point, he was a classic loose end. Abdor denied killing him as well—said it was Ishaq."

"Humph, at least Abdor was consistent. What finally happened to him?"

Justin shrugged. "He's off to Cherson—he'll be given a little money to live on there, if being in Cherson can be called living. It should be snowing there most any day now. For someone from Egypt, I imagine that would be like dying and going to the bad place."

Sophie smiled. "Well, the city is going to be a quieter place for a while, or at least I hope so. Have all of your problem people left, been killed or exiled?"

"I think so. The delegation from the pope has gone back to that pile of ruins they call Rome. I have to say that more than one of them expressed a desire to stay here, but duty called. I do have a new ally in Romanus, who is the pope's brother, and who may be pope himself someday. That could come in handy!"

Sophie frowned. "He didn't seem like a religious man. Is he?"

"No, not at all. He told me one time that if he got selected to be pope—he'd have to be ordained as a priest first! What a crazy system! Still, he seemed like a reasonable man, unlike our patriarch."

"Ah, Sergius," Sophie sighed, "not one of my favorite people, nor am I one of his, I dare say. Did he sign off on whatever kind of deal you brokered?"

Justin nodded. "Yes, after much bickering the two sides agreed to disagree on priestly celibacy, when to celebrate Easter and what kind of bread to use in communion. As for the wording in the Nicene Creed, I got them to agree that the Latin and Greek terms expressed the same thing in a slightly different way."

Sophie looked at her husband with surprise. "No wonder you were so tired back then—dealing with that and the Varangian murders at the same time! Do you think this is the end of the problem with the church in Rome?"

Justin's tone turned darker. "No, dear, I don't. In the long term, we're just too different. Still, may that long term be longer than we have left."

Sophie gave a sniff and said, "Speak for yourself! I intend to be around for a long time!" Then, after sitting in silence for a few minutes, she took Justin's hand and said, "It's humbling to think that without the manuscript and the locket we never could have solved this case. Do you think we'll ever know for sure who sent them?"

"With certainty? No, unless I talk to Sitt al-Mulk again, and I can't see how that would ever happen. Still, it had to be her—she made sure I saw the locket when I was summoned to talk with her with no curtain in between. It was genius really—if someone went through my luggage, there was nothing to implicate her. An obscure scientific journal would mean nothing to anyone, while it's to be expected that a man returning from a trip would get something for his wife. As the caliph's sister, she's above suspicion. That leaves only the scientist. While you and I know it wasn't al-Haytham's idea, any more than using the device was, the Caliph has long ears, and I have figured out a way to cover for the innocent scientist."

"You mean that book you found? I assumed you're going to send it to him. How about the letter you talked about—did you ever finish it?"

"Yes, I did, although Anwar actually wrote as I dictated. He writes in a classical script, very lovely. I didn't do anything with it for awhile, since I couldn't figure out how to deliver it. Now at last I've thought of something. When Alexius comes by soon, I'll know if my idea works. Why do you ask?"

"Oh, no reason really. It's just that I have something to send, too. Here it is!"

Justin gave out a low whistle. "By Saint George! You really got her to donate that? I am impressed, Sophie, I am impressed!"

Philip appeared at the door but before he could say anything, Alexius had blown on through. "You called, Boss?"

"Yes, Alexius, I have a question. Does Levi still have contacts in Egypt?"

Alexius looked puzzled. "I'm sure he does. He talks about a cousin of his all the time who lives in Cairo, I think. Why do you ask?"

"I have a letter for him to send, along with a book. I'll give both of you more directions on Monday."

"Oh, Alexius," said Sophie, "I've got something too. It's in this sealed pouch, and if you open it I will call down 'Loviatar' to cut off your nose. Understand?"

Alexius stared at Sophie for a long moment before replying, "Sure, sure, 'Scalpel,' whatever you say. You are kidding, aren't you?"

"About what part? Thanks, you're a dear!"

After Alexius departed with more than one look over his shoulder, Sophie shook her head and sighed before saying, "Any doubt in your mind that the caliph was behind all of this?"

Justin answered immediately. "No, none. He knows he's not strong enough to challenge Basil militarily, so he tried to destabilize the empire from within, undermining the Varangians through 'Loviatar' and weakening the heir to the throne through his poisoner.

The funny thing is, Sophie, both Basil and Prefect Comnenus have to see this too, yet no one wants to say his name. The prefect doesn't want to aggravate the emperor, while Basil knows that he has unfinished business in Bulgaria. After that's over, look out!"

Sophie shook her head. "You know, I feel sorry for the caliph and even more so for the people of his realm. He focuses only on destroying things, never doing anything good. He also scares me. I don't ever want to be anywhere near him again!"

"Neither do I. The way the caliph's mind works—poisoning Constantine would either cause Basil to lose faith in him or actually kill him—a win either way. He may have not won this time, but he's still out there, and he won't give up."

The couple sat in silence for a few minutes until Sophie smiled and gave her hand to Justin. "Husband, husband, what a few weeks we've had! I guess we've lived to prove the old saying 'Everyone loves drama, but they hate change!'"

Justin took her hand and kissed it. "With you, Sophie, every change is for the better!"

EPILOGUE

A few weeks later, evening came to the Fatimid capital of Cairo. It was mid-September, and the evenings provided very pleasant escapes from the still-oppressive heat of the days. The hoopoes had finished their nesting duties for the year, and so were free to roam as they willed. Still, old habits die hard, and they continued to seek out the places where they had hunted during the breeding season. The old male and his mate, who had made their nest in the hole on the side of the observatory, still frequented the place where the men who were around the building during the day had left scraps out for them. As the sun set across the river and the last light of day glinted off the tops of the pyramids, the hoopoe looked forward to bedding down for the night.

    Around the observatory, activity continued, for Caliph Al-Hakim had been in attendance that afternoon, consulting with various scientists about their latest experiments. Among the men he spoke with was Hasan Ibn al-Haytham, who had initially feared for his life once the news came from Constantinople about Musa al-Hadi's fate. Once the full facts became known, as received from Fatimid agents unknown to Alexius and his network, the Caliph quickly made it known that he attached no fault to al-Haytham. Now, after the evening meal had been concluded, he intended to emphasize the point in a private meeting with the scientist, to be conducted on the same bench he had shared with his sister in June.

After summoning his guard to bring al-Haytham to him, the Caliph took a moment to take in the beauty of the sunset and the appearance of lights across the city which lay stretched out below him. It had not been an easy year—the harvest across lower Egypt and Palestine had only been fair, and the cost of basic food items was still high enough to excite occasional popular unrest. While the Yemenis had been put down without difficulty, the situation in Spain was one of anarchy which was spilling over into Morocco. His schemes in Constantinople had come to naught, and he was no closer to getting control of Baghdad than before. Still, he thought, it was the will of Allah, and another year lay ahead.

He was still staring into the west, admiring the last rays of the sun glinting off the Nile, when his guards returned with al-Haytham. The scientist was quiet but then again, in the Caliph's experience he had never been very talkative. He decided to open the conversation.

"Very well, guards, you are dismissed. We have no further need for you." Turning to his guest, he said, "Please, sit by us. The evening is quite beautiful." Even as he said this, however, the Caliph's eye caught a package which al-Haytham was carrying by his side. Given that everyone who came near him was searched, he had no fear of a hidden weapon, not that the scientist seemed like assassin material. So, the question remained, what was it? Before getting to that point, however, preliminary matters had to be addressed.

"Thank you, Scientist, for seeing us this evening. We wish to convey our appreciation for your assistance in our recent efforts to use your knowledge in the city of our enemies. While the ultimate outcome was not to our wishes, we feel that the ultimate failure of Musa al-Hadi was not yours. We wish you to know that."

Al-Haytham seemed to relax upon hearing this, as if his body was deflated. "Thank you Highness, that is wonderful to hear. I swear to you as Allah is my judge that al-Hadi assured me he understood how to set up the device when I spoke to him in Crete. He assured me that all was going well. I do not see what more I could have done."

At this, the Caliph said nothing, but instead continued to stare at the scientist. Then, he looked off to the heavens and remained quiet for what seemed an eternity. Finally, he looked back to al-Haytham, or rather to the package the man continued to cradle on his lap before saying, "We agree. Pray, what is that?"

Relieved about the change of subject, al-Haytham supplied a ready answer. "Thank you, Highness, you are most kind. As for what I have here, your summons came at a most opportune time. I received this package from a messenger who came from the Coptic Christian pope here in Cairo. The pope had in turn received it from Constantinople, by means of a Russian trading ship which docked in the harbor today."

At the mention of Constantinople, the Caliph's interest was immediately piqued. He said nothing, however, but motioned to his guest to continue.

"When I opened it up, I found two things. The first was a copy of a work by the Greek philosopher Euclid called *Optics*. As I set forth in my report of the Crete meetings, during one of our conversations, I mentioned my desire to obtain a copy of this work to Treasurer Cataphlates. He replied that it seemed only proper, since he had earlier been provided with some works he desired by your Highness during his visit. In any event, it will fill a large hole in our understanding of the subject, as it gives a mathematical explanation…"

"Of course, of course," interrupted the Caliph, completely bored with this extraneous language. "And the second item, what was it?"

"A letter, Highness, sealed, bearing your name."

"And it remains sealed?"

"Yes, of course."

"That is well for you. Thank you for your attention to this matter and for your discretion. You are dismissed, and you will never speak to anyone of this again, understood?"

Seeing the familiar widening of al-Haytham's eyes before he mumbled his assent, the Caliph was content that the matter would go no further. While the light was fading when the scientist left, he decided to examine the enclosed message, and opened the letter to find the following, written in flowing Arabic script:

To His Eminence abu Ali Al-Mansur Al-Hakim Bi-amr Al-lah (or just 'Ali'),

"I write you now because it is to the benefit to the Empire which I serve. If the prefect or the emperors had positive proof of your involvement in the events of the last few weeks, believe me that all contact would cease and open warfare would begin. However, it is also my belief that it is better in the long run to keep the channels of communication open. But, 'Ali', know this—if the prefect or the emperors ask me a direct question about your involvement, I will not lie.

I do not pretend to understand what motivates you to do the things you do—to kidnap an imperial princess, to destroy places of worship which the Prophet (Peace Be Upon Him) deemed to belong to People of the Book, to cause men to die who could never pose any conceivable threat to you, and so on. This I do know—in due time, you will be answerable to Allah, as will we all.

I also know that the Quran recognizes the prophets of what we call the Old Testament as having been sent from Allah to the Jewish people, before the final revelations you believe were brought by the Prophet (PBUH). Hear the words of one such prophet, Nahum, who foretold the downfall of a mighty empire: "Allah is jealous, and revengeth; he revengeth and is furious; he will take vengeance on his adversaries, and he reserveth wrath for his enemies. He is slow to anger, and great in power, and will not at all acquit the wicked." While the empire in question was not yours, it could as well be. Take thought on this.

Finally, also know this—by now you have heard about the fate of al-Hadi and his men from the other agents you still had in the city. I say 'have heard', for you will not be hearing from any of them again, as they now have all been rounded up. By my count, that makes a total of nine. As Allah is my judge, if you send any more assassins to Constantinople, we will send a single one to Cairo, and we will not need to send a second. Content yourself with what Allah has given you, and leave us in peace to do the same."

I remain,
Justin Cataphlates
Treasurer of Rome

Upon finishing the letter, the Caliph read it again, and yet one more time. Finally, he gave a sigh, and proceeded to tear it into tiny pieces, which he scattered to the wind which was coming up from the south, as it did every evening. After he had walked back to the observatory, the male hoopoe swooped down to check out the pieces in the hopes that they were edible. Disappointed in this he flew off, leaving the fragments to merge with the sands of the Sahara, under the light of the distant and unfeeling stars.

At about the same time, a mute eunuch delivered a package to the quarters of Sitt al-Mulk in the women's wing of the Great Palace. After making sure she was alone, she opened it and found a pouch which contained an emerald necklace that was once the property of Zoe Porphyrogenita, Imperial Princess of the Roman Empire. While there was no note, none was needed. Sitt smiled to herself, tried the necklace on, admired it for a while in a mirror, and then concealed it in a place in her quarters known only to herself.

THE END

HISTORICAL NOTES

Like <u>Year of the Dolphin</u>, its predecessor book, this novel is a work of fiction based on historical facts. Zoe, Theodora, Basil, Constantine and the various patriarchs were all real people, as was Caliph al-Hamid. New to this story are Sitt al-Mulk, the older half-sister of the caliph who proved to be a true survivor, and Ibn al-Haytham, who is recognized even today as the father of modern optics. The device he designed to project images is quite real, and was known to medieval Europeans by its Latin name, 'camera obscura', even if its use by the fictional villain Musa al-Hadi is not.

It bears repeating that in referring to the Empire as Roman, I use the term Justin and Sophie would have been familiar with. The term "Byzantine" to describe the empire of Basil and Constantine first appeared in 1557, and was not widely used until the nineteenth century. Anyone labelling the people as Greeks would have gotten the same reaction as the delegation from Rome gets, i.e., negative.

While the first Justin and Sophie book saw our intrepid heroes travel across the Empire and beyond, this book is for the most part set in Constantinople, apart from Justin's brief but fateful journey to Crete. I have tried to make my descriptions of the city and its streets, buildings and churches as close to what existed as possible. Some of the places named exist to this day (Hagia Sophia, St. Irene, and the land walls, and the Cistern of Aspar, albeit as a football pitch) while the palaces are sadly but memories. The outline of the Hippodrome can still be seen, and some of the monuments in the middle also remain.

It may surprise some readers that the delegation from Rome is depicted as speaking Italian rather than Latin. All languages change over time, and Latin is no exception. As early as 700 A.D., an English visitor to Rome (St. Boniface) found that he could barely understand the pope of the day, even though Boniface had been educated by monks in pure Ciceronian Latin. Justin and Sophie would not have had that problem, in that their church used a form of Greek (Koine) which had been spoken for centuries. It also helped that their part of the Empire had never been occupied by non-native speakers for any period of time.

While Justin and Sophie may also be criticized, as Alexius in fact does in the novel, as being unbelievably good at anything they do, the world of 1016 A.D. was both simpler and yet more demanding. With fewer people and much less technology, people had to be experts in many areas. Multi-lingualism was likely very prevalent in the Empire at the time, and if Justin was more of a polyglot than most, well, so be it. Sophie is on the other side of the coin, at home in the worlds of high fashion and anatomy at the same time. Her knowledge of Norse was just a bonus.

Finally, this novel introduces two new groups who play a significant part in the story. The first, the Varangians, are well documented in history, and were actually formed by Basil at the beginning of his reign. As pure mercenaries, they are the final step away from the citizen legionnaires of ancient Rome. Still, their loyalty was beyond question, and while Hetman Siggurdsen is a creation of fiction, there were many men like him over many years in the Empire. One, Harald Hardrada, went back after his service in Mikkelgard to become King of Norway and made it to the semi-finals for the English throne in 1066, losing to Harald Godwinson, who then lost in a thrilling final match to William, Duke of Normandy, whose bloodline continues on the throne of Great Britain to this day.

The other are the cross-dressers, personified by Matthew/'Daphne'/'Loviatar'. While I do not have the weight of historical sources to support their presence, they were undoubtedly present in Constantinople, as Sophie says, "just people trying to live like the rest of us." I like to think that, second to halting the murders of the Varangians, Sophie and Justin most enjoyed helping alleviate the plight of these misunderstood and persecuted people. Like espionage, cross-dressing is not an invention of our modern world.

Finally, you may have noticed that the language my characters use does not sound very 'classical' in content. That was a deliberate decision on my part. I am not a scholar of ancient Greek, and even if I was, it would not be the same Greek as that spoken by Sophie, Justin and their contemporaries. As noted earlier with Latin, Greek changed too over time, and it doesn't take that long—I daresay the Greek spoken by Dr. Lascaris is different than that which will spoken by his grandchildren. I did make an effort to keep modern idioms to a minimum, but if one or two slip through, I trust you will not let that stand in the way of your enjoyment of the story.

Jeff Southard, 2021

ABOUT THE AUTHOR

Jeff Southard is a fifth-generation Kansan who was born in Wichita in 1953, the 500th anniversary of the fall of the Roman/Byzantine Empire. While an undergraduate at the University of Kansas, one of his majors was medieval history with an emphasis on the Byzantine Empire. Although he followed in his father's footsteps and became an attorney, he always retained an interest in the subject. Now retired, he can devote more time to that fascinating yet rarely-studied period in history. Year of the Hoopoe is his second published work, and continues the adventures of Sophie and Justin as they fight crime in 11th Century Constantinople.

Jeff lives in an historic neighborhood in Lawrence, Kansas, with his wife Peggy and their dog. He rejoices in KU basketball, continues to endure KU football, and is active in his church and the community.

CPSIA information can be obtained
at www.ICGtesting.com
Printed in the USA
LVHW030454250821
696024LV00001B/6